Caroline England was born _____ nd studied Law at the University of Manchester. She was a divorce and professional indemnity lawyer before leaving the law to bring up her three daughters and turning her hand to writing. As well as *The Stranger Beside Me*, Caroline is the author of *The Sinner*, *The Wife's Secret* (previously called *Beneath the Skin*), the top-ten ebook bestseller *My Husband's Lies*, *Betray Her* and *Truth Games*. She has also been shortlisted for a CWA Dagger for her short story 'Blindsided'. She lives in Manchester with her family.

To find out more about Caroline, visit her website
www.carolineenglandauthor.co.uk
or follow her on social media:

Twitter: @CazEngland
Facebook: www.facebook.com/CazEngland1
Instagram: www.instagram.com/cazengland1

CAROLINE ENGLAND

THE STRANGER BESIDE ME

PIATKUS

PIATKUS

First published in Great Britain in 2023 by Piatkus

1 3 5 7 9 10 8 6 4 2

A CIP catalogue record for this book is available from the British Library.

ISBN 978-0-349-43149-9

Typeset in Garamond by M Rules
Printed and bound in Great Britain by Clays Ltd, Elcograf S.p.A.

Papers used by Piatkus are from well-managed forests
and other responsible sources.

Piatkus
An imprint of
Little, Brown Book Group
Carmelite House
50 Victoria Embankment
London EC4Y 0DZ

An Hachette UK Company
www.hachette.co.uk

www.littlebrown.co.uk

To my airport Johnnie Walker-swigging cohorts: Liz, Charl, Emily and Jonathan. Thank you for Paris. Love you all so much!

So tired, too tired in the car next to Dad. The flash of his features and the comforting smell of his aftershave in the dark.

Black night, slim moon, smooth wheels and soft warmth. And so very sleepy.

Sudden headlights burn her eyes. A bend and, oh God, that familiar canopy of trees. He has to slow down; it's too dangerous, he's driving too fast.

'Stop. Dad, stop! You have to stop!'

She tries to form words but she's dumb. It's coming, it's coming, the film on repeat: the headlights, the bend, the trees. The curse and the swerve, the screech and the stench. Sizzling rubber, sweaty terror, jangling fear. The almighty jolt, the sickening sound of crushing metal; the shaky silence perfumed by firework-like fumes.

And inevitably the weight, constricting her chest and her body, pinning and pushing her down.

Paralysis and panic, suffocating, stuck. Blind, solid blind. Except for the blood, the brightest red blood. And her lovely mum's face she must always remember.

1

Sibeal

Save for her red shoes, Sibeal Matthews is all dressed in black.

Despite her clanging agitation, her eyes sweep the stifling room with a will of their own. A waxed leather sofa and low tables, lantern lights and wicker cushions. Even an artificial bamboo. No doubt there's a tea house or a pagoda on the lawn at the back.

A snort of derision escapes. Camouflaged by the plethora of suburban trees, she's watched this modern build in Wilmslow from outside many times, and now she's finally crossed the threshold. Just one of many fucking, fucking ironies. How often did she covet it from afar? The house that should have been hers. And yet now she's here, it's so depressingly tasteless.

She reverts to the salt and pepper crown of the bloke in the queue ahead of her. A bald patch is developing and she can smell the sour stench of his body odour from here; he's probably unaware of both. Blissfully smug and unknowing like she was. Ignorant of what loitered, pernicious and deadly. What became that devastating and irrevocable knockout blow.

The man gravely murmurs to the four-person line-up, shakes

hands and walks away. Like taking communion in church, it's her turn to step forward and open her mouth. Can she? Can she do it without roaring alcoholic fire in their faces? Or crying, misbehaving, making a scene? Or maybe just bolting. But Gabriel is beside her, his hand cupping her elbow.

Though his tiny frame draws her like a magnet, she tries not to glance at the boy. She can't bear to look at *her* either, but she said she'd be here if this day ever came. Standing tall and beautiful and civilised, her make-up perfect, her crimson lipstick bright, she's here as she promised.

She focuses on the wife's knuckles, white and sharp on the child's narrow shoulders. Robin's boy. And *hers*. Yes, hers, Sibeal Matthews, from his sandy blond hair to his dimpled square chin and hazel brown eyes. At four years of age he's too young for a funeral, for shaking hands with tearful adults, for *this*. He should be outdoors, playing on the pristine square of grass at the front, kicking a ball, laughing and carefree. Not on display like ... a medal? No, like a possession, like proof.

A second passes, then another. She's never been this close to Joseph before. Can she really hold back from peeping at him? Staring and touching, stroking his silky locks, caressing his warm flesh and inhaling his smell? Absorbing the living, breathing clone of her lover? But of course that's a no-no, even for her, and she promised Gabriel she'd behave. So she allows her gaze to slip and sucks in his mini-Robin features for as many moments as she can. Same as last week, last month, through that pane of glass. His boy, Robin's boy, who changed everything.

Gabriel clears his throat loudly and her words fall out. 'I'm sorry for your loss.' She turns to the parents. 'Sibeal and Gabriel Matthews,' she says, using the phonetic 'Sibeeal' she adopted at eleven rather than the Irish pronunciation her saintly mum gave her. She gestures to her brother. 'We went to university with Robin. We're so—'

The mother's eloquent tone cuts in. 'Yes, of course,' she says. 'Please help yourself to beverages from the kitchen island.'

'Thank you.'

His hand in the small of her back, Gabe guides her away like a minder, a carer. Or perhaps a jailer. And why the hell is he here anyway? 'Robin has no interest in anyone but himself,' he said only weeks ago. And as always she knows what her older sibling will say moments before he utters it.

'You didn't go to university with Robin,' he hisses.

Her dear lovely Gabe. Pedantic to the nth degree.

'You don't say.' She turns to his scowl and mimics the mother. '"Beverages from the kitchen island." As opposed to from the *fabby* chabudai. That's the short-legged table in the . . .' She sighs at Gabe's frown. 'Never mind. I don't know why you've come. Why did you come, Gabriel?'

'Because I did go to uni with Robin. He was a close friend for seventeen years,' he replies tersely. 'More to the point, why did you come?'

She turns to the boy. If only she could have kissed his soft, apple cheek. 'Funeral practising,' she replies. 'I told you last night.'

'For God's sake, Sibeal, stop acting so, so . . .' He picks up two drinks and hands one to her. 'Well, weird.'

'Weird. Hmm, how charming.' She nudges him playfully. 'Is that why you're at the end of your tether, as you so eloquently put it? Have I inherited the freak gene from our dearest Imelda?'

'Mum wasn't a freak, Sibeal. And I said that because of the drinking. It's not just wine these days, you're on the hard stuff

5

too. It's embarrassing. You become ... Well, someone I don't recognise.'

'Or like?'

'I didn't say that.'

'It's a good job Dad loves me.'

'If you say so.'

A stab of hurt hits her chest, but it feels so familiar she shrugs it away. She theatrically wafts her glass. 'At least this friend is reliable.' Anticipating the consoling burn, she inhales the fruity alcohol, then slugs it all back in one go. 'Cheap plonk, but who cares. I'm getting another.'

Gabriel catches her wrist. 'Not now, Sibeal. You can do what you like in the privacy of your own home, but you behave when you're with me. Understood?'

His handsome father-brother face clouds with irritation. Hiding her alarm with a grin, she slicks back his dark fringe. 'Absolutely, my darling, sensible Gabe. You know your wish is always my command.'

He flinches away. 'Don't mock me.'

'I'm not, I'm really not.' How she hates it when Gabe's angry, when he sucks in his cheeks and says 'end of his tether' types of thing. Though she swallows, she has to say it. 'You just said Dad doesn't love me.'

His cheeks lightly flush. 'Don't be silly, Sib. I didn't say that at all.'

'Not in so many words. But you said—'

'No, Sib.' He looks her in the eyes. 'I was just annoyed. What you said about Mum. And Dad loves us both very much, OK? You just need to stop the booze, or at least cut down. He doesn't like it and nor do I.'

6

'I don't drink when I see Dad—'

'I know and that's great. It shows you don't always have to.' He moves to the lounge door and watches the milling mourners for a while. When the wife clearly clocks him, he finally turns back, his eyes shiny with emotion. 'I see what you mean about the chabudai table. And too much black leather for my taste.' He offers his arm. 'Come on, little sis. There's nothing for us here any more. And I am your friend, your forever friend. You know that.'

2

Katy

It's the local village fete, so of course it's raining. Though Katy splashes through the downpour as fast as her wellies will allow, Bridget is already in position by the park gate. 'Sorry I'm later than we planned; I was chatting to Dad.' She turns towards the wind to blow back the ribs of her brolly. 'So, what are we supposed to do again?'

The blue reflective vest almost reaching her knees, Bridget looks the part. She narrows her eyes and studies Katy for a moment or two before speaking. 'We're to stop cars from coming in this way.' As if it's an indicator of Katy's well-being, she peers at Katy's old cagoule. 'I can do it on my own if you're not feeling—'

'I'm fine. Really. And I promised I'd keep you company.' She takes a quick breath and smooths her hair. 'I can cope with a drop of rain, even if these damned tresses can't! Shame for the kids though.'

'That's what happens when the powers that be decide on May. Will you bring Milo later?'

'Yeah. Or Dad will.' Katy gives up on the umbrella and lobs the torn remains into the bin. 'He's to blame for my tardiness.

Dad, that is. A letter arrived in the post just as I was leaving. Some guy asking him to visit.' She pictures her father's ashen face as he studied the notepaper. 'He's in a hospice, poor man, so . . .'

'Oh no. Anyone we know?'

'Some old schoolfriend of his I've never heard of. He's fifty-five, same as Dad, so far too young to be dying.' Her chest tingles at the thought. 'Dad looked pretty horrified. He—'

'Oh look, it's Harry,' Bridget cuts in. She waves enthusiastically to a man with a dog, so Katy steps back and contemplates whether it's too late to lift her hood. The trickle of cold water down her spine suggests it is, so she smiles politely at the families trundling in, then reverts to Bridget, noting with some envy that Harry has sensibly opted for a baker boy cap. As she watches Bridget, she chuckles to herself: she's talking animatedly, barely pausing to breathe as usual. Not that Katy minds, it's great to have a friend who launches into embarrassing silences to break them, as it saves her from struggling to do it, and generally not succeeding. Though is 'friend' the right word?

'Did you hear that, Katy?' Bridget's eloquent Scottish tones interrupt her internal debate. She goes back to Harry. 'How can you possibly hate him? He's so cute.'

Gathering they're discussing the dog, Katy eyes the silver pug at the man's feet. It looks familiar, but most local ones do, as it's infinitely easier to communicate with pet than owner.

'A golden retriever, a handsome black lab, even a German shepherd. But this is what I got,' Harry says. 'What did Lydia say when she brought him home? "I like him. I'll walk him and I'll feed him, so that's pretty much that."'

Bridget laughs her high trill, then turns to her. 'You've met Rex before, haven't you, Katy?'

9

Though in all honesty 'cute' isn't the description she'd use, she has met him before on a tromp with Milo, but the keeper was a woman, not a tall guy with a broad grin and dimples who's clearly flirting with Bridget.

'*Doctor* Harry said he always wanted a dog called Rex, so that's what he got,' Bridget says, lifting her eyebrows meaningfully.

The penny finally dropping, Katy studies him. So this is *the* Harry Bridget's always wittering on about. With his trendy clothes, striking eyes and fair hair, he's pretty much as she described. He's not Katy's type, though. What that once was, she can barely remember.

Bridget continues to chatter, so Katy lifts her hand to another mum from Milo's class, then glances around the sodden scene. The red hawthorn blossom is shedding from the trees, landing on hats and hoods like confetti. It's quite a comical sight, but when she follows its journey to the ground, she can't help but equate the trodden petals to blood spatter. Forcing the image away, she focuses on another stream of wet and dejected fete-goers entering the park. She's lived in the village for all her life, but it feels strange to be in this familiar place, out and about, yet feigning confidence. She's much better these days, but she can still feel the anxiety just under her skin like a bruise.

'Bye, Katy,' she hears, so she turns. Harry gazes a moment too long for comfort. 'Nice to meet you again.'

Again? As he walks away, she racks her brains for a previous meeting, but Bridget is speaking, her voice squeaky with pleasure. 'Did you see that? A hug *and* a kiss on both cheeks. Wait until I tell Andrew.'

'So Andrew fancies him too?'

She laughs. 'Absolutely, who doesn't. Though rumour has it

that—' She abruptly stops as a van tries to enter the gates. 'What the . . .? Right. Watch this!'

She trots to the offending vehicle and converses with the driver for some time. Bridget is so open about everything, who knows what she might be discussing with the poor man. Eventually accepting defeat, he closes his window and reverses to join the wet traffic queue.

'So this friend of Alexander who's in the hospice,' she says when she returns, as though the intermission hasn't happened. 'Who is he and how come he's in touch? Apart from the obvious?'

Katy shifts her thoughts to earlier. From the initials on the front, she'd assumed the handwritten envelope was for her, so she opened it and glanced at the first sentence before twigging that it wasn't and calling her dad. He motioned her apology away with an, 'Oh, don't worry', but his face paled when he read it. Which was hardly surprising. Her father is still youthful and athletic, fitting in tennis and squash between his long working hours, so it must've been a dreadful shock to learn that an old pal was dying, a reminder of his own mortality.

Here one minute, gone the next.

Swallowing the usual jolt of grief, she comes back to Bridget's inquisitive peer and considers the question. 'Oh, the letter; I don't know. There wasn't time to talk about it in detail . . .' Instinctively knowing he's near, she rotates to the pavement. Wearing a bucket hat someone must have left at their home, her father is approaching, holding her son's hand. 'But talk of the devil. Here he is. You can ask him yourself.'

He bends to kiss Bridget's cheek. 'Made the mistake of telling Milo about the goldfish Katy won here many moons ago.' He theatrically lowers his voice. 'Between you and me, we were

11

relying on a quick exit, but the damned thing lived for years. Tried everything from solitary confinement to starvation, but it seems goldfish like being neglected.'

'As though you'd neglect anyone, Alexander.' Bridget laughs, the trill back. 'Though I believe it isn't PC to sell them at fairs any more. A pet shop's the thing and these days they vet you. Make sure the tank is large enough and so on. Probably do a spot visit from time to time, check the fish is getting five a day.'

'Oh lord.'

Milo tugs his hand. 'That's a swear word, Grandad. And you promised me a fish.'

Katy squeezes her son's shoulder. 'Sorry, Milo, but with Grandad's fishy history, I don't think they'll let him buy one. Best stick with Poppy.'

'Poppy's so old. All she does is—' Milo begins to reply, but he's stopped short by a loud wailing from the park. A windswept lady is trotting towards them, her arms tightly around a little girl.

'Anyone from the police? Is there a police officer anywhere?'

Blue uniform flashes in. Thrown back in time, Katy freezes, but when she resumes her respiration, her father is lightly holding the woman's elbow. 'What can I do? Slowly inhale and exhale. Don't panic, I'm here to help.' Like a father to a child, he crouches on one knee, gently pressing her with questions. Breathe deeply. What's the problem? Where exactly did it happen? How long ago? What did the man look like?

Clutching Milo's hand, Katy watches intently as her father steps away, makes a call on his mobile, then leads the woman to the administrator's tent. Though worried about the mother's clear distress, alarmed by the thought of what must have happened to her daughter, she can't help feeling a flush of pride for her dad.

After ten minutes, he returns. 'A man flashing from the bushes, today of all days. I know people like that need help, but when it comes to children ... Bloody disgrace. Of course he'll be long gone, but I'll give Dave Masters a call and fill him in.' He ruffles his grandson's hair. 'Nothing for you to worry about, Milo. Some people are plain bad, but most people aren't. Look, the sun's peeping out. I think it's time for me to buy my special boy an ice cream.'

3

Sibeal

Merged as it has into her dream, it takes Sibeal several minutes to realise the hammering is for real.

'Sibeal? Sibeal, for God's sake wake up.'

The rap of pebbles against glass and Gabriel's deep voice finally reach her. She scoops up her mobile to peer at the time, but she turned the damn thing off. Closure before bed. That desperate need to prevent the spurt of expectation and pleasure at the sound of the ringtone before brutal reality slapped them down.

Robin is dead; he'll always be dead.

Rushing from the bedroom, she almost slips on the stairs, but grabs the banister just in time to stop her breaking her bloody neck. When the dizziness finally passes, she flings open the front door and the fragrant Yorkshire air breezes in.

'What?' she says to Gabriel's shadowy features. 'What's happened?'

'Dad,' he replies. 'The hospice have called. They say he's near the end.'

'That can't be right. They said months. And he was fine when we saw him last week.' She finds herself shouting. 'He

14

was laughing, Gabe. He said he'd be there for my bloody thirtieth!'

'Shush; it's four o'clock in the morning; you'll wake the neighbours.' He ushers her back into the house. 'I know; I'm shocked too, but you have to get dressed.' He puts his hands either side of her shoulders. 'Are you listening, Sib? It'll take an hour and a half to get there. We need to go now.'

She digs her toes into the soft carpet. 'No,' she says. Though her brain is rebelling, her jaw, her fingers, her whole body seems to know. She folds her arms to stop the shuddering. 'Maybe they're wrong. How can they possibly tell?'

'I've no idea, Sib, but they can. Get dressed quickly. We have to go.'

Lifting her chin like she did as a toddler, an infant, a girl, Sibeal takes a huge breath and steps into the dim hospice room.

It's a death chamber, she knows, yet her immediate thoughts are of the sweet shop at the top of her childhood road. Pear drops, she decides, or perhaps those sugary candies in the shape of a Coke bottle or teeth or a dummy. An innocent smell, which is ironic given that she used to steal them.

'The acetone odour is caused by changes in the metabolism . . .' Gabe mutters, as though he's a flaming doctor, rather than a musician. He gently presses her towards a bedside chair. 'You sit here and I'll go the other side.'

Glad she swigged the mouthful of whisky before leaving the house, she does as she's told, but instead of facing grim reality, she closes her eyes.

Gabe's clotted voice breaks her cusp of sleep. 'Take his hand if you like.'

15

She squints at her brother's terse features. 'Really? Have you?'

'Yes.'

'OK.'

Beginning at the outline of the prone figure's feet, she works her way up the bed to the arms. They're covered by the stripy pyjamas which belong to her dad, but when she reaches the hand, it's huge, far too lifelike and human in comparison to the shrunken shape. Perhaps it isn't her father James Matthews after all; maybe it's an imposter who wears the same Claddagh wedding band. But that's little Sibeal being silly or running away, so she continues her journey to look at his face.

Oh God, it is him. Though he's pallid and waxy and gaunt, though his gossamer skin is stretched over his cheekbones like latex, it's definitely him, her daddy. Asleep, unconscious or dead? His mouth is slack; she can't tell.

'He looks like a skeleton, a fucking skeleton, Gabe,' she says over the clatter of her thrashing heart. Then, more quietly, 'How can that happen in just a few days?'

Gabriel shakes his head, but she needs him to speak, to pierce the threatening panic. 'He's so cold. These fingers, these skeleton fingers are icy, Gabe. Are yours? Or did you go for the warm hand, the *right* side of Dad?'

He smiles faintly. 'Both are the same, Sib.'

Her pulse slowing, she stares at their father. He'd be unrecognisable if she passed him in the street. A good thing or not? Better to lose someone who's no longer her dad? She jerks back at the abrupt bubble of sound from his throat. 'Bloody hell, Gabe. He's gurgling. Is that normal?'

'He's dying, Sib. Nothing will be normal today. You have to go with it. OK?'

'Sure, but how about ditching the patronising tone? I'm nearly thirty, not three.'

'I'm not—'

Her father, alarmingly, yawns. 'Should we call a nurse? Perhaps it won't be today. Maybe they've got it—'

'You heard what they said. Twitching, moving, sighing. It's all usual.' Gabriel stands and walks over. 'Do you want me to leave the room so you can say goodbye?'

'God no!' Then, after a moment's thought, 'Why? Do you? I mean, do you want me to go?'

'Maybe just for a minute?'

Like a claustrophobic cloud of smoke, the old image descends: their mother smiling and whispering in her cherished Gabriel's ear; that intimate, cosy club of just two.

'But why?' she asks. 'Why would you want to speak to Dad without me?'

'No reason.' He pulls her into a hug. 'I just feel embarrassed, that's all,' he says into her hair. 'Stay, please stay, it's fine. Just pretend you can't hear.'

Though she wants to hang on to his solid warmth and reassuring patchouli smell, she disentangles herself. 'Sorry,' she says. 'Sorry for being ...' Paranoid? Jealous? Hurt? Yes, all those things, despite the years of feigning deafness. 'For being stupid. I'll give you a few minutes.'

Once in the corridor, she hunches down on the floor and rests her throbbing head on her knees. As the seconds pass, her thoughts snap to Robin. Robin, *her* Robin, regardless of what the world thinks. She pictures the woman in her widow's weeds, the strange glance between her and Gabe before they left. Did she sit beside him as he died? Was he transformed, turned to bones like her dad? She doesn't know because she can't ask anyone, not even Gabe.

'Go to the funeral service by all means, but who attends the wake of someone they briefly dated at sixteen?' he'd said. 'If it was in a hotel or church hall, fair enough, but it's at his home, so it's meant for family and close friends.'

'It was more than briefly.'

'Fourteen years ago.'

'Well I'm going.'

'OK. But why?'

Gabe's croaky voice in her ear brings her back to the present. 'Your turn,' he says. 'Your turn to say goodbye.'

'Not without—'

'I know. I'll come too.'

As she follows him inside, the thin curtains billow. He's opened the window – not for fresh air as most people would suppose, but for family tradition. 'You've set him free.'

His expression tight and unbearably sad, he smiles thinly in reply. Her lovely, lovely big brother. The only person in the world who speaks the same language. He's desperate to cry but he's being brave for her, just like always.

She kisses her father's forehead. 'Bye, Dad,' she says, guilt sizzling in her chest at her own lack of tears. After all, this is a man she's entitled to grieve for. As a daughter she can shout her anguish from the rooftops or the trees; she can beat her chest, weep and wail. Have people say they are sorry for her loss. Host a tasteful bloody wake.

'His breathing is more laboured,' Gabriel mutters. 'I think that means he's near the end.'

Retaking their seats, they listen in silence. Sound in reverse.

18

Waiting for the rattle of death. But no final noise comes, just a couple of pants, then the rasp of their own lives.

'Do you think that's it?' she whispers eventually.

'I don't know. Fucking hell, Sib. Is this surreal or what?'

Her Gabe, who's usually so steady, suddenly guffaws so much, it makes his shoulders shake. Consumed with flat panic, she simply gapes, but after a few moments his strange laughter stops.

He rakes his fingers through his hair. 'Thank God,' he says. 'Thank God it's all over.'

4

Sibeal

Although it's pitch black when she wakes, Sibeal immediately knows where she is from the cold. And the bloody smell. Dank and fusty, Brook House always had the aroma of old things – from the plethora of antique furniture and decaying tomes which clutter every room, to chalky floorboards, dead mice and ancient wax. Then there was the tang of oil paints, liquin, linseed and turps, mixed with the stench of her dad's tobacco. She just didn't notice any of it until she returned the first Christmas after starting university in Durham.

'Oh my God, Gabe, it stinks in this house,' she declared, hurling herself next to him on the scuffed Chesterfield sofa.

'Yup,' he replied, his attention on the newspaper he consumed from cover to cover. 'You just never noticed, like you don't notice anything.'

'What a load of old tosh. As it happens, I observe everything. Dad's secret stash of a million cigarettes, whatever you're currently hiding in your sock drawer, for starters. In fact, I haven't had a nosy in your bedroom for aeons. I need to investigate what Santa's buying me this year . . .'

As ever, he didn't rise to the bait. 'You only see what you want to see, Sib. That's how you are.'

Though only five years older, Gabriel was her father-mother-brother even then. She would have had an apposite answer, but she can't remember it now.

Surprised at the darkness, she gropes for her mobile. There's strangely no bedside table, but a standard lamp on the floor. When dull light finally floods the room, she realises it's the front parlour and not her bedroom, which explains the toasty warmth from the leather beneath her body, the scratchy blanket above.

Wondering if she does only see – and smell – what she wants to, she squints at her surroundings. It's undoubtedly shabby now, but from the fiery red Moroccan rug, the 1940s marble fireplace and the lion's paws sideboard, to the heavy pinch-pleat curtains and shutters behind, the room still has stately elegance. Her eyes catch a brown and yellow damp patch on the far ceiling cornice, so she follows the bumps in the textured wallpaper down to the tiered skirting, snug against the worn carpet. No doubt it's a leak from the bathroom, the roof, a radiator, the sink in the attic or the decrepit toilet closet; like her private outpour of grief, there's a constant trickle of water from somewhere in Brook House.

Self-pity surfacing, she presses her eyes. When she moved to Yorkshire, she deliberately bought a new build with easy-to-clean units, modern plumbing, plain walls and coving. But in truth she missed this, the aromas and her dad.

James Matthews, her lovely, gentle father. Bloody hell, the man in the hospice is deceased, gone for ever. She saw it for herself, and yet it feels improbable, impossible, outlandish. As though waiting for the credits of an old black and white movie, she and Gabe stayed pinned to their seats for over an hour, wanting to seek out the fresh air but feeling too rotten to leave. A nurse finally appeared and gave them dispensation to go. They'd intended to drown their sorrows in a pub, any pub, but instead they drove here to Brook House, their forever home. Gabe put the key in the lock with shaking fingers, opened up and they tiptoed across the freezing hallway like thieves.

'So he is dead,' she said when they stood in this room. 'The skeleton in the hospice *was* him.'

Gabe frowned, but she knew he understood. They'd both watched their father take his last breath, but it was only here that she finally felt his absence – James was the one thing that had warmed this old house.

Gabriel responded with a shrug. 'I need a drink.' He stepped to the mahogany display cupboard and inspected the dusty bottles that had been there, untouched, for as long as she could remember. A faint smile on his lips, he pulled one out. 'The Rémy Martin, I think, don't you?'

Now sitting up, Sibeal tests her head by shaking it. Surprisingly, there's no raging hangover, despite the ancient brandy, a somewhat inappropriate gift of thanks to a Methodist teetotaller. She pictures the crucifix her mother always wore. So, it wasn't OK for James to drink alcohol, but it was fine for him to marry a staunch Irish left-footer. A child accepts their lot as it is, yet now she contemplates it, the two ideals seem to clash.

She looks down at her fingers and flexes them. Yes, clash, like her and Saint Imelda, her perfect, perfect absent mother.

Cramp pinching her stomach, she pulls up her knees. Absence, abandonment, death. Her mother, her father and— Oh God, for moments she forgets, then realisation strikes, hammering her harder than ever. Robin has gone, gone for ever. He's *dead*; she'll never hear the sound of his voice, feel his warm arms, his skin and his lips. No one will ever love her as he did.

Christ, she needs a drink, needs to seek out that parallel world where life is more bearable. Forgetting the lamp in her haste, she plunges ahead, trips on the flex and pulls out the plug. Falling to her knees, she madly gropes in the dark until she reaches the lion's trusty paws, then she snaps open the first bottle she finds, swigs back the peaty liquid and swallows.

Though the whisky burns her throat, she continues to gulp, waiting a beat between mouthfuls for the heady alcohol to do its thing. Finally registering the arthritic twinge in her hands, she sits back and drily chuckles. A psychiatrist would have a field day analysing why booze numbs everything but them. Yet her body is pimpled and shivering, so the room must be very cold.

She glances at the fireplace. Yup, that's dead too. Gabe built it and lit it 'for the brandy' last night, but he hurried down his measure, then disappeared upstairs. If he returned, she was asleep by then. Yet she was covered by the blanket, so he must have.

Gabe. Always silently there. She'd be nowhere without him.

Swaying through the double doors, she leaves the parlour behind and pauses in the hallway. A funeral dirge echoes back, but that's nothing new, so she shrugs the sound away and slowly climbs the stairs, careful not to slip with her too-heavy feet.

On the landing she pauses, momentarily confused. 'Gabe?' she calls. The hoarse and slurred voice is apparently her own. She tries again. 'Gabriel, where are you?'

'I'm in here. Where else?'

'Righty-ho.' She sniggers. 'Incoming!'

Once she's wobbled to his door, she pats the wall for the

switch, but his grumpy tone cuts in. 'Don't turn it on. I'm asleep, Sibeal. Go to your own room.'

'Well of course you're not asleep, my darling Archangel. People who are asleep don't talk.'

She yanks back the duvet and climbs in, hitches to his side and absorbs the warmth of his back.

'You're freezing,' he says. 'Go away.'

'Near hypothermia, you mean. That's why you need to heat me up.'

'For God's sake, Sibeal. Put on some clothes. Get in your own bed.'

She slots her knees into his. 'You didn't used to mind.'

'That was a long time ago.'

'But still you didn't.'

'You needed me then.'

'I still do now, Gabe. More than ever.'

He's silent for some time. Then, when she has almost fallen asleep, 'OK, just for tonight. But for God's sake, turn off that bloody light.'

5

Katy

Short-winded at the prospect of today, Katy watches the windscreen wipers do their thing and tries to puff out her anxiety. The thought of a body in a coffin makes her want to go home and hide, but her dad's unusual silence suggests he's dreading this too, so she can't let him down.

'Not only the slowest moving traffic known to man, but behind a funeral cortège. Ironic,' she says eventually to fill the quietness. She leans to one side, trying to make out the floral words in the hearse ahead. 'Could this be for James, do you think?'

Her father taps the wheel of the Jaguar and doesn't reply. He hates to be late for anything; easy-going, personable and scrupulously fair, it's the one thing that winds him up. Back in her work experience days at his chambers, she had stood at the photocopier almost holding her breath, steeling herself to overhear criticism or snippets of gossip about him she didn't want to know, but his irritation with tardiness of any sort was as far as any fault-finding went.

'Finally,' he says, swerving through the handsome crematorium gates. 'Now the challenge of finding a space.'

Spotting one eventually, they tumble out and dash towards the immaculate flower beds overflowing with spring colour. When they reach the pillared entrance, her dad smiles reassuringly, offers one arm and opens the heavy door with the other.

'OK, darling?' he murmurs.

Though her heart feels fit to burst, Katy nods and walks quickly inside. There's only a handful of mourners in the chapel, but one or two turn, and from their small frowns she guesses the service has already begun. But the celebrant pauses, greets them with a 'welcome' and a grin, so they hitch along an empty bench at the back.

Conscious of a hefty woman gawping from the adjacent pew, Katy picks up the order of service and sucks in some air. Her dad asked her to come, so she has. A crematorium, he said, so it would be completely different to their local church. Yet it's still a funeral, a gathering to 'celebrate' a person's life. Pushing that inappropriate word away, she sets her eye-line on the domed orange wall above the wicker casket and tunes in to what the celebrant is saying.

Like a beardless Santa Claus, his face is pink and dimpled. 'James Matthews was a man many remember for his art and his unique sense of humour, talents he put together at grammar school and university. He sadly lost his wife Imelda too young, but was blessed with a son Gabriel and a daughter Sibeal . . .'

Her throat suddenly tight, and her body both sweaty and chilled, Katy focuses on an image of Milo and her dad splashing through the sparkling water at a sun-drenched, sandy beach. It's soon followed by her own swimming, not in the Mediterranean sea – she was too weak for that – but at their local leisure centre. She uses the indoor pool when she's up to taking Milo for fun, but he was at a party a few weeks ago, so on impulse she decided to use the outdoor lido instead, despite it being a chilly March morning. The experience was a revelation, the sensations sublime. The open sky and cool breeze above her, the warm depths below. Buoyant, supportive, calming. And yet energising too ...

A noise snaps her back to the present. A woman is making her way to the lectern. Katy stares at her angular face and shock of dark hair. She's seen her before, hasn't she? A friend of Bridget's? Someone from the village?

Despite the dark grooves of grief beneath her eyes, the woman stands tall. 'Thank you all for coming,' she says. 'My father was teetotal, so it's a little ironic that his favourite poet was Dylan Thomas.' Her drawn expression is transformed by a dazzling smile. She gestures to the front row. 'Gabriel, my genius brother, inherited Dad's artistic side. I don't know impressionism from pop art, a sonnet from a limerick, a Ming from a Qing, but here goes ...'

It's clearly Sibeal, James's daughter. Mesmerised by her apparent mix of indifference and emotion, Katy observes her open a somewhat tatty edition of *In Country Sleep*, toss back her head, then begin the opening of 'Do not go gentle into that good night', in a clear and loud tone. But as the stanzas fade away, so does her voice.

She stops, bites her lip and holds out the collection. 'Gabe,' she croaks.

Her equally tall, slim and dark-haired brother joins her, takes her hand and recites the rest of the poem by heart. Finding it too unbearable to watch, Katy looks at her father. This will be her one day, a motherless child saying goodbye to him. How on earth will she cope? He's been her anchor all her life; the thought of him leaving her is unbearable.

As though reading her thoughts, he turns with soulful eyes. But as ever his nod, his thin smile and whole demeanour is solid and reassuring; he doesn't have to say the, 'I'm here, I'm strong, I'm not going anywhere' mantra these days.

The celebrant speaks again. 'And now a time for reflection.'

As her ears catch the tinny sounds of 'Let It Be', Katy breathes deeply from her diaphragm. She can do this. It's someone else's loss, not hers today. That poor woman's, her brother's. She can't quite say why, but she wants to reach out and offer them comfort.

A sudden loud sob pierces the near-silent music. It isn't from Sibeal or Gabriel, but the older woman who'd stared. As if offended by the sound, or perhaps short of time, the celebrant rushes through the committal, says a few concluding remarks and shows the gathering the door. Alexander waits for the others to shuffle out, steps back for Katy, then turns to the curtains, slowly enveloping the coffin.

'Poor James. A close friend for many years and a lovely man. Such a shame he died before I had a chance to see him and say goodbye. At least with your mum—'

'I know, Dad,' she says quickly.

'Sorry, love. I know you're still fragile, but sometimes it helps to share.' He takes a sharp breath and rubs Katy's back. 'Onwards and upwards, eh? Pay my respects to the children, then I'd better get into chambers. My desk is cluttered with paperwork.'

The sun's cracking a smile through the drizzle when they emerge outside, but there's no sign of the mourners.

'Ah, what a pity, they seem to have scattered. Drop you home before heading into town, darling?' he asks.

28

'If it isn't too much trouble. Though I can easily catch the—'

A voice interrupts. 'Hello?' Then louder, 'Hello! We're over here.'

Model-like in a wide-legged trouser suit, Sibeal strides towards them. 'Thanks for coming.' She narrows her eyes at Katy, then Alexander. 'I feel as though we've met before, but I don't know your names or who you are.' She lifts her shoulders indifferently. 'Don't be offended, I'm crap at remembering people. I'm Sibeal.'

Alexander steps forward and offers his hand. 'Alexander Henry and my daughter Kathryn. I'm very sorry for your loss. Your father and I were at school together back in the day. Sadly we hadn't seen each other since—'

'My aunt assures me there's a nice pub nearby.' Clearly uninterested in Alexander's introduction, Sibeal gestures to a couple climbing in a people carrier. 'Not lived here for years so don't blame me if it's dire, but you're welcome to join us for a toast to Dad. Not many of us, but how many do you need for these things?'

Alexander raises his arms in a gesture of apology. 'That would've been lovely but I'm afraid I have to get back to the grind and I promised to drop Kathryn home. I have a trial next week, so I have rather a lot of reading to get through.'

'A trial? Interesting.' Sibeal gazes at him appraisingly. 'Lawyer, judge or the accused?'

'On this occasion, the judge.'

'A hanging judge?' she asks.

'Lord, no. Quite the opposite, I'm afraid.'

As though sensing him behind her, Sibeal turns to her brother emerging from the red-brick building. 'OK,' she replies, apparently losing her snap of curiosity. 'Good of you to make the effort.'

'I'll come.'

Katy's words pop out, surprising herself. There's something appealing about this woman and her wavy-haired sibling. And besides, she has nothing else to do until she collects Milo from school at four. As Gabriel approaches, she finds herself gabbling. 'I'll come,' she repeats. 'I'd love to join you. We don't live a million miles from here so I can grab a bus or a taxi later. I'm Katy, by the way. Only my parents ...' She starts again. 'Only Dad calls me Kathryn.'

A shadow of emotion flits through Sibeal's eyes. 'Funny that. Only my mother calls me Sibeal,' she says, pronouncing the name as 'Shibale'.

Her use of the present tense is somewhat strange, but Sibeal blinks the moment away. 'Bye, Mr Judge. Enjoy your trial.' Smiling that stunning smile, she holds out her elbow. 'Come on then, little Kat. I've no idea where Gabriel's parked the car. He's the leader because he's driving and he's hidden the keys as usual.'

She waits for him to catch up, then she slips her other arm into his. 'Gabe, meet Kat; Kat, meet Gabe. I have an awful suspicion this place isn't going to be even remotely tasteful, so that's all the more reason to party.'

6

Katy

Reeking of fried breakfast even from outside, the pub's a new-build chain restaurant. With an appalled expression, Sibeal stalls on the threshold, but after a moment she snorts.

'So much for good intentions. But beggars and all that,' she says.

She strides to a high table and gestures Katy to a seat between her and Gabriel. Conscious that he still hasn't acknowledged her, Katy takes her place and watches the large lady from the crematorium bustle towards them. She sits on the other side of Sibeal, directs her Jack Sprat skinny husband to sit opposite, then looks around.

'I was right. I thought this would do nicely for our James.' She's clearly the aunt Sibeal mentioned. She takes a huge breath. 'But I do wish—'

'Yes, you've already said. It's done now.'

The woman ignores her niece's dismissive tone. 'I did think there'd be a proper service at the church on Withington Road. I know the congregation has changed since your grandad's time but—'

'We're the children, we chose.'

'But not even hymns. How can that be right?' Clearly undaunted by Sibeal's sharp tone, the woman looks at Katy. 'James was a late addition to the family. I can picture him singing "Thine Be the Glory" even now. He loved singing hymns when he was a little boy. I know he lost his way, but he found his faith again after Imelda—'

'Well, we don't sing and we're not religious, so just drop it, Valerie.' Sibeal looks at her brother. 'We don't believe in God, do we, Gabe?'

He finally speaks. 'It was a nice service. Dad would have liked it.' Then, as though realising why they are there, 'Right, I'll get some drinks in. What's everyone having?'

Aunt Valerie picks up the menu. 'Very reasonable prices.' She turns to her husband and bellows into his ear. 'I'm a little peckish, aren't you, Fred? Perhaps a snack or a sandwich to see us over until lunch. Brunch, I believe that's what you young people call it.'

Ignoring her aunt's prattle as she debates what to eat, Sibeal turns to Katy. 'Haute cuisine not, methinks. There's nothing like this in our village, thank God. Saxton is small but perfectly formed.' She nods to her brother, still waiting for his aunt to decide on her order. 'Gabe couldn't live without me, so he followed me to Yorkshire.'

'That isn't entirely true, Sib.' He removes his wire-framed glasses and looks at Katy briefly. 'I was already in York. I went to university there and stayed.'

Sibeal laughs. 'He followed me.'

'Why young people move from their home towns, I have no idea,' Valerie says. She focuses on Katy. 'My lot and these two

32

were born at the hospital down this very road. We all had boys so everyone was well pleased when this one appeared. "A little girl," I said to Imelda. "Aren't you lucky."' She raises her voice again. 'We were well pleased when little Sibby was born, weren't we, Fred? Even if she was a right squawker.'

Sibeal glances at Gabriel. '*Lucky*, she wasn't,' she mutters.

'So, you guys lived near here when you were younger?' Katy asks after several beats of uncomfortable silence.

'Whalley Range,' Valerie answers. 'The Matthews family lived there back in the day before it got its ... reputation. It's gone back, mind. Sought-after again, when you look at the prices. Which shows James wasn't such a fool after all.' She slaps her palm to her mouth. 'Sorry, loves, but you know what I mean.' She leans in to Katy. 'Well, you must know, living locally. Brook House is beautiful, but the area went right down the pan. Red light, if you take my meaning. Most people sold, everything turned into horrible bedsits, but James held on, even though he was the youngest. James held on, didn't he, Fred? Held on to Brook House. Paid you your share and held on?'

Fred nods. 'He did, that.'

'But goodness me, these two will have their work cut out,' she continues. 'Chock-a-block with clutter, it is. I don't think anything has been thrown out since it was bought. That'll have been in the 1920s. Is that right, Fred?' She shouts again at her husband. 'The house. When will your folks have bought it? The 1920s?'

'About then, aye.'

'And they'll need to tart it up if they want a good price. Nothing's been done to it since ...' Her eyes flicker. 'Well, houses need a woman's touch, don't they? Still, I'm happy to get stuck in. Begin in the attic room and work down to the cellar. As I said to

Fred, who knows what we might find?' She fingers her chunky beads, tight on her neck. 'I'm hoping for family heirlooms, not mice, mind.'

Sibeal smiles stiffly. 'Gabriel and I have it sorted, thanks.' Then when he doesn't reply, 'Gabe? We'll manage with the house, won't we?'

'Yes.' He seems to shake himself to the present and addresses his sister as though the others aren't there. 'But I'll need to get back, Sib. We've already talked about this. My job isn't moveable like yours; I've got my regular lessons and a backlog of tunings. I can't stay for ever.'

'That's sorted then,' the aunt says with a satisfied beam. 'I'll get out the bin liners and my Marigolds as soon as we've had some sustenance.' She nudges her husband. 'You'll be there to brew up, won't you, Fred? Then there'll be three of us. Perfect number!'

'There's already three of us, actually,' Katy says, the words flying out before she can stop them. 'Sibeal, and Gabriel, of course, for as long as he can. And me.'

For a pulse of time, everyone stares, and just when Katy thinks she will die from embarrassment, Sibeal speaks. 'That's right, we have our heavenly trio, Valerie. Can we order now, please?' She squeezes Katy's hand. 'Tomorrow at eleven. It'll be an adventure, little Kat! God knows what we'll find.'

7

Sibeal

Sibeal sits up with a jolt. It's dark and Gabriel is there by the bed.

The cold air pinches her flesh. 'What is it? What's happened?'

Lit by a shaft of light through the bedroom door, her brother is holding a mug. 'Nothing's happened, Sib. It's quarter to eleven. You asked that girl to come at eleven, so you need to get up.' He stares for a moment, then touches her shoulder. 'We're at Dad's, Sib. Remember?'

It takes a few seconds to adjust, to inhale the earthy aroma of coffee, to absorb Gabe's tense, handsome face. Of course; Dad is dead, his funeral was yesterday. Never to return, like Robin. The thought grasps her throat. 'You're wrong,' she says, swallowing, 'it can't be eleven, it's still dark.'

Gabe strides to the brocade curtains and yanks them back. 'See? Daylight.'

She flops back against the pillow and groans. She feels unbelievably groggy, her head like a scratchy sandbag. 'What bloody girl?'

'A woman, I suppose. Fringe and a high ponytail. No idea who she is. Daughter of one of Dad's friends or something—'

'One we've never bloody heard of.'

'An old schoolfriend, you said. Forty plus years ago, so it's unlikely we would. Now a judge? It was good of him to come.'

'After several decades? Weird, if you ask me.'

Gabe folds his arms. 'Like you turning up at Robin's?'

Robin. Oh God, the ache. She tried to numb it with whisky last night, but she was still awake in the early hours, just thinking of him. How he smelled, how he felt, how he spoke, that hint of northern twang infecting his posh vowels. How much she fucking missed him. And here it is again, pain in technicolour, just at the mention of his name.

'Did you know her?' she asks.

'Who?'

'His wife.'

'Zoe?'

Zoe. Fucking, fucking Zoe. 'Yeah.'

'Not really.' Gabe's eyes seem to flicker. 'I went to the wedding, and so did you. Why do you ask?'

'No reason.' She slips down the bed. 'So what does this girl-woman want?'

'To help with all this. Your room, mine. Dad's.' He ruffles his dark hair. 'And the rest. It's an impossible task, Sib. God knows where we'll start.'

Hugging the pillow, she closes her eyes. 'Good luck with that. It's too bloody cold to climb out.'

'You should've worn pyjamas. Come on, get up. You asked her to come, Sibeal.' There's an edge of irritation in his voice. 'You liked her yesterday. She seemed very shy, but you encouraged her.'

'Did I?' She thinks back to the girl in the pub. Bit younger than her, probably, fair-haired, pretty, sweet-looking. Not her

36

type at all. But then again, she doesn't have a type, she doesn't have friends, she doesn't want them. She doesn't want anyone or anything except Robin, and Robin has gone.

'Come on, Sib, make an effort. She seemed a nice person; she offered to help. Katy, I think she said her name was.'

Though she can't see her brother's face, she knows he's pushing back his glasses, a frown of love in his beautiful blue gaze. 'Come on. I know it isn't easy, but try, Sib. Please.'

'So you *do* remember her name. I might get jealous if you're not careful.' She throws back the duvet and strides out of the bed. 'Time me. Three minutes to get washed and dressed. And of course to look beautiful. Need to keep an eye on the competition.'

8

Katy

Katy retraces her steps along the wide tree-lined road. Though her heart is clattering loud in her ears, she tries to concentrate on the smell of newly mown grass and the pink and yellow blossom bursting from the branches. When she woke with the dawn this morning, she wondered if she'd really travel to Whalley Range, but after waving her dad off to work and dropping Milo at school, the rest of the day felt like a gaping chasm, so she walked straight from the playground to the bus stop, holding in her anxiety like a big gulp of air.

She arrived far too early, so she hurried past the sleeping house towards Alexandra Park, not even turning to the closed curtains in case she was seen. Then she strolled around the walkways of the expansive, dappled gardens and shelved her apprehension by watching her own footsteps and inhaling the spring air.

Now at the gate of Brook House, she pauses to absorb its façade. Large and detached, it has a flat window and a bay either side of the wooden porch, and though it's undoubtedly worn and faded, it's still dignified and handsome, somehow, like Laurence Olivier in his dotage. Like her own dad will be one day. She hopes, God, she hopes. Not like Sibeal and Gabriel's father who has died far too young. But she doesn't want to think of death. She's pushing herself out of her comfort zone, so today's a good day.

Taking a sharp breath, she strides to the front door and raps with the knocker. Nothing happens for a while, so she moves to one side, searching for a bell behind the dark, creeping ivy. She rubs the cobwebs from her hands, and when she looks up, the brother is on the threshold.

'Oh hi.' She nervously chuckles. 'Sorry, I didn't hear you—'

'Hello.' He gazes absently for a moment, then looks at a stash of paperwork in his hands. 'Sorry, I was in my bedroom. Nothing is ever where it's supposed to be.' His frown clearing, he rakes back his floppy fringe. 'It's Katy, isn't it? Sib is just getting ...' He gestures towards a polished wooden staircase. 'Well, she'll be down in a—'

Sibeal's voice echoes through. 'Let her in, for God's sake, Gabriel.'

He stands back. 'Sorry, yes, of course. Come on in.'

'Morning, little Kat!'

Wearing only her underwear, Sibeal rubs her arms theatrically from the landing above. 'Old bloody houses. Bet it's warmer out there than in here. Which means it's haunted, of course. Gabriel, what happened to the heating? It's freezing.'

His eyes blue and almost feminine, Gabriel scans Katy briefly, then motions to the panelled hallway. 'Come through to the kitchen. It's warmer in there.'

'OK, thanks.' Sweaty and shy from his appraisal, Katy follows him past one closed door. She stops and examines a wall hanging to give her hot face time to cool before reaching the next. 'This is nice.' She points to a faded monochrome photograph. 'Is it ...'

'Yup, it's here.' Gabriel joins her. 'Hard to believe it, but Whalley Range was one of the city's earliest suburbs. It was built by someone called Samuel Brooks from 1834 onwards.' He clears his throat. 'Brooks called the area "a desirable estate for gentlemen and families". You know, so the rich and privileged could escape the city's dirt and congestion. Ironic, don't you think? Still, someone thought it fit to name this house after him.'

Surprised to hear him speak for so long, Katy considers how to reply, but she's saved by the unexpected sound of Sibeal's sardonic tone close behind her. 'And this, little Kat, is our beloved Roman Catholic church of English Martyrs.'

Now dressed in an oversized sweater, Sibeal's finger is pressed against the glass of another framed image, this time of a church. She looks at her brother with raised eyebrows. 'Our local, you might say. Just a stone's throw away for compulsory attendance. Truly beloved, isn't it, Gabe?'

He snorts faintly without reply and heads to the end room, but Sibeal doesn't move. She stares at the old picture. 'Remind me to show you *the* painting,' she mutters. Then, abruptly rotating with a grin, 'Actually, let's look now. Gabe will make us a drink.'

Taking Katy's hand, she leads her up the first flight of stairs, then stops at the front bedroom. 'Are you ready?' she asks, opening the door with a flourish. She flicks a light switch. 'Ta-da!'

It takes a moment for Katy's eyes to adjust. Reminding her of the antiques village she and Milo recently visited with her dad, the dimly lit area is stuffed from floor to ceiling. Sturdy dark furniture, a grandfather clock, old newspapers, books, a commode, rugs and bureaus. Similar to the vintage bazaar, the woody aroma of tobacco, period pieces and old tomes fragrances the air. It isn't unpleasant; indeed, it feels like a study Sherlock Holmes might have just vacated.

Aware of Sibeal's intense expression, she searches for suitable words. But her new friend fills the silence. 'The smell?' she asks. 'Or should I say stink? You'll get used to it. Come in, but be careful not to trip. This is the junk room. Not that the others are exempt, as you'll see. I think we should start in here when we're ready, though. I'll be more brutal than Gabe and he won't know when I get bored and chuck everything out.' She pauses. 'The dining room's a different ball game, though. It's Gabe's baby.'

'Oh?'

'If you hear Chopin, that's where it's coming from.' She looks at her hands and flexes her long fingers. 'Not that anyone has played music in there for years. Gabe's the musician; I definitely am not.'

Though a shiver passes through her, Katy smiles and says, 'I see.' She glances around, but the atmosphere feels foggy. As if having the same thought, Sibeal strides to the window and opens the shutters.

She peers out of the dusty glass. 'No car. Don't you drive?'

As the sunlight streams in, Katy ponders how to answer. Her crippled real life will spill out at some point, but she may as well try to minimise it for now. 'Not these days. Pathetic really, but the thought of being behind a wheel unnerves me. I should get over it but—'

'So that's why your dad was so keen to whisk you home yesterday? In the Jag?'

'I guess so.'

'But you stayed.' Sibeal's dark eyes are sharp. 'And now you're here.'

Still pleased with her impetuous decision, Katy can't help smiling. 'Yes, I did, didn't I?' She spreads her arms and laughs. 'There's quite a task ahead! I'm looking forward to helping. Do you have a plan?'

Dropping into a sixties-style swivel chair, Sibeal swings from side to side and assesses her surroundings. 'No. I don't do plans. But I'm up and dressed in Gabe's jumper, and you're sweetly here, so that's a start.' Her gaze rests beyond Katy's shoulders. 'It's a monstrosity, isn't it? But I like it.'

Both intrigued and alarmed, Katy turns. Almost hidden behind the stuffed bookcases, a life-sized oil painting hangs from the picture rail. A blend of fine art and abstract, it's of a woman's face, her gaze sparkling from the shaft of sunshine through the window.

'What do you think?' Sibeal asks eventually.

Though Katy can't put her finger on what, the canvas resonates with *something*. 'It's interesting. It's as though the artist painted a traditional portrait and then covered it in random shadows. Except the eyes. They seem alive.'

Sibeal laughs without mirth. 'They aren't, I assure you. A trick of the light, that's all.' Her jaw tight, she stares at the portrait a moment longer, then sighs. 'It's of my mother. As painted by my dad after she died. You'll find more around the house that look more . . .' She appears to search for a word. 'Human.'

Katy nods; the celebrant said the wife had died too young. And those references in the pub she'd been too awed to fully absorb. She flushes again. 'Sorry, I didn't mean to be rude.'

'You weren't. Random shadows, I like it. You were actually spot on.' She frowns. 'Like ghosts, phantoms, spirits. Or whatever one likes to call the haunting.' She regains her focus and stands.

'I'm bored of this room already. Shall we procrastinate? Last I looked it was trying to be early summer outside. In this bubble I have no idea of the time. Is it too early for a large glass of red?' Her grin large and perfect, she laughs. 'I can tell by your look that it is, but consider this. If you were on holiday, would nearly noon be too early?'

Katy returns the smile. This house, this woman. So different to her closed life and compliance, she likes her and her rebellion already. That blend of indifference and emotion, too. 'Well, when you put it like that . . .'

Sibeal moves to the door. 'Come on then, little Kat. I know Gabriel will approve of you.'

'Oh?'

Pain seems to pass through her features, yet Sibeal casually shrugs. 'You can be my new whisky.'

9

Katy

Careful not to get her hair wet today, Katy keeps her head above the water and glides through the leisure club's warm lido. She would have brought Milo for a splash around in the kids' pool, but he was a little snotty when he woke, so her dad suggested he stay at home. Poor Milo's shoulders slumped, but in fairness his sniffles can soon turn to full-blown colds unless kept in check, and her dad soon distracted him with the need for 'Grandad pie-making help'.

Though it's time to get out and quickly change, she allows herself another couple of lengths. These lone swimming minutes are usually empty, sensations engaged but deep thought suspended. Yet this Sunday her mind is in Whalley Range, inside that house.

The property she shares with her father is a clean and tidy 1990s modern detached which she very much appreciates, so the desire to quarry in those old nooks and crannies, to unearth the secrets they hide, is strange. Not that she and Sibeal did any digging yesterday. After chatting upstairs, they joined Gabriel in the kitchen.

He pushed back his glasses and looked at his sister pointedly. 'I'll make another pot. That one will be cold.'

'We're here for vino,' she replied.

'No you're not,' he said. 'It's still morning and you haven't eaten yet.' His terse expression seemed to ease. 'Save it for later. You'll enjoy it more then. OK, Sib?'

'Fine!' she replied, widening her dark eyes at Katy. 'Ply me with bloody caffeine, see if I care!'

Watching the brother and sister again was captivating. Katy can't quite make them out. On the face of it Sibeal is the more dominant – and certainly more vocal – sibling, and yet the balance of power appears pretty equal overall. And it was good to study Gabriel more closely this time. Like his sister he's tall, broad-shouldered and slim, but it's as though he has inherited the more feminine features, she the male. And yet Sibeal is the spit of her mother, 'Saint Imelda', as she called her several times. When they left the junk room, she gestured to the far landing wall, then turned on a picture light which lit up a patchwork of portraits.

'Wow! Did you have to pose for them all?' Katy asked. They appeared to be in a variety of mediums, from pencil to charcoal to watercolour. She wanted to look closer, to examine and touch and drink them all in, but Sibeal shook her head. 'It's Saint Imelda, not me. Come on, time for wine.'

Conversation filtering over from the doorway brings Katy back to today. A gym bag over his shoulder and wearing a matching designer kit, the guy is turned away, but his hair and his voice are familiar. Oh heck, it's Bridget's friend *Doctor* Harry. Hoping he won't clock her, she continues her final metres of breaststroke as silently as she can. When she turns back for the steps, he's gone, thank goodness.

*

Glad she didn't incur the extra time of having to dry her thick barnet, Katy glances at her watch and hurries past the car park barrier. At times like this she wishes she still had a runaround, but home is only fifteen minutes away, less when she ups the pace. Yet as ever she has to be practical; she feels great today, but the crippling exhaustion can strike unexpectedly, so she mustn't risk pushing it.

She adopts her half-walk, half-jog as she leaves the tree-lined complex, but a sixth sense makes her stop. As she turns, a sleek sports car pulls up beside her. Anticipating a request for directions, she takes a big breath, but when the window winds down, it's those same amber eyes.

Harry grins. 'Small world. I thought it was you.'

'It is. I'm just—'

'Couch to 5K?'

She cringes with the usual embarrassment, but there's annoyance too. Back in her teens she was a bloody good athlete. 'No.'

'Got it. An Ironman.'

'Ha.'

'Are you always this chatty?'

'I'm in a hurry to get home, so . . .'

'Can I give you a lift?'

She relents with a polite smile. Alexander is unfailingly polite; he wouldn't approve of her surliness. 'No thank you, I'm fine.'

'Are you sure? I think it's about to rain.'

She looks up to the sky. 'I think I'll be OK.'

'Fair enough.' He studies her for another beat. 'I'd better let you get off, then. Rain in five minutes, just you see.'

Wet and cold from the downpour, Katy squeezes the rain from her ponytail and slips her trainers off outside the house.

Intending to head straight for a hot shower, she makes for the stairs, but a high titter echoes through from the kitchen. Should she leave Bridget to it? On balance, she decides to say hi.

'Hello, Bridget.'

'Katy!' She puts a hand to her chest. 'You made me jump. I didn't hear you come in.' Recovering herself from her cosy tête-à-tête with Alexander, she perches on a stool at the island and lifts her wine glass. 'Are you joining me? Remind me not to drop in when your dad's preparing lunch. He made me get stuck in with some peeling and I think this nail's a goner.'

Breathing away the surprising smart of irritation, Katy inhales the cooking aromas and watches her dad baste the beef joint. When he's finished turning the roast vegetables, he rotates and pecks her hair. 'Looks like you got caught. You should have given me a bell.' He nods to his companion. 'Bridget offered to help so I did a kindness by nominating her for the carrots. Onions always make me cry, but like the true gent I am . . .'

Bridget laughs. 'That would've been cruel, Alexander. Smelly hands as well as a broken acrylic.'

'I'll do it.' Katy picks up a chopping board and a knife. 'How do you want it, Dad? Sliced, diced, quartered—'

'Thought I'd toss it through the potatoes. So thick sliced, I'd say.'

'Okey-dokey. Where's Milo?'

'Upstairs. Ferociously colouring, the last time I looked in.'

Bridget takes a slug of her wine. 'You do know how lucky you are, don't you, Katy? A man in the house who can not only cook, but who does it willingly.'

'I'd be more than happy to do it, but Dad—'

'After years of being a dinosaur, I discovered I enjoyed it,

47

so it's now a hobby of sorts. And I rather think I've passed it down the line as my grandson prepared an apple and blackberry crumble earlier. It looks delicious. You are very welcome to join us, Bridget.'

'I'd love to, but Andrew might be offended, even if he has deserted me for his mountain bike this morning. I only popped in to catch up with Katy, see what she's been up to all week.'

'Not much,' Katy replies, noting that despite being a twenty-seven-year-old adult, she's being referred to in the third person. Again. And why does Bridget 'pop in' at this time on a Sunday when she knows she'll be at David Lloyd? But Bridget's flirtatiousness with her dad was ever thus. What irritates her far more is the dig about meals. She is perfectly willing and able to do it herself; Alexander doing the honours is just a habit they fell into.

Oblivious to Katy's tart reply, Bridget flashes another smile. 'This claret is delicious. You shouldn't tempt me so early in the day, Alexander.' Her eyes shiny with interest, she lowers her voice. 'Seeing as Milo's busy, I can ask about the funeral. It was Thursday, wasn't it? An old schoolfriend, I think you or Katy said? How did it go? A wife and kids?' Then looking from him to Katy, 'I take it there was a wake.'

'Quick, to be honest,' Alexander replies. 'Not helped by me having to shoot off to chambers. A fascinating case, though. Internet fraud is growing daily. This one has it all: email compromise, data breach, denial of service, malware, phishing, spoofing, ransomware. The list goes on. If you're staying, I could—'

'Perhaps another time.' Bridget stands. 'I'd better get off and see if the cyclist has returned.'

Katy carefully continues slicing the onions and inwardly smiles. Never one to offend, her dad always seamlessly changes the subject when he doesn't want to talk about something. Or, more to the point, when he knows Katy doesn't want to. She'd saved the story of her surreal visit to Brook House to please – and astonish – both him and Bridget; indeed, she'd been looking forward to regaling them with each and every detail about her strange yet fascinating new friends but, on reflection, the thought of keeping them secret a little while longer feels rather nice.

10

Sibeal

Intermittent pearls of rain fall from the gloomy sky, land on the SUV windscreen, then splatter and spread like globules of spittle. Sibeal opens the glovebox, selects the first pair of sunglasses she finds, slips them on and pulls down the mirror flap. It's Gabe's fault she's here. They had a row this morning at breakfast, which might just have been lunch, and she had to get out.

Despite her sheer misery, she snorts to herself. She shouldn't have been such a good girl. To please Gabe she'd dropped the empty J&B bottle in the brown bin, more or less leaving the evidence in plain sight.

'What's this?' he asked, wafting his find when she flopped to the kitchen table.

'Recycling, I think one calls it.'

'It was half full when I went to bed last night. Apart from your well-being, whisky costs money. How much a go? Twenty pounds?'

'Insulting, Gabe. I don't drink the cheap stuff. Maybe thirty quid? Thirty-five?'

'Bloody hell.'

'That's nothing.'

'Maybe to you. It's a whole hour of teaching time.'

Her head badly thumped. The last thing she needed was a lecture. 'Then charge those ghastly parents more for lessons. Or ditch the snivelling kids for your London piano tuning. Anything to stop you constantly moaning about money.' She looked at his uniform of jeans and a shirt. 'What do you do with it anyway? You're always skint, you dress like a pauper, your car's a million years old . . .'

'Off subject, Sibeal. You'd already had plenty of wine before I left. The amount you're throwing back isn't good for your health. You drink more than you eat. You've lost weight and your face—'

'Stop lecturing!' There was no need for him to get personal; commenting on her looks was below the bloody belt. And how would she possibly begin to explain about the parallel world she needs to escape to? Not just now, but for ever. 'For one minute shut up. You're not my bloody father.'

'More's the pity. You didn't drink when he was in the house. He might be dead, but the least you can do is respect it now.'

'So it's OK for you to do it, but not me.'

'I don't become offensive—'

'Offensive? How?'

'All that Saint Imelda stuff. You even did it with a complete stranger.'

'What?'

'Katy, the other day.' He mimicked her voice. '"Here's our beloved church . . ."'

Emotion caught in her throat then. She didn't want to fall out with Gabe of all people; she just missed Robin so bloody much. 'I don't mean anything by it. You know I'm just joking,' she managed. 'Sorry, Gabe, I'll stop saying it, I promise.'

She reached out for a hug, but he pulled away. 'I'm going out. I might even give our "beloved church" a go seeing as it's Sunday.'

That's when she scraped back her chair, stomped to her car keys and left the building. She had to leave before Gabe did; the music and bad dreams were still tangible, the thought of being alone with them unbearable. A coffee to cool off might have been the plan, but she didn't bring her handbag, not even a coat, and she found herself here. So it's Gabe's fault, absolutely. Here in Wilmslow when she promised herself she'd never do it again.

She glances around the leafy street, the affluent houses set back either side. She should go, she really should. Yet a few moments won't hurt, a minute to squint beyond the begonias, sweet peas and petunias surrounding the manicured lawn, to the window beyond.

She pictures the widow-wife in her weeds. Zoe. Has she reverted to the more familiar – and yes, too bloody attractive – woman in the Facebook photographs? The horsey face and enhanced lips, the top-heavy yet gym-toned body? How she'd hated to look at her Hollywood-white smile, but like a masochism of sorts, each night she'd been unable to resist before sleep. A really stupid move because the happy family snaps would be etched on her mind. *Me and my two handsome boys* at the beach or the zoo. Eating a hot dog or a Mr Whippy ice cream. At the park, on the seesaw, the climbing frame, the swings. Or in the garden, *this* fucking pristine garden.

Then there were the posed, pouty selfies with Robin. *How did I get so lucky?*; *Couldn't wish for a better hubby*; *Date night tonight!*

With a yelp of frustration, Sibeal searches for a better scene in her head. Yes, there's one. *Her* and Robin, sweaty and naked in her king-sized bed. Chest to chest, lip to lip, breath to breath. His gorgeous, gorgeous post-sex grin. So loving, so vital. So fucking *alive*. Did he say it? Did he really quip: 'If I die, promise you'll come to my funeral. Promise you'll wear red and knock them all dead.'

She taps her head against the steering wheel. 'What the hell happened, Robin?' she mutters out loud. 'You were with me in that bed only the evening before . . .'

Should she have known? Should she have felt something momentous when he died? All she can remember of their last tryst was them falling asleep and him having to bolt out of the house without even taking a shower. It wasn't his lack of texts or replies that she noticed over the following days but Gabe's, so much so that she marched round to his house to confront him in person.

'Why aren't you answering my messages?' she demanded when he finally opened the door. Then, clocking his red eyes, 'What's happened, Gabriel?'

'It's Robin.'

'Robin? What about him?'

'It's unbelievable—'

'What is, Gabe?'

'He's died.'

'What?'

'Robin is dead, Sib.'

'When?'

Gabe squinted in thought. 'Christ, the first.'

Four days previously; April Fool's. His words were so surreal they felt like a joke. Yet his distraught face said otherwise. 'What? He can't be, he . . . What happened?'

'He . . .'

She wanted to shake every last detail from him. 'He *what*, Gabe?'

'He died in hospital.'

'Of what?'

Gabe raked a trembling hand through his hair. 'I could hardly phone Zoe and demand chapter and verse from the poor woman.'

She couldn't listen to more. The shock, the devastation, the certainty that bitch had done *something* to Robin was so jammed in her chest she couldn't breathe. But she should have stayed and probed for more information instead of lurching away.

'What the hell happened, Robin?' she asks again.

As though he's been listening, an upstairs bedroom floods with light and a face appears at the window. Sure she's been seen, Sibeal slips down the seat and turns on the ignition. Bloody ironic, really. How many times did she sit in this very spot, wanting to be caught? There's no point now, no point at all. And yet the need is still there, pumping through her veins. A desire to punish *her* when no one else will.

Then, of course, there's the boy. Robin's boy, the baby that should have been hers. She'd planned to call him Joseph.

Hateful, hateful woman. She even stole his name.

11

Katy

Still stuffed from the Sunday roast, Katy lies on the sofa with the novel she's reading for her book group and stifles yet another yawn. It seems as though she's been on the same paragraph all evening, so it's a good job she read it years ago; in those days she'd consume anything and everything she could lay her hands on, from her dad's childhood set of Alexandre Dumas books to the Scandinavian noir her mum loved to read. Henning and his Wallander outlived Elke, but not for long. Though, did Wallander actually die? She isn't sure, but the character had Alzheimer's and, as her dad says, that particular disease is a 'living death' even before it kills one. And he should know – he lost both parents to it in quick succession.

Sniffing the dismal thoughts away, she watches her son doodle on his tablet. She's tempted to close her eyes at the same time as him, but there's a programme she fancies in an hour, so she'll force herself to stay awake until then. And tonight her drowsiness is simply from a glass of wine at lunch, so it feels important to fight it.

'It's seven thirty. Teeth, then time for bed, Milo.'

Like a balloon with a puncture, he deflates into the soft cushions of the chair. She can't help but smile; she used to do pretty much the same at five years of age; sitting very still and holding her breath at the start of *Corrie*, as though that might make her invisible.

She stands and offers her hand. 'It's school tomorrow. A nice new week!' Then, when he pouts, 'Come on, love. You know the rules.'

'It isn't fair. Dylan says he's allowed to watch—'

A rich voice interrupts from behind them. 'I bet Dylan's grandad doesn't read him not one but two bedtime stories.'

Milo punches the air. 'Yes!'

Katy studies her father's drawn features. 'Are you sure, Dad? You were knee deep in paperwork the last time I looked. It's for your trial tomorrow, isn't it?'

He takes off his reading glasses and rubs his eyes. 'To be honest, I need a break. A change of genre is just the thing. How about some more Penelope Dreadful, Milo? See what mystery she's uncovering this time.'

'Yes.' Milo grins. 'And then a powder nap, Grandad?'

He puts a finger to his lips. 'That's a secret, remember? Don't want Mummy to find out.'

Milo tightens the belt of his dressing gown and giggles. 'Sometimes *I* tell the story and Grandad falls asleep. He says it's a powder nap. It's what grown-ups do to charge their batteries.' He lifts his arms for a hug. 'But grown-ups don't really have batteries, do they, Mummy?'

Love swelling in her chest, she scoops him up and absorbs the smell of shampoo and innocence. 'No, Milo, they don't, but your grandad is so full of beans, sometimes I wonder.'

He pulls away, his eyes like brown shiny buttons. 'Baked beans, Mummy? Grandad always says: "Heinz every time. A bean won't pass my lips unless it's Heinz!"'

Impressed at his mimicry, Katy laughs. 'Think I've heard that one too, just once or twice.' Suddenly realising her boy will be too heavy to lift fairly soon, she hands him to her father. 'Night night, gorgeous. Don't forget to clean your teeth! See you in the morning, bright and early.'

Once the door clicks to, she wryly smiles at the thought of *powder* naps. How nice it would be to cure her lethargy with a quick siesta, but once her eyelids droop, she's immediately dragged into black, tarry sleep, and although she tries to climb out, she just can't. More recently, she's learned not to fight it. Better to defer the calling of her bed's comforts for as long as she can, though it's rarely later than nine when she's feeling like that.

But this evening she's just tired like anyone else. Isn't she? To convince herself, she extends her arms high, then touches her toes several times. The action summons a flash of Doctor Harry in his ridiculous Lycra doing stretches as he chatted to his pal this morning. As if he was a professional sportsman, the idiot. Yet in fairness, it did rain as he'd predicted the moment he drove away, so perhaps she's the fool after all. And with her track history . . .

Shaking off that thought, she pads to the kitchen and stares at the Nespresso machine. Another coffee or wait for her bedtime cocoa? She went onto decaf several months ago to help with the jitters, the heartburn and anxiety, but sadly not for insomnia. The cure was self-prescribed, an internet search as usual, the same one which said most decaffeinated drinks still contain some caffeine. But it made her feel better. Progress; a step in the right direction, like the swimming these days.

Her ears prick at the distant peal of her mobile. When she finally locates it beneath Milo's pile of soft toys, it's a number she doesn't recognise. The unknown still scares her, but she focuses on *progress* and *steps*, and answers it.

'Hello?'

'Robin left me. He left me all alone.'

It takes a moment to work out the slurred voice. 'Sibeal? Is that you?'

'He left me all alone. Robin, my beautiful man.'

What on earth . . .? 'It's Katy here, Katy Henry. Is that you, Sibeal? Are you OK?'

'I know it's you. My little Kit Kat. I'm all on my own. He's gone.'

'Who's gone?'

'Gabriel. We argued and now he's fucked off somewhere. He never tells me where. He's hiding something, I know. He always has, little Kat. Why doesn't he tell me? He's supposed to love me.'

'Oh, I don't—'

'Well, I don't care anyway! Wherever he's gone, he can stay there. But you need to come. Please? Will you come, keep me company for a bit?'

Katy pauses to consider her request. This call is most odd, and if Sibeal's incoherent rambling is anything to go by, she must have drunk a *lot*. And yet there's a warm, spreading glow in her chest. Her strange but fascinating new *friend* needs her. Because only a friend would ask, right?

'Yes, of course I'll come. It's just . . .' She falters. Her dad's with Milo; it's past Milo's bedtime; she can't drag them out. How will she get there?

'Thank you, thank you . . .' Sibeal's voice appeals. 'Now,

Kat? You will come now, won't you? Come and turn off the bloody piano.'

Katy stares into space as she thinks. Her dad uses black cabs; they're sturdy and safe, aren't they? 'Yeah, sure. I'll call a taxi now. I don't know how long I'll be, but I'll have my phone, so if you need to call . . .'

'Kind Kat. I knew you would be.'

'OK. See you very soon.'

Her heart thrashing with adrenalin and purpose, Katy orders a cab, then darts up the stairs. At the top she inhales deeply, gently pushes down Milo's handle and takes in the picture of grandfather and grandson, so strikingly similar and peaceful in sleep. Retracing her steps, she thanks her lucky stars, slips on her trainers and scrawls a message to her dad. Then, puffing out her tingling energy, she opens the front door to a new world outside.

12

Katy

Wondering if she'll recognise the house through the dusk, Katy peers through the taxi's grimy window. She spots the ivy-clad wooden porch. 'Just here, please. How much?'

'Eight pounds, please, love.'

She does another take. Though the gate is still latched, the front door of Brook House is clearly ajar. Fumbling with her purse, she pulls out a tenner and hands it to the driver.

'You all right, love?'

So used to that question, Katy barely hears it. Besides, she's too alarmed by the memory of Sibeal's teary, drunken blather. Suppose something is badly wrong? Could she cope on her own, without her dad, without Bridget? Yet she finds herself tumbling out, belting up the path and bursting in.

Though the hallway is in darkness, a dull beam from the kitchen bathes Sibeal's motionless body like a spotlight. Her head tucked in her chest and her arms around her knees, she's in the foetal position, a pose Katy understands all too well. Scanning for any signs of blood or injury, she crouches beside her.

'Sibeal? Are you OK? It's Katy.' Fear grips her chest as she stares.

Oh God, she's been here before. But this isn't about her, not today. 'Sibeal?' she says again. 'Wake up, it's Katy. You called me.'

A beat of time passes, then two and three. Then just as Katy puts out a trembling hand to touch her, Sibeal lifts her head and extends her legs. A bottle rolls from her lap, rocking on the polished floorboards before coming to a standstill.

Her dark gaze takes several seconds to clear. 'It's Kat, little Kat. Hello,' she says eventually. Gathering up her long limbs, she stands, unsteady but graceful, like a newborn foal. 'You came.' She gestures to the front room as though nothing is amiss. 'Please come through to the parlour. We've never been la-di-da but we always called it a parlour. Is that odd? No fire, I'm afraid, that's Gabe's department, but I found a . . .' She gestures to a fan heater. 'No idea what you call these things, but we need to . . . We need electricity! Can you see a socket?'

Katy flicks on the light and searches the 'parlour' for a plug. It has a jaded elegance about it, but there's a definite hue of decay, from the dank smell to the jigsaw of damp patches on the ceiling and the yellowing gloss.

Clearly as old as the hills, the machine puffs out a thin stream of balmy air. 'There we go. You need to warm up. Where do you want to . . .'

But Sibeal has already settled on the scuffed leather sofa. 'Gabriel would say I'm drunk, but I'm not.' She pats the seat beside her. 'Do sit. Am I inebriated, little Kat? If one can say the word without stumbling over it, one can't possibly be that, can one? Or even intoxicated! See? Beautifully enunciated.'

Resting her head on the arm, she dozes for a while, then re-animates herself again. 'I haven't offered you something to drink. That's rude. Gabe would say I'm rude. But he's fucked off so he can't climb on his horse and say that he's at the end of his tether. How very charming.' She burps. 'Do you think Gabriel's charming? He can be, you know, gives cuddles if you ask. But he just fucked off when he knows I hate the silence. When it's quiet I hear it; I hear *her*. He knows that. So why would he leave me? But you'll stay, won't you, little Kat?'

'Yes.' So noble, so tragic, so pissed. And so very needy. Katy finds herself squeezing her new friend's hand. 'Yes, I'll stay for as long as I can, but I'll need to go back before it gets too late. Sometimes Milo wakes up and Alexander has to leave early for his train in the morning.'

Sibeal frowns. 'Who's Alexander?'

'My dad. He came to the funeral.'

'Ah, the handsome hanging judge.' She snorts. 'My father's car is a Jaguar, he drives it rather fast! Shiny nouveau riche little Kat.' She brings her fingers to her face like whiskers. 'Not poor old-money church mice like us. Like Gabriel. What the fuck does he do with his cash? Tell me; it worries me.'

'I have no—'

'So, who's Milo?'

'My son. He's just turned five. He's . . .'

But Sibeal's attention has gone again. She's staring at the grate, her eyes shiny as though it is lit. 'I was promised one. A beautiful baby called Joseph.' She spirals around. 'Shall I tell you a secret about my man? A secret about Robin?'

Though the smell of sour alcohol hits her, Katy doesn't recoil. She recognises the desperation in this woman's very being; she needs to talk, to let something out. 'Yes, of course.'

The fan heater clatters, loud in the silence. Eventually Sibeal speaks. '*She* killed him. That's what he told me. That he'd end up strangled.' Her gaze wide, she flops back. 'Should I tell? Who should I tell?'

Katy blows out her trapped breath. 'I don't know. I'm sorry, I don't even know who you're talking—'

Sibeal grabs both her hands and laughs. 'Your face, little Kat! Your pretty, pretty face! Don't worry, we don't tell, do we? Rule number one, some things we never tell.'

'Sibeal. Stop.'

Both jumping at the sound, they snap around to the doorway. Gabriel's expression is stony, his jaw tight.

Sibeal rocks forward. 'You left. You left me alone!'

'No I didn't, Sib. I had to go home to . . . to do stuff. I left you a note.'

Finally up from the sofa, Sibeal points her finger. 'No, you did not.'

He disappears, then returns with a scrap of paper. 'Next to the telephone. A text too. Look at your mobile, Sib.' He glances at the elegantly shaped coffee table. 'No drink? Sorry, Katy, that's rude. What can I get you?'

'Rude . . .' Sibeal whispers loudly.

Though she smirks, the tension between the siblings is palpable. 'I'm fine, thanks.' Katy stands. 'It's probably time for me to go anyway. I'll just call a taxi.'

'No, absolutely not. It was good of you to come. I'll drop you home. If we go now the car will still be warm.' Gabriel looks at his sister. 'OK with you? I'll be twenty minutes.'

'Warm car. Very sensible.' Sibeal shuffles away. 'The junk room,' she says over her shoulder. 'Tomorrow, Kat. No, Tuesday. I'll text.'

*

63

Save for the steady rhythm of the wipers, Gabriel drives his old Volvo in silence. But at the temporary traffic lights, he turns, his eyes hazy and troubled.

'I teach music near home. Home being a village between Leeds and York. Close to the battlefield of Towton? And I have to travel a fair bit ...' He clears his throat. 'Both for teaching and tuning pianos. So I can't always be around. I spend time in London too. I have ... I have commitments there.'

Katy waits for more, but when he doesn't elaborate, she smiles. 'I got to grade eight, but I haven't touched our upright for years. It probably needs a good old tuning.' Then after a moment, 'Not that I'm asking you to—'

'It all depends what you want from your piano. Take jazz, for example. You need that hard and crisp hammer, but something cosy like the blues ... Well, some tuners shred the felt to get a softer sound.'

'That's interesting. I didn't know that.'

'Yeah.' He takes a big breath. 'Sib. Whatever she's said about Mum ... Well, she wasn't that bad. In fact, not bad at all, really. She suffered from severe post-natal depression after Sib was born, and despite medication and counselling, she never recovered.' He rakes his hair and sighs. 'Look, I know mother and daughter relationships can be fraught at the best of times and I love Sib; she's fun, unbelievably intelligent, a brilliant businesswoman, but sometimes ... Well, you've probably gathered she can be a bit dramatic when the fancy takes her.'

His look is so intense, it's all Katy can do to maintain eye contact, but she's saved by a beep from behind them.

'Thanks so much for the lift,' she says when she finally climbs out. 'I hope she's OK.'

His cloudy features are transformed by an unexpected smile. 'Sibeal is always OK. And all the better for having a friend, so thank you for coming.'

Feeling his gaze burn her spine, Katy strides over the driveway and fumbles to insert the front door key. Though it's nearly midnight, she's exhilarated, excited and wide, wide awake. What a surreal and compelling couple of hours. So very different to her closeted, mundane life. As she heads for the stairs, she chuckles to herself. How on earth will she manage to sleep?

13

Sibeal

Inhaling the satisfying smell of new leather, Sibeal pulls up the SUV outside little Kat's house and presses the horn. After over-thinking how shit her life was during a work-related trip yesterday, she woke up strangely cheerful, excited by the prospect of hanging out with her. Not that her new friend is actually so little. She's shorter than her, but most girls are. It's more her petite pretty face, all neat and symmetrical and shiny like a dolly's. Why that's appealing, Sibeal doesn't know. She had zero interest in the 'tick-box' dolls, babies and Barbies – and all the girlie paraphernalia that went with them – she was bought as a kid. Gabe's presents seemed so much more exciting. *Were* more exciting, because he was older, from the Gameboy, Ninja Turtles and Power Rangers to his beloved Tamagotchi. As for the sheet music and notepads, the endless pencils or erasers embossed with crotchets and quavers, she didn't covet them, per se; it was more the naked, indulgent love that was bestowed with them.

Sighing deeply, she pushes that particular image away. She's spent the last nineteen years blocking out her mother – sometimes more successfully than others – but the bloody woman came back big time with James's death.

If Saint Imelda ever left in the first place . . .

Great-Aunt Sibeal's imposing figure, duly garbed in black, flashes in behind her eyes. What a bloody namesake! Remembering the old bat's look of horror, she gives an involuntary little shiver.

She clenches her jaw. Nope, she won't let her mother in, she won't allow her to tunnel and chip away at her psyche, her confidence and self-worth. Instead she focuses on today and the moss-free driveway of Kat's well-to-do home.

'My father's car is a Jaguar . . .' she mutters.

Had she actually known he drove one? Or did the hanging judge just look like that respectable, wealthy but not overly flashy sort who sends their kids to elocution lessons? He's parked it to one side, as though leaving space for another. Kat's? No, she said something about not driving and nerves. Yup, she can see that, the way her blue eyes slide away when she talks for too long. And her propensity to blush, though the two spots of pink on her cheeks make her look even sweeter.

Donning her WebLife 'hat', she scans the handsome house and considers how she'd describe it online for her networking business. Next to the leafy local park and with the mandatory electronic gates, the retro-modern building looks around the same age as hers. Not that her and Gabe's tiny homes have what looks like five en-suite bedrooms and high ceilings, classical bay windows, Cheshire brickwork and smart double garages. She sniggers to herself. If she needed a tagline it'd be: 'the sort of property the liberal rich tend to buy'.

She glances at her watch. Should she honk again? Stride up

and hammer on the door? Nope; after Gabriel's admonishment, it wouldn't do to show her general lack of patience – or manners – and make a scene. A polite 'I've been waiting five minutes; are you bloody well coming?' text is the thing. Yet when she looks to the passenger seat for her mobile, it isn't there, nor underneath, in the footwell, nor on the dash. Did she even bring it after waking late and hurtling from Brook House? Christ, she isn't sure. It's usually glued to her hand; her soul, her heart, waiting for its chime, a sound that would make her salivate like Pavlov's bloody dog.

Scrunching her eyes, she breathes through a new wave of grief. She doesn't want to move on, be indifferent or blasé. She needs Robin still tangible; to sense him, to smell him, to feel his presence. She can't let him go; she won't. Her shoulders relax as he steps into the frame of a memory. He's still there, thank God, tugging her towards the crumpled sheets; his eyes, his smile, the citrus aroma of his aftershave. His neatly trimmed beard, toned chest and those bloody tight buttocks. The kisses and caresses, the love, making love. That intense, roisterous release . . .

The scene grips her throat, but the impulse to jump out and roar at the sky is punctured by a slamming sound. It's Kat at last, her high ponytail jaunty but her face hesitant and pale.

She opens the door. 'So sorry for the wait. I just needed to sort out a few things. It's very good of you to collect me,' she says breathlessly, as though she's been running. 'You didn't need to put yourself out; I could've caught the bus.'

Surprised at her friend's demeanour, Sibeal shelves her own angst. Kat's expression is serious, almost tearful. What to say to her? Best make her smile.

'I got told off by my brother big time about Sunday, so I had no option. Poor old Gabe. Still, his life would be dull without me causing him grief, so I'm doing him a favour when I'm being badly behaved.' She gestures to the scarf she hurriedly tied around her head before leaving. 'What do you think? Charlady or what?'

Kat's features relax as she looks. The smile's nearly there. A little push more. 'God knows who it belongs to. Not my pot-bellied aunt Valerie, I hope! Though it's really to cover my greasy locks as I had no time for a shower. I probably stink of BO. You don't mind labouring with a smelly co-worker, do you?'

Kat's lips twitch as she sniffs the air. 'I don't detect any bromhidrosis as yet. Still, if we work up a good sweat today, I might get lucky.'

'Hark at you with your "bromhidrosis". Medically qualified or what?'

Kat's gaze falters. 'Just a geeky swat, probably.' She rallies. 'Pot-bellied aunt! Cruel! Brook House is so huge. Clearing the junk room to start, I think you said.'

'Did I?' She feels a stab of guilt as reality hits. Her lovely dad is dead and she's barely given him a thought. James Matthews isn't slowly expiring in the hospice any more. Like Robin, he's gone, forever gone. 'Truth is, I don't want to begin anywhere, do anything with the house. I want to leave it preserved like a tomb. I don't want to unsettle it,' she says quietly.

Briefly touching her hand, Kat studies her inquisitively. 'Unsettle what?'

'Ghosts, of course.'

An honest reply and so rare. She doesn't know why she said any of it. Perhaps it's Kat's quiet guilelessness, but there's an impulse to share. She snorts to cover her agitation. 'All old houses have them, don't they? Apparitions, phantoms, evil spirits?' She gestures through the windscreen. 'Yours is modern, but that's no excuse. It's still probably built on an ancient graveyard, a witches' coven or similar . . .'

'An orchard apparently. Opulent top soil, which the developers sold, replacing it with rubbish cheap earth, according to Dad . . . We've been here since I was born, so it still has lots of history . . .' She seems to shake her thoughts away. 'But I'm all yours today. Your wish is my command until it's time to collect Milo from school.'

A spike of jealousy hitting, Sibeal starts the engine and doesn't reply. Her child, Robin's. The one she never had . . . Christ, what's wrong with her today? Ignoring the loud blare of an oncoming car, she clears the emotion stuck in her throat. 'So, was I badly behaved the other night?' She grimaces. 'Oh God, I can tell by your silence I was. Go on, spit it out. What did I say?'

A beat of time passes, then: 'You were talking about Robin.'

Robin. Hearing his name from someone else's lips is both exquisite and unbearable. She takes a breath to change the subject, but the whispered truth slips out. 'Robin was my lover.'

'I sort of gathered that. But he left you?'

'No, he did not!' Her reply emerges more harshly than she intends, but it's important to explain, so she pulls the car onto the pavement. 'He died, Kat,' she says, the words bubbling out. 'And because I was his secret I can't grieve, I can't cry, I can't bloody breathe. I can't say that I miss him out loud. That I miss him, I miss him. I fucking miss him!' She stares at Kat's startled expression. 'It's stifling me, suffocating me. You won't understand, nobody understands, no one can.'

For several moments, Kat doesn't reply. When she finally speaks, her voice is tremulous, yet clipped. 'I do a little, actually.

My mum died. In a car crash.' She clears her throat. 'She was with Dad. She died and he didn't, so people thought I was lucky. You know, only to lose one parent when I could have lost both. And I was twenty-two, an adult, so it was indulgent to make a fuss. But it wasn't just that.' She frowns as though searching for the words. 'They were devoted, Mum and Dad. He lost his wife, his best friend. It didn't feel fair to add to his grief. I don't have a brother or a sister, so I just held it in.'

'Wow.' Sibeal whistles softly and rejoins the traffic. So, they've both lost a mother. How strange. But perhaps that's what draws her to this quiet, contained girl. Yet what is more 'normal': Kat's selfless silence, or her constant demand for attention at eleven, at thirteen and fourteen, hell, even now?

She turns to Kat at the pelican crossing. 'Didn't you want to kick and cry and let it all out?'

Kat polishes the face of her watch. 'At first. Sometimes I wanted to scream "What about me? What about me? Don't I matter too?" Then, as time passed, I got so used to holding it in that it sort of became comfortable.' She pauses again, her features thoughtful. 'But it got stuck inside here.' She puts her palm on her chest. 'To the point where I couldn't talk about it at all . . .'

Sibeal shrugs. 'You're telling me now.' Then after a moment, 'Like I told you about Robin.'

'I know!' The tension in Kat's jaw is replaced with a smile. 'I know. How weird is that?'

14

Katy

Trying to quell her thrashing heart, Katy spends the rest of the journey silently studying her hands. Her ability to speak about the accident has got a touch better, yet it's still pretty poor after five long years. Not that they've felt very long – in her zombified state she's been half absent – asleep, mostly, but frustratingly weary, useless and incapacitated when conscious. And though it goes in the face of psychological advice, she still prefers to 'bottle' her mum. She can't explain why, but it's as though she gives a little part of her away every time she's mentioned. Yet today has been a sea-change of sorts. Talking to Sibeal feels different. Maybe because she has suffered loss too.

A sudden jolting movement brings her back to the present. She whips up her head, then sighs, feeling foolish. It's fine; they've arrived at Brook House; it's only the high kerb and Sibeal's erratic driving.

'No Gabe,' she's saying, scanning the road through the windscreen. Then clearly remembering, 'Ah, bin liners. That's where he'll be. Come on.'

Katy follows her down the weed-strewn path. Sibeal stops at

a cracked plant pot and gestures to a woody and leafless azalea with two plucky purple flowers. 'Dead but not dead like . . .' She shakes her head. 'Like my dad at the hospice.' She extracts her find and wafts it. '*La clé de la porte!*'

Surprised people really do hide a key in plain sight, Katy steps inside the old house. From the double window locks, to the alarm, to his new video doorbell, her own dad is fanatical about security.

'When you've been so long in the law . . .' he wryly says when Bridget makes her frequent 'Fort Knox' comment.

Sibeal reads her thoughts. 'Well, there's nothing to steal,' she throws over her shoulder.

Scooping the post up en route, she heads straight to the kitchen and flops down at the table. 'Unless you're into junk and more junk. Though don't say that to Gabe as he likes to call them "antiques".' She raises her arched eyebrows. 'He thinks we'll make a bob or two from the contents, but I'm not convinced. I'd personally hand it all over to a house clearer, auction place or whatever, but he's insisting we go through everything first. Drawers, chests, bureaus, wardrobes. Find paperwork, family memorabilia, hidden bloody ivory. To be honest I'm exhausted just thinking about it and I woke up at an ungodly hour. Bloody noisy old house. Pipes, doors, floorboards. Clunking, chugging, *clanking* . . .' She laughs. 'And that's just Gabe in the bathroom.' She yawns theatrically. 'I need a pint of fresh coffee, but instant will have to do.'

Glad to feel full of beans – for now – Katy turns to the kettle. 'I'll make it. How do you like it?'

'However it appears.' Sibeal stretches. 'You can come again. You're very calm and I like that. Same as Gabe, you're . . . I don't know, serene. Yup, serene.'

'Not entirely,' Kat replies, busying herself with the mugs to cover her embarrassment.

The abridged version of her mum's death didn't include her hysteria when two police officers knocked at the door in the early hours; her inability to focus on their words after 'your mother and father have been in a road accident . . .'; her certainty that both parents were dead, even as she sat by her dad's bedside and watched the regular rhythm of his chest. Her complete and utter panic and terror even though she'd been on medication since university; stabilisers for anxiety; hypnotics to help her sleep.

Truly ironic when it's all she can do to stay awake these days.

'Gabe's like that.'

'Sorry?'

Sibeal pulls the scarf from her head and ruffles her glossy hair. 'Not *entirely* calm.' She laughs, a joyous loud peal. 'But that's usually because I'm driving him mad.' Her face suddenly stills. 'By the way, don't mention Robin to him.'

'Course not. I wouldn't dream of—'

'He thought Robin was a selfish prick. I don't know why, really. They were best mates at uni.'

'Oh?' Katy waits for Sibeal to say more about the man's death. Something about strangulation, she said the other night. But then again, she was drunk, paralytic almost, and making no sense.

'Gabe has no taste, Kat. You've seen his clothes and that wreck of a car. Men, women, dogs – his judgement's impaired. Badly.' She shrugs and snorts. 'That's what comes of only ever loving his saintly mother.'

'*Our* mother, Sibeal.'

74

Carrying two bags of shopping, Gabriel scowls from the door. He wafts the famous black liners, then balances them on a tower of newspapers stacked against the wall.

'These are from upstairs,' he says stiffly. 'No idea why Dad kept them, but I suggest you briefly look at each date and head-line and if nothing grabs your attention, they can go in the blue recycling bin.' He stares at Sibeal briefly before turning away. 'Do something useful while you're baring your soul.'

'For Christ's sake!' She scrapes back her chair. 'The world doesn't revolve around her, Gabriel. You're thirty-five. Why don't you grow up? Get a life, even have fun once in a while.'

His jaw tight, he slowly rotates. 'Get a life, should I? Like you have? Then why are you still having a go at her, even now? Mum's been dead for nearly twenty bloody years—'

'I wasn't "having a go". We weren't even talking about her. She isn't the sole topic of conversation.' She lifts her chin. 'But seeing as you've brought up the subject of *our* mother, tell me, Gabe, which mother was *ours*? The one who couldn't do enough for her precious Gabriel or the one who couldn't bear to look at her daughter's face, let alone kiss or cuddle or pretend to love her?'

'That isn't true, Sib. She did love you very much, of course she did.' He massages his forehead. 'Sometimes she was low. That's all. It wasn't her fault. She was ill.' His expression softens. 'You know this, Sib. We've talked about it many, many—'

'Quite right; it wasn't her fault. It was mine for being born, wasn't it?' Despite her defiant stance, her voice catches. 'If I hadn't appeared, she'd still be your lovely happy mummy. I think that's the theory, isn't it, Gabriel?'

'I've never said that.'

Hardly daring to breathe, Katy waits on the sidelines for someone to speak. When the silence becomes oppressive, she turns to her chore, pours steaming water into three mugs and places them on the table. Like Narnians turned to stone, neither of them have moved. 'Does anyone take sugar?' she asks. 'I wasn't sure where to find—'

'But it's what you *think*, isn't it?' Sibeal says, as though the intermission hasn't happened. 'I could see it in your eyes, Gabe. When she died, you wished it was me, didn't you? You wished I'd gone and not her?'

His blue eyes flicker and Katy knows he needs to be truthful. 'For an iota, Sib. A blink of an eye. I was just sixteen. I was meant to be a man, but I still desperately needed her.'

'And I suppose you think a girl who hadn't even hit puberty didn't,' Sibeal mutters. 'At least my crazy hoarder dad loved me.'

She scoops a *Westmorland Gazette* from the pile, scans it and adopts a newsreader's tone. 'Today's headlines. "Brewery celebrates one year of business with the launch of three new beers." "Barn to be turned into a holiday let." "Alleged sex offender has a solid alibi. Police hunt continues." "Hundreds of animal cruelty calls in Cumbria over three years."' She guffaws. 'Bloody hell, who would've thought life was so exciting in the eighties.'

Gabriel becomes animated too. 'Talking of which, guess what was on the radio on the way here?' He mimes someone playing a saxophone, then puts his hand to his chest and a finger to his lips.

Sib laughs. 'Who broke my heart?'

He gyrates and points. 'You did, you did.'

Astonished at the change in both siblings' demeanour, Katy watches them belt out the refrain of various eighties hits. When they've finally exhausted their repertoire, Gabriel passes the invisible microphone to her.

He smiles his sister's compelling smile. 'Here we go, Katy. Your turn,' he says.

15

Katy

The doorbell rings at six on the dot as usual. Bridget shakes the rain from her umbrella and steps in.

'How's tricks?' she asks, removing her coat.

'Good, actually,' Katy replies, thrilled that it is.

After Sibeal beeped her horn this morning, she honestly thought she'd never leave the house. She'd taken Milo to school with a spring in her step and trotted home quickly to do some chores before Sibeal arrived. She stripped all the beds, bunged the towels in the basket and lugged it down the stairs. Sibeal sent a text saying she'd be another half an hour, so she had time to fill the washing machine, dust the dining room and lounge, and still have ten minutes to spare. Waiting at the kitchen window seemed too keen, so she'd sat in the study where she could glimpse the road through the blinds.

Only a touch apprehensive, she'd swung in her dad's leather chair, absently gazing at her old school photographs which adorned the side wall. As if an artist had gradually shaded her features with a graphite pencil, the huge eyes, round face, plump cheeks and turned-up nose had become more defined, shaped and solid as the years progressed. She still looked like the neat-haired A-level student in the final portrait, but she felt no connection with her sure smile. The academic achievements had come so easily then – when had the crippling uncertainty set in?

Hearing the low summon of Sibeal's car, she'd grabbed her handbag and made for the front door. But just as she put her fingers on the handle, there it was, out of nowhere, that sudden surge of overwhelming anxiety and fear. Her heart had pounded; she could barely suck in air.

For agonising moments the old terror had consumed her: she was ill, she was dying, she'd have to stagger out and ask a virtual stranger for help. It took her several minutes to rein in the hysteria with a paper bag and deep breathing. Then despondency set in. Not just dismay, but bitter disappointment. Where had *that* come from? She hadn't had an actual panic attack for well over a year.

Bridget's melodic tones now bring her back. 'Well, you look very well,' she's saying. She opens a cupboard and extracts the box of coffee pods, dragging her finger over the coloured lids before deciding which to select.

'Gasping for a hot drink. Been on my feet all day,' she says. 'What about you? Have you been out at all?' Without waiting for a reply she peers around the snug area. 'Hmm, no TV, no Milo. Where is our little chap?'

Katy takes a moment before replying. Are she and Bridget really *friends*? Despite the age difference, she's always thought so, yet today she feels irked by her familiarity, her busy presence, the way she always calls Milo 'ours'.

But she bats the irritation away. She's still buzzing after her day with Sib and Gabe, and quite frankly wants to share their alarming yet compelling relationship. She addresses the Milo question first.

'He's upstairs with his friend. When I took them some juice they looked furtive. Goodness knows how, but they'd clearly been in Dad's wardrobe and managed to fetch down his High Chaparral box. Well, that's what he called it when I was little. It's basically a cowboy game.' Her thoughts apparently elsewhere, Bridget blows on her coffee and sips.

'You know, cowboys and Indians? With a few horses and trees thrown in?' Katy continues. 'Well, they'd strategically dotted the little plastic figures around Milo's bedroom ...'

Bridget seems to rally. 'Indians? Oops, not very PC. I'm surprised Alexander kept them.'

'Me too. Memories of childhood and his parents, I suppose. Some things are too hard to throw out.' Like her mum's clothes in that very closet ... Elke's penchant for leopard print and stylish trouser suits, her neat row of colour-coded shoes, the wedding hat still in its box ...

Katy shifts her mental picture to the pile of old board games on the shelf above. 'He's kept Colditz, Battleship, Treasure Island and Buccaneer too. Save for the sparkling gems, I always considered them to be boys' games, but I did relent when it came to Mouse Trap. They're all pristine, of course.' She comes back to the memory of her son's guilty flush. 'Fortunately the Indians were in a defensive cluster, so I was able to whisk them away. They weren't impressed. The boys, that is, not the Indians, so it took a while to relieve them of the cowboys.'

'I rather think Alexander would suit a Stetson.' Bridget giggles. 'Along with the rest of the ... ensemble.'

The annoyance edging back, Katy looks at her watch. 'Actually, it's probably time to clear up and wipe Strummer's spaghetti-smeared face. His mum will be here to collect him soon.'

Bridget crinkles her nose. 'Did you really say Strummer? Please tell me that's not actually his name.'

'I like it; it's a bit different. Anyway, children grow into whatever they're called. I wasn't keen on the name Miles but you and Dad convinced me, and now I can't imagine calling him anything else. Except Milo, of course.'

'He looked like a Miles the moment we saw him.' Katy clocks her glance, sharp as flint. 'No tiredness this week? No napping today?'

The heat of irritation rising, Katy shakes her head. Thank God she didn't mention the panic attack. 'Not yet, though it is only Tuesday, Bridget. You might have more luck asking me on Thursday.'

The moment it's out, she regrets her sarcasm. Yet still . . . She knows her dad and Bridget mean well, but she's not a child; she doesn't need checking on at six o'clock every other bloody evening; if she needs help she can ask for it. And it suddenly feels strange that this woman saw her newborn before she did.

'Good, good,' Bridget replies, apparently oblivious to her loaded tone. She opens the fridge, extracts a bowl, peels back the clingfilm and sniffs it. 'Smells like one of Alexander's curries. Weren't you hungry? Looks delicious. Beef from the roast?'

'I expect so. Have it, if you fancy. Though it's probably past its best. I had lunch out.'

'Oh yeah?' Bridget says the words casually, but her stance shows surprise.

'At a friend's house.'

'Really?' She sits in the snug armchair and curls up her legs.

'You have *other* friends? I'm hurt! Anyone I know? Chapter and verse, please!'

It's an 'in' joke, Katy knows, and she's usually pleased to describe her tiny triumphs, but it suddenly feels private, as though she's part of a trio, a secret club that no one else would understand. After the shocking spat between the siblings, the tense atmosphere lifted as abruptly as it had fallen, thank goodness. Though she laughingly declined Gabe's invitation to sing, the three of them sat at the kitchen table for over an hour, amiably chatting as they sorted through more newspapers, pamphlets and magazines.

Sibeal related comical childhood stories about 'Gabriel the prize nerd'. More at ease than she'd seen him before, he responded with wry humour, describing himself as 'cool, actually, Ray-Ban Aviators and biker leather included'.

Eventually Sibeal looked at the clock. 'I'm bloody starving. What have you bought us for lunch?' she asked him.

'Oh yeah, the shopping,' he replied, turning to the paper bags he'd left by the door.

Sibeal delved in, making a running commentary like the *Generation Game* as she lined up items on the worktop. 'Crumpets and butter, fair enough, but a small loaf and one tin of sardines ...' She snorted. 'What's this? The gospel according to St Gabriel? Feeding the five thousand? You can tell he's a single man, can't you?'

Katy tensed at the religious angle, especially the word 'saint', and a pulse of time passed before Gabriel laughed. He raked his hands through his hair. 'See your point. I'll take that as fish and chips for three. Sib likes a ridiculous amount of salt and vinegar on hers. How about you, Katy?'

'And . . .?'

Katy comes back to Bridget's wide gaze and finds herself relenting. 'My *other* friend is called Sibeal and she's as intriguing as her name. She has a brother called—'

But the doorbell interrupts and Bridget's attention snaps away. 'Strummer's mum, I take it? Oh, excellent. I can't wait to see what she's like.'

16

Katy

The honeyed images crumble on waking, but still Katy feels a warm sense of contentment. She hasn't had a nice dream for months, and she knows her mum was in it, smiling and happy and *there*. Rather than tears, her fond smile is amazing progress, same as telling Sibeal about the car crash and finally wearing Elke's gold watch. It even took time to fall asleep last night. Like every evening since Tuesday, her mind fizzed and buzzed, reviewing the day and her small achievements this week: helping Gabe and Sib at Brook House, chatting to the other mums at the school gate, preparing meals for her and Milo whilst her dad's been away. Even baking him a Shaun the Sheep cake!

The sun bright through the curtains, she closes her eyes. It's so nice to lie here and deliberate over her plans for today without that gluey grogginess dragging her back into darkness. Or being exhausted from that strange limbo between consciousness and deep sleep, where dreamland seems so very real. Almost like post-traumatic stress disorder, the nightmare is always the same – she's in the passenger seat of the Jag, and though she's warm and sleepy, she knows her dad is there from the comforting smell of his aftershave. Then sudden headlights burn her eyes and she knows what's coming. The bend, the familiar canopy of trees. She tries to form words but she's dumb. It's coming, it's coming, the film on repeat: the headlights, the bend, the trees. The curse and the swerve, the screech and the stench. Sizzling rubber, sweaty terror, jangling fear. The almighty jolt, the sickening sound of crushing metal; the shaky silence perfumed by firework-like fumes. Then the airbag, constricting her chest, pinning her body and pushing her down.

Only she wasn't in the car. She wasn't there to witness her mum's final moments, her death by 'catastrophic injuries'. Whatever that actually meant. Too *catastrophic* to contemplate, she had to work hard to stop her imagination going there. But she knew there'd be blood, the brightest red blood.

Pushing away those negative thoughts, she turns to her sleeping son. He's spread out like a windmill, taking more than his fair share of the bed. Ironically he had a bad dream and climbed in at some point, tearful and clingy and so very lovable despite his snotty face. She kisses his hair, still downy like a toddler's. As if the transition from nursery to 'proper school' would change him overnight, she had expected it to become more boy-like when he began in reception last September. But Milo is her first and she's never had siblings; her mum passed away before he was even born, so motherhood is a huge learning curve. Thank goodness she has Dad. And Bridget, in fairness.

She slips from the bed, pads to her en-suite bathroom and inspects herself in the mirror. Funny how she longed to lose weight at university. Looking back, she wasn't remotely fat, yet she worried about her arms, her legs, her less-than-flat stomach, like she worried about everything. The anxiety was constant, the fear of having a panic attack in public more crippling than any actual episode. Then, of course, the worst happened, like a punishment of sorts: *You thought a panic attack was bad? Try this . . .*

'That's in the past,' she says to her pink-faced reflection. 'This is the new me.'

But one step at a time; she's learned *that* the hard way.

When she returns to her starfish son, his closed, sleepy face takes her back to his operation. His cryptorchidism had been noted at birth, and she'd known a surgical procedure would be necessary if the testicles didn't descend into the scrotum by six months, yet the notion of anaesthetic and incisions in such a tiny tot was still horrible. The advice about fertility problems and an increased risk of developing testicular cancer made the decision to go ahead with the orchidopexy easy, but it brought home the responsibility of being a parent: her baby was only nine months old and she was having to make decisions about his adult life and future well-being already.

She now nudges him gently.

'Time to wake up, Milo. It's the first of the month. We have to say rabbits!'

He rolls into a tight ball. 'Go away, I'm still sleepy, Mummy.'

'It's Friday, the best day of the week because . . .?'

He opens an eye. 'I didn't like that lolly last week. It was really sour.'

'But you did like your purple tongue.'

He responds with a reluctant smile.

'And it's a good job there's a whole counter of sweets so you can choose something different this time.'

'Will Grandad be back today?'

'You'll probably be fast asleep when he gets home tonight, but you can wake him up tomorrow morning. Take him his boiled eggs on a tray.'

He finally sits up. 'With soldiers?'

'Of course.'

He stretches and yawns, then does another take. 'What are you wearing, Mummy?'

'My running kit. New resolution, Milo. I'll walk you to school every day, then jog home afterwards.'

'Like the wind?'

'Spot on, Milo. I'm going to run like the wind.'

17

Katy

Katy runs, properly runs, like she did as a teenager. The thwack of her footfall is muffled by the damp, muddy pathways, but the sound of parakeets and the early summer breeze propels her through the woods. The lime green buds have now sprung open and the hillocks of crocuses and daffodils have been usurped by pink and red tulips. Can she really smell the fresh aroma of their delicate petals? Unlikely, she supposes, but today it feels that way.

Feeling somewhat bashful in her leggings and vest top, she dropped Milo off at the school door and said hi to the 'mum crowd' before pacing away. 'You look like a flipping gazelle,' one of them shouted. 'We're going for coffee at Cocoon. Join us if you've got time after your workout.'

Though Katy waved in acknowledgement, she didn't want to interrupt her new resolve. In the past she was often wiped out with exhaustion by Friday, lifting her heavy head and unwilling legs from the bed, shuffling to the shower and forcing a fake smile for her son at breakfast. The only way she'd have enough strength for a walk with Milo on Sunday would be a day of complete rest on the Saturday. Yet look at her this week – the past couple, in fact!

As she slows down for a puddle, she laughs at her zest. She had dreaded the build-up to Milo starting at nursery last year, knew she had to emerge from her hiding place and face life outside. And it was hard. Not only summoning up the energy to tromp to school and back, but to reconnect with people she knew and face their condolences or questions about Elke, who was well known and accepted in the village, despite the remaining twang of her German accent. Yet those fears were silly; by then four years had passed since the accident and, as her dad put it, people were far more interested in themselves than them.

As ever, he was right. It took a few months, but she eventually lifted her head as she walked home, made eye contact with both dogs *and* their owners, sometimes even saying hi. Each week, a small win. Yet it's now as if she's woken up and 'got a life', as Sib put it, and it feels bloody great. The cliquey mums asked her to coffee again; she belted out the 'Hallelujah Chorus' in the shower; she has a beautiful starfish son and she's pacing the glorious woodland of Bruntwood Park. Then there's the icing on the cake – Sib and Gabe Matthews, her enchanting new friends.

She pulls up by the railings to watch a family of ducks bobbing on the glistening water below. The image and the smell of wild garlic invoke a memory of trying to throw bread to the ducklings from this very spot. Her mum's soft hand and beautiful smile; her dad's laughter as the wind blew the crusts back. Though she usually tries not to regress, the flash of nostalgia is surprisingly warm and pleasant. Of course she can summon up each and every step of her childhood if she wants to, but the day of Elke's death became the 'new normal'; it was best to look forward, her dad advised; glancing back was painful and pointless.

As though reading her thoughts, the blue sky disappears and the pond surface dimples. Rain, yet again. She considers sheltering beneath a tree, but decides it's a light shower she can brave, so she continues the two-mile loop she used to run back in the day. Fine but persistent, the downpour doesn't stop. Finally accepting the superior power of the weather gods, she squelches across a hilly meadow and makes for the gates.

Once on solid ground, she peers through her wet fringe and smiles grimly. So much for flaming optimism; she's knackered after all and cold water has seeped into her trainers. As ever wondering who once lived in Bruntwood Hall, she trudges towards the old pavilion.

'Hello?' she hears through the drizzle.

Sure no one is speaking to her, she continues her weary tromp past the tea rooms.

'Hello! Bridget's friend, hello!'

Looking up to the patio, she squints at the man. Bloody hell, not again. If it wasn't for the silver pug at his side, she'd worry he was stalking her. Her instinct is to jog on and pretend she hasn't heard, but he knows Bridget and she doesn't want to appear odd. Her face, her hair and her clothes are streaming, though, so she's sure to appear as mad as a drowned hatter anyway.

'Hello to you too. I would stop, but it's somewhat ...' She gestures to her surroundings. 'Wet.'

Dry as a flipping bone, the thirty-something guy is sitting at a metal table beneath his golf umbrella. 'The rainy city, eh?' he says easily. He stands. 'You've still a way to go. Come and shelter until it passes.'

Struggling to find a reply, she self-consciously hops up the steps and joins him. The tissue from her pocket is damp, but she attempts to repair some of the damage and wipes her nose. Certain her cheeks are bright pink from embarrassment, she looks at him sideways. 'Thanks.' He's attractive, she supposes, if you like that strange combination of fairish hair and darker brows. His handsome features are drawn today, she notices, the grooves beneath his eyes smudged with grey shadows.

He stifles a yawn and nods to the café doors. 'A coffee to keep me going would've been nice but it's closed. Too early, I expect. Or perhaps they had the foresight to check the weather.'

Feeling uncomfortable in such close proximity to a stranger, Katy takes a breath to reply, but Harry gestures to his pet. 'The plan was to leave him outside and hope he gets stolen, but the deluge has put off would-be dog thieves. However, you've appeared like providence, so perhaps there's some hope for sleep after all. Do you fancy taking an ugly . . .' He theatrically clears his throat. 'A beautiful and obedient hound off my hands?'

'He seems very well behaved to me.'

'Hmm, perhaps now, but not when you're back from a long and hard shift. You know, when you're desperate to crawl into the sack and sleep, yet he thinks it's time for walkies.' Rex cocks his head and pricks up his ears. 'See what I mean? It's all "me, me, me . . ."'

Despite herself, Katy chuckles. 'Don't you know animals always come first?' she says. 'I don't suppose his mistress would be impressed if you arrived home empty-handed.'

'His mistress has buggered off and left me with sole custody.' He grimaces. 'Aren't couples meant to argue over who keeps the dog, not the other way around? Maybe I should get the law on

91

my side.' Though he's clearly joking, his look is intent, interested. 'Your dad's a lawyer. A barrister, isn't he?'

And yes, it's also invasive, somehow. The prickle of unease is immediate. Questions, bloody questions, how Katy hates them. She slides her own gaze to the ground. 'Not any longer.'

'Oh, right.'

Trying for normality, she shrugs. 'He's actually a circuit judge now.' She steps back and lifts her hand. 'I'd better get off. The rain is easing and I'm due to meet friends. I hope you manage some sleep.'

'Me too,' she hears as she moves away. 'By the way, if you like the outdoors, have you tried wild swimming? The lake at Sale Water Park is sublime.' Then, as she breaks into a trot, 'It's usual to swim in pairs, especially the first time. It's safer to have a partner. Maybe see you there one day.'

18

Sibeal

Wondering if she can really resist a little diversion from her planned journey to Nantwich, Sibeal drives down the parkway towards the M56. Her heart quickens at the tempting thought, soon followed by tingling from her stomach to her toes, the customary sensation which precedes a knee-jerk decision. They range from something relatively harmless like nicking a newspaper or a sandwich from Tesco to, well, slightly more hot-headed things such as driving against the flow on a one-way street to avoid heavy traffic, or mounting the pavement for similar reasons. Then there was the outdoor sex with Robin. In the car, against a tree, in a field. Down a town centre alleyway, the oblivious world walking by.

Her innate impatience aside, it's the desire for a high, she knows. The need for a buzz, a reaction or simply attention has always been part of her psyche. Prodding, provoking, needling – both herself and others – for *something*. She did it to the few friends she had, the transient boyfriends, Gabe, her too-passive father. And especially her mother, the Saint, looking for the response she never quite received. All except for Robin, her lover, her soulmate, her other half. He understood her and loved her just as she was, impatient, flawed and badly behaved. When he declared his love, she *believed* him.

She swallows the sob searing up through her body, focusing instead on the approaching Wilmslow exit. She could just do a loop, the slightest of diversions for a fillip, a little boost to brighten her morning. But what would be the point? Friday's a school day and it's drizzling. Even if her boy was at home today, he'd hardly be playing outside. And besides, the thought of stalking him feels a touch uncomfortable after her conversation with Kat. Until then she'd never thought of it as that. 'Stalking' is an ugly word; the sort of headline used in trashy tabloids to describe someone obsessed or deranged.

'He thought he was Odysseus,' Kat said yesterday. 'Why the man thought being a Greek god made the stalking any more palatable is beyond me.'

They were lying on a four-poster bed and Kat was nattering away. Not as quiet as she first appeared, she's opened up over the past few days of house clearing. So far they've only tackled a few cupboards and drawers, so the actual *clearing* has been pretty minimal, but it has been nice to hang out, drink coffee and chat. About precisely what, Sibeal couldn't say, but the conversations have felt easy, the need to dominate or control them noticeable by its absence. But she knows she's been zoning out, only returning to the present when a word or a phrase drags her back from Robin land.

'Odysseus? Start again. What man?'

'The stalker my dad sentenced to community service the other week. It was in the *London Gazette*.' Clearly pleased at the press mention, Katy laughed brightly. 'It quoted Dad describing the guy's behaviour as "shameful".'

'What did the "shameful" man do exactly?'

'Loads of inappropriate things. Appearing outside the woman's house at all hours; peeping into her windows.'

'Well that's hardly a crime.'

'Course it is! Only weird, obsessive people do that, Sib. And other stuff too. Bombarding her with texts, Facebook and Instagram stalking which went further than—'

'Well, we all do that.'

'Except me.' Kat flushed. 'I don't do social media. Well, not these days.'

'Really? Why not? Facebook was particularly brilliant when I started WebLife. Making "friends" with all and sundry, creating a million pages, asking my newly beloved pals to like them. In fairness, everyone has been pretty nice about the business. They clearly like me more online than in real life. Not that I care, it's too much hard work trying to please them.' She pulled Kat's silky ponytail. 'Except you, little Kat. So why did you stop social media?'

Her blush deepened. 'Seems silly now, but it was . . . stressful. After Mum died I went into that shell I told you about. People tried to tell me stuff I didn't want to know. Or they'd strike up a conversation about it in a nosy way. Tell me they'd read about the crash or seen a photograph in the newspaper. They'd say how shocked and sorry they were, but really? I didn't want to think about it, let alone visualise it, so . . .'

'So, what? You became a hermit?'

'Pretty much.' She smiled. 'But I was pregnant with Milo, so I didn't feel alone. And of course I had Dad and close friends.'

'Fair enough,' Sibeal replied, not wanting to talk about it any more. Kat had had *her* baby and she was getting pretty bored of hearing about her perfect bloody father. Then there was the 'stalker' niggle. Did her own behaviour really qualify her as one? Occasionally stopping by someone's house and simply watching was surely not that.

Gabriel put his head around the door, saying that the surveyor had arrived, so that stymied any further analysis, thank God, and she was relieved when Kat said she would leave them to it. But on the way out, she bit her lip. 'By the way,' she said hesitantly when Gabe was out of earshot, 'I know everyone's different, but if you ever want to talk about Robin and stuff, I'm all ears.' Touching Sibeal's arm lightly, she smiled ruefully. 'That's the benefit of having a hermit friend. There's pretty much no one for her to tell!'

Now shooting past the slip road to Wilmslow, Sibeal relaxes her jaw. Good little Kat. Yes, she'll talk to her about her man. Tell her about the promises and the plans they made before the bloody boy got in the way. Show her there's no way she's an obsessed loony who's out of control.

19

Sibeal

Pleased with her resolve about the Robin chat, Sibeal parks down a side street, flings her camera case across her shoulder and asks for directions to the independent bookshop. She normally subcontracts any photography to someone local, but she fancied taking these snaps after idly researching Nantwich on the internet. She was immediately intrigued about the medieval hamlet which had been famous for salt since Roman times, so she decided to have a mooch around and look for herself. She laughs at her sudden interest in the past; from houses to furniture to belongings, she's spent her adult life shrinking away from anything old. History too; world history, her history. What good comes from looking back? You can't change what's set in stone, as much as you'd like to.

Purchasing a modern, functional flat had been the plan after finishing university. She couldn't shape why, but buying and owning, having something that was hers, felt important, so she worked like a demon to scrape up enough money for a deposit. At one time she had three jobs – stacking supermarket shelves at dawn, cleaning middle-class homes during the day and working in a wine bar at night. What else did one do with a degree in bloody maths? It didn't really matter where she lived, so long as it was draught- and odour-free, yet she found her home by chance on the way to see Gabe at his new digs in York. Taking a wrong turn, like so often in her life. But this worked out to be the right one.

Maybe it was the silence and the sun's warm rays, but there was something about the small parish that made her pull up the car, climb out and stroll around that day. A pale brick house was for sale, so she knocked on the door and asked if she could go in for a recce. Nude carpets and walls, functional kitchen appliances, windows that actually opened. No smells ingrained in the floors. And though the village was classed as 'affluent', she was able to afford the small property with her dad's help, a loan that turned into a generous gift, a surprisingly large amount from an itinerant artist with no money.

Replacing the image of that white skeleton face with her kindly father's, she sniffs away the memory and comes back to the busy precinct and her mission to check out the bookshop as a networking venue. A smart canopy is attached to the Gothic terrace, announcing it as a coffee lounge too, yet there's something about the ancient black and white timber façade that brings on a shudder. She shrugs it off and moves inside, surprised to see the Tardis-like ground floor is modern and light, the walls stuffed with brightly coloured books.

A huddle of pensioners are milling at the bookshelves and chatting. Dabbers, she guesses from her research – someone born within the town's ancient boundaries. A little like cockneys, she supposes, a label showing one belongs. She chuckles to herself: 'belongs' – well, wouldn't that be nice!

'Hi, I'm Sibeal Matthews, here from WebLife to take a few

98

photos,' she says to a young woman at the till. 'It's all arranged, so is it OK if I just get on with it?'

'Yeah, sure. I'll just fetch Steve or Denise—'

'No thanks. Experiencing it with virgin ears and eyes is all important.'

'Oh, OK.'

'Cheers.'

Following the aroma of coffee, she makes her way upstairs and takes in the area. More in keeping with the Elizabethan building, one half is lined with grainy pews and wooden benches, the other resembles a gentleman's den with its elegant round tables, panelled walls, leather sofas and matching armchairs. She nods approvingly and takes a few snaps. Yes, it's definitely something a little different for a business luncheon or other professional event.

Feeling eyes burn her back, she turns. 'I'm here to take pics,' she says to a fresh-faced guy behind the counter. 'Is this everything?'

'There's more up there.' He gestures to a velvet curtain. 'Say hi to Santa.'

'Last I heard it was June.'

He lifts his bony shoulders. 'The attic used to be his grotto when I was a kid. Help yourself.'

'Yeah, will do.'

Her mouth dry, Sib swallows. Bloody hell, even the word 'attic' causes a visceral response. Chiding herself for being so pathetic, she pulls back the heavy drape and pauses to identify the fusty aromas. The resinous tang of old timber, certainly, but alcohol and cigarette smoke too. Can she really smell it, fetid and sickly? Or is it simply her imagination?

'By the way, the . . .' she hears as the cloak drops behind her.

She takes two steps, then another. It's dark, too dark, and her heart is wildly thrashing. Continue or just bolt? But as she turns back to drag in some air, a shaft of brightness hits her eyes.

'The switch is tricky to find if you don't know where it is,' the café guy says from below. 'Careful of the banister, it disappears.'

She forces sound through her throat. 'OK, thanks.'

A dull beam lights the two rooms at the top. Why people like to live in the shadows, Sibeal doesn't know. Hotel rooms, restaurants and toilets. She likes things to be clear, to see where she's going.

Taking a deep breath, she glances around. If the remains of trodden tinsel are anything to go by, Santa's grotto was on the right. Her shoulders relax at the sight. It's just a room, a happy place, Father Christmas duly surrounded by parcels, a pink-faced, avid child sitting on his knee. Even she can remember the sheer excitement of that. Today the area is lined with more books in display units. She steps over to peep. Old tomes, not the 'pre-loved' selection downstairs, but what looks like valuable first editions. How hard would it be to ram open the doors or smash the glass? Sneaking out a signed copy of *Alice's Adventures in Wonderland* could be today's fillip.

She lifts the Canon and takes several snaps. That little boost she can resist. There's plenty of antiquated rubbish at her dad's, she and Kat slowly sorting and throwing and talking. She finds herself smiling. Yes, a pleasant therapy of sorts.

Turning to the left, she takes in the crooked, leaded casement she noticed from outside, and though she wryly mutters 'at least there's a window', the triangle of dark eaves and wooden beams is unavoidable. And there it is again, that stench of spirits and smoke. And perfume. She'd forgotten about that.

100

She closes her eyes and breathes through the memory.

'Mummy, can I come in?'

No reply.

'Mummy, please can I come in? I've done you a drawing.'

Nothing but the sound of her own respiration. Is Mummy all right?

'Mummy, are you there? You'll really like it.'

Finally – and thankfully – her voice. 'I'm just resting, Sibeal. I'll come down at teatime.'

'It's of you and Gabe. I'll only be two minutes. I've coloured it too, really neatly . . .'

'The door's locked and I'm too sleepy to move. Show me it later. Off you go now . . .'

Locked, always locked. Locking herself in, but mostly locking little Sibby out.

20

Katy

'Kathryn?' Her dad's voice filters through the thick tar of sleep. 'I've brought you some breakfast. Can you manage to sit up?'

It's morning, Katy knows, has been daytime for minutes, maybe hours. She's clocked light through the curtains, felt the vibration of her mobile, heard chatter from downstairs. But only for moments, scrambled seconds of consciousness before being sucked back inside.

'It's porridge, darling. A touch of cream and a smattering of brown sugar. Perhaps not terribly seasonal for such a lovely warm day, but I thought it might give you some energy.'

She peels back her eyelids. A frown of love mars her dad's handsome face.

'What time is it?' she asks.

He settles the tray on her lap, smooths his dark fringe into place and pulls up his cuff to look at his watch. 'Goodness, it's noon already! So I suppose I should really call my offering brunch. Come on, eat up while it's warm, love. Your tea is duly stewed, as you like it.'

'Thanks, Dad. Where's Milo?'

'He's just gone out for a walk with Bridget and the dog.' He sits on the wicker chair and crosses his legs. 'He popped in to check on you a few times and said you were still sleeping "like a princess". He even brought your mobile downstairs so it wouldn't wake you. Sweet little man.'

He steeples his fingers and taps his chin, the usual sign that he's worried. 'Everything OK, Dad?' she asks.

'Absolutely. Just over-thinking last week's trial.'

'The fraud case?'

'No, not in the end. There were last minute shenanigans so it got adjourned and I ended up with another. A trial for rape. Date rape, I suppose, though I hate that expression. Both parties are students at university, bright kids, nice families, upstanding citizens. It's a dreadful no-win situation for anyone, and the evidence is so finely balanced, I have no idea of the outcome.'

'Oh no, that sounds horrible,' she replies. 'Though I guess the police charged him, so . . .'

'No smoke without fire? On the one hand that's the worry for him. Yet on the other, prosecutions for sexual offences are at an all-time low, so the CPS wouldn't have made the decision lightly.'

'Do you think he did it? What's your gut feeling?'

'I really don't know, love. But even if he's acquitted, his name's out there, folk will think the worst. Would you offer him a job? Would I?' He sighs. 'Still, the law is the law. I'm just glad I don't have to decide either way. That's down to the jury, thank goodness.'

He continues to tap and Katy knows the question is coming despite his work digression. 'So, other than your jaunts to Brook House, how was your week?' he asks. 'Bridget popping in as usual?'

Spooning the oatmeal in her mouth, she battles with the niggle of irritation. Right now she feels like a baby in a high chair, yet she can't blame her dad for his concern: she's still in the sack at midday, still feels horribly groggy, which is so, so disappointing after her optimistic week.

He arrived home earlier than she'd expected yesterday, so she abandoned her plans for fish fingers with Milo for tea, opting for one of his delicacies instead. Once she'd given Milo a bath and put him to bed, she watched him create a beef stew that was much more than that. Mouth-watering strips of best steak sautéed with half a bottle of claret and every vegetable in the house. Not able to hide her grin, she sipped a glass of wine and told him about Sib, Gabe and Brook House. She described the mammoth task ahead – from the junk and art materials to the books, newspapers and journals, but mostly she regaled him with descriptions of the oil paintings and floor lamps, the shabby-chic sofas, curtains and chairs, the rich mahogany furniture, even a four-poster bed. They stayed up to chuckle at *Gogglebox*, and when she finally went upstairs she was tired, but in a good way.

Deeply sighing, she now shakes her head. So frustrating! One step forward and two back as always. It's bloody demoralising.

She reverts to her dad's quizzical gaze. 'Yeah, a good week. It's been pretty standard fare.'

'Milo says you jogged home from school yesterday. "Like the wind", as he put it.'

Katy feels herself flushing. 'I was just full of energy, so I thought, why not . . .'

'Good to hear. Very good to hear.' Alexander stands and stretches. 'And don't feel bad about another lie-in. If folk think it's indulgent, let them. There's no harm recharging the batteries once in a while; we all need "powder" naps. No doubt I'll be doing the same after a brisk game of tennis. Dave's determined to make a comeback after last week's thrashing. You'll be home alone for a couple of hours, so there's no need to rush out of bed; I'll bring up the newspaper, then I'm off.'

As the door clicks to, a surge of dizziness hits. Her dad was too nice to say it out loud but there's no doubt she overdid yesterday's run. Like Milo, she's susceptible to colds and chills and the soaking won't have helped. She should've stopped to shelter beneath Harry's umbrella for longer, instead of being so touchy and aloof.

Trying to search for a positive, she closes her eyes. It's noon, only noon, the sort of hour Sib rises every day, for heaven's sake. And she's not due at Brook House until three. A long shower and a hair wash will wake her up. A minute or two more of shut-eye, then she'll be completely fine.

21

Sibeal

Sibeal checks the time on her laptop again. She's been at it since her darling brother woke her at ten with the mandatory noisy shower, rattling pipes and slamming doors. Still, it's probably a good thing as she's fallen behind with work correspondence. Ignoring general emails is fair enough, but it pays to be on top of professional matters – literally pays, and pretty damn well. Since she set it up seven years ago, WebLife has gone from strength to strength, particularly during the pandemic when all the tools were already in place to network and meet online when it couldn't be done in person.

She takes off her reading glasses and rubs her eyes. She wouldn't say it to anyone, but she's proud of her business. Bloody ecstatic, in fact. She'd like all those spoilt posh girls from her halls in Durham to put her salary in their pipe and smoke it. 'A puppet master' she always says if anyone asks what she does. Pulling strings for A to meet B and C, or indeed the whole alphabet, then book the venue and charge the client a fee for the introduction and an extortionate uplift on the accommodation cost. And the beauty is that she can do the admin from anywhere, from Saxton or Switzerland, Timbuktu or the toilet, which actually has been known. In all honesty it's money for nothing; people can 'network' in the pub if they put their minds to it. She rarely makes an appearance herself, but someone nominated WebLife for a new business award, so she felt compelled to attend a few sessions before the ceremony itself, dragging Gabe with her when she longed to take Robin. Not winning was eye-opening, as it hurt – surprisingly so – and the only person she could tell was—

She lets out a shriek of frustration. She forgets him for seconds, for minutes, even hours, but when her thoughts flip to him, it squeezes her windpipe, as agonising as ever. Stilling, she claps a hand over her mouth. She never told Gabe about the affair. Of course he'd have disapproved of the adultery in that 'end of his tether' type of way, but the reason she didn't was Robin. He asked her not to. She's never been one to make promises, a practice she finds inconvenient or too hard to maintain, but she always kept the ones made to him. Weird, really. But he was her first love, an almost disabling crush the moment Gabe introduced her to him at fifteen. Thank God the attraction was mutual. They first had sex within hours, yet they could never quite get enough; a prelude to their reunion ten years later, perhaps. Was their five-year age gap appropriate? Her under the age of consent and him a grown man of twenty? Probably not, but she didn't have a mother to object and, lost in his artwork, her dad didn't notice things like that.

She sighs at the thought of her dear passive father. He was reliable and solid when she asked him for help, but he didn't twig developments off his own bat, so they had to be flagged. Puberty, periods, parties; larger clothes, a first bra. There were parents' evenings and decisions about choices of A levels and uni too, but it was the girls' stuff that mattered mainly, things a mum should've been there to care about.

Flinging open the back door, she stares at the broken sky. It's ready to cry, like she is. Now she's on the Robin track, there'll be no stopping the memories and images, the bloody agonising what-ifs, especially as they are her own bloody fault. She groans at the memory of her eighteen-year-old self: she'd started at university and realised he was old. Hardly *old* at twenty-three, but he had a job, a car and a flat. The domesticity seemed predictable and boring. Suffocating too. And his hairy chest and beard felt grubby compared with the smooth-skinned adolescents she was snogging most nights. So she ended it briskly by text.

Her mobile beeps. Thank God, a distraction at last! Kat was supposed to be here at three, but hoping she could come earlier, Sibeal called her at ten, eleven and two without any luck. She peers at the screen. Great; a message from Vodafone. Where the hell is Kat? She needs to talk about Robin, to let out this leaden ball of angst; if she doesn't she'll bloody rupture.

After a moment she nods, strides back to the laptop, bangs down the lid and scoops up her keys. Needs must. If the mountain won't come to Muhammad, then Muhammad must bloody insist.

22

Sibeal

Both chilly and clammy, Sibeal pulls up the SUV outside the post office and stares at the Tesco Express opposite. Continue to Kat's place or buy a bottle of wine and retreat? She looks up to the blue sky and laughs without mirth. 'How the sun shines on the righteous,' she mutters.

Bloody typical; the downpour occurred during the thirty seconds it took to dash from her front door to her car. No doubt it was arranged by the gods especially for her. Of course she could have waited or sheltered or dug out some flea-bitten umbrella, but once she'd made the decision to see Kat, she strode right on through it. It was only when she'd driven halfway here that she realised her top was stuck to her chest, making her appear like some wet T-shirt bimbo type. Now her resolve to see Kat is as damp as her hair and the thought of alcohol-induced oblivion is a-calling. Besides, her little pal is probably not even home but out with her son, doing all the Saturday afternoon things mums do with their kids. Normal mothers, at least. Sweet shops and swings, baking and bubbles and craft.

She sighs. If she was in Saxton, getting pissed would be a

no-brainer. But as she jumped into her car, she clocked a shadow in an upstairs window. Whether it was Gabe or their mother, she couldn't say, but neither his frown nor her ghost make good drinking companions.

Deciding a drive out somewhere will clear her head, she joins the busy traffic. If that 'somewhere' happens to be Wilmslow, so much the better, but as she crawls through the village and watches the joggers and families and shoppers, the desire for company outweighs the need to glimpse her boy, so when she reaches the park, she swings to the left. Cars are parked on the pavement either side of Kat's house, so she pulls onto the drive-way and stops next to the Jag.

Looking akin to a guardian hen, a black moggy eyes her from the doormat. She actually likes cats, loves the feel of their fur, the warmth of their bodies. A touch thing, she supposes ... *Touch*, if only. Breathing through another jolt of self-pity, she climbs out, lifts her chin and strides to the porch. She rings the bell, and though the moggy stretches and lines up expectantly beside her, nobody answers.

'Anybody in?' she asks the cat. 'Should I stay or should I go?' She squats down to stroke it. 'How about you keeping me company for a while? We could buy Whiskas and wine and go on a road trip.'

The scrape of keys makes her jump, but when the door opens it isn't Kat. Dressed in a striped dressing gown and towelling his hair, it's her father.

He looks as surprised as she is, but after a moment or two, he recovers himself. 'James's girl?' He squints in thought. 'Siobhan? Serena? Sorry, I—'

'Sibeal.'

'Yes, of course I knew that. And apologies, you're a young woman, not a girl. How lovely to see you again. Please come in.'

Feeling unaccountably shy, Sibeal looks at her feet and fights the deep flush. Perhaps it's the glimpse of his chest, the easy smile or the smell of shower gel, but he reminds her of Robin. Bloody hell; what's wrong with her? This is Kat's dad, the same age as hers, which makes him mid-fifties. Yet now she's over the threshold, she can't just scarper. Picturing Gabriel's raised eyebrows, she nods in acknowledgement. Kat's father – Alexander – is a proper grown-up; it's time to behave.

He gestures to the first room on the right. 'Come on through and I'll put on the kettle.' She dumbly follows his eloquent timbre, as Gabriel would describe it, and when he turns at the granite island, he studies her for a beat. 'It looks like you've been caught by the rain.' He holds out his bath towel. 'Feel free to share.'

Praying her T-shirt is no longer glued around her nipples, Sibeal puts a hand to her hair. It's only a touch wet, but his expression is affable, so perhaps he's only joking.

'Yes, an unexpected summer shower, I'm afraid,' she replies, sounding more like him than herself. Mirroring of some sort, she supposes. Despite her ridiculous nerves, she chuckles inwardly. Is she subconsciously trying to build a rapport with this man? She doubts it; it feels like she's been summoned to a headmaster's study for a lecture or a reprimand. Not that her school's headteacher was a master who had a study. If Alexander's accent is anything to go by, he probably had both. Though he was educated with her dad, of course. Grammar school, then, so she's probably right.

'Oh no, poor you.' His courteous gaze unwavering, he rakes

back his thick fringe. 'My hair doesn't like rain.' He gestures to a hat on the counter. 'Hence the Oasis look. Though . . .' He tightens his belt and chuckles. 'I'm sure Liam doesn't greet his guests dressed like this. I had a somewhat tough game of tennis, then discovered there was no hot water at the club. It wasn't a pretty sight – or indeed smell – when I got home, so I got straight in the shower.' He nods at a chrome bar stool. 'Sit, please sit. Can I get you a drink? I recently invested in a coffee machine, so there's a choice of pods. Then we have all manner of tea. Peppermint, camomile, lemon, green and so on. Kathryn likes to—'

'A latte if you have it, thanks. Is she here?'

Alexander pauses and blinks. Then he lowers his voice. 'She's a little under the weather – a bug going round, I expect. She went for a nap, but she might be awake now. I could give her a knock, though she's probably heard us and will be down in a minute.'

As he draws breath to say more, Sibeal readies herself for some gen about Kat or her mum and her death, but his actual words catch her short.

'I'm sorry to stare, but you look strikingly like your mother.'

Bloody hell, she hasn't heard that for a very long time. *What a gorgeous child, the very spit of you, Imelda. So beautiful!* She tries to float above the old memories, but they descend anyway: little Sibby's hopeful gaze, searching for her mummy's approval for *something*. Yet even at that age she didn't need to be told that you have to be beautiful on the inside as well as out, and that neither of them were.

Alexander's brown eyes are polite and attentive, so she gropes for her mental promise to behave. 'Oh right; so you knew my mum.'

'Yes, I did.' He turns and deftly operates the Nespresso

112

machine without speaking for a minute or two. When he's finished his task he carries the mugs to a sofa area and places them on a low table covered in animal jigsaws. 'My grandson loves elephants, as you can see. This is his den, but he's very inclusive and allows the adults to play too.'

Relieved the Imelda conversation has passed, she searches for a jaunty riposte, but Alexander sighs and shakes his head. 'A long time ago now. As it happens we were there the night your parents met.' Tapping his chin, he smiles thoughtfully. 'The three of us had gone off to different universities but we were still tight in those days, so we had a lads' boozy weekend every six months or so . . .'

Wondering who the 'three of them' were and where this agonising story might go, Sibeal picks up her cup. Christ, her hands are trembling, and though the coffee is scalding, she slurps it nonetheless. Where the hell is Kat? She needs her to appear and stop this man talking. But he continues to speak with a chuckle of reminiscence.

'That particular weekend was Dublin, of course. She worked in the hotel we were staying at. Only a small place, so she'd be there on reception, cleaning rooms, pulling us pints of Guinness from behind the bar. Always with that huge, stunning smile. Then, when she played the piano, well . . . we were all pretty starstruck. Kenny was especially, thought your mum was *the* one, but it was your dad who caught her eye.' His gaze sparkles with amusement. 'Kenny was used to having the pick of the bunch, so he never quite got over it. Though he could match us pint for pint, your dad was a quieter character, of course. He painted her from memory; that's how striking she was. They kept in touch, she came over and they got married within a few months . . .' He

113

flushes lightly. 'Not that they wouldn't have anyway; they were very much in love. And such a handsome couple. Well, I'm sure you've heard it all before.'

'Dad was teetotal,' she replies, stuck for any other comment.

She certainly hasn't 'heard it all before', yet she doesn't focus on the astonishing image of her mum behind a bar with a 'huge, stunning smile'. Instead she reflects on the paltry numbers at her dad's funeral. Did she and Gabe make enough effort to contact his old mates? They didn't know about his friendship with Alexander, let alone anyone called Kenny. James had some pals he saw from time to time, but those few had already been frightened off by his cancer, his slow but steady decline from human being to just a thing, as if it was contagious. But she didn't really blame them; if she hadn't been his daughter, she'd have buggered off too.

Alexander nods. 'Ah, he must have taken the pledge later, like his father. And his grandfather too, as I recall.'

'This guy, Kenny,' she asks, only because she knows Gabe would want her to find out more. 'Was he close to Dad? Should we have told him about his death and the funeral? We didn't know—'

'Kenny Philippe? No, I wouldn't worry. Last I heard he was living in the Lakes – Coniston or Buttermere, I think. I haven't seen him for years.' Alexander smiles a regretful smile. 'Same with me and your dad, of course. Hindsight is a wonderful thing, but I should have tried harder. We kept in touch for a long time, went to each other's weddings . . .' He pauses, his brow puckering in thought. 'How old are you? If you don't mind me asking.'

'Thirty in July—'

'That's right! Your birth and my wedding pretty much

coincided. Your mum couldn't come for obvious reasons, but James was there, proud as punch because he'd got the baby girl he wanted. We talked on the telephone occasionally but life gets in the way, priorities change. I'm sure you must know.' He peers intently. 'The death of a parent is tough, but both ... Loss is a dreadful thing. Until you experience bereavement, you can't quite understand it. It's simply missing that person which hurts the most. Touching, holding, talking, just being. It must be difficult, very hard for you at times. I'm so sorry, Sibeal.'

She gropes for words, but knows she can't speak. Instead she throws back the coffee and stands. He rises too and puts a hand on her shoulder. 'I do apologise, I've upset you. That wasn't my intention. On the contrary, I'd like to help if I can—'

Speech finally bursts out. 'Well you can't, so just stop.' She taps at her temple. 'You have no idea, so just stop.'

He holds out his palms. 'Try me. People say I'm a good listener. Let's sit down and—'

His sentence is cut short by the opening door and a dark-haired little boy who flies at him. 'It's Milo the explorer!' he says, scooping him up high. 'What have you been up to today?'

A woman calls from the hallway. 'His wellies are out here, Alex.' Her accent is Scottish posh. 'I'll drop the hound home and be back in five minutes. Pour me a glass, it's definitely wine time.'

Pressing his cheek to Alexander's, the boy plays with his hair. 'Is Mummy still asleep?' he asks.

Alexander puts him down. 'Why don't you go and see? Tell her to come down and say hello to her friend here.'

'You come too, Grandad. Like Sleeping Beauty, you said.' He tugs his hand. 'Come on, Grandad. Let's wake up Mummy.'

'OK.' Turning to Sibeal, he shrugs apologetically. 'Grandchildren, eh? Give me two minutes and I'll be right with you.'

Rooted and frozen, she doesn't move for a moment. Then, when she's sure they've really gone, she lets out her breath, strides to the front door and runs out.

23

Sibeal

The tender scene of boy and grandfather clawing at her heart, Sibeal indicates right for Sainsbury's and oblivion, but the road is chock-a-block with traffic and no one is prepared to let her in. She yelps in frustration but, like aversion therapy, an image of her mother pulling pints in a bar elbows in. Then her eyes catch the highway sign: Wilmslow. She snorts at the serendipity. All roads lead to Wilmslow! She should have gone there first instead of being tempted by a rogue need for companionship.

Since fate has decided it for her, she allows her shoulders to relax and takes the countryside route. As though Robin is sitting beside her, she scores each house along Styal Road out of ten, then points out the field where they once stopped to have sex. In fairness, they'd thought they'd be hidden in the long grass, but a tractor appeared and saw them off.

'Like that film with the truck,' she says out loud. 'The one where there's no driver. Bloody hell, what's it called?'

She thrums the steering wheel as she drives. Is it normal to talk to oneself? Does she even care? There's no one here to judge her. Except, of course, herself.

'*Duel!*' she says out loud. 'And thank God for that; there's nothing worse than having something so nearly in reach and yet ...'

She comes back to the leafy view through the windscreen. Good God, she's found herself on the right street in Wilmslow without even trying. Imprinted. Autopilot. It feels like an augury.

Not able to find a space near the house, she drives straight past to the Costa on Alderley Road and pulls up on the corner. The late afternoon is so balmy, she considers sitting outside for a drink to get rid of the sour taste of bloody Alexander's coffee, but a sixth sense tells her the boy is at home and she needs that boost, just a little something to lift a shit day, so she buys a fresh juice with the twenty-pound note in her pocket. When she returns, she finds her regular spot is free, so she settles down in her seat for half an hour of window shopping.

She jerks at the sound of voices nearby. Bloody hell, she fell asleep. She straightens herself, but immediately slips downwards again. Christ, it's her. Wearing leggings and a baggy sweatshirt, her swinging hair in a high plait, Zoe's striding towards her.

Though her heart is in her mouth, Sibeal finds herself staring. Did this woman really cause Robin's death? Strangulation or stabbing or poisoning, even hiring a hitman? If she challenges her for being here, she'll bloody challenge her back. Yet if she did something criminal, she'd hardly be here as large as life, smiling and ... yes, thank God, oblivious to her and jogging past.

A second athlete, calling commands, passes by. Male, this time, duly tanned and musclebound. An evening run with one's personal trainer? Sibeal hasn't donned even a plimsoll since school, let alone broken a sweat for 'fun', but she recently created an arm of WebLife to match wealthy clients with non-gym PTs and she charges them silly money, so she isn't complaining. As she watches them disappear in the rear-view mirror, a notion snaps in. The front bedroom curtains were open before, now they're closed. It's eight o'clock at night. Has Zoe left Joseph alone? Has she nipped out for a run and left Robin's precious boy in the house on his own?

Without thinking it through, she jumps from the car, strides over the road and walks up the driveway. When she steps to the large window and peers in, a teenage girl is curled up on the Vivere Zen wooden sofa, eating crisps.

She quickly pulls back. How old is this babysitter? How old should she be to care for a three-year-old? Though Joseph's no longer three. He turned four without a father. Her nose smarts again. Each birthday she gave Robin an old-fashioned teddy she'd have bought her own son. How she'd loved the thought of it entering this very home disguised as a gift from his daddy. The boy touching, cuddling and kissing it. Something of her infecting, infusing, pervading this house. She'd done the same this year; oblivious to the devastation that would come a week later, she'd purchased a soft toy to hand over to Robin on that final Wednesday. But it was in the boot of her car and she forgot to bring it inside.

She jolts around to her SUV. Perfect! It's still there and the babysitter is just a kid . . .

Armed with the gift bag, she retraces her steps and knocks at the front door. The girl soon answers, clearly alarmed at the unexpected visit. 'Yes?'

'Hi, is Zoe in? I'm just dropping off a present for Joseph. A bit belated, I know.'

'She isn't in, so . . .'

'It's actually from my brother, Gabriel. He was mates with Robin, so it felt important to remember Joseph's birthday this year.'

'Oh, right.'

'Here you go. I hope he likes it.' Sibeal pulls a suitably desperate yet comical face. 'I've drunk too much today. Would you mind if I use the loo while I'm here? I could wait until Zoe's back, but I might have to pee in my coffee cup before then.'

The teenager relents and stands back. 'Sure. Do you know where it is?'

'I do, thanks. The pressie is only wrapped in tissue paper, by the way, so feel free to have a peep.' She makes for the downstairs toilet. 'Thanks so much for this – you're a lifesaver.'

When the girl returns to the lounge, Sibeal doubles back and climbs the stairs. On the landing she stops and inhales the familiar smell of Robin's shirts. It's only detergent, she knows, but it brings on a need to see where he slept. Guessing it's the room at the back, she tiptoes across and peers in. It's tasteless, of course, and there's no apparent sign he's ever been here, but when she reaches the wardrobe, it's as though he left it open just for her. She gently fingers the T-shirts, the boxers and socks on the shelves, but when it comes to the ties she shakes her head. He always carried one in his pocket, and though she approved of the Gucci label and liked the soft feel of silk against her throat, she couldn't go there. She was open to pretty much anything sexually, but not that, so he'd use it to tie her wrists instead. His gold puppytooth-patterned one doesn't seem to be there, so she quickly puts another in her back pocket, then creeps along the landing to the front.

Though the door sticks on the thick pile of the carpet, she

finally slips into the bedroom, listens for movement from the lounge beneath, then turns her attention to the sweet sound of the boy's light, feathery breathing. Her eyes becoming accustomed to the gloom, she moves to the bed and gasps with sheer longing. Dark lashes on pale cheeks and downy hair. So beautiful and so very small; she could scoop him up in her arms and take him away, just like that. It's serendipity she's here; she could—

'What are you doing?'

Though her heart thunders, Sibeal turns with a reassuring smile. It's only the babysitter, thank God. 'Sorry, I was too embarrassed to ask you, but I was looking for a tampon or a liner. I thought this might be the bathroom, then when I saw this little chap ... Well, I couldn't resist taking a peek.' Moving out, she pulls an awkward face. 'So, a tampon or a towel, even a wad of tissues? Really sorry to put you on the spot, but ...'

Her face tight with worry, the girl stares. Then she gestures to a door. 'That's the bathroom. I'll wait,' she says, folding her arms.

Her whole body shaking, Sibeal sits on the loo and forces out a pee. Oh God, will the babysitter tell Zoe? But as she washes her hands, the panic is replaced by pure anger. The Tom Ford aftershave she bought Robin is there on the shelf for anyone to use. *Her* fucking Robin! She reaches out to take it, but the girl's voice cuts in.

'Have you finished?'

'Yup, coming.' She forces a smile. 'That feels a whole lot better. Thanks, you've been a star.' She follows the kid down to the hallway. 'So what's the going rate for babysitting these days?'

She snorts. 'A packet of Doritos.' Then she shrugs her slim shoulders. 'It's only for half an hour, so ...'

Sibeal rolls her eyes. 'Yup, I remember being ripped off too.'

She delves into her pocket, pulls out the Costa change and presses it into her hand. 'Toilet attendant's fee. Thanks again for being a star. See ya.'

The perspiration wet behind her knees, Sibeal climbs into the SUV and presses the ignition. Will the girl tell Zoe what happened? Does she even care? The pain in her chest is too fucking much. She has to get home and have a stiff drink; she needs to obliterate the scent of Persil and Tom Ford aftershave, and particularly the imprint of that perfect little boy, from her head.

24

Katy

Savouring his clammy grip, Katy holds Milo's hand and listens to him chatter about his afternoon with Bridget yesterday. His joy and his laughter makes her breathless with both disquiet and envy. She shouldn't feel jealous of her friend, but she is. Bridget's time with Milo doesn't feel like 'borrowing', as she puts it; it feels like she's *taking* something that isn't hers.

Yet it's Katy's own fault, she knows that. She slept all Saturday, only coming to the surface when Milo woke her at five with his soft puckered lips on her cheek. A lovely moment.

'My handsome prince,' she said, opening her eyes. Though in truth she'd been awake before the kiss. She'd smelled the scent of his afternoon with Bridget first: dog, damp hair, cut grass and fresh air.

Yes, it's her own bloody deficiencies. She's crippled and pathetic, incapable of looking after her own son. And it wasn't just one step back yesterday; it was hundreds. So frustrating and annoying when she'd felt incredibly well in the week.

Deeply sighing, she looks up to the spreading boughs. Though there's still a damp chill from last night's downpour, the sky is a bright and cloudless blue today. It's a perfect morning for a run; indeed, she could have done one. She woke up early, and though her joints were stiff, she felt alert, clear-headed and starving. She crept downstairs and made a whole pile of Marmite on toast, only struggling to finish the last piece. She hadn't eaten since the porridge, so it was no flaming wonder.

Full of energy, she itched to go out and 'run like the wind'. Or at least stretch her limbs. She even spent a moment or two considering it: it was early, she could sneak out before her dad and Milo woke; they'd be none the wiser. But that felt dishonest and, more importantly, she couldn't risk another day in bed. She had Milo to look after and—

With a jolt of dismay she realised she'd missed her date with Sib yesterday. She hunted for her mobile and when she finally found it beneath a stack of toys, there were several missed calls. Suppose she'd offended her? She'd really hate that.

Shaking away the vexation, she comes back to the balmy day and her picturesque surroundings. Small achievements, she remembers. She may only be having a gander rather than actually dipping into the lagoon, but when her dad awoke she asked if he'd drive them here before he settled down in his study.

'Could you drop us at Sale Water Park?' she asked.

'Of course. Does Milo have a party there?'

She almost mentioned the open swimming but thought better of it. 'I think Bridget exhausted Bruntwood Park yesterday, so I thought a change of scene. Not to mention the lake, the boats and bird hide. And we can come back on the tram. Fancy that, Milo?'

So, all in all, life isn't that bad. She's here with her son, her beautiful boy in his yellow wellies, her avoiding the muddy puddles along the wooded pathway, him squelching straight through them. His hair is messy from the breeze and his cheeks are rosy with mirth. These are moments to treasure and bottle.

Milo tugs at her hand. 'Mummy?'

'Yes?'

He stops and gawps. 'There are people in the river!'

Katy looks too. A section of the water is clearly earmarked for swimmers. 'They look like baby seals.' Noting swimming caps but no wetsuits, she points to a jetty. 'Ah, that's where they get in and out. Do you fancy doing it one day?'

He wrinkles his nose. 'Maybe when I'm a big boy.'

'Right, that's a date.'

Milo takes up a story and they continue to amble. 'Then Murphy stole another dog's ball and Bridget had to chase him.' He puts his hand to his mouth to stifle the giggle. 'He wouldn't come back and she really shouted. Her face went all red like a balloon.'

'Oh dear. What happened then?'

'She said sorry to the man with the puppy, but he was still cross. He said the ball cost twelve pounds! Do dog balls really cost twelve pounds?'

'Goodness, I don't know, love, but that does sound expensive—'

'That's what Bridget said.' He mimics her voice. '"Then you've been robbed. You can buy those in Poundland!"' Milo chortles again. 'Then after we'd walked for a bit, Murphy dropped the ball, so she had to run back to the man and give it to him. It was so funny, Mummy. I wish you'd been there. It's not the same without you.'

Katy picks him up and spins him around. 'Do you know how much I love you?'

He laughs as he flies. 'To the moon and back!'

'And how many times?'

'Zillions!'

Once on the ground, she rakes his fringe from his eyes. 'Thirty seconds' rest, dizzy won't do.'

'Won't do for what?'

'Well, I believe there's a café.'

'Why are we going there?' he asks, though his sparkling eyes already know the answer.

'For an ice cream, of course!'

25

Katy

Propelled by the wind and their chatter about whether there'll be strawberry *and* chocolate chip, Katy and Milo finally reach the benches outside Tree Tops. She points to a placard by the entry.

'Can you see that sign with a picture of a whippet? Guess what it says?'

His eyes wide, Milo hops from foot to foot. 'I don't know.'

'It says "Scoops. A frozen treat for dogs that gets their tails wagging". Right, let's investigate what will make your tail wag.'

Remembering the puddles, Katy crouches down to inspect Milo's wellies.

'Hmm. I think I'd better—'

'You had salted caramel tart last time we went to a café,' Milo cuts in.

She chuckles, amazed as always at his eloquence and his memory. Would she have known about anything 'salted' at five years of age? Though she probably did. *Typical only child*, she once heard a teacher murmur to another when she was in infants. It was a confusing moment she still clearly remembers. The woman's derogatory tone didn't match all the enthusiastic red ticks on her homework. Similar comments followed as her education progressed, but it was the word 'precocious' that hurt the most. There was always a sneer, which really wasn't fair. She couldn't help being clever; she was hardly going to get poor marks on purpose; it was just the way she was. Until university, of course.

'Hello! You came.' A familiar voice interrupts her reverie. 'Did you swim or . . .' Harry drags a hand through his wet hair. 'I'm guessing just a walk.'

Feeling her deep blush, she struggles – in a somewhat ungainly way – upright. Oh God. Does he think she came here on purpose to bump into him? 'I didn't know you swam on . . . Yes, I thought a change of scene would be . . .' Cupping Milo's shoulders, she rallies. 'We're here for an ice cream but I thought I'd inspect the muddy damage before we traipse inside to choose which one. This is Milo.'

'Hi.' Harry holds out his hand. 'I'm Harry, pleased to meet you. So what flavours are your favourite?'

'Strawberry and chocolate chip.'

'Good choice. I'm taking it you like them together? In a cone with sprinkles?'

Milo chuckles behind his fist and nods.

'Right, I'll do the honours.' Harry turns to Katy. 'What can I get you?'

She tries not to return his winning smile, but her mouth flaming betrays her. She takes a breath to reply, but he speaks again.

'Or shall I surprise you?'

She actually hates surprises of any kind, but she finds herself grinning again. 'Sure, that would be—'

'Salted caramel tart! That's Mummy's favourite!'

Harry taps his nose. 'Thanks, Milo. Message received and understood.'

128

Trying to ignore the ridiculous flutter in her belly, Katy sits next to Milo at a table, points out a bank of swans and chats while they wait. When Harry returns, he looks ruefully at the tray he's carrying.

'I've more or less succeeded with Milo's order, but we'll have to save yours for our next date, I'm afraid, Katy.' His amber eyes catch hers. 'Blueberry muffin, carrot cake, flapjack and a cookie. Hopefully there's something that might take your fancy.'

Quickly breaking their gaze, she laughs. 'Well, I'm peckish, but not *that* peckish, so I hope we're all sharing.'

'That, I like the sound of.' He lifts the teapot lid and stirs. 'Builders' tea?'

'Yes please.'

Katy looks at the people, the bushes, the plants and trees as they eat their delicacies. At anything other than the handsome man opposite. When she reaches the swimmers, he speaks. 'You should try it. It's great exercise, supercharges your immune system, crushes fatigue, burns fat and stimulates the release of feel-good endorphins and so on, but it's also ...' Squinting thoughtfully, he seems to search for what he wants to say. 'Well, it's therapeutic, I guess.' He smiles thinly. 'Good for working things through.'

Remembering his comment about Rex's mistress 'buggering off', Katy considers how to respond, but Harry addresses Milo. 'Is that as tasty as it looks?'

Milo doesn't reply. His attention has been caught by a girl flicking her long braids on a nearby bench. Katy touches his shoulder and turns to him before speaking. The hearing in his good ear is fine, his regular mimicry is evidence of that, but it's an instruction she keenly obeyed when they discovered his partial deafness: make sure you have your baby's attention and eye contact before speaking; move closer to him when you are talking, rather than raising your voice. Yet another trauma she had to ride.

'Milo? Harry is asking you a question.'

When he turns, Harry asks again. 'Is that as tasty as it looks? A sundae on a Sunday!'

'A gelato. That's what Bridget calls them. "A chocolate gelato, Milo?"' he says in an impressive Scottish accent. 'Do you know Bridget?'

'I do, actually.'

'How do you know her?'

Harry's eyes flicker to Katy's. 'Our dogs know each other.'

'Really? You have a dog? What type of dog? Bridget's is a . . .'

Her shoulders relaxing, Katy zones out and picks up a sachet of sugar. The subject of Bridget shouldn't stress her, and she has nothing to hide, not really. But it would be nice to be normal, just for once in her life.

Kneading absently, her thoughts drift to her dad. En route to Sale he got a call about a burst water pipe in his chambers. The plumber in question had been rushed to hospital with bad burns. Even as he drove he was formulating a plan to raise cash for the poor workman. She should prepare something for dinner in his absence. Maybe a nice casserole for when he gets home. What did she see in the fridge? Chicken, definitely . . .

Milo's high voice brings her back to the conversation. 'She's Grandad's friend too,' he's saying. 'They're always "sharing a joke". She looks after me when Mummy gets sad or sleepy.'

'I don't get sad, Milo.' Despite the punch of guilt, Katy tries for a smile. 'Occasionally a bit sleepy, but not for a long—'

130

'You sometimes look sad.' Milo lowers his head and pulls at his T-shirt. 'And you were sleepy all day yesterday.'

Harry clears his throat. He has a fine scar on his chin, she notices. 'Your mummy doesn't look tired today, Milo. In fact, just the opposite. How are you guys getting home?'

'I believe there's a tram stop nearby.'

Milo slumps. 'Not more walking . . .'

'See that sleek, shiny Lexus over there?' Harry points to a black sports car. 'The back seat isn't huge, but it's big enough for a little one. How about I give you and your mummy a ride home?'

'No thanks.' The angsty response pops out before Katy can stop it. Bloody hell, what about being *normal* for once? She tempers her tone. 'We don't have Milo's booster seat, so . . .'

Harry's brow puckers. 'Sorry, I should have thought before—' He offers his arms to Milo. 'A shoulder lift to the tram stop instead?'

'OK. But next time I'm defo going to bring my seat.' Milo looks from Katy to Harry and rolls his shiny eyes. 'When we go on our next date, of course.'

26

Sibeal

Jolting awake, Sibeal holds her breath, her ears tuned for sound. There's no resonance, no refrain, thank God. The oppressive, slow dirge has finally stopped. She lets out the trapped, ragged air from her lungs. She's so cold, bloody freezing. Where the hell is she? She lifts her leaden head and takes in her bearings. What the fuck is she doing on the attic landing?

She stills at a creaking sound from below. It's Gabriel, at last. 'Gabe?' Her throat rasps, so she tries again. 'Gabe, I'm up here.'

A voice echoes back, but it's female. 'Sib? Where are you? It's Katy. The back door was unlocked . . .'

Her body soon follows. Trainers, skinny jeans and a baggy jumper as always. Her pretty face creases. 'Gosh, are you OK?' She crouches down, the warmth radiating from her like a hot-water bottle. 'Did you fall? Have you hurt yourself?'

'Nope and I don't think so.'

'Shall I help you up?'

'I'm fine.' Her limbs stiff and heavy, Sib struggles upright. Christ, something has come loose, pounding her skull. She tries to think back to last night. Yup, fossilised ancient port after a shedload of wine.

Kat scans the area, and though her gaze is questioning, she doesn't probe. Instead she pulls Sib towards her and softly rubs her back as if comforting a child. In this particular place, it feels so very apt and sad and ironic that tears sting her eyes.

Surprised at the desire to stay wrapped for ever, Sibeal melts into the embrace, but after a few moments the stench of puke reaches her senses. Her own bloody vomit, of course. She pulls away and grimaces at the lumpy mess on her dressing gown. And it has transferred to poor Kat's top. 'God, I'm sorry. Cockburn's Old Tawny chunder. Not nice. When I can move, I'll put it in the washer. You can borrow one of mine.'

'Oh, it's fine,' Kat says absently. 'You're frozen. You must have been here for a while. Maybe you should warm up in the shower.'

An unstoppable yawn rattling her head, Sibeal squints in thought. In truth, she can't remember how long she's been up here; it might have been minutes; it could have been hours. Sleepwalking or alcohol? Imagined music or real? And that persistent waft of cheap perfume . . . Not that it makes much odds. It adds up to the same thing.

She returns to Kat. She'd like to explain, but despite her friend's guileless blue gaze, it's still too raw to broach, even as a grown adult. 'Gabe's fault,' she mutters. 'He said he'd stay last night and go back this morning. But we had an argument and he pissed off.'

It was a row about her slipping into his bed again. She should have known better, but she was still out of kilter from her stalking on Saturday. Though in reality it was more than just that, wasn't it? She went into the boy's room; she absorbed his innocence, his beauty, his smell. If the babysitter hadn't appeared the moment she did, God knows what might have happened.

She blinks away a shiver. Of fear or excitement, she can't quite say. 'Who but Gabe would get out of a cosy bed and stomp off in the early hours? Stubborn man. He could've stayed until daylight.' And then, the thought popping out without warning, 'Did your mum cuddle you when you were little? When you were small and smooth and sweet? When your hair was still feathery and your hands soft and tiny?'

Shock passes through Kat's neat features. Perhaps that sounded a little too Gothic, even creepy; sometimes it's difficult to judge with a hangover.

'In short, did she hug you?'

'Yes, of course. She was very affectionate.'

Sibeal pulls herself to her feet. 'But she died.'

'Yes.'

'And you still miss her?'

'Yes.'

'How did she die?'

Kat visibly stiffens. 'I told you before. She was in an accident.'

'Yeah, sorry, you—'

'A car crash. She was the passenger.' As though summoning her resolve, Kat lifts her chin. 'She died from catastrophic injuries, whatever that means. In all likelihood she would have lived if the airbag had worked. Whiplash instead of death. So there you have it.'

'Bloody hell.'

She nods.

'Did you sue?'

Her cheeks flooding with colour, Kat turns away. 'What was

the point of that? Her death was inordinately painful for me and my dad. Raking everything up would have just made it worse,' she says crisply. 'All the money in the world wouldn't have brought her back to us.'

Sibeal shrugs and tightens her belt. 'Dosh helps. Trust me, it does.' She steps tentatively to the stairs and clutches the banister. 'But what do I know? I hated my fucking mother.'

27

Katy

Unsure if she's offended, angry or somehow liberated, Katy watches Sibeal wobble down the stairs.

'Bathroom,' she says when they reach the next floor. She wafts an arm. 'Help yourself to a clean top. They're in the overnight bag.'

'Thanks.' Katy pushes the first door and peers in. From the framed prints of string instruments to its tidiness and smell, it's clearly Gabe's. She smiles despite herself. Suppose he'd been here? Asleep or even naked? How embarrassing would that be?

A flash of Harry's sculpted chest flies in. She wasn't looking, absolutely not, but at David Lloyd she couldn't help noticing how his Lycra top and shorts left little to the imagination. She thrusts the image away. She's not in the market for romance, and from his cloudy look when he mentioned the therapeutic benefits of open water swimming, neither is he.

She reverts to Gabe's quarters. Does he have a love interest? Intrigued to find out more, she moves further inside. Tall, neatly stacked bookcases line one of the walls, dark wooden furniture the other, but when she turns towards the bed, she smiles. The pillows are higgledy, the duvet in disarray and a pile of discarded underwear is scattered on the floor. So he does have a girlfriend! Clearly one who wears the same designer clothes label as Sib.

Katy taps the tabletop as she waits for Sibeal. Milo had a sniffle when he woke up this morning. Did she do right to chivvy him out of bed and to school?

She puffs her angst away. He's absolutely fine. Indeed, he skipped all the way, only pulling to a stop by the gate to say, 'Is our date with Harry today?' Little rascal. It was the first thing he said to Alexander when they arrived home on Sunday. 'Mummy is going on a date and I'm coming too.'

'No, I'm not, Milo, and neither are you!' she cut in.

Preoccupied by the young plumber's injuries, her dad was miles away. To prevent water damage to the old building's furnishings, the lad had bravely stemmed the burning flow with a tool and his feet until his mate turned off the supply. But a shoot had escaped and scalded his legs and torso. If he had a claim against chambers, they'd make sure to fast-track it, Alexander murmured. In the meantime, he'd started a collection.

The thought of the poor guy's injuries brings Katy full circle to her doctor friend again. There's no doubt he deflected Milo's comments about Bridget and sadness and sleeping. Then there was the way he'd said 'I should have thought before' about the lift in his car. Is she just being paranoid or has Bridget said something?

'Can I borrow your phone?' he said when they arrived at the tram stop.

She assumed he'd forgotten his mobile and needed to make an urgent call, but his own phone rang from his pocket. He ruffled Milo's hair. 'Salted caramel date soon,' he said.

Feeling somewhat hot, she now loosens the neck of Sibeal's cashmere jumper. Though hers were in a variety of pastel colours, it's the sort of thing her mum used to sport. She was wearing one in lilac the year 'Father Christmas' brought Katy an Instamatic camera.

'Maybe ration them, sweetheart,' Elke said. 'Otherwise you'll run out of film before you've opened the rest of your pressies.' Then to her dad with a chuckle, 'And keep your mitts off it too, Alexon. I know what you're like once you start taking snaps.'

Of course the instant gratification was too much to resist, and the photographs were all of her parents, goofing and laughing and in love, but for the first time in years she's glad that she did, so she can look at them later. Though her nose stings, today's grief is mixed with fondness. Perhaps she is making progress after all. Sib's questions about her mum's death were somewhat direct, but Katy did say 'catastrophic injuries' and 'airbag' out loud, which is a flaming miracle. The one time she tried to drive her own car after the event, she found herself seeing blood and hyperventilating, so the shiny new Polo stayed on their driveway for months. In the end her dad gave it to Bridget, a company car of sorts.

'Was I rude?' Dropping a cardboard crate on the table, Sib smiles that stunning smile. 'Gabe says I can be rude. Or tactless. Depending on whether I'm in his good books or not. So sorry if I was, I don't do it intentionally.' She pops out two pills from a blister pack. 'You can take ibuprofen and paracetamol at the same time, right? I was fine with the wine but the port was probably fermented to a hundred and ninety per cent proof. Not that I can remember what it tasted like. Anyway, look what I found. You're going to like this, little Kat.' She taps the box. 'Busted.'

'Busted?'

Save for the dark smudges beneath Sibeal's eyes, it's as though her semi-conscious state never happened. She pulls a face. 'You *have* heard of Busted? Pop punk band from Southend-on-Sea? Or maybe schoolgirl crushes weren't allowed in your posh educational establishment?'

Katy laughs. 'What makes you think it was a posh school?'

'Well, apart from the accent, let's see. Barrister to judiciary dad, house in Cheadle *with gates*. You always say please and thank you. I expect you were head girl.' She stares. 'Oh God, you were. You do know that's annoying? A star bloody student too, I bet. Which university? No, don't tell me, it'll be Oxbridge.' She narrows her eyes. 'Law or Medicine? A first?'

Katy shifts in her seat. 'I never sat my finals. So, back to Busted . . . I take it they were your schoolgirl crush.'

'Not "they", Kat. "He".' She drags off the lid, scoops out two palmfuls of paper and spreads it out on the table. 'My Charlie. God, how I adored him.'

'You don't say!' Katy picks through the images and selects one trimmed around the guy's knowing gaze. 'This one?'

'So he only had eyes for me.'

'And that?' she asks, pointing to one that has clearly been cut into pieces then sellotaped back together.

'The scissors came out whenever he had a new girlfriend.'

'Yup, I can see that you loved him, just a little.'

'This is nothing. He was plastered all over my bedroom wall. I went to any concert within a million-mile radius, hung outside the stage door, desperate for a glimpse.' She picks up a CD still in its cellophane. 'Bought several copies of each album, calendars, annuals. They'll all be here somewhere; Dad wouldn't have dared to throw them out.'

'Wow.' Wondering what to say, Katy smiles politely. It's a little ... well, obsessive. She had her fair share of pop star squeezes as a teenager, but nothing compared to this. 'What do you think of Charlie now?' she asks.

Sibeal brushes the memorabilia back into its container. 'Nothing,' she says. She picks up one last photo, stares for a moment, then drops it in. 'Absolutely nothing. I binned Charlie for Robin.'

28

Sibeal

Sibeal observes Kat pat her mouth with the ancient kitchen roll they found under the sink. Her countenance is open and kind. 'You were going to tell me about Robin,' she says again. A small frown creases her forehead. 'But only if you want to.'

She does, she really does, but it's difficult. She's already procrastinated by brewing up and putting eight frozen croissants in a heap in the microwave. They were limp and piping hot, so she should have obeyed the instructions by baking them in the oven, but she was too bloody starving to wait. And all that time she felt Kat's watchful eyes on her spine. *Tell me*, they said. *You can trust me; you can tell me everything and I won't mention it to another soul.* But after years of holding it in, it's so hard to let it out. She loved him so much; he wasn't a poster on the wall; he was real, he was human, he was perfect and she—

'I binned him too. Robin.'

Kat stops picking at the crumbs on her plate and looks up in surprise. 'Oh, right, I thought . . .'

'That he died? He did. That was later.'

Oh God, the bloody pain, the ragged bloody pain. She puts

141

her fist to her breast; she can feel it right there, like a blunt knife ripping through her flesh.

Taking a deep breath, she blocks the urgent need to wail. 'He was my first boyfriend, but I finished it. We went our own ways. I was a stupid, stupid fool. If I hadn't chucked him, he'd never have met *her*. She wouldn't have killed him.'

Kat slowly nods as she processes the information. 'You said that before. How do you know?'

'He told me. "If I end up strangled . . ." That's what he said. Which is why . . .'

'Why what?'

She puffs through the memory of the funeral service. How she didn't make a scene, she'll never know. 'Why we talked about his funeral. He said if he died I was to go, wear red and knock them all . . .' She swallows the word.

'Wow.' Kat clears her throat. 'Do you know how he . . .'

'Not really. Gabe muttered something about a cardiac arrest, but the bitch isn't about to tell the truth, is she?'

'I guess not. It's just . . . well . . . surely the paramedics or hospital would have informed the police if there was anything suspicious . . .'

But Sibeal isn't listening. 'First love. You know when you can't get enough of someone? When you want to be with them all the time?' She closes her eyes, trying to find words to describe how she felt back then. 'I wanted to breathe him, eat him, invade him. Be his undies, his T-shirt, his jeans. He consumed my every last thought. There was no room for anyone or anything else. I spent every weekend and holiday at his digs in York. More, if I could get away with it.'

Remembering how lost she'd been when her dad begged her to

come home for lessons or exams, she glances around the kitchen. 'I was miserable without him.'

'But you finished with him?'

'Yeah. Weird really. I forgot he existed for over five years. Then Gabe took me as his plus one to his wedding.' Smiling wryly, she snorts. 'I only went to have a nosy at the bloody woman. See what she looked like, find out how tacky I knew the gown would be. Robin was there with this guy called Crispin at the altar, waiting for his bride.'

Picturing the image, she stops, the agony still physical. 'It was like a hard punch to the stomach. I was winded, couldn't breathe. Then I cried through the service. Tears of happiness, people thought, not bitterness, self-loathing, jealousy. But later I knew he'd be back. As soon as his eyes locked onto mine, I knew. We had sex the day he returned from his honeymoon and I was right back to how I'd been at fifteen. Needing and wanting constantly. Only this time he belonged to someone else.'

Listening to the clunk of old pipes, neither of them speak for some time. 'Why did you break it off with him?' Kat asks eventually.

Sib covers her face. Boys her own age and freedom. That's what she said to Gabe and her dad. To herself too. But of course it's not the whole story.

Behind her wet fingers she whispers the words.

'I can't hear you, Sib,' Kat says. 'Tell me again.'

She shakes her head. She's said them once, she can't repeat them.

'It's fine, you don't have to tell me.' Kat's warm arms envelop her again. 'We all keep things to ourselves. Sometimes it's better that way.'

'I got pregnant and aborted it. Nothing felt the same after that.' Then, pulling away from the soft jumper and wiping her face, 'I knew he'd persuade me to keep it if I told him. He wanted babies, he wanted *my* baby. But I'd just started at Durham, freshers' week and fun. I didn't want to be tied down. And Robin suddenly felt too hairy, too old.'

The frustration overwhelming, she stands and paces. Kat's startled eyes flick to the upturned chair, but Sib has to get the sheer injustice out. 'So when we got together again, I said, "Let's have that baby you wanted." He was thrilled, said he would leave her.' Her hands shake. 'But she got there first. That bitch had my baby.'

29

Sibeal

When the wind turbines wave, Sibeal turns off the radio and opens the car window as usual. She draws in the rural aromas, still amazed at how much she likes the smell of manure, then she takes the road which cuts a swathe through fields of tight green vegetation. God knows what's growing there, but they resemble huge sprouts. Feeling her shoulders loosen, she expels the remaining tension with a long breath through her nose. She's surrounded by meadows, shrubs and sheep, all silently ignoring her. It feels good, really good, which is strange for someone who loves noise. And attention. Yearning for it each night before sleep. Craving it, needing it, demanding it every day.

She inwardly groans. If only she could say that was just as a child.

She continues along the country lane, past the Crooked Billet pub, the huge pylon and the thicket of woods. The church of All Saints' turret appears, a comforting square tower above the yew trees. The Anglican Grade I listed building is her home place of prayer. She doesn't attend but perhaps she should; it would make Saint Imelda turn in her grave. It'd annoy Gabe too; that might be fun.

Goading Gabriel, poor Gabriel; she really must stop.

The sunny quietness hits as she drives through the centre. One pub, a village hall and a cricket club. A 'sleepy' hamlet, she supposes, the sort of jargon she uses on the website. But this place is more like comatose. Other than dog owners heading for the fields, she rarely sees anyone walking the pretty paths. It suits her completely; though she'll wave at anonymous cars passing by, there's no need to stop and say hi.

Pulling up on her driveway, she notes the cloudless blue sky. It rains here sometimes, sleets and thunders and even floods, but it doesn't feel that way. It snows, of course, heavy dumb snowfall. But she welcomes that.

The thud of the car door breaks the stillness. Go inside for a coffee or head straight to Gabe's? Well, that's a no-brainer; she won't settle until she makes peace with him. Now three days have passed, she can barely remember Sunday night. But he was angry, that's for sure; she can picture his white face.

Slinging her bag over her shoulder, she sets off along the narrow pavement. At least she has good news to report. Over the last few days she and Kat have made pretty good progress with the house *and* her mental state. She'd never dream of seeing a shrink, but her time with Kat is how she imagines counselling would be – freely reminiscing about Robin, describing memories and moments, their few stolen weekends away, as well as the frustration and impotence of them being a secret. It was so nice to have someone listening and interested as they piled books into boxes for Oxfam, threw out cracked crockery, ancient appliances and broken ornaments. They were careful with what they selected, of course, using the litmus test of 'would Gabriel approve?' But when it came to Sibeal's own possessions, there was no holding back. She simply scooped old clothes, toys and dolls straight from cupboards and drawers into the sturdy bin liners. Without a pang of regret she even said goodbye to Charlic.

'I think this calls for a toast, don't you?' she asked Kat and they clinked their coffee cups even though she had chilled wine in the fridge.

Would Gabriel approve? It has been the acid test her whole adult life. Mostly failing it, and often deliberately, but always wanting his endorsement nonetheless.

When she reaches his white door, she lifts her knuckles to knock, then notices the closed blinds and the muted sound of a string instrument. He's clearly teaching; it's best she uses her keys. She quietly steps in, but to her surprise, a lampshade-cum-dog greets her.

'What the fuck?' she blurts loudly, then lowers her voice. 'Where did you come from?'

Though the Labrador sniffs her and pads away uninterestedly, the damage is done. The wistful melody of '*Le cygne*' stops and Gabriel appears, his jaw tight with irritation.

'I have a pupil here; I'm teaching.'

'I know, sorry. I tried to be silent, but the . . .' She gestures to the pet. 'Look, I'll be as quiet as a mouse until you finish. You won't know I'm here—'

'That's not the point, Sibeal. You can't just barge into someone's house.' His voice is staccato, his lips barely moving. 'You can't use keys to waltz in. You wait until you're invited—'

'Well, that wasn't going to happen. You haven't even

147

answered my calls or my texts. If you had, then I wouldn't have had to . . .'

She looks beyond Gabe's shoulder. A flaxen-haired youth of sixteen or so has appeared at the door with his cello. 'I think you're wanted.' She taps her watch. 'I'll rustle up something for lunch. Quiet as a mouse! See you in a bit.'

When the slow strain of the dying swan recommences, Sibeal doesn't make for the kitchen but heads upstairs. What the hell is an animal doing here? Though her brother is fond of dogs, his peripatetic life has never allowed him to have one. And if Gabe hasn't told her about it, what else hasn't he mentioned?

The bathroom reveals nothing she doesn't already know. Gabriel is scrupulously tidy and clean; he likes to buy ethical toiletries and the fennel toothpaste is revolting. She peers into the box room. It's still his alphabetically book-lined study, so he hasn't moved a Labrador-owning lodger in. Unless that person's sharing with him, of course. Disturbed by that thought, she moves to his door and turns the handle. The bed is made, thank God, and there's no sign or smell of sex. Releasing her breath, she casts her eyes around the room. The sunshine is streaming in through the window, but there's no dust to light up like in hers. A freshly ironed shirt hangs from the wardrobe and there's a neat pile of T-shirts clearly ready to be put away.

Without thinking about it too deeply, she steps to a high chest and opens the top drawer. He always kept his boxers and socks in the right-hand one at Brook House and he's predictably done the same here, save he's added handkerchiefs, belts, a tie and . . . She pulls out an emerald green silk scarf. Well, that's an eye-opener; perhaps he does have a woman . . . But she pauses in thought. Gabe appointed himself in charge of clearing their parents' bedroom, so in all likelihood it belonged to their mother. Putting it to her nose, she inhales the familiar earthy and sweet smell of her brother's aftershave.

She nods to herself. This was his secret place back in the day. *Story of O*, that year's Valentine's card, a couple of spliffs and a lighter. And of course his stash of well-thumbed mammy and son photographs.

Looking for inspiration, she glances around. Gabe's hiding something, she's sure. Those incommunicado days and his increasing caginess ... Hearing voices from below, she quickly replaces her find and slips from the room. The youth, the dog, Gabe and the huge instrument are struggling to fit in the hallway.

'Can you manage?' Gabe is saying, handing over the lead. 'Sally looks keen for a walk. You could collect the cello later if you like? My sister is here, so there's no rush.'

The teenager digs in his pockets and pulls out a poo bag. 'Yeah, probably a good idea.' He looks up to Sib as she comes down the stairs. 'So, see you later. Thanks.'

Sibeal brushes past her brother when the door clicks to. 'I see you're still using that soap with no lather,' she comments. 'So, your new girlfriend's called *Sally*. She's a bit pongy, don't you think? Is this the latest add-on to your talents? Music lessons-cum-kennels?'

Gabe follows her through to the kitchen. 'She's had an operation so I could hardly say no.' He removes his glasses and rubs his cheeks. 'Anyway, why are you here?'

Turning away, Sibeal busies herself with the kettle. 'I thought

I was being attacked by a bloody standard lamp when I arrived.' Then, 'I live just up the road, remember?'

'I have work to do, pupils to see. You can't just walk in. I'll take back my keys if you—'

'I came to say I was sorry.' Tears prick her eyes. 'You haven't been in touch since Sunday. So I'm sorry. I have a big mouth, I blurt stupid things, but you know I don't mean it.'

She thinks back to the bloody awful weekend, the sighting of Zoe, the scent of Persil and Tom Ford aftershave, that perfect little boy. But on reflection her erratic feelings and behaviour started at Kat's house when Alexander gushed about the wonderful and talented Imelda. Everyone inevitably smitten, including some bloke called Kenny. Then later at home, she wanted Gabe to say, just for once, 'You are right, Sib. She might have been a good mum to me, but she wasn't to you. You weren't loved, but that wasn't your fault.'

He didn't, of course.

So she drank steadily all Sunday, went early to bed, then woke to the sound of . . .

'I heard the piano, Gabe.'

'No, you didn't. No one plays it. No one. It's all in your mind or your dreams.'

'Well I hear it. What difference does it make? I heard it and I was frightened.' Her voice is annoyingly tremulous. 'You're my brother. You're all I've got. You're supposed to love me and take care of me.'

'I do love you. You know that.' He pauses and sighs. 'But the point is that I am your brother. You can't just come in my bedroom, climb in my bed when it suits you. It isn't right, Sib. It isn't fair to put me in that—'

'It's only when I'm scared. I just need to be reassured, comforted. I don't mean anything by it.'

'You took off your clothes, all of them; you wanted more than comfort, Sib.'

'You didn't always turn me away,' she mutters.

She reaches for the kitchen roll, wipes her face, then moves across to the fridge and opens it. 'Hmm. Eggs, cheese and ham. How about an omelette?' She finally turns with a wry smile. 'Almost bloody cremated, just how you like it?'

His lips twitch and she knows she's forgiven.

'Kat's been helping me chuck things out but we have a huge pile of maybes you need to look at.'

Gabriel pulls out a chair. 'I'm sure you can decide; I trust you to make the right call.' He massages his forehead. 'I have to work, Sib. I have lessons here as normal. Then I'm off to London next week with tunings back to back, so . . .'

'But you'll come when you can?'

'You know I will.' He taps the table. 'I'll be in London on Thursday for ten days or so. I'll come before then.'

The slow dirge of Chopin's 'Marche Funèbre' echoes in Sibeal's head. Always that. 'Because it's you who said we had to go through everything before they came for the furniture.'

'I know. It seemed respectful to Mum and Dad. Handing it over to someone else felt—'

'When will they come?'

'No date yet.'

'Will they take everything when they do?'

'Unless there's anything you want, Sib.'

Her throat is tight; she just has to ask. 'Including the piano?'

'Yes.'

'Are you sure? Don't you want it?'

Shadows pass through her brother's eyes. 'No, I don't want it.' He nods. 'Yes, including the piano. It'll do us both good to put that in the past.'

30

Katy

The sun warm on her back, Katy ambles away from school with a new mum from Milo's class. She gathers from Lizzie's chatter that her husband had a project abroad so they leased their house out for a year.

'You should try it,' she says with a chuckle. 'The tenants painted all the walls with Farrow and Ball, no less, overhauled the flower beds and added some pretty expensive-looking decking. Feel free to pop in if you're passing. How about you? Where are you and your other half based?'

She draws breath to reply but is saved by the ding of a text. 'I think this might be my friend, demanding my instant attention, so if you don't mind . . .'

'Sure, go ahead.'

She pulls out her mobile and idly glances at the screen.

Are you free for a drink tonight?

Bloody hell, it's from Harry.

'Are you OK?' Lizzie asks.

'Yes, absolutely!'

'Oh, OK. You just looked a little alarmed. You know, from the text.'

Bloody typical. Right from being small her face always gave her away. Although her pulse is still rushing, she tries for a casual reply. 'It's nothing important. So, what are your plans for today?'

'Breakfast at Costa, which sounds nice, but I'm meeting some girls I used to work with and they're pretty hard work. Very much the "why would anyone let a baby get in the way of one's career" types.' She looks at Katy and her eyes light like candles. 'Hey, that's an idea. Do you fancy joining us? It would be amazing if you'd come and help me out.'

Katy takes a breath. It would be mean to say no. Besides, the flip and fizz from Harry's message has affected her power of speech, so she simply nods and says, 'Sure.'

The two polished woman sitting opposite seem nice, but Katy struggles to make small talk about management consultancy work. Or maybe it's because she's both anxious and excited about the text burning a hole in her pocket. Is she free for a drink tonight? Does she *want* to go for a drink with Harry? Her dad is away, so the first is a no. As for the second? It's no, not sure, maybe.

After twenty minutes, she can't bear the waiting any longer. Lizzie clearly senses her imminent departure as she quickly speaks. 'I'll get you another coffee, Katy. Cappuccino again?' she asks, her face imploring.

'Great, thanks. I'll just nip to the loo.'

She reads the message again in the dimly lit cubicle. *Are you free for a drink tonight?*

Well, she already knows the answer to that, so she hurriedly replies to get the churning over with.

Sorry, Dad's working away.

When she returns to the table, the smell of cheese toasties greets her.

'Help yourself,' Lizzie says.

'Oh, thanks very much.'

The conversation has moved on to the easier topic of *Stranger Things*, thank goodness, yet Katy's unable to focus on anything except her damned reply. She should have thought about it for longer. It was too short and blunt. She should have mentioned Milo. But then Harry might have suggested asking Bridget to mind Milo as per his comment about her sleepiness. And sadness. Oh God, how embarrassing. But one thing is for sure, she doesn't want Bridget involved. If she ever gets an evening life again, she'll find a babysitter. Her neighbour has a smiley and sensible fifteen-year-old daughter. She could ask her. Well, she could've if she hadn't already turned down the date. Though was it really a *date*? He'd only asked if she was free for a drink, for heaven's sake!

Almost laughing to herself for her wasted agitation, Katy shoves the phone back in her pocket and heads for home. For the past hour and a half there has been no reply from Harry at all. Still, the management consultants turned out to be human. Though her whole body remained alert to a beep or vibration from her mobile, she managed to tune in to the conversation and listened to tales of their extracurricular exploits. The world of work sounded fun, actually – five-star hotels here and there; early mornings and hard graft; spas, expensive bathroom products and saunas; cocktails she'd never heard of, late-night parties and general revelry.

Deciding to divert to the park, she inhales the smell of newly mown grass, and takes in the undoubted beauty of the earth. From the purple borders to the white magnolias and the raspberry-pink Dianthus, it's bursting with colour. She woke so full of zip, she considered jogging home after dropping Milo at school, but it felt a little like tempting fate, and she didn't want to risk another 'Mummy ran home like the wind' comment by him at the weekend. Her dad is never cross, but somehow his silent 'are you sure you're up to it?' look is so much worse.

She clenches her jaw. Well, she is 'up to it', actually. She's been busy all week at Brook House. Lugging and lifting and packing. Doing far more than Sib who sat with her feet up and mostly watched and gave directions between her smiling accounts of Robin. Some were quite graphic, far more detailed than she would have shared. Not that she's seen or been touched by a man's naked body parts for some considerable time.

She groans at that particular thought; she might have been able to put that right, but she was pathetic and weak instead of having some bloody spirit.

Fingering the phone in her pocket, she looks up to the sky. In all honesty she's tempted to yell with exasperation. She is the Oxbridge girl who had so much potential once upon a time, yet she's marching to an empty house with nothing to do. No future, no plans, no focus. Few proper friends. No one to kiss and cuddle, let alone shag. Though that's hardly surprising. She never had any trouble getting boyfriends; keeping them was the problem. So maybe she was dull or boring or spotty or fat. Perhaps she slept with them too soon or not soon enough. Whatever it was, she did *something* wrong. And today she's obviously pissed off the one man who seemed remotely interested.

Not wanting to retreat to her echoey house just yet, she thumps down on a bench next to the play area and folds her arms. Trying to shake off her frustration, she watches two toddlers dart from the slide to the swings. She has a child, a beautiful child; she'd trade nothing for him. So she's fortunate, really. Yes, life has dealt her a poor hand in some ways, but she has Milo and her dad. She has Sib and her mum pals. She's just held her own over coffee with a new friend and two strangers. Two years ago she'd have barely stepped out of the driveway, let alone sat in a public area and be *seen*.

Determined not to look again at her mobile, she tightens her grip. What the hell is wrong with her anyway? She has no interest in dating. Guys bugger off when you've just got to like them. And yet remembering Sib's words, she can't help but shuffle on her seat and smile.

'You know my favourite part of a man?' she'd asked, her eyes dreamy.

Katy sat back from her chore and grinned. 'Their ability to multitask?'

Sib raised her dark eyebrows. 'It's not what you think but it's close.' She stood and demonstrated with her hand. 'This bit. Between his belly button and his . . . tool.'

That made Katy laugh. 'His *tool*? How very functional!'

'The more functional the better, I'd say,' Sib replied. 'Why, what do you call them?'

Katy tried to think back but the only names that came to

157

mind were poetical ones suitable for a small child. Yet visualising one now, her thoughts are far more prosaic.

'That's a nice smile.'

She looks across the grass. Rex is pulling his owner towards her. Wishing she could hide the burning embarrassment rushing from her toes to her nose, she takes in Harry's dimples, his wide and white grin. And yes, his lithe body. Slightly limping, he finally reaches her. He leans in to peck her cheek, then sits down beside her.

'It dazzled me from the path,' he says. 'That smile.' He studies her with those dark amber eyes. 'I wonder what you were thinking about.'

Too disconcerted to reply, Katy dumbly studies a line of busy ants on ground. Then she notices his loosely laced trainer on one foot. 'You seem to be struggling with that ankle,' she says, finally rallying. 'You should see a doctor.'

'Witty as well as pretty,' he replies. 'A dog who shall remain anonymous for his own protection got in my way and I bashed it.' He lifts his right leg. 'A couple of days ago, so you're probably right. I should get an X-ray.'

'Can't you write yourself a referral at work? Like mates' rates, get to the top of the waiting list?'

He squints into the distance. 'Yeah, something like that.' He turns. 'So, are you free for our date tonight?'

'I don't do dates and no.' The words pop out more contemptuously than she intends, but Harry just laughs.

'OK. It's not a date. A date would be going out in public, right? What about if I rustled something up at home? Though I say so myself, I'm not a bad cook. If you're vegan, vegetarian, pescatarian, best let me know, otherwise—'

Katy stands. *Going out in public.* How does he know? It can only be bloody Bridget, flirting and gossiping like she does with her dad. 'No thank you,' she says stiffly. She looks at her watch. 'It's time for me to go.'

'What did I say wrong?' Harry reaches for her hand. 'I said something to upset you. What was it?'

She gazes at his face, his sweetly crestfallen face. She's sick of small steps; she wants to take strides and that's down to her. 'Don't you ever look at your mobile?'

'Ah, no. I've been walking . . .' He looks at Rex. 'Painfully slow walking, thanks to someone.'

He feels his jeans' pockets, takes out his phone and reads her text. 'Very chatty,' he comments. He nods, his expression earnest. 'Of course, you have Milo in the evenings, stupid of me not to think that through. OK, fair enough.' Lightly tugging the dog's lead, he starts to walk away. Then he stops and looks back. 'Come on. Lunch it is, then. I've no idea what I've got in. Hope you like . . .' His brow creases in thought. 'Cereal? Yup, I definitely have cereal. And tailored kibble, of course.' He laughs. 'Who was it that said "animals come first"? This bloody dog rules my life.'

31

Katy

It takes ten minutes to arrive at Harry's detached house, which is situated at the far side of the village. Feeling self-conscious and nervous, Katy follows him up the path.

He steps into the porch, opens up and gestures her in. 'Go through and make yourself comfortable.' As the dog scuttles past, he crouches down to his trainers. 'I'll inspect the damage and be right with you.'

Her eyes as big as saucers, Katy moves into the front room and looks around. It's longer than she expected and very much open plan, the lounge one end, the window-lined kitchen the other. Unsure of the etiquette, she makes for a dark leather sofa, perches on the edge and listens to the clink of Rex's water bowl as he pushes it around the tiled floor.

Sure she's seen the retro elm bookcases, sideboard and cabinets in the John Lewis brochure, she inhales the smell of floral cleaning products and tries to remember Bridget's gossip over the years. They're both doctors, she recalls, a 'golden couple' as she called them. The wife was Linda or Lydia, but of course she left him and the dog, her dog. A pretty strange thing to do; she must have had a reason. Though Katy senses her belongings are still very much here.

The sound of an upstairs tap breaks the quietness, then finally Harry's voice. 'Sorry to keep you.' He looks down to his foot. 'I think I've overdone the walking today.'

She drags her gaze from the wedding portrait of him and his new bride prominently displayed on a side table. Like the happiness forever snap in her head of her parents, they look so exuberant and content. A stab of sorrow takes her breath. Yes, the past frozen in celluloid, telling lies.

Though Harry's face is pale, he tries for a grin. 'Not that a throbbing ankle affects my cooking prowess. A couple of ibuprofen and I'll be in the cereal cupboard like a shot.'

'I don't mind helping out. I'm a dab hand at filling the kettle. I could even pour milk on cornflakes if you tell me where to—'

'She accepted a post in Berlin,' he cuts in. His eyes slide away from the photograph and meet Katy's. 'Coincidentally following one of her colleagues, a female colleague.' He flops next to Katy and looks at the ceiling. 'More a blow to my ego than anything else. I knew they were close but . . .' He laughs drily. 'Not *that* close.'

Katy studies him. Though his dimples show either side of his wry smile, she senses the hurt radiating through. He rocks his head towards her and clears his throat. 'It's fine; we'd known each other since freshers' week, so it wasn't the grand romance. You know, more like friendship.' He shakes his head. 'I suppose "friendship" should've told me something; I should've seen it coming but I didn't. I came home from work one Tuesday and her bags were packed, the taxi waiting. No time for an argument, I guess. No time to persuade her to change her mind. Bit of a shock, really.'

Taking in his troubled gaze, Katy nods. She understands all too well the violence of the unexpected, the way it doesn't just take away your breath, but everything else too; the ground, your stability, your reality, your trust.

'It's hard to describe where I'm at. Working shifts . . . well, we weren't always home at the same time, so being here alone isn't unusual. It still feels unreal; I'm in limbo, I suppose. She only packed a couple of suitcases, so her stuff is still everywhere . . .'

Like Elke's, Katy thinks. Her mum died but the house stayed the same; her vases, her crockery, her books; her boots, hats and coats in the cupboard beneath the stairs; her dresses and blouses, her trousers and skirts neatly hung in her side of the wardrobe. But when do you draw the line? How do you draw the line? Like Gabriel and Sibeal, it's difficult to know. Making choices, emotional decisions. Leave those you love in the past.

The droll smile is there again. 'I suppose I could gather everything up and take it to charity, even build a huge bonfire,' Harry says, as though reading her mind. 'But that would feel petty.' His eyes cloud as they sweep the room. 'And this is her house as much as mine. We bought stuff together. That's what married couples do. Where would I begin to sort the wheat from the chaff? It's a nightmare even thinking about it, to be honest.'

He comes back to Katy and gently rakes an escaped lock of hair behind her ear. Just as she thinks she'll expire from holding her breath, his expression transforms with a grin. 'Right, sorry, enough of my misery. I'm actually fine, more than fine. And me spilling out my life story as though I'm in the psychiatrist's chair is not why you're here. Free me from your beautiful gaze and I'll get on with lunch. Shall we start our date with a drink?

Something cold? Tea or coffee? I have wine and beer and spirits too. What takes your fancy?'

She smiles at the word 'fancy'. If the tingling from his touch is anything to go by, she certainly does. 'It's not a date, remember?' She traces the fine scar on his chin with a finger. 'How did that happen?'

He colours lightly. 'I spent hours of overtime to buy the shiny new car I'd lusted after for years, but the steering wheel decided to punch me.'

'Which means?'

'Not very heroic, I'm afraid. I liked the high of speeding. A stupid boy racer, basically. I bashed it on the wheel. It bled like buggery and needed stitches.'

'Poor you. It must have hurt.' Then, surprising herself, she leans in and pecks it gently.

He pulls a mock sad face. 'Yup, hurts very much,' he replies. 'In fact, did I mention that it wasn't just my—'

Stopping his words, she puts her lips to his. He cups her face and kisses her back, soft, slow and melting, and meaningful somehow. When they finally pull away, he wraps her in his arms and holds her tightly. 'Oh God, that feels so nice,' he says into her hair.

'It does.'

It really does feel so bloody lovely. Like waking from hibernation, the old sensations are pumping and flooding Katy's veins. Desire and wonderful craving, hot and gluey in her chest, her stomach, every fibre of her body.

Laughing and kissing, warm minutes pass. 'So,' Harry says eventually. 'I'm being a bad host. I'll get you a drink first, then I'll make us something to eat . . .'

But Katy isn't thinking about food. Strides, she's thinking. She wants to take bloody strides. She nods at his injured ankle. 'Shouldn't you be resting that? Looks pretty swollen to me.' She knows she's flushing deeply despite her resolve. 'I'm no expert, but I believe you're meant to raise it above the level of your heart or something like that.'

Harry pulls a grave face. 'That's very true. It would involve lying down, though.'

She stands and holds out her hand. 'Come on. Lying down it is, then.'

32

Katy

'Grandad!' Milo beats Katy to the door and flings his arms around Alexander's waist. 'Grandad, finally!'

He ruffles Milo's hair and laughs. 'Hello to you too. You sound more like your mummy every day.'

He kisses her on the cheek. 'Hello, darling, you look well. Sorry about the extra night this week, but what a good evening it was. The usual suspects were there and they all send their best wishes. I was a touch the worse for wear when I woke this morning, so I thought I'd have another half an hour. When I looked at my watch, I was astonished to see—'

Milo squints up with a frown. 'What does "worse for wear" mean?'

Katy laughs. 'It means Grandad had too many brandies with his friends at his posh dinner last night. Or red wine. And Champagne?'

'All of them, and in no particular order. The food was as dreadful as ever, but I suppose catering for that number isn't easy. Lamb, I was told, but I wasn't convinced. Still, I do like mint sauce occasionally. What about you, Milo? Fancy a condiment tasting like Polo mints?'

Milo sneezes. 'What's a condiment?'

'Something to look up in the dictionary.' Alexander crouches down and peers at his face. 'Have you got the sniffles again?'

'Dunno,' Milo replies with a shrug.

'I think that's a "I don't know, Grandad", Milo,' Katy says, beating her dad to it. 'What did we decide to rustle up for Grandad's tea tonight?'

Tonight. Tonight she has a *date* with Harry. They've chatted on the phone several times since Thursday, but she hasn't actually seen him. She glances at her dad. *If* he'll babysit Milo. It's no big deal, she just has to casually ask him if he's around this evening. Yet it does feel flaming huge.

'What did we decide in the end?' she prompts Milo. 'We bought mince from Pimlott's on the way home from school yesterday and had a long chat, didn't we?'

He wrinkles his nose. 'Spaghetti Bolognese, lasagne or … I can't remember what the other one is called, but Strummer's mum makes it and sometimes he eats it cold for his lunch. Those purple things look like cockroaches. I tried one and it was revolting.'

'Kidney beans.' Alexander chuckles. 'I didn't like them when I was your age either. Like olives and coffee and sauce tasting like Polo mints, they're an acquired taste.'

'Acquired taste,' Milo repeats thoughtfully, ambling away.

Katy takes her dad's overnight bag. 'He'll be mulling that one for a while. And condiments! I bet you're starving.' She heads for the kitchen and gestures to the French stick on the counter. 'Fresh from Greenhalgh's if you fancy a sandwich. Tea or coffee or something cold?'

The phrase makes her squirm. She wishes she could stop, but

Harry has been constantly on her mind since Thursday. His toned body, his smile, his tingling kisses. Despite her craving the feel of him inside her, they didn't end up having sex. Well, not actual intercourse, as their interlude wasn't planned and neither of them had contraception. She inwardly guffaws. Not that a condom was effective nearly six years ago. She found herself pregnant, unexpectedly so. It was a massive shock, not least because her mum noticed the tell-tale signs before she did. It turned out to be the very best blessing, though; Milo is her joy; she couldn't imagine life without him.

'A butty would be perfect.' She comes back to her father's interested gaze. 'Yes, you do look well, very well.' He pulls out a stool. 'What have you and Milo been up to all week? Seen much of Bridget?'

'No, just an exchange of messages. I think she's been pretty busy.'

Katy pre-empted it by getting a text in herself on Monday, saying she had a full week. To keep Bridget in the loop, she sent a few chatty messages, but it was nice to keep her at arm's length for a change. And anyway, Bridget said something about a night or two away with her hubby at Royal Lytham, so it worked out perfectly. 'I'm sure she'll pop in for a glass of wine at some point today or tomorrow, though.'

Her dad laughs. 'I'm sure she will, bless her.' He stifles a yawn. 'Been helping out at Brook House again? I remember it well—'

'You've been there?' Katy blurts in surprise. But of course her dad and James were at school together; she's so preoccupied by her babysitting request, she isn't thinking straight. 'Sorry. School days. I forgot.'

'No, not then, actually. Whalley Range was too far to travel from Prestbury, but you're right about it being James's home as a boy. He stayed after his parents moved out to run a Methodist nursing home or the like, and eventually took it on. Nice father; I met him a few times. Sweet, caring type.'

Alexander snorts faintly. He rarely speaks about his own childhood, but he once described his father as a 'bit of a tyrant', the reason why he loathes bullies with a vengeance, no doubt.

'It was later,' he continues, his expression thoughtful. 'When was the first time? That's it! Gabriel's baptism. We hadn't seen James for a while but Kenny and I were invited to the service and the celebration at the house afterwards—'

'Kenny?'

'Kenny Philippe. One of the Three Musketeers.' He smiles fondly. 'The wittiest guy I've ever met. Sporty, handsome and gregarious too. You know how some young men have it all? He'd been pretty miffed when Imelda chose James over him ... Indeed, he tried to knock a hole in a Dublin toilet cubicle. A rage punch, I think they call them these days. More damage to his pride and his hand than the door. Still, he was over his infatuation by the time of the christening.' His lips twitch. 'He rather had to be, what with Imelda getting pregnant by James, then being propelled up the aisle by her very angry father and a shotgun not long after Dublin. Anyway, Gabriel's baptism broke the ice and after that we were invited to stay at Brook House from time to time, Imelda feeding us poor students with chunks of soda bread and Irish stew around that huge dining table.'

The story is fascinating; Katy wishes she could picture the scene. 'I haven't actually been in that room yet.' Is it odd that she hasn't? Yet Sibeal said something about it being Gabriel's domain, so probably not.

'Really?' Alexander pops a cherry tomato in his mouth. 'Presumably the piano is still there.' He smiles. 'We'd persuade Imelda to play us a tune, and though she was bashful, there was absolutely no need. She was exceptionally talented and could jump between classical, modern and jazz without batting an eyelid. She had some involvement with the Hallé, the choral academy, I think.' He clicks his fingers. 'The Hallé, that's right; I remember seeing her at a concert a few years later. Not playing, just in the foyer. I was about to say hello when I thought I saw . . .' He pauses and frowns.

'Who?'

'Well, the rage punch man himself—'

'What? This Kenny guy?'

'I thought so, but it was a fleeting glimpse as they went in the auditorium. He'd moved to Cumbria by then, so I was probably mistaken. But Imelda, yes, instinctively musical, gifted like some people are.'

Katy pictures Gabe's fine eyes and inwardly laughs at her previous slight crush. 'Like Gabriel. Apparently he can play everything from viola to bassoon. And the piano, of course.'

'He was the apple of his mother's eye, right from the start. Though that sounds rather familiar.' He leans back and calls to Milo in his snug. 'Are you the apple of your mummy's eye, Milo?'

'Yes!'

'And Grandad's?'

'I am!'

It's the perfect time for her request. Feeling herself flushing, Katy cuts the baguette into two, then slices it in half. 'Talking of Milo, are you free to mind him tonight?'

'Of course, anytime.'

'Thanks. Bavarian ham from the deli OK? With mustard?' she asks, her heart thumping loudly.

'Sounds perfect. Are you going anywhere nice?'

'Just into the village for a drink.'

'How lovely to get out on a Saturday night.' He calls to Milo again. 'It's just you and me this evening, Milo, so we'll have the spaghetti tomorrow. What's the plan? Pizza or pizza?'

Milo appears and hands his colouring pad to Katy. 'I haven't gone over the edges but the blue felt tip ran out.' He frowns. 'Is this the date with Harry, Mummy?'

'No, love, it's just a grown-ups' drink down the road. We won't be eating ice cream, I promise.'

Alexander chuckles. 'No flies on your son, Kathryn.'

'Yuck, I hope not,' Milo replies. 'His doggy is friends with Bridget's.'

Alexander lifts him up and kisses his cheek. 'It just goes to show what a very small dog world it is.' He settles him on a bar stool. 'Sandwich time. What are you having?' He gestures to the sandwich. 'Maybe not quite as big as this one, eh? You'll need to keep space for your monster-sized pizza.'

33

Katy

Katy checks her make-up in the hall mirror. Or perhaps the lack of it. She tried foundation and light bronzer, which actually looked fine on her face. Her pale neck was the problem. 'Long, like a swan,' as her mum used to say. Yeah, a bloody white one. She contemplated spreading the beige tint to her collarbone, but what about her décolletage? Where did one draw the tanned-look line? Then there was the eyeshadow. A panda bear horror story. It all had to come off.

Turning away, she sighs. The artwork was a ruse, she knows that, something to pass the time and take her mind off her stupid decision to go out. Not just out of the house, but out of her comfort zone. Big time.

'Stay a bit longer,' Harry said on Thursday, playfully grabbing her waist when she tried to climb out. 'I haven't even fed you yet!'

'Designer kibble?' She patted her stomach. 'Don't I know it. I'd love to stay but it's time to collect Milo, I'm afraid.'

'So let's make another date . . .' He flopped back on the mattress. 'Damn, I'm working all day tomorrow. Please tell me we can arrange something at some point in the evening.'

171

'Dad's away until Saturday . . .'

'Perfect. Saturday night, then. Do you want to come here or go out?'

'How about both?' At that moment she felt so wanted, so attractive and confident, she was up for anything, but doubt immediately wormed its way in.

'Are you sure? Either or both is fine by me.'

It was a tough one. Stupid at nearly twenty-eight years of age, but she didn't want her dad to know she was going to a man's house and it felt easier not to set up a lie. But now it's time to leave, apprehension is fluttering in her chest.

She reverts to her reflection, inhales deeply and straightens her spine. The posture reminds her of Sib. What would she do? Well, that's an easy answer; she'd do what *she* wanted, not let stupid anxiety hold her back from having fun. She went to her lover's funeral wearing crimson stiletto heels and matching lipstick, for goodness' sake!

Slamming the door behind her, she lifts her chin. 'Having fun,' she says inwardly as she walks across the drive and along the length of the tall boundary wall. But by the time she reaches the corner, the fluttering has become battering and she's struggling to swallow.

Her slogan all forgotten, she drops her head and replaces it with another mantra: Breathe, Katy, breathe. Breathe from your abdomen. Then another stern voice: You have to go onwards. You can hardly go back and face Dad after three minutes. Yes, he looked so pleased, so proud of her progress, of her. 'Stunning,' he said from the kitchen. 'My daughter is stunning. Have a wonderful time.'

The air starts to flow; in and out, in and out. Strides, not steps, she remembers. Or at least one foot in front of the other. Pulling up her jacket collar, she continues to walk, but thoughts of old boyfriends and failures nudge back, prodding and poking like they did in the old days: does he really like her? Will he actually be there? Suppose he's changed his mind? She'd look such a fool. It's happened before, more than once. Can she really bear to go through it again?

As she walks along the high street, she eyes up the wine bars and cafés. So many beginning or ending with the letters C and O! She could pop in for a coffee or a glass of wine until enough time passes, then return with a confident smile for her dad, go up to her bedroom and hide.

'Katy?' She looks up to Harry's tall frame. 'Sorry, I didn't mean to make you jump. I was waiting outside Costa and saw you. Thought I'd join you halfway despite the old limp.'

'Oh, hi.' His fringe in a quiff, he's dressed in the collarless leather bomber he wore at the fete.

He kisses her cheek. 'Your hair looks nice down.' He studies her and frowns lightly. 'Are you OK? Are you cold?'

She releases the grip on her collar. 'Oh, I didn't realise—'

'Trying for incognito? Married man and all that?'

He's only joking, of course, but he's right. She's reverting to that need to be invisible. 'No, it's just that . . .'

'Second thoughts?' His smile fades and he steps away. 'It's fine. I understand.'

'No!' She laughs nervously and tries again in a less hysterical tone. 'No, not at all. Why would you think that?'

He looks at his feet and shuffles. 'Given that my wife left me . . .' he says stiffly. 'Well, it involves a considerable amount of self-reflection. You might not want to take on damaged goods.'

Tension melting away, Katy blows out the air trapped in her lungs. Like a party popper released, she feels light and liberated. 'Damaged goods,' she says, slipping her arm into his. 'Then we make a good pair.'

34

Katy

Snug in Harry's bed, Katy drifts from exertion, exhaustion and sheer bloody pleasure. Even with her chequered daring history, some sexual encounters were better than others. The act was occasionally too prolonged – resulting in soreness and a possible orgasm – but mostly it was too quick – resulting in no climax at all. Today, however, was just perfect, even if she did embarrass herself by possibly sharing the highlights with Harry's neighbours.

Hearing the sound of his footsteps, she opens her eyes. 'Is it time to get up? I can't move. I should have a wash, but I don't think my legs would work even if I tried. They feel dead.' She smiles. 'In a nice way; in a very nice way.'

He sits and strokes a strand of hair from her cheek. 'It's a good job you don't have to. I've brought up fizz and crisps. Best Kettle and a choice of flavours.'

She peers at the tray on the bedside table. 'Thank God the service has improved since Thursday.'

He pecks her lips. 'That's because I couldn't bear to leave you on Thursday. You might have absconded.' He looks at her pointedly. 'You have form. I offered you a lift, to keep you sheltered from the rain. And if Milo hadn't been with you at the water park . . .'

She laughs. 'Point taken, but if I'd known about your culinary skills . . .'

'And tonight. I could see it in your face. Before you saw me.'

She reaches for his hand. 'The cafés ending with an O were a-calling.' Then, more seriously, 'I thought about diverting there and hiding. But I didn't.'

'No, you didn't. I'm glad.'

He pops the Champagne cork and pours it into the flutes. As though listening to the bubbles, they fall silent for a few moments. Still turned away, Harry clears his throat. 'Who is Milo's dad?'

Katy sighs. A red-headed boy she loved once; at least she thought so. But he was airbrushed out by circumstance and trauma. Occasionally she feels bad for not having told him, but there was never a good time and now it's far, far too late. 'Do you know, you're the first person who has ever asked me?'

He rotates to look at her. 'Seriously? How come?'

There's that feeling of lightness again. His question doesn't feel intrusive or judgemental; she doesn't mind answering. 'It all happened at once, I suppose. Life, death, beginnings, endings . . .'

He climbs back beneath the duvet, so she nestles into his shoulder and tries to put the tangled tale into some semblance of order. Funny, really – she's lived it, she's breathed it, she's floated around it for five years, but she's never had to unpick it before.

'I met Jake in a bar in my third year at uni. He was studying at Oxford Brookes *and* was from the north, so it was quite refreshing . . . Anyhow, we dated for a few months, I liked him, he liked me. Or so I thought.' She almost laughs at the same old story. 'So . . . we're really into each other, inseparable for weeks. I meet his parents, he meets mine and everyone gets on brilliantly. Then he dumps me out of nowhere, and I'm still reeling from that, even though I sort of get it, when my mum takes me to one side and asks if I'm OK.' She pauses in thought. 'I was already deeply worried about my course, and I guess she was concerned that I'd developed bulimia . . .' She takes a shuddery breath. 'When I explain about the nausea, she asks about my periods and I realise I haven't had one for a couple of months. The penny finally drops that I'm pregnant. When I think life can't get any worse, my parents are in a road accident, father unconscious, mother dead.'

She feels Harry's visceral reaction through his warm chest. 'I know,' she says, glancing at his furrowed brow. 'I was a mess for a long time; still am, I suppose. So the baby continued to grow inside me, and no one asked or cared who the dad was.'

'Bloody hell,' he says eventually. 'I'm so sorry. If you don't want to talk, it's—'

'No, it's fine,' she replies. And it is, it really is. She tilts her head up to kiss him. 'Ask me anything. What do you want to know?'

'Nothing. It's just so much to take in, I guess.' He peers at her and frowns. 'You're a lovely person, you're interesting, smart, beautiful. Why did you "sort of get it" about being dumped?'

'Damaged goods, sums it up.' Yes, that's how she felt, how she still does in many ways. 'I was rubbish at relationships. As soon as I relaxed, decided I liked them and came out to friends and family, so to speak, they chucked me. They liked the chase, I suppose. Or perhaps I was too much . . . But I "got it" because I felt such a failure. Stupid and fat . . .'

'Were you stupid and fat?'

She thinks for a moment. Needing a size 12 pair of jeans at one point . . . Hmm, hardly *fat*, looking back. But she definitely struggled with the course. She tried her best but learning no longer came easily; she wasn't top of the class any more, not by a long shot, and the disappointment was crushing.

'Probably not. But I was severely anxious and it put me in a horrible tailspin that . . . Well, it stopped me thinking straight, that's for sure. Goodness, I shouldn't be telling you this, it'll put you off me.'

'I doubt it.' He kisses her hair. 'I'm so sorry about your mum. Your dad too, of course. He made a full recovery? After his loss of consciousness?'

'Yes, thank God. He had serious concussion from his head injury and was completely out for some time. When I arrived at the hospital I thought he was dead . . .' She covers her face. 'It was dreadful; the police had already told me about Mum and though I struggled to listen properly to anything they said, some part of my subconscious must have heard them say "alive". Then I saw him like that, unresponsive like a corpse . . .'

Harry pulls her closer. 'I'm upsetting you. Let's talk about something else.'

The old image of her dad flashes behind her closed eyes. She digs in deep to push it away, but when it comes into focus, the colours and the intensity have somehow diluted. And her heart isn't racing, her face isn't wet.

She lifts her head to Harry's. Handsome, sensitive, concerned.

'It's fine,' she says. 'He sort of came back from the dead, didn't he? I've never seen it this way before, but in some respects, it's like a happy ending.'

35

Sibeal

Deep in dreamland there's a smile in Robin's voice. 'Come on, Sib, don't be cross with me. I have to go in half an hour.' He's kissing her hip bone, her waist, working up slowly along her arm to her shoulder and finally her neck. He knows she loves that. Not pressing or compressing, but that nuzzling that makes her feel loved. 'Let's make the most of it . . .'

His warm hands sweep her buttocks, moving over her belly then up to her breasts where they linger, his fingers teasing her nipples. She needs him to kiss her but she doesn't want to turn. If she faces him, he'll see she's been crying.

He pulls away and the cold chasm of loneliness, of rejection is already there. 'Sib? Come on, what's up?'

She stares at the white wall. How can she begin to describe it? She can't; she never could. 'Do you love me?'

'You know I do. I never stopped loving you. Never.'

'Do you love her?'

'No.'

'Do you have sex with her?'

A snort. 'God, no.'

'Then why don't you leave her?'

He falls back on the pillow. The abyss grows wider. 'You know why.' He sighs. 'If things had been different . . .'

She'd like to read the truth in his features, but she doesn't rotate. She hates her weeping; she loathes her weakness for asking, almost pleading. 'But Joseph is only a baby. How will he know if you're there or not?'

'Even babies know, Sib.' He pulls her around and peers intently. 'I long to be here, but I want to be there with him too. Watch him grow. Not just every other weekend as a part-time dad, but each morning and night. Even during the ten hours between work and coming home he develops and changes, so I need to be there. You can see that, can't you?'

Her tears freely flow. She can no longer hide them, so she closes her eyes. 'Just go then.'

'Sibeal? Look at me, Sib. It isn't easy pretending. You are my love; my *only* love. I want no one but you. I'm with you whenever I can, you know that. But I have to be honest about Joseph. That's important, isn't it? That's what's special about this, us? Our honesty and trust?'

When she doesn't reply, he slips out of the bed. 'Time's ticking. I'd better have a shower, then get off.' He says the words but doesn't move. 'Perhaps when he's older. It might be different then.'

That bloody glimmer of light; she both loves and loathes him for it. Reaching out to his hand, she tugs him towards her, then she kneels and slowly kisses the tapering hair from his belly button to his—

Sibeal bursts awake. It's bright, the sun shining through the

180

voile curtains. She's at home in Saxton, Robin's side of the bed is warm as though he's only just stepped out.

'The bathroom,' she mutters, tumbling from the mattress. Yet even as she yanks open the door, she knows he's not there. Feeling the retch gurgle up, she leans on the sink to spit the bile out. When she lifts her face to the mirror it's still wet from the tears in her dream. Angular and hollow. Empty, abandoned, unloved. Not just her reflection, but at the heart of her very being.

36

Katy

Katy says goodbye to the dog, pulls closed the front door and locks it with the spare keys Harry gave her last night.

'I have a favour to ask,' he said before accompanying her home.

She wondered what on earth it would be, but she liked the request. It had a permanence about it, which was particularly reassuring after her earlier – shocking – soul baring. 'Sure.'

'I have a long shift tomorrow and the dogsitter isn't available. Could you pop round here to walk Rex at some point? A short one will be fine. Then feed him before you leave? Oh, and feel free to make yourself at home; help yourself to whatever you find in the fridge or the larder.'

The balmy June breeze on her neck, she smiles as she trots homeward. Not only a *favour*, but keys! She has no idea how the metamorphosis has happened, but right now it's as though she's walking on air. New friends, a handsome guy she really likes – who appears to like her too – and glorious sex. She glances at her watch. And to top it all it's nearly time for a Sunday roast with her dad and her son. Life can't get any better than this.

She tugs off her trainers at the door and pads towards the cooking aromas. Wearing a striped apron, Alexander is turned to the oven.

He glances over his shoulder. 'Hello, darling. Good walk?'

'Yes. The weather's lovely. Windy but warm.'

She watches him stick a skewer in the beef joint. On waking she considered offering to do the honours today, but she knew he'd decline. He likes his head-chef crown, and though he's away during the week with his judging these days, it is his kitchen, after all. Save for shared student digs, she's never had her own. Or house, for that matter. She's never considered – or wanted – that before.

'A pug, did you say?' her dad asks over the chatter on the radio.

Keen as he is to meet Harry's dog, it was actually Milo who said it. She knew she couldn't say no, but as much as she loves her inquisitive son, she wasn't sure about him going to Harry's place or how she'd answer all his perspicacious questions. But she was saved by Bridget and her Airedale terrier at eleven. Could she *borrow* Milo for an hour? Walkies were so much more fun with '*our* little man'. A week ago her request would have severely grated, but today Katy was relieved.

'Yes, a silver one,' she replies. A silver pug belonging to Harry's wife ... 'Given the choice I'd go for something with a prettier face, though.'

Clearly listening to a song, her dad doesn't respond, so she picks at the thought of her lover's spouse some more. She didn't 'make herself at home' at Harry's, but she did spend a few moments gliding her fingers over the smart granite surfaces of his new kitchen and guiltily peeping in a couple of units. Of course it's Lydia's house too, but despite framed photographs of various holidays adorning one wall and a drawer clearly dedicated to their joint knick-knacks – the Matchbox collection of fast cars his, she guessed, the blingy key rings hers – it somehow felt uncluttered by sentiment. Unlike this room and the huge knot of emotion that plasters the hole . . .

As if reading her mind, her dad turns down the sound. 'It's as though your mum is here today.' He smiles reflectively. 'Maybe it's the music. She did always love . . . Sorry, darling. Sometimes it's nice to reminisce, that's all.'

'It's fine, Dad. Go ahead, I don't mind.' And she doesn't, she really doesn't. It feels like she's been given a miracle cure.

'It's double edged, of course, thinking about the good times. Better to have loved and lost, as they say.' He frowns. 'Yet it's those happy days which makes the what-ifs so much worse . . .'

Shaking the shadows away, he pulls out a stool and sits next to Katy. 'Still, I'm glad we had the party, aren't you? Lord, it took some persuasion; Elke really didn't want it, did she! "Who wants to celebrate being fifty?" Yet she was the best-looking woman there. Youthful, beautiful, still blonde.' He pats Katy's knee. 'Like you. You inherited the Scandinavian gene, not this old mug.'

'Your mug isn't old, and it's very handsome, as well you know.'

'Is it?' He rakes back his dark hair. To her surprise, it's lightly streaked with silver.

'Yes, it is. Are you OK, Dad? You seem a bit jaded.'

'Too much booze on Friday, I expect. Left me feeling a bit maudlin.' He taps the worktop and sighs. 'I always try to be impartial, as fair to the accused as to the victim. Bend too far back, some would say. There are always at least two points of view, all valid in some way or another. Mostly, anyway . . .'

Wondering where the conversation's going, Katy nods. It's work-related, she supposes; he's often described the conflict between the legal and ethical aspects of being a judge.

He continues to speak. 'Even bad people have a reason why they do what they do, but to cause an accident, then drive on without a second's thought of the consequences . . .' His jaw tightens. 'Or worse, being a coward and not facing up to one's actions. Drink driving, I expect. But even if it was simply running late for an early shift or a call-out . . . Well, not making an anonymous call to the emergency services is appalling. It's delays like that which make the difference between life and death.'

An instant frost on her skin, Katy realises what he's saying. The accident. Catastrophic injuries. Elke's death. 'But I thought . . .'

What does she think? She doesn't know the events leading up to the crash. She only understands what happened to her: idly waving her parents off to a meal on a Saturday evening; going to bed, racked with anxiety about the pregnancy and her mum's surprisingly less-than-supportive response, even hints about abortion. Being woken by an insistent rapping noise, groggily peering at her watch. Wondering who'd be knocking at the door so early on a Sunday and why her dad wasn't answering. Not for a moment absorbing what it might mean. Padding down the stairs and opening it. A rush of cold wind, two uniformed officers and words: accident, parents, hospital, death.

Her dad is tapping his lips. 'Even now I can't look at a Porsche logo without it all tumbling back. A car's headlights far too close behind us. "Bloody idiot," I said to Elke, not really thinking he'd try to overtake.' His voice quavers. 'But he did. A flash of red enamel as he passed. Showing off its speed, no doubt. But at a blind spot on a narrow country lane . . . A vehicle coming the other way felt inevitable somehow. Unfortunately I was right. I immediately hit the brakes but . . .'

Swallowing the sob, Katy grasps his hand. It's his trauma, not hers, she wasn't there. And though the terror of hearing his account batters her chest, she understands he needs to let it out.

'Of course I blacked out on impact,' he continues, 'but there's no chance, no possibility he wouldn't have seen the collision in his rear-view mirror. Not just seen, but heard it. That's what I can't forgive. If he had stopped, called an ambulance . . .' He looks at Katy through teary eyes. 'Without that delay, your mum might have had a chance.'

Katy stays frozen, her mind torpid. Too much information, so much grief, so much to absorb. *She might have had a chance.* Was she conscious, in agony? And blood, that bright bubbly blood she sees in her dreams. She clears the huge clot from her throat. 'How long did it take for the emergency services to arrive?'

Alexander sighs. 'I don't know exactly. Too long, love.'

He stands and increases the volume for the news, listens for a few moments, then turns with a thin smile. 'Sorry, darling. I don't know where that came from. It wasn't fair of me to burden you and I'm breaking my own rules by not looking forward.' He glances at his watch. 'Goodness, it's time to drain the veg. Cauliflower, broccoli, and thinly diced carrots for Milo.' He kisses Katy's forehead. 'Cheese sauce for the cauli?'

Still stunned from the conversation, Katy tries to focus on the mundane question. 'No, don't worry, no one else likes it.'

He lifts a lid. 'Already done. It just needs reheating. Right; gravy and we're ready. Talking of my grandson, where is he?'

They both turn to the sound of the doorbell. 'His wellies,' Katy says, coming back to today, 'No doubt they're dirty. He's a good boy to remember not to run in. I'll get it.'

37

Sibeal

Wondering what the hell she's doing here, Sibeal waits at the blue door and looks at the mismatched pumps on her feet. The habitual sensations of loneliness, isolation and rejection jerk in her chest along with her heart, but they're more powerful today. Should she ring the bell again? They may not have heard it. Or perhaps she should quickly retreat and drive to a café to eat. Though she's not actually hungry. She doesn't need food; she needs people and company; she needs love.

Fighting back the ridiculous self-pity, she turns to her SUV. The sunshine is highlighting the dried evidence of country lanes and motorway dust. Maybe she should get it cleaned, sit in a carwash and sob along with the streams of soapy water. She should definitely leave anyway; she's already been spurned once today. After waking from her dream about Robin, she dragged on the first clothes to hand and sprinted to Gabriel's house. But even as she approached his cottage, the sound of Vivaldi breezed through the open window. Not just one instrument, but two, a cello–violin duet. He had company, a *purpose* with somebody else. Though logically she knew it was simply his job, it still really hurt, so she stalked back to her house, grabbed her bag and drove the sixty miles here without breathing. Or so it felt.

The unmistakable tang of roast beef makes her turn. Kat's teary expression is replaced with a beam. 'Sib!' she exclaims. 'Sib! How lovely to see you!'

Emotion grips Sibeal's throat, but she tries for the nonchalant, sardonic woman everyone thinks that they know. 'I've come to hang out with the cat. We bonded the last time I came so—'

'Poppy will be thrilled!' Kat tugs her inside and gives a tight hug. She smells of sweet lavender and it's all Sibeal can do not to blubber like a baby.

When she pulls away, Kat sniffs too. 'Perfect timing. We're just about to sit down for a late lunch. Are you hungry? Please join us.'

'If you're sure . . .'

'I am, absolutely. Come on through.'

Sibeal follows Kat into the kitchen and self-consciously watches Alexander pour glossy gravy into a boat. Bloody hell. She didn't think this through properly. How will he react after her wacky behaviour the last time she was here? After a moment he turns, and though his expression shows surprise, a warm smile soon follows.

'Hello! Sorry, I was expecting to see my muddy grandson. How nice to see you.'

'I thought *Sibeal* could join us for lunch, Dad.'

He laughs and pats Kat's shoulder. 'See how subtly my daughter does it? I'm dreadful with names but I hadn't forgotten yours. Yes, please join us, Sibeal. I was just about to—'

The front door clatters open. 'Wellies, Milo!' Kat calls, making for the door.

Her son charges past her. 'Already taken them off, Mummy!' He comes to a halt at Alexander and lifts his pink face.

The scene takes Sibeal's breath. Like Joseph, this boy has flawless skin and neat features. And such beautiful hair, windswept and feathery. It's hard not to stare.

'Bridget says sorry we're late,' he's saying. 'We dropped Murphy off at her house and the phone rang. I called Andrew's name but he wasn't there because he's on a golfing week.' He crinkles his face in thought, then shrugs. 'He's gone somewhere in Scotland with his friends. They think it's OK to eat and drink too much just because they've played eighteen holes.' He rolls his dark eyes. 'Bridget didn't go even though she's Scottish!'

'Out of the mouths of babes,' Alexander remarks with a chuckle. 'Then we'd better invite Bridget for lunch too.'

But the petite, sinewy woman is already bustling towards them. 'Sorry we're late. Something smells incredible,' she says in that same Anglo-Scottish accent Sib heard before. Pinning her helmet of hair behind her ears, she lifts a tureen lid. 'Wonderful! Alexander's famous roast potatoes,' she says. She turns to Sibeal, her tidy features creasing. 'I'm Bridget. I think we might have met before. Let me—'

'Please sit before the food gets cold, everybody.' Alexander gestures to Milo, already at the table. 'Like my hungry grandson. Are you joining us, Bridget? Do sit.'

Kat seems to shake away her small frown. She guides Sibeal to a chair. 'You have this one next to Dad. I'll just grab some more cutlery.'

She's handed a warm plate laden with pink beef. 'Don't worry if it's too much. Just leave what you can't manage.' Alexander ruffles Milo's soft locks. 'What do we do with the leftovers?'

190

'Make a curry.' He wrinkles his nose. 'I don't like curry; it's too . . .'

'Spicy.'

Bridget helps herself to the vegetables. 'Alexander is a feeder,' she says. Her piercing eyes study Sibeal with open interest. 'You must be Katy's new friend. "Sibeeal", I believe, rather than the usual Irish pronunciation.'

'The kids at school got it wrong, so—'

'It was easier to run with the pack?'

'Sure,' she replies, though it was actually a protest rather than any need to conform.

Kat offers a tureen. 'Cauliflower, Sib? I find it a bit plain on its own, but these guys don't like cheese sauce.'

'It's gloopy,' Milo says. 'Grandad thinks so too.'

Kat chuckles. 'Precisely, Milo. That's the best part about it. How about you, Sib?'

Dragging her eyes from the child, she finds her voice. 'I'm a huge cheese fan. Any and every type going.'

'Alleluia!' Kat scrapes back her chair.

'I wouldn't, love. It smelled a bit dodgy when I heated it. Out-of-date milk, I expect.' Alexander offers Sibeal a bowl of relish. 'Special home-made horseradish for the beef.' He leans across and whispers theatrically. 'The home-made bit involves adding a huge dollop of cream to Aldi's best, but don't tell anyone.'

'That's cheating, Grandad. Bridget says it's cheating, don't you?'

Everyone chuckles, but the woman doesn't seem perturbed. 'Home-made means from scratch, Alexander, so hoodwinking us, yes you are. Still, my Andrew doesn't know the difference between pancetta and bruschetta, let alone do any cooking, so I'm not complaining.'

'They're both from Italy,' Milo says.

'So they are,' Alexander replies with a proud grin. 'No—'

'Flies on me.' Milo titters behind his hand. 'Yuck, like on cow poo. Me and Bridget saw some today . . .'

Listening and swallowing, Sibeal fixes a smile. The boy is so perfect; this house and this meal is lovely, too lovely, too much like a proper family. She only has Gabe and he's so aloof and distant right now. And spirits, of course. A loving and loyal ghost in Saxton; a hostile phantom in Whalley Range. She's no longer sure which is the easiest to bear.

Even before she turns to his eloquent, low voice, she senses Alexander's gaze. 'It's so lovely to have you join us, Sibeal. You must come to us more often.' His eyes are warm. 'Any time, and I mean it. Promise me you won't be a stranger.'

38

Sibeal

The shuddering floors and banging pipes echo around her, but Sibeal doesn't mind being roused early. She's sleepy and content, still half in the fantasy, trying to pull it back. A boy, her boy in her arms. Tiny, like a foetus, but alive, responsive and hers. And though she knows it was a dream, a temporary possession, it doesn't bother her today; she's feeling positive and loved. After a faltering start at Kat's yesterday, she finally relaxed and found she was hungry. Bloody ravenous, in fact. A beef joint and all the trimmings. She hadn't had a roast at anyone's home, let alone her own, for a year at least. Her dad wasn't a great cook but he tried to do a traditional dish when she and Gabe were both around. Which wasn't nearly as often as it should have been.

The realisation hit halfway through the meal. Her dad, her poor harmless and steady father; he'd died in a horrible, painful way and she'd almost forgotten him again. Her nose stung and tears pricked at the back of her eyes, but she was saved by the beautiful boy who made another comment which might have come from the mouth of a fifty-year-old. Some would call him precocious, but she found him rather cute and appealing; he lifted her spirits along with everyone else's. Based around his chatter, the conversation flowed, loving and funny. She could sense the kindness and warmth from Alexander and Kat too, both glancing her way, making sure she was included.

She'd felt the inquisitive gaze of the Scottish nanny or helper, or whatever she was, from the moment they sat down, but the woman didn't start her full interrogation until after dessert. Like a flaming terrier, right down to her small teeth and those flinty eyes, she didn't want to let go. How long had Sibeal known Alexander and Kathryn? She herself had been close friends with them both since before Milo was born. Was Sibeal married or had a significant other half?

The woman's huge crush on Alexander was plain to see, and despite being closer in age to him, she clearly felt threatened by Sibeal's presence. That's when Kat picked up her coffee cup and said, 'Come on, Sib, I'll show you around. We can drink these in my bedroom.'

She now turns the pillow and smiles. It was fun, really nice. She and Kat had a quick tour of the upstairs, Milo's red and green bedroom cluttered with toys, a minimalist spare room and the fully tiled bathroom. Alexander's quarters were immaculately tidy, and as her eyes swept his plush but somehow manly divan, she fleetingly pondered if he'd a girlfriend since Elke died; five years had passed and he was pretty good-looking for an older guy, but even she knew better than to ask that. She followed Kat to her suite at the back, and it was the nicest room in the house. Floral, light and with millions of soft cushions, she genuinely liked the Laura Ashley furnishings, even though she wasn't usually a fan. Kat put down the coffee cups, pounced on the bed and patted the other side.

'Chocolate,' she said, opening the bedside drawer. 'I'm sure I still have Christmas chocolate somewhere.'

Like best friends, Sibeal now thinks. Of course they'd done similar at Brook House but Kat's sunny personal space felt completely different. They were at a clever head pupil's home, the popular and pretty type who wouldn't have looked at her twice at school. She'd always said to Gabe that she'd hated those girls and those godawful cliques, that she was more than happy to strut away and revel in her aloofness. But was that true? Was that really, really true?

Gabriel's voice from the landing breaks her thoughts. 'Sib, are you up?'

'I might be,' she replies. 'Why?'

Her lovely, reliable brother puts his head around the door. Despite her doubts yesterday, he fulfilled his promise to return and he was already here by the time she came back from Kat's. Carrying a crate of stuff and looking absent, rattled and so very adorable, he'd greeted her at the door.

'Gabe! You came!'

'I said I would.' He looked at the box. 'Still not convinced I've found everything yet. Have you moved anything?'

'Like what?'

He flushed. 'My old compositions and the like . . .'

'Thinking of forming a boy band again?' She kissed his cheek. 'No, Brownies promise.'

'You weren't a Brownie, Sib.'

'Hmm, you got me. However, music and paperwork are your department, darling bro, so I wouldn't dare touch them.'

She focuses on him now. The blue eyes are serious. 'What?' she asks.

'You're still in bed. I told you last night. The solicitor's appointment at noon?'

She peers at her watch. 'There's plenty of time.'

'You promised to collect Katy from Cheadle.'

Oh yes, a Kat day today; until yesterday she hadn't realised the journey to Whalley Range involved two separate buses. Still, she won't mind ... She scoops up her mobile.

'Sib ...' Gabe says slowly, as though telepathic.

'OK, OK, promises are promises,' she says, standing from the bed. 'I'll be ten minutes! Though if you want to make sure it's not twenty, a large coffee would help.'

39

Katy

A thin beep alerts Katy to Sib's arrival. She quickly grabs the bouquet of lilies and her bag, but to her surprise, Gabe's battered old Volvo is waiting on the kerb.

'Jump in,' Sib says from the passenger window. 'A fresh new week of sunshine and smiles so I thought you'd like to be chauffeured in style!'

'Thanks, Gabriel.'

Pushing an instrument case to one side, Katy climbs into the back seat. She suddenly feels bashful. Has Sib told him about Harry?

'Come on, Kat, spill the beans,' she'd said mid-conversation about another subject yesterday. 'You're excited about something, I can tell.'

She found herself laughing. 'Oh, God. Is it that obvious?' Then the words joyfully tumbled from her lips. 'I'm seeing someone really nice. At least I think so! But the point is I had sex for the first time since getting pregnant with Milo. Well, not actual sex on our first date—'

'Everything but?'

'Yes, exactly! Then on Friday, the full monty.'

'And was it good? Was his tool fully functional? No, don't tell me; I can see by your smile that it was. So, give me the low-down. What's his name and what does he look like? Surely even you have a photo . . .'

Katy took a deep, excited breath to describe her new man, but the door was flung open and Milo dived on the bed, snuggling in between them. She detected a strange stiffness and a shadow pass through Sib's features, but Milo didn't give her a chance to object, turning to her with his wide, inquisitive eyes and plying her with questions from her age, to her favourite subject at school, to the spelling of her 'funny' name. Ten minutes later, the two of them were like old friends, impressively on the same wavelength for 'I-spy'.

'Ready, Kat?'

Katy comes back from her thoughts. They're outside Brook House and Sib is addressing her. 'Sorry, what was that?'

'Birth certificate, passport, height, sexual preference, the lot.'

'OK . . .'

'The solicitor's! We've got to prove we're not scammers so we're dropping you off first.' She lifts her eyebrows meaningfully. 'You were daydreaming, little Kat. I can't think what about. Remember where the keys are hidden?'

'Sure, but what should I do whilst I'm—'

'Find Gabe's very important missing paperwork, of course.'

Katy pulls the door handle. 'Oh, right, so where should I—'

'She's only teasing,' Gabe says through the mirror. 'No need to do anything. We won't be long.'

Sib guffaws. 'That's what Gabe always says, but coffee at the ready would be good.'

Waving the Volvo away, Katy turns to the weathered door and inserts the key in the lock. It feels intrusive stepping into someone else's empty home. Like Harry's, though at least she was greeted by an enthusiastic pug there. She sniffs the air. Funny how every home has a smell. Yesterday's was a light mix of bacon, lemon and dog; today's is a much heavier affair, a blend of the past and the present, somehow: tobacco, charred wood, parchment; shower gel, coffee and toast. What about the home she shares with Alexander and Milo? There's sure to be an aroma she's unaware of.

Finding a new shiny carafe in the kitchen, she spoons in fresh coffee and sits at the table whilst she waits. Images of Harry sneak in: his white grin, toned chest, his thoughtful eyes. She likes him, she fancies him, that's for sure, but how much does she know about him? Her dad didn't ask anything other than, 'Have a lovely time last night?' at breakfast on Sunday, yet she knew what he thought behind his *Sunday Times:* It's been a long time. You've had so many disappointments in the past. How much do you know this man, Kathryn? I'd hate you to get hurt.

Or perhaps it's her own niggle, something Harry said or didn't say, a look or a hint.

'Anxiety,' she whispers. 'Just silly anxiety.'

Pushing the uncomfortable notion aside, she ambles to the front and looks into the parlour. Her gaze rests on the scuffed leather sofa. Picturing Sib the first time she came in here, she chuckles out loud. It was both strange and compelling to see someone so charming and rambling and utterly drunk, but she's used to her now. She's occasionally a little wild or blunt or too intense, and she's ridiculously demanding of her brother, but that's just Sibeal. She rubs her arms. As with the dank chilliness

199

of this place, she's become acclimatised to her new friend.

Coming back to the hallway, she traces the dust along the dado rail and peers at the old images of the church and the house. 'Saint Imelda' who died. Loved by Gabe and allegedly loathed by Sibeal. Their mother's post-natal depression must have been awful for them both, but especially for her, the 'cause' of it. She glances at the handsome staircase. Sibeal shrugged off her comatose state on that top landing, made peculiar very normal. She's actually anything other than 'normal', of course, and Katy loves her for that.

When she reaches the next room, she pauses. This is the one her dad mentioned, the dining room where Imelda served Irish stew. She's never seen the siblings go in here. Memories of their mother, or something else? Taking a quick breath, she opens up and peers inside. A wall of fustiness hits as she takes in the panelled walls and dark mahogany furniture. It's far more sophisticated than anywhere else in the house: the polished table sits on an elaborate Chinese rug and a spectacular chandelier hangs above; the glass sideboard sparkles with crystal glassware and the open fireplace is adorned by a gilt mirror.

As she turns to the left, she's caught short by the piano. Yet it's silly to be surprised; Gabe tunes them for a living and her dad described the joy of listening to Imelda play it back in the day. She probably forgot because she's never heard it.

Picturing the way Sibeal flexes her fingers, she frowns in thought. What did she say that first day? *If you hear Chopin, that's where it's coming from . . . Not that anyone has played music in there for years. Gabe's the musician; I definitely am not.*

Though she gives a little shudder, she moves towards the handsome upright and inwardly laughs at her desire to play it. Like

200

most things during her carefree private school days, reading the notes, instructions and annotations came easily. Will her grade eight piece come flooding back?

Careful not to smudge the layer of fine grime, she lifts the lid, compresses the keys and plays a basic chord. The rich sound is alarmingly loud in the silence but she spends a few moments working through minors and majors from A through to G like she did as a beginner. She'd wondered whether the memories they invoked might make her sad, but it's fine, she feels strong. Like when her dad mentioned her mum and the accident on Sunday, she's coping. Maybe facing the past isn't as bad as she feared.

A rich peal of laughter makes her jump from her skin. 'So beautiful, so compliant, your skin like alabaster,' ricochets in the air. Putting a hand to her breast, she stills to listen for more. Did she really hear it? And whose voice was it? Almost expecting to see the university students around the table like ghosts, she slowly turns around. It's empty, of course, the only movement the rushing pelt of her own heart. Assuming the echo must have come from outside, she quickly shuts the lid and slips from the room.

When she reaches the front door, the outline of the siblings is smudged through the stained glass. Her chest pounding with something she can't quite grasp, she opens up to their chatter.

40

Katy

Holding the flowers, Sibeal steps in.

'Gabe's feeling smug, Kat. For once he was right,' she says. 'Two minutes and a ten thousand quid bill, probably. Bloody extortionate lawyers. Are these for me? Hope so! I love lilies. They're so spectacular when they open and reveal their swollen pistil, then get somewhat disgusting when they've had their day.' She laughs. 'I think there's a metaphor in there somewhere. But we mustn't *stigmatise* them, must we, Gabe? Do we have chocolate? Please say we have chocolate to go with the coffee. That's how they do it in Kat's house.'

Though Gabriel rakes his hair, his lips twitch. 'I'll go now.'

Sibeal waves her credit card wallet. 'And whatever else your heart desires. The corner shop is your oyster.'

'You are rotten to poor Gabe,' Katy says when he's gone. 'Wish I'd had a brother or sister. Maybe I'd have been more ...' She searches for a word. 'Well ... single child syndrome and apple of both parents' eyes doesn't bode well for being ... *rounded*, I guess. Being the centre of attention was great in some ways, but leaving home for university was a pretty big shock. A whole new learning curve which took some adjustment.'

Sib stares, a flare of irritation in her eyes. She strides to the kitchen, shoves the flowers in a sink and loads provisions for their drinks on a tray. 'If you want sugar,' she says, 'it's tough.'

Conscious she's upset or offended Sib somehow, Katy follows up the stairs. Instead of stopping at her floor, Sib continues upwards. 'Dad's clothes. Got to tackle them sometime.'

Once in the sparse room, her tone softens. 'I haven't been in here since he was taken to the hospice.' She gestures to the open drawers and half-filled bin liners. 'I was so angry. Gabe told me to leave it, but as I put it to him, nobody recovers at a freaking hospice. After all those appointments, the chemo, the pain that meant the end, there was no maybe any more.'

'I'm so sorry, Sib.' Katy doesn't know what's worse, the shock of instant death or a drawn-out illness. At least with the latter one can say goodbye.

'Of course I didn't really think that,' Sibeal continues. 'I was still in flat denial, so it didn't feel remotely real. But logic told me to pack up his belongings, say goodbye to them whilst he was alive.' She barks a mirthless laugh. 'But I didn't know Robin would steal that unbearable grief.'

Reminding herself poor Sib has suffered both versions of loss, she touches her shoulder. 'Are you OK? We don't have to do this now if you're not ready.'

'It's fine.' She turns. 'Sorry for being ratty. Let's toast Dad with our coffee.' She drags two pillows to the worn carpet and sits down. 'You can tell he was a Methodist. No creature comforts. Parents, eh? Low church and high church; chalk and cheese. A weekend fling is understandable, but for the long term ...' She glances at Katy. 'Though something your dad said ...'

Feeling herself flush, Katy pours the strong coffee. 'Really? What was that?'

'He didn't say it in so many words, but ...' She lifts her eyebrows. 'Crikey, Gabe was a love child, wasn't he? I wonder if a marriage certificate is what he's searching for.'

'Would he mind?' Kat asks, still uncomfortable that she already knew about the pre-marriage pregnancy. 'As a child, you might be shocked, but as an adult—'

'Imelda was a fucking saint, remember?' Two spots of deep colour appear on her cheeks. 'You have Milo, right?'

'Yes ...'

'Do you help him to get dressed and tie his shoelaces? I don't know ... do you run him a bath, scrub his back, wash or comb his hair?'

Katy nods. Sib said similar when she was up in the attic.

'I'm not even talking cuddles and kisses. Just the practical things an auntie or a teacher might do. Even the bloody neighbour, for God's sake. But she never touched me. Dad did, Gabriel did, but not her. I felt like a leper.'

When the door slams below, she lowers her voice. 'On the contrary, she adored him. He says she was ill, depressed, devoid of emotion towards us all, but I *heard* them, Kat.' She looks at her hands. 'I asked her to teach me the piano, but she said I didn't have the patience, that I never finished what I started.' She glances around the room, looks at the ceiling and snorts. 'Touché, Mother. I guess you were right.'

When they've both drunk their coffees, Katy scoops up a bin liner. 'Right then. Everything, or are we being discerning today?'

'Everything.' Sib picks up a dogtooth jacket and puts it to her face. 'Still reeks of tobacco. No alcohol, tick, but he smoked thirty cigs a day. Look at the elbow patches. Even if I was going to be sentimental, which I'm not, nothing's worth keeping. Everything is threadbare and smells of turps.' Tears well in her eyes. 'He was a nice man, you know. Loving and kind in a quiet way like Gabe. Taking of which, where's that bloody chocolate? Be a doll and see what he's brought us.'

'OK.' Kat hovers. 'Are you sure you're—'

'Yup, five minutes and I'll be fine. I think we'll need more caffeine.'

When Katy steps out, she covers her face. She's ashamed, actually. Fate took away her lovely mum but she has absolutely no doubt she was dearly loved. Sib wasn't, or at least didn't *feel* it. What does any child need the most in life? *Touch*. Hugs and kisses, the simple act of holding hands. Skin to skin is the first thing they try to do in the delivery suite. In her case it took several desperate minutes for Milo to transition, but she finally heard a cry and her dad handed him over. 'A boy,' he said, wiping away a tear. 'Darling clever girl, we have a boy.' From that moment, she adored her baby; it's truly impossible to imagine anything else.

Taking a steadying breath, she makes her way down the first set of stairs. Gabriel is on the landing below, holding a music case and apparently muttering to himself. Hanging back in the shadows, she watches him hurry down to the ground floor. Intrigued despite her emotion, she tiptoes further down, peers over the banister and sees him enter the dining room. That same shiver from earlier flutters in but anticipation soon overtakes it. Gabe is going to play the piano! Her ears prick for the sound of music, but he emerges moments later.

Seeming to sense that she's there, he jerks up his head. 'Katy! It's you.'

'Sorry to make you jump.' She bashfully joins him. 'Sib sent me for ...'

'Chocolate?' His face clears and he smiles. 'You shouldn't let her boss you around. Once she starts ... Well, look at me, I'm a lost cause.' He gestures to the kitchen. 'I had no idea what you like, so ...'

She follows him in, takes in the huge array of confectionery and laughs. 'Goodness. My son would think he was in heaven!'

Gabe looks down at the music case, still beneath his arm. 'Could he make use of this? It's from when I was a boy. It could go on Sib's bonfire, but it's made of kid leather and it doesn't have a scratch on it.'

Katy takes his offering. 'Thank you. It's beautiful,' she says. 'Are you sure you don't you want to keep it? Memories of child-hood and all that?'

Rubbing his glasses on his shirt, he doesn't answer for a while. 'Soft focus,' he says when he eventually looks up. 'Please have it. You'd be doing me a huge favour.'

41

Katy

It's finally Wednesday, Katy's 'day date' with Harry. Though she's been pacing the hallway since ten to, she still jumps when she hears the low thrum of his car. Grateful there's a breeze to cool her hot cheeks, she hurries across the drive and climbs in.

She feels ridiculously gauche. They've spoken on the phone every day, but she hasn't seen him since Saturday.

'Hello,' he says. 'You look lovely.'

'Thanks.' She can't quite meet his gaze, so she babbles instead. 'Gosh, these seats are low. It must be quite new. You can smell the leather.'

He reaches for her hand. 'Everything OK? Are you all set for a Magical Mystery Tour?'

'Of course.' Is she, though? Is she really ready? This isn't her dad's car or a sturdy black cab.

'Katy?' Harry dips his head. 'I can tell you where we're going if you prefer. I thought a drive to the countryside and a pub lunch. If you're not sure, we can—'

'No, it's fine.' Bloody hell, if she can brave Sibeal's driving, she can brave anything. 'Sorry, I just feel a bit shy.'

He leans in for a soft kiss. 'I do too. Well, a bit. In fairness I'm probably more excited than shy. I've missed you.' He nods at the Jaguar parked in the drive. 'Is Kenton home?'

'Kenton?'

'Sorry, your dad.'

'Alexon, you numpty! Only my mum called him that for fun. The original was an ancient Greek mercenary, apparently.'

When Katy spoke to her dad on the telephone last night, he said he hadn't felt great all day. Her stomach had flipped; it's generally her who's the weakling, not him, but he said not to worry, that it was probably nothing more than a passing bug.

She comes back to Harry's inquisitive gaze. 'No, when he's sitting in London he gets the train.'

'Sounds sensible.' He puts the car into gear. 'Hungry?'

'My breakfast crumpet is all forgotten.'

'Excellent. I'll take the scenic route.'

'This is so lovely,' she says after a while. 'The steady hum reminds me of when Milo was a baby. He had colic and the only thing that would settle him was the sound of the vacuum cleaner . . .'

Katy stops speaking. God knows why she mentioned it. The effort it took her to plug in the damned thing had been immeasurable, let alone trying to actually use it.

The silence feels odd. 'It was Bridget's idea about the Hoover,' she says to fill it. 'From her days as a health visitor, I guess. She's stuffed with good ideas, which can be annoying at times.'

'My mother's like that. She's nearly always right.' He grins. 'Only nearly. Drives my dad nuts.'

'You have parents!' she says, glad of the subject change. 'Tell me about them.'

'Well, they bicker a lot, but I guess that's the norm . . .'

Though Katy smiles and nods, hers weren't the bickering sort. The only major thing she can recall were their views on her pregnancy, which were the polar opposite of what she'd expected.

'They live in the sticks beyond Altrincham. In fact, that's where we're going. I told Mum all about you, so she's made the special Persian recipe passed down from her mother. It takes her hours to cook, so I hope you like it . . .' He glances at her and laughs. 'Your face! I'm only joking. They do live pretty close to where we're going but that's just coincidental. Well, sort of. The Three-Legged Mare was my teenage local and it happens to offer the best lunch ever. Have you never been?'

She shakes her head. She's been nowhere really. Three disastrous years at university, then home and isolation. Bloody hell – *isolation*! She starts at her own choice of word. Until this very moment her home has always equated to *safety* rather than seclusion.

Harry continues to speak. 'Next to Dunham Massey Hall?'

'Yes! We went there for school trips at ten and eleven, dressed up in cloth caps and made coloured candles or bread. Then we were let loose in the grounds.' She thinks back and smiles. 'Well, in a group with a parent in charge. Mum came both times, so I was put with the naughty boys.'

'You were a naughty boy?'

'Ha, no!'

'I wish I could say the same.'

Surprised at his tone, she turns to look at him. 'Really? You were—'

'A bad lad, yes, but that was when I was older.' He sighs. 'Things I'm not proud of . . .'

'Well, you should have met my mum,' she says to lighten the atmosphere. 'You'd have been putty in her hands. The rascals were on best behaviour when she was around, hence the teacher's logic. They fought over who'd each take an arm.'

'Was she beautiful?'

'Yes, she was.'

He reaches for Katy's hand and squeezes. 'Like putty,' he says. 'That makes sense.'

42

Katy

Katy sits at a table and looks around the dog-friendly pub. Although balmy outside, the log fire is burning and a pleasant hum of conversation surrounds her. It's busy enough to feel unnoticeable but not overwhelming. She snaps an invisible rubber band on her wrist. Those are the thoughts of an 'isolated' person. Today's a new day; she's going to damned well enjoy it.

Harry pulls out a chair. 'Sorry about that. Phil's a great lad, but he likes to chat. Be warned; he'll present you with what he deems you should eat and drink rather than give you any choice.'

'Sounds fantastic.' She inhales the delicious food aromas. 'I can't wait to see what I'm given! Thank you for bringing me. Though poor little Rex ...' Her eyes wide, she counts on her fingers. 'Let's see, one doggie, two. Three doggie, four. Oh, and one in the corner ...'

'I knew it! The moment I stepped in, I knew it was coming. You like that bloody hound better than me, don't you?'

'Even-stevens at the moment.' She leans in to give him a peck, but a large shadow interrupts. 'Bad moment? I'm Phil and I gather you are Katy.' He flourishes a bottle of red wine, then pours a measure in her glass. 'Château Clos Floridène. This one's been breathing all morning.'

'Cheers,' Harry says when he's gone. 'Just this one for me. You enjoy the rest, but no snoozing and snoring on the way home.'

Katy fingers her stem for a moment or two. 'Sleepy', she thinks. And 'sad'. Words from the mouth of a babe. Her gorgeous babe. She likes Harry, she really likes him; what does she have to fear? He's honest and open with her.

She clears her throat. 'After Mum died, I got ill . . .'

He nods but says nothing.

'I had no energy; I felt exhausted all the time. Some days were better than others, but on occasions it was a struggle to get out of bed. I spent hours just sleeping. Dad was worried, of course, but he had to go back to work at some point, so he employed—'

'Bridget.'

'So you knew? Bridget told you?'

'No, not at all. She nurses privately. Putting together that with what Milo said . . .'

'Ah, Milo.' She takes a shuddery breath. 'That was the worst of it. I was determined not to let the tiredness get the better of me. I had a son to care for and distract me from the loss of Mum, but as much as I wanted to be fully hands-on, sometimes I had to give in to sleep.'

'Did you get a diagnosis?' Harry asks quietly.

'Myalgic encephalomyelitis, chronic fatigue syndrome, ME, CFS or whatever the term is. No one really knows, do they? But I read it can be brought on by depression and emotional trauma, so I guess that makes sense.' She tries for a smile. 'Anyway, there you have it. A veritable nutcase! But I'm so much better now. More steps forwards than backwards, thank God.'

She waits for judgement or even recoil. 'You're not a nutcase, Katy. And you shouldn't feel ashamed.'

'But I do.' She covers her face. 'I'm such a failure. I couldn't hack uni; couldn't help my dad with his grief; couldn't play with my own son at times. The list is endless.'

'You are not a failure. You've faced your fears by telling me, so you're strong. Katy?' He waits for eye contact. 'We're all just human; we all wish we could turn back the clock.' His dark gaze is loaded with something she can't quite fathom. 'In fact, there's something I need to tell you too—'

Phil's voice cuts in. 'Salmon fishcakes with crème fraîche, and king prawns with chilli and garlic,' he says, placing two serving dishes on the table. 'Mushrooms baked with Stilton and breaded Brie with cranberry coming up.'

'Wow, thank you. This looks amazing.'

'Do start whilst it's hot. I'll be back!'

As Phil moves away, she takes a breath to continue their conversation, but a loud clattering sound makes her turn.

'Oh God, she's choking. For God's sake do something!' a woman shrieks. 'She's swallowed it!'

Harry drags back his chair and Katy follows. A musclebound man is roughly slapping a girl's back. Harry draws him away and kneels next to the child. 'Can you cough?'

'Who the fuck—'

'I'm a doctor. We need to be calm. Can you give me room, please?'

The man puffs out his broad chest. 'Get your hands off . . .' Then, 'Bloody hell, it's you. One of us, then it turns out you're a—'

'Don't start now, Gary.' Her face puce with anger, the woman jabs a finger at him. 'She's choking, for God's sake!'

213

Breath trapped in her chest, Katy watches Harry expertly strike the child between her shoulder blades with the heel of his hand. But Gary lunges forward, so she grabs his belt to hold him back.

'Your little girl needs space . . .' she begins, but she's silenced by the impact of his elbow in her face.

Stumbling back, she lands on the soft cushion of a person behind her. 'God, I'm so sorry. Are you OK?' she asks the startled woman.

If there's a reply she doesn't hear it; it's mercifully stifled by the peal of a child's cry.

43

Katy

Harry pulls up the car outside Katy's house. 'Are you sure you're OK?' He gently touches her cheekbone. 'It's bruising already.'

'I'm fine.' She's far more than fine; she's happy, bloody happy. 'Perhaps it's inappropriate, but I've had a really fun day.'

'A child almost asphyxiated, a man assaulting you . . .' He kisses her lightly. 'Yup, a fun day. We should do it again.'

'In fairness I did shock him—'

'Gary drinks too much. He was like that at school.'

Katy nods but doesn't comment. Once the audience had dispersed and the little girl settled down, she returned to the table. But she clocked Harry speaking to Gary before he joined her. She doesn't know what passed between the two men, but it appeared heated.

She now looks at her watch. 'Nearly time to collect Milo. I'd better get . . . Oh, Dad must be home. The light's on in his study.'

'If he's up for babysitting tonight, maybe you could have a sleepover at mine? I'm off all day tomorrow.'

'Yes; maybe. I'm not sure . . .' Oh God, her dad must be quite ill to come home mid-week. 'I'll call you.'

Waving Harry away, she trots to the house and fumbles for her keys.

'In here,' she hears as she closes the door.

He's sitting at the paper-strewn desk. 'Hello, darling. Had a good day? Where have you . . .?' His expression darkens. 'What's happened to your face? Has someone hit you?'

'Yes, but not deliberately; there's a story behind it. How about you? Are you OK?'

'I felt rotten when I woke, but two hours' snoozing on the train seems to have sorted me out.'

'Oh, great.' She glances at the window. In her haste she forgot to thank Harry; she barely said goodbye. She takes a quick breath. 'Dad, tonight; I was wondering if—'

'Already done. With this bit of a cold, I can't smell it myself, but I've prepared our Wednesday special. Just needs popping in the oven later.' He chuckles. 'Let's see if we can still hoodwink Milo with the hidden broccoli.'

'That's great, thanks. After dinner could you—'

'And the pièce de résistance I spotted at Euston . . .' He rustles in his briefcase and brings out a DVD. 'Remember we missed this at the cinema? I know it's probably on Netflix or similar, but if it is, don't tell me!'

Her emotions still conflicted, Katy leans back against the pillow. Milo was surprised and delighted to find his grandad home, so the afternoon and evening was busy and joyful. Yet she found herself fingering the mobile in her pocket, wanting to phone Harry or to text him at least, to say sorry for bolting so abruptly, and thank him for such a lovely day. To say: *I'd have loved to stay over tonight; it's just that . . .*

216

She felt guilty for the ping of resentment in her chest, but it was replaced by another niggle which popped up out of nowhere. Harry had been going to say something before Phil served the food. Such a serious face. What on earth was it?

But she's now finally alone in her bedroom. Her dad made two mugs of hot chocolate and smiled wryly. 'It feels wrong not to finish special Wednesday the traditional way. I'm taking mine up to bed, then lights out for me.'

'Good idea. Me too.'

The scent of cocoa perfuming the room, she finally looks at her phone. Oh God, there's a message waiting from Harry. She's left her texting too late. She should've sent one earlier. She shouldn't have told him about her illness, let alone her disastrous dating history . . .

Just knowing a 'step backwards' is about to slap her down, she quickly opens it.

In the sack and thinking about you. Can't you escape and slip in beside me?

It's all she can do not to squeal with delight.

Tomorrow. I promise tomorrow.

44

Sibeal

Sib sighs deeply. Each time she falls asleep, she seems to wake up seconds later. Sometimes that can happen with moderate drinking; she'll drop off the moment she flops back against the mattress, then wake again around three. But she hasn't touched a flaming drop of alcohol since politely sipping a glass of red at Kat's place on Sunday.

After all Kat's blather about the trials of being an only kid and the centre of attention, Sib had been tempted to snap open a bottle on Monday instead of their coffee, but it was stupid to take out her personal angst on her friend. She only marched to her dad's bedroom through pique, but she was glad of the diversion in the end. Even though he was no longer there, she reverted to the Sibby who wanted to please him. Funny, that; she always behaved for him. Not from anything he did or said but because she wanted to, and that included abstaining from booze whilst in this house.

Digging deep for good Sibby, she focuses on the last couple of days. With James somehow by her side, she's been fine without Gabe. The less jumbled the house has become, the more cosy she's felt. She said so to him on the phone and he laughed.

'Typical Sibeal. Contrary to the end.'

'Mock all you like,' she replied. 'I'm just telling you how I feel. Anyway, how's London?'

'Busy.'

'Staying in the squat with Crispin and Vivienne?'

'I'm not sure they'd describe this beautiful house as that, but yes.'

Squatting, albeit for many years, added up to a squat in anyone's view, but she didn't say that to Gabe, nor did she explain that the uncluttering has felt symbolic, a release of the emotions invested in *stuff*, belongings that are meaningless, actually. Calm and relaxed, she's motored through a backlog of WebLife admin, made herself proper food with vegetables and even gone for walks.

Exorcising ghosts, she's said to herself once or twice with the hint of a smile. But she's been too effective, too bloody efficacious, as the clearing has included Robin.

The fantasy still tangible, Sibeal stirs. Sensuous kisses and stroking, Robin's bedtime soapy smell. He's back, thank God, he's back! But his face ... She can't remember his face. Tightly screwing her eyes, she tries to climb back into the dream. Fuck, it's gone. So has he. What did he look like? The image in her mind has become vaporous, insubstantial, unreliable. How can this be? What the hell is wrong with her?

Hitching herself up the bed, she reaches for her phone and swipes through her photos. Yet it's a fruitless search, she knows that. Robin didn't let her take them. When she tried, he laughingly deleted the snap. She didn't need to ask why. The boy, the boy, always the boy.

'What if Zoe found out about us?' she'd ask.

'I don't care if she does, per se. We don't have a marriage. But if she left me, she'd take Joseph with her and I can't risk that, Sib. Not while he's little.'

'Then maybe you should go to her now.'

'Don't be like that. I love you, only you. It's just that . . .'

He didn't need to say that it was her own bloody fault, that she'd finished with him and left him free to marry who the fuck he'd wanted to.

Now noting the time, she pummels the pillow with frustration. It's only four o'clock and she's completely awake. She needs her parallel land; it's the only way she'll ever see Robin again. Fending off her dad with the flat of her hand, she pads to the bathroom and looks behind the loo. Her emergency reserves are where she left them a week ago. Well, this is an emergency.

She slugs back a measure, then another, grimacing a little less each time the fiery liquid hits her throat. As she closes her eyes, the boy steps into the frame. If it wasn't for him . . . But she likes Joseph, doesn't she? *Stalking* the boy. No, not stalking. Just watching, that's all. Even when he was sleeping. The boy so like his father.

She peers a little closer. He's the image of his dad. And Wilmslow's only just down the road. Then she'd see Robin's face, his mini-boy-face.

45

Katy

Katy throws back the duvet, drags open her curtains and smiles at the thought of her trip to the other side of the village after she's dropped Milo off at school. Yesterday's resentment and guilt have cleared from her head. Instead she feels giddy and light yet strong, like Harry described, prepared for any challenges which might face her today.

She pads to the bathroom. Her clothes are in a heap on the bidet, her bedtime drink untouched, toothpaste smeared in the sink and the lid on the floor. She chuckles at the rare disarray. Such was her excitement after her text tête-à-tête with Harry.

Peering into the mirror, she traces the bruise below her eye. She thought her dad might ask about it again, but he didn't, thank goodness. She has nothing to hide, but it's one of those incidents where you had to be there.

Eventually refreshed from her shower, she finds her dad with his laptop in the snug. 'Egg with soldiers?' he asks over his shoulder.

Katy laughs. 'That sounds lovely,' she says, 'but it's me. Milo's still upstairs.'

He turns, his face showing his surprise. 'Kathryn! I thought you'd be asleep.'

'It's Thursday, remember?' She kisses his cheek. 'A school day.'

'Of course! Sorry, darling, I'm so used to being away all week.'

She peers at his screen. 'So what are you ...? Ah, I spy a holiday.'

He playfully twists it away. 'No peeping until I've done all my research. Looks like there are some great deals but they're all long haul. What do you think? Would you and Milo be up for that?'

She pauses. Milo was a toddler the one time they ventured abroad. Even with her dad's help, the week was exhausting. But she's so much better now. She takes a breath to reply, but he speaks again.

'Have a think about it. You look nice. What are you up to today?'

'I'm—'

She's interrupted by the noisy entrance of Milo. He hurtles to Alexander and grabs him around the waist. 'You're taking me to school!'

'Well, I certainly can. A bit of fresh air will do my cold good.' He looks at Katy. 'In fact, if you fancy a walk?'

She bends down to scoop up Poppy. 'Maybe later,' she says, burying her face in her fur. 'I'm promised to Sibeal today. Milo is having tea at Strummer's house, so I might not be back until ...'

Her voice tails off but it's fine; grandad and grandson have moved on to their mission for breakfast. She puffs out her relief; no need to hide her burning fibbing cheeks any more.

46

Sibeal

Driving in the outside lane, Sibeal squints at the speedometer. Not too fast or too slow is the thing. Not that Gabe's old heap of junk goes that bloody quickly. And she doesn't need to worry about being over the limit really. She didn't drink *that* much whisky, did she? And anyway, it was hours ago. Well, three or four hours ago. She didn't dream, but at least she fell asleep almost immediately, forcing herself awake when the alarm beeped at seven thirty. She considered drifting into oblivion again, but only for a second as memory kicked in. She'd promised herself a trip to Wilmslow! The boy would see her through the day and the week, but she had to look sharp; she had no idea what time he'd leave for nursery, but if she didn't get her skates on, she might miss him.

The traffic slows and Sibeal looks to her left. A fat man glares back. He flashed his headlights at her earlier, wanting to get past. Ha, look at him now, stuck in the morning rush like everyone else. She thinks about giving him the V sign, but instead she dons a bright smile. Today is a good day. She's had the sense not to drive her own car, so she can take a little peek at that beautiful face, then move on, maybe collect Kat, go for lunch and chill out. She's wearing her new white capri trousers and heels, ready for fun.

She turns on the radio and waits for the carriageway to clear.

'It's just a question of being patient, Sib,' she hears in her head.

Gabe, of course, piano tuner to the stars! Not that they're celebs she's ever heard of.

'They're the *real* musicians,' he says with a tut. 'Professionals. Session instrumentalists and concert pianists. It's an honour to be asked.'

She pictures the squat that's not a squat. In fairness to him, the massive house in Greenwich isn't quite the run-down hovel she'd imagined. The actors who live there are quite Sloaney, and the one time she visited, Vivienne gracefully presented her with a smoked salmon bagel on a Wedgwood plate like a silver service waitress. Fine-boned, wrinkled and old enough to be his mother, she shares a bed with Crispin, Robin's best man.

Pushing the image away, she reverts to the chock-a-block road. The gridlock is easing, thank God. Concentrate, Sib, you're nearly there; not too fast or too slow; not too odd or too erratic; just negotiate the roundabout, head towards Wilmslow, then park up and wait.

Her chest tingling with anticipation, she carefully negotiates the long, leafy road. When she's finally there, she indicates left. Her usual place is taken, but she doesn't panic. It's early, these posh people are still in their homes, devouring a healthy breakfast. Her own stomach is churning with hunger, now she thinks of it. Perhaps she should have eaten something to soak up the slight alcohol fuzz. Not that it's affecting her one little bit. She'll drive down further and turn around.

The three-point turn takes five or six goes. Finally facing the

224

right direction, she looks in the rear-view mirror. A school! Little children and their parents are milling towards it. With a smile of satisfaction, she pulls onto the kerb to watch.

'What the hell do you think—'

Sibeal snaps around. The driver's door has been opened and the bitch is leaning in.

'Sorry, I thought it was ...' Zoe's eyes narrow. 'It's you.' Comprehension flashes through her gaze. 'You brought a teddy the other week. You wheedled your way into my house.' Pulling Joseph behind her, she points a finger. 'Robin warned me about you. The sister, the loopy ex who couldn't let go.'

'That's a lie!'

'Proving it by turning up to his wake, dressed like a tart.'

'He asked me to.'

'You're deranged.'

Her condescending sneer is too fucking much. 'We were lovers,' Sib hisses. 'He loved me until the day he died.'

Zoe snorts derisively. 'You're delusional and pathetic. If he was in love with anyone it was ...' She shakes her head and steps away. 'Get out of here and don't come back.'

Frozen with shock, Sibeal stares at the woman's midriff. The personal-trainer-toned stomach from the old Facebook photographs is no longer there. Her fitted polo shirt is stretched to its limit. Zoe is pregnant, quite noticeably pregnant. 'Get out of here,' she repeats. 'Or I'll call the police.'

Her body on autopilot, Sib puts the Volvo into gear and somehow drives away. What the fuck, what the fuck? rattles in her head. They didn't have sex, they didn't *have a marriage*. Maybe she's wrong; perhaps the bloody woman has just put on weight ...

Pulling up where she can, she fumbles for her phone and opens up Facebook. Her fingers shake as she scrolls through the pictures, but eventually she finds it. A scan photo of a foetus and a sentence: *Still grieving for my beautiful Robin, but part of him is still with me, so I'm lucky, really.*

Bile froths and lurches in her chest. Opening the door just in time, she vomits onto the double yellow lines. Oblivious to the acrid boozy stench, she wipes her mouth with her sleeve and stares vacantly into space. Who says that it's Robin's? *She*, the bitch, does. The woman who killed him. What did he die of, what did he really die of? Gabriel will know more. Phone Gabe; yes, call Gabe.

His number rings out until voicemail kicks in. She tries again, then again. Where the hell is he? Hurling the mobile into the passenger footwell, she tries to rise above the fuddle, the panic and frustration.

London, of course. Gabe's in London.

47

Katy

Though Katy hears the door slam, she heads for her dad's bedroom and peeps through the window to make sure that they're
gone. Embarrassed by her teenage-like behaviour, a nervous
chuckle bubbles out. She was actually a late developer so she
didn't date boys until university, but her parents were open and
interested, encouraging her to bring the guy here for Sunday
lunch or a meal out, so God knows why she's being so secretive
now. She could've just told her dad she was spending the day with
Harry, even if not in front of Milo and his little ears. Bloody hell,
she even lied!

She turns to the neatly made divan. Well, there's a thought.
How would she feel if her dad starting seeing someone? Dismayed
or delighted or a bit miffed? A little vexed, if she's honest, not for
herself but for her beautiful mum.

Pushing that notion away, she hurries down the stairs, grabs
her thin jacket and leaves the house. She almost takes the short-
cut through the park, but reminds herself just in time that it's
Milo's preferred route to school, so she strides through the village,
hoping there's no one she recognises today.

She guffaws to herself. She needs to get a grip. People aren't generally telepathic. The school secretary, the butcher or the chirpy fruit-shop owner, heck, even Bridget can't read her mind. Nor can they study the text exchange between her and Harry which became more unrestrained as last night rolled on. She couldn't bring herself to delete them.

When she reaches Harry's door, she fingers the keys in her pocket. Dare she use them? *You have keys! Feel free to surprise me anytime.*

Knowing she can't do it, she steps back and rings the bell. Its chime is quite distinct through the glass porch, but nobody answers. The curtains are open in the front bedroom; he clearly isn't in.

She turns to the road, but a smiling voice stops her in her tracks. 'Another beautiful sight to behold this sunny morning.'

His hair disarrayed, Harry's on the drive at the other side of the house with a sponge and a bucket.

'"Another"?' she asks.

He nods to his car. 'Now she's all polished and shiny. Though seeing you side by side . . .'

He kisses her. 'Sorry, I'm a bit sweaty. I woke with the dawn, so I thought I'd attend to my . . . my recently relegated second love.'

She laughs. 'Boys and their toys.'

'Hey, I'm improving with age. The last one was a vermilion red. I felt black was progress. Maybe grey next time.'

He leads Katy to the back door. 'Are you ready? Rex has been waiting; he'll be delighted to see you. A quick shower, then I'm all yours.' He kisses her again. 'Did I mention how delighted I am to see you too?'

48

Sibeal

Groggy and disorientated, Sibeal opens her eyes. Where is she? On the Manchester tram? But a whooshing noise hits and it's dark beyond the windows. Perhaps she's on her way to hell. Wondering what they've done to deserve their fate, she studies her companions. A bearded old guy; a woman with the sharpest grey nails and ladybird earrings; a tousled blond teenager with a ring on his thumb swinging a purple 'Eat' carrier. Two girls, surely sisters, with exotic eyes and plaited hair. One of them has spider buckles on her shoes, the other clutches a green Harrods bag . . .

Bloody hell, that's right; she's in London on the DLR, hurtling towards Gabriel. How she arrived in the carriage, only God knows.

The train pulls to a stop at Greenwich. Unbelievably thirsty, she forces her legs to stand, work their way through the clog of commuters and up the unending station steps. She eventually pops into light and drizzle and wind, so she pulls up her blazer collar and shuffles along the busy road, squinting at the shops, pubs and cafés, wishing she had sunglasses. Registering a sharp sting, she looks down to her shoes. Bloody blisters. Never mind,

Gabe will have plasters to alleviate the pain. She puts a hand to her breast. Christ, she hopes so.

She continues to walk, past the picture house and church, until the street forks. 'The Road Not Taken', she remembers from school. But she only wants to take the path to Gabe in a house with a baby grand piano in the downstairs front room. Finally she stops at a flat-roofed property that looks familiar. A dull yellow-brick terrace sits on one side, a smarter red detached on the other. Staggering towards it, she now remembers the wine. A man at Milton Keynes woke her, insisting the seat was his, so she bought three small bottles from the buffet car, sat opposite the pedantic shit and downed them. Still, she's only a little light-headed, so she takes a deep breath and knocks at the door.

Best behaviour, Sibeal, she muses inwardly. Gabriel didn't actually say it the last time she was here, but she knew that's what he was thinking.

A girl in a green floral dress answers. Nope, she's never seen this one before. Sib guffaws to herself. Perhaps Crispin has ditched Vivienne for a much younger model.

'Is Gabriel in?' she asks. Then, as an afterthought, 'Please.'

The plain Jane frowns. 'Who's Gabriel?'

'He's my brother. He's staying here.'

The girl opens her arms to prevent her from entering. 'Hey, you can't just—'

'Gabriel?' Sib calls, pushing past. Then louder, 'Gabe? Are you here?' Suddenly fearful her plan to see her brother will collapse like everything else, she makes for the stairs and calls again. 'Gabriel? It's Sibeal. I need to talk to you.'

A door opens. Almost blinded by panic she stares at the man in the shadows. 'Gabriel? Is that you?'

'No, it's Crispin. Sibeal? What are you doing here?'

The strong smell of incense knocks her sick. 'I need to talk to Gabe.'

'He isn't here.'

'He is; I know he is. I can feel it.' She makes for another bedroom, but Crispin blocks her path.

'He isn't here, Sibeal. Has something happened?'

She stares at him. Floppy-haired and posh, so similar to Robin. 'No. I need to talk to my brother. Let me past. I need to talk to him fucking now!'

Her yellow tresses in a candy-floss cloud and wearing a silk wrap, Vivienne appears. Putting a finger to her lips, she guides Sibeal inside and gestures to a chaise longue set against the far wall. Folding her hands in her lap, she sits next to Sib and silently gazes. Bloody Buddhists, Sib remembers. But her rebellion soon falters and dies. With her damned sanctimonious restraint and reprimand without words, Vivienne is too like her mother. Yet this woman's eyes are gentle.

'What did you need to talk to Gabriel about?' she asks quietly. 'Perhaps I can help.'

Sib shrugs like a kid, stares at the wall hangings and tightens her lips, but Vivienne's peer and her silence become too much, so she breaks it eventually. She turns to Crispin, still standing at the door. 'You didn't go to Robin's funeral. Neither of you did.'

'We were on tour in Devon. *Hamlet.*' Then after a beat, 'Crispin will make us a nice cup of tea, won't you, darling.' She pats Sib's thigh. 'And maybe something to eat?'

She is bloody hungry, but that's not why she's here. She takes off her shoes and explores the sores on her feet. 'I saw his wife, Robin's wife, recently. I didn't know she was pregnant . . .'

'Oh really? That's so lovely.' The relief in Vivienne's tone makes Sibeal look up. 'I didn't know that. It's a little ... Well, like karma, I suppose.' Then as though answering Sib's unspoken question, 'They'd been trying for another baby since the little boy.'

Like breezy snowflakes, the words take moments to catch. 'Who? Who was trying for a baby?'

'Robin and Zoe, of course. He'd always adored children, so after Joseph was born, he was understandably keen for—'

But Sibeal can't bear to hear more. Up from the sofa and down the stairs, she pelts from the truth like a firecracker.

49

Katy

Contented and warm, Katy watches the patterns on the ceiling move with the breeze through the open window. It's the sunlight through the tree at the front of the house, but they feel like Christmas lights, those sparkles of excitement, anticipation, delight. Until now she'd forgotten how much she missed them and the happy feelings they evoked.

The need to wee overwhelming, she slips from the bed, reaches for a robe to cover her nakedness and pads to the bathroom. It feels too intrusive to shower, so she washes herself at the sink, almost embarrassed to lift her face and witness her pink reflection in the mirror. Even with the bruise she knows she looks nice. Was she always so pretty? Maybe she was, but never really *felt* it. Which is silly when she was told it all the time by her parents.

Tightening the belt around her waist, she returns to the landing and stops at the photographs of Lydia and Harry in various exotic locations. A record of their life, their love, frozen in frames. But they don't bother her; she understands why they're still here. It's far easier to do nothing than something. Dig in deep and survive rather than face the grief and the heartbreak. Perhaps that's why she slept, a self-imposed cure.

As she yawns, a portrait of an older couple catches her eye. Tall, handsome and fair, the man is undoubtedly Harry's father, so the woman must be his mum. With her dark hair, glowing eyes and sculpted cheekbones, she's stunning. Persian food, Harry said, so presumably she's Iranian. He's a mix, as she is; she likes that.

Returning to the bedroom, she tiptoes to the bed and studies him in sleep. Without his mum's dark amber gaze he looks different. It evokes that image of her 'dead' dad, but only for a fleeting moment, so she shrugs it away and climbs in.

He stirs, kisses her nose and pulls her to his shoulder. 'Ten minutes more. So tired. Can't think why,' he mutters with a smile.

She yawns again. God, she's so sleepy too. But it's such a nice weariness, gently pulling her in.

'Stop! You have to stop!'

The sound of her own voice jerks Katy awake. Bolting upright, she stares until the smoke clears. It isn't her dad but Harry beside her, his face sharp with concern.

'Katy? Are you OK?'

She lets out a gasp. 'Yes.' Then, 'God, I'm so sorry. I must have frightened you to death.'

'No, it's OK. What happened?'

'Just a dream.' Her cheeks burn with embarrassment. 'Nightmare, more like. It's gone now, but it's always the same.'

'Tell me.'

Leaning forward, she studies her trembling hands. As if the fumes were real, her throat feels sore.

Harry rubs her shoulder. 'Everything is fine, Katy. You're safe.'

'The dream . . .' She swallows. 'I'm in the car with Dad instead of Mum. I know the crash is coming but there's nothing I can do to stop it. I'm paralysed, stuck. It's horrible.' She briefly looks at him. 'Sorry, it hasn't happened for ages. But earlier I watched you sleeping and it reminded me of the hospital. You know, when I thought Dad was dead.' Feeling stupid, she groans. 'You must think I'm completely crackers.'

He gently pulls her back and circles her with his arms. Then he kisses her shoulder. 'Watching me sleep, eh? It must be love.' He sighs. 'Don't apologise. It's your mind still processing a deeply traumatic experience. Trying to make sense of it; trying to make the outcome different.'

He falls silent for some time, so she turns. 'I've spooked you, haven't I?'

'No, you haven't, not at all.' He pecks her forehead but his eyes are perturbed. 'Let's get dressed and have some lunch.' He looks at his watch. 'Four o'clock! Bloody hell, how did that happen? I guess we need to call it high tea. Still, you got lucky. After I dropped you off yesterday, I plundered the deli counter in Waitrose.' He smiles his lovely smile and stands from the bed. 'Hope you like fromage. I'll grab a shower. Feel free to raid the fridge while you're waiting.'

Heavy-hearted, Katy dresses and plods down the stairs. She's done it again, hasn't she? Without even knowing it, she's pushed Harry away. Another bloody failure. What's the problem with her? Perching on the sofa, she drifts and waits. But eventually she takes a swift breath of resolve. It's better to know, surely? Preferable to face the music for once in her life.

Harry finally appears. 'Did you find anything you fancy?'

Lifting her chin, Katy stands. 'What did I do wrong?'

235

'What? No, nothing—'

'I'm not a complete idiot. What just happened?'

He rakes his damp hair. 'You did nothing, Katy.' He sighs. 'It's not you, it's me. There's something I haven't told you. Look, why don't you sit and I'll explain.'

Katy's mouth is dry as she takes a seat. Something is wrong, very wrong.

He inhales deeply. 'I was the person who . . .' His gaze faltering, he pauses and frowns. 'You know I'm based at the hospital, right?'

She nods.

'As an A&E doctor, a specialist registrar dealing with emergencies?'

A strange paralysis sets in. What is he saying? Does she really want to know?

'Well, the night of your parents' accident, or should I say morning, I was on the early shift, so I . . . I was on duty that day, Katy. I was there when the paramedics brought them in.'

Her mind numb, it takes several painfully slow moments to add up his words. Harry's an accident and emergency doctor; a *specialist* registrar. He works at the hospital. He was *there*, he was there when her mum . . . Catastrophic injuries, oh God. She doesn't need to hear more.

She holds out her palm to stop him, but his lips are moving. 'We . . . I . . . tried my best, but there was nothing I could do.'

Struggling to her feet, she steps away. Stop, he needs to stop! She doesn't want to know; she doesn't want to fucking know! Yet her mind has already switched to overdrive. Too intimate, too intimate. This man, this *stranger*, was with her mother when she died. There was *nothing he could do*. The one dreadful thing that wiped five years from her life. Why the hell didn't he tell

236

her? She liked him, she almost loved him. She slept with him; she *trusted* him.

She scoops up her jacket and bag, brushes by him and heads for the door. Though almost too winded to speak, she knows she must say it. 'You didn't tell me; it's unforgivable. Don't ever contact me again.'

50

Sibeal

As she indicates for Cheadle, Sibeal's mobile shrills from the passenger seat, so she winds down the window and drops it out. Another call from fucking Gabe. It's always the same; he ignores her when she needs him, yet persistently rings when it suits him, when it's all too bloody late. Well, he can fuck off along with Hamlet and his Gertrude. No doubt the bloody woman rushed to phone him the moment Sib was gone, her received pronunciation squeaky, shocked and worried.

'Sibeal was here acting tremendously oddly. I think she'd had a drink or two. Is everything all right, darling? I feel we should do something, but goodness knows what ...'

No doubt she passed the call to Crispin for his tuppence. 'Sorry, Gabriel, but quite frankly her behaviour was out of order ...'

She glances at the parking tickets, still stuck to the windscreen. Bloody serves her brother right. Divine retribution for not being there when she was desperate to speak to him, to find out more about Zoe and her pregnancy. Did he know about it? And if he did, why the fuck didn't he tell her?

The words 'the loopy ex', 'deranged' and 'delusional' filter in, but she can't go there; on top of the new baby it's just too, too painful. And what about *If he was in love with anyone it was . . .*? She pushes them all away. The bitch just said them to be hurtful. Sticks and stones and all that. And yet, what did she say? *Robin warned me . . .* That can't be true, can it?

She pulls down the mirror flap to protect her eyes. The burning soreness is from sheer tiredness and the insistent Manchester sunshine, she'd say to anyone who might ask. But the truth is she cried like never before. From that Sloaney squat to Greenwich station, from there to Euston where she'd just missed a train, the tears dripped. Then after buying wine from M&S Simply Food, she sat on a bench with the smokers outside and positively sobbed.

'What's up, love?' some kind soul asked eventually.

'I want my dad,' she replied, surprising herself.

It was true. Perhaps it was the older crowd or the comforting smell of cigarettes, but for the first time since his death she really needed her solid, abstemious, chain-smoking father. He was the only person in the world who'd just hold her tightly without reservation. Not like bloody Gabe, ever fearful of the consequences. And that was long ago, even before Robin.

Robin warned me . . . Robin, fucking, fucking Robin. Her nose stings but she won't cry again. When she climbed from the train and peered at the sign for Wilmslow, she decided that was it. She firmly nods to her reflection. Yes, she's done with bloody weeping, she's completely done with the past. All she needs is five minutes of being comforted and she'll be fine. Little Kat will hold her; warm-hearted Kat will listen and not judge.

The lights finally change. Not too fast or too slow, she

remembers, as she heads towards her house. Almost missing the turn at the church, she swerves to the right and trundles along until she sees her oasis. Squeezing her swollen feet into her shoes, she stumbles from the Volvo and makes for the blue door. Like magic, it opens before she knocks.

Alexander lifts his dark eyebrows in surprise. 'Sibeal, it's you.' He gestures to the bay window. 'I was in the lounge and I didn't recognise the car.' He does a double-take. 'Goodness, what's happened?'

'It's Gabriel's car . . .'

'Ah, I see.' His eyes kindly, he offers his hand. 'Kathryn isn't here at the moment, but do come in. You look as though you could do with a sit-down and a hot drink. What can I get you? Tea or coffee?' He smiles wryly. 'Perhaps a glass of water to start?'

'Thank you,' she manages, following him into the hallway. But the warm smell of a home and his solidness is all too much. 'Actually,' she says through a fresh onset of tears. 'What I need is . . .'

'Yes? How can I help?'

'Hold me, please hold me. I need someone to hold me.'

'Of course I will.'

He folds her in his arms and hugs her for an age. When he finally pulls away, he offers her a handkerchief from his pocket, then dips his face to hers. 'Whatever it is, Sibeal, I'm sure we can fix it.'

The snivelling starts again. *Deranged, delusional, pathetic.* 'It can't be fixed. *I* can't be fixed. I thought he loved me.'

'Who doesn't love you?'

'Robin.'

'And who is—'

'It doesn't matter, he's dead.'

Alexander smiles a small smile. 'Well, perhaps that's a good thing.'

'Why?'

'Closure; dreadful though it is, death gives finality. Maybe you can move on now and give your heart to somebody else. Let me get you that drink and we can have a long chat about it.'

Too weary to speak, she nods but doesn't move. She's so tired, very tired, she has to lie down.

Alexander cocks his head and gives a wonky smile. 'Am I detecting a need for another hug first?'

Yes, one more embrace like her lovely dad's. Slipping her hands around his waist, she clings to him tightly. His arms respond, but so does his body.

The usual consequences, she thinks. But that's fine; right now, she just needs to be loved.

51

Katy

Katy holds Milo's hand and absently listens to his chatter as they amble through the sunlit park. Not wanting to arrive home earlier than she'd said and face her dad's questions, she'd hurried from Harry's to Starbucks, hiding in a corner and nursing the same mug of tea for over an hour. There was only one other person tapping away at her laptop, so it should've been an ideal opportunity to unravel the knot of emotion in both her heart and her head.

Rotating her mum's Omega as though it burned, she tried to work it out. The sensations included anger, humiliation and betrayal, but when she attempted to analyse why she felt so floored, her mind simply chased its tail, so she ended up staring through the window and watching the village close for dinner. Everyone seemed to be smiling: the pet shop staff, the volunteers in Oxfam, the young woman rolling back the florist's canopy. Desperate to escape their apparent contentment, she set off for Strummer's flat and collected Milo early.

His high voice brings her back to their road. 'Look, Mummy. Whose is that car?' He crinkles his nose. 'It's a Volvo Estate. It's the advert with the snow but this one's old.'

It's Gabriel's car. Oh heck, what did Katy tell her dad about today? The lie she told him. But Milo flies through the front door before she has the chance to summon up an excuse, so she follows him in. Almost sliding to the television in his snug corner, he holds up the DVD he borrowed from Strummer.

'Can I watch it now, Mummy?'

'OK, just this once.'

Despite being told that the boys had been glued to it non-stop since school, she's glad of the distraction. Why on earth is Gabriel Matthews here? Has something happened to Sib? The thought is unbearable. She likes Sib tremendously; she's her only real friend.

Breath caught in her chest, she looks into the lounge. There's nobody in there, nor in the conservatory, the dining room or even outside. Perplexed and alarmed, she climbs the stairs cautiously and calls out, 'Hello?'

A cloud of steam following him like an aura, her dad is leaving the main bathroom, wrapped in a towel. He doesn't notice her at first and when he does he stops humming and gives a small jerk. 'Katy, you're home!' Then in a hushed voice, 'Had a good day, darling?'

For a moment she's stumped for a reply. 'Yes, I ended up going into town with another mum,' she answers, hoping another fib doesn't show in her face.

He puts a finger to his lips. 'Ssh,' he says.

Despite wondering why, Katy lowers her tone. 'Why were you in the bathroom?'

'Having a shower, of course.'

'I didn't mean that. You don't normally use the main—'

'We have a visitor.'

'What? Gabriel?'

He chuckles. 'Of course not; Sibeal.'

She studies his bright eyes, his light-hearted demeanour. And there's something about the way he says Sib's name. Like he's savouring it, almost. 'Sibeal Matthews is in your en suite?'

'Under my quilt, actually. Fast asleep, poor girl. Think it's best that we leave her.'

What? Her fastidious father has offered his bed? Katy gestures to the spare room. 'Why not . . .'

'She turned up tired and emotional, not to mention the worse for wear, poor thing. My bedroom happened to be the one she wandered into. I didn't mind one jot. No harm done, eh?'

'Mummy? Mummy!' Milo has appeared at the bottom of the stairs. He holds out a mini carton of fruit juice. 'Am I allowed to open this? I forgot to have it at school.' He lifts up his soiled palm. 'It's a bit sticky. The Frubes tube burst in my lunch box.'

Alexander pulls his 'Uh-oh, fingerprints!' face, so she leans over the banister. 'I'm coming, love. Don't touch anything.'

She dutifully hurries down to the kitchen. Any rogue traces of yoghurt simply wouldn't do! They're her dad's walls, after all. His walls, his bedroom, his kitchen, his whole bloody house.

Thoroughly wiping Milo's hands, she tries to calm down. Of course it's her home too; it's just . . .

She ambles to the lounge, slumps on the sofa and groans. An exquisitely good day turned so astonishingly crap. If she was to share it with somebody, she wouldn't know where to start. And anyway, who would she tell? The man she really liked has hoodwinked her, her father is being weird – too smiley, too sparkly – and her special friend, Sib . . . well, what? She doesn't know what to think, but she's apparently asleep in her father's bed and he's just had a shower. It doesn't feel right, and anyway, isn't Sibeal meant to be *her* friend, not his?

Irritation swelling again, she taps her foot. She doesn't want to think about Harry and his guilty eyes. As for Sib turning up drunk, perhaps that's not a surprise, but why didn't she call or text *her* like she has in the past? And her father is supposed to be ill; why the hell is he so flaming jolly?

'All right, darling?' he asks from behind her. She turns in surprise, not only at the sound of his voice, but the strong aroma of aftershave.

He's wearing a smart jacket. 'Are you going somewhere?' she asks.

He lifts a rakish eyebrow. 'What makes you think that? A few drinks in town with Dave Masters.' His smile fades. 'I can stay in if you'd rather . . .'

She silently puffs out her stupid angst and her dreadful misjudgement. The shower and his excitement was for this, a night out with his pal, not whatever her addled mind had thought. 'No, of course not. Go out and have fun!'

He pulls her into a hug. 'Are you OK? You seem a little . . . sapped.' He pulls back and examines her face. 'Not feeling . . .'

'No, nothing like that. I'm a bit tetchy through hunger; I haven't eaten since breakfast.'

He stands and straightens his trousers. 'Then it's a good job you have such a fabulous father. There's fresh pasta in the fridge, sauce on the hob. Garlic and parmesan and rather tasty, though I say so myself.' He checks his watch. 'Right, see you later. Be kind to your friend when she wakes up; she's in a bad place. We've been there, haven't we?' He steps away and turns back. 'By the way, I've just promised Milo to take him to school tomorrow, so there's no need to rush up in the morning. Love you.'

The door clicks to but Katy doesn't move. Like a bloody pendulum, the relief didn't last long. She feels rebuked, reprimanded, chastened. In the nicest possible way, of course. 'You're acting spoilt and uncharitable,' is what her dad really meant.

She sighs deeply. Sometimes she wishes he'd just spit it out. 'You've put on weight, Kathryn', instead of, 'Not quite as sylph-like as usual, but you'll soon lose it, darling'. Or, 'Sixty-five per cent in your exam isn't good enough', instead of, 'It's a little disappointing, but you'll reach your potential next time, love.' But she knows she's being a single-child-syndrome brat. And she *is* bloody starving, bless him.

She stands and stretches. Food is definitely the thing to cheer her up. She'll give Milo a bath, put him to bed and check in on Sib. Then she'll eat a big bowl of pasta with a huge fuck-off glass of wine.

52

Sibeal

The sound of a slamming door jerks Sib awake. She's in a strange room; unfussy fitted wardrobes, thick stripy curtains with matching cushions on the floor and, save for a single aviation art print, plain papered walls. She smiles. She's in a hotel with Robin! She was with him last night; the sheets are tangled and damp, the smell of his sweat still clings to her body . . .

Her thumping temples and reality set in. Robin. The man who loved her, the one who had no marriage; the one who never had any intention of leaving that bitch. The boy was never hers, not even for a moment.

It hurts, *she* hurts so badly. The heartache almost physical, she curls into a ball. She felt fine driving here yesterday. Robin was in the past; his boy was history; she was going to look forward. Who was she kidding? She was anaesthetised by alcohol, that's all.

She pulls down a pillow to rest her throbbing head. The aroma of aftershave breathes back. Ah, Alexander. Mellow, like the man himself. So gentle and kind, just when she needed it. Yes, she remembers a little more now. Closure, he said when she arrived here. Robin's death gave her an ending to work with. But what about the boy, Joseph? They talked about him too, didn't they? Or was that later?

Too much effort and pounding to tune her brain now, she scrunches her eyes and tries for sleep, but the need for the toilet and water and painkillers eventually becomes so imperative that she drags back the quilt and launches from the bed. It takes several moments for the dizziness to pass, then she covers her goosebumped flesh with a towel and heads for the en-suite bathroom. Her clothes are in a huddle on the floor. Oh Christ, she stripped, didn't she? Embarrassing even by her standards. Jumping in the Volvo and making her escape right now is the thing. Worry about what she did or didn't do later.

Though she can smell her stale armpits and the stench of her breath, she finishes her pee, quickly dresses and quietly heads for the stairs. At the bottom she sneezes, the rattle in her skull ricocheting through her body. Expecting some movement from somewhere in the house, she stills, but the atmosphere remains eerily silent. It's empty, thank God; everyone must have left for work or school. She just needs her shoes. Where the hell did she leave them? And the keys to Gabe's car?

Almost gagging on the stench of bacon, she tiptoes across the kitchen to the snug area at the side. No footwear or keys, but there's a crystal decanter on the low table next to the broken jigsaw. Recall flutters in. That's right; she woke to the sound of Alexander bumping into the hallway during the early hours, came down and found him here drinking brandy.

'Nightcap,' he said, his eloquent enunciation slightly slurred. He stood and fetched a crystal glass from a cupboard. 'Please come and join me.'

So she did and she drank and she talked and she cried. Then

she drank more. At some point he pulled her to his shoulder and kissed her forehead, her hair.

'Kathryn wouldn't approve,' he said.

'Approve of what?'

She groans out loud. Did she really say that teasingly?

He gave a slow smile. 'Of brandy, when I've already had a skinful,' he replied.

Cringing again, she shakes her head to expel the memory, but something inside clatters and clanks. She needs those painkillers PDQ. Where the hell do they keep them? Wiping her palms on her grimy trousers, she shuffles to the gleaming sink and opens the cupboards above.

As she's busy rifling through a Tupperware box containing a variety of blister packs, Alexander's voice from behind makes her jump out of her skin. 'Are you looking for something? Can I help you?'

She spins around. 'Sorry, I was searching for paracetamol or ibuprofen? There weren't any in your bathroom, so . . .'

His shoulder rubbing hers, he examines the sachet she's holding and chuckles. 'Feel free to help yourself if you have heartburn.' Then he turns with that disarming smile. 'But my guess is a headache, a pretty dreadful one, so I'd try two of these.'

Conscious of her stale breath and how she must look, Sib accepts the proffered pills and steps back. 'I'll take these and get out of your hair. Sorry for intruding; I thought you'd be at work this morning.'

'Not today. I've just walked Milo to school. Gave his mum a lie-in.' He studies her for a beat. 'There's no need to rush off. Why don't you stay a little longer? Have a bite of lunch with Kathryn and me?'

'That's very kind, thank you, but . . .' She almost guffaws at this polite person coming out of her mouth. Headmaster's study syndrome again, no doubt. 'I need to . . . well, do my ablutions and don some clean clothes.' She glances at the worktops. 'My shoes and my keys. I don't suppose you know where they are?'

Alexander's brow puckers. 'Maybe leave it a few more hours before you drive?' Then, when she starts to protest, 'It's none of my business, Sibeal, but when you turned up here yesterday afternoon, you were more than a touch the worse for wear. Then our brandies . . . I wouldn't want you to hurt yourself.' He looks at her sternly. 'Or anyone else.'

'Right, then I'll call a—'

He strides to the hall and picks up his keys. 'Come on, young lady, I'll drive you.'

53

Katy

Finally clawing herself from sludgy sleep, Katy peels opens her eyelids and hitches herself upright. She peers at the bedside clock, pleased to see a pint glass half full of water. It has lost its fizz, but it quenches her raging thirst nonetheless. Wiping her lips, she leans back, trying to separate the dream and reality. Her dad and Sibeal; Sibeal and her dad. What the hell went on yesterday?

She rubs her sticky eyes. Nothing inappropriate, surely? He was full of zip because he was heading out for an evening with Dave. But he was definitely taken aback when she appeared home earlier than she'd said. And when she checked on their guest before sleep, she was . . . Bloody hell, yes, Sibeal was splayed between the sheets, clearly stark naked. Why on earth would she do that?

Katy folds her arms. Sib can drink, become downright paralytic, in fact, so perhaps that was it. They've joked about sex and men over the weeks, but *this* man is her dad, for God's sake. Her mum's clothes still hang in the wardrobe. Whatever the circumstances, you don't pursue a friend's father.

With a frown, she looks at the empty tumbler. A dream or not? Sib's voice, slurry and tearful: *He was my boy. He should've been my boy. He promised me a baby!* Followed by, *So perfect, so very small. I should have taken him then, made him mine. It's not fucking fair! Why should she have another when I don't have any?*

Agitated and hot, she climbs from the bed. It's nearly ten o'clock, yet she's still so dazed. But that's down to her, drinking two large glasses of Barolo to drown her sorrows last night. The hurt fizzles in her chest. Harry and his confession, his astonishing betrayal, not just an omission but his downright lie ...

His apologetic expression flashes in, but she firmly pushes it away. She won't forgive him, ever.

Sighing deeply, she returns to thoughts of Sibeal. Drinking to expunge heartache ... Perhaps they're not so different after all. Maybe she should take her dad's advice and make an effort to be kind. With that notion in mind, she makes her way to his bedroom and taps on the door.

'Sib? Dad? Anyone there?'

When there's no reply, she lets herself in and puffs out her trapped breath. It's empty, the window open, the divan neatly made. She does the same in the spare room, eyeing up the bedding to glean whether it was slept in last night.

With a nod of satisfaction, she heads down the stairs. There's a damp patch on the carpet halfway down. Oh yes, that was her, seeking out liquid in the night like a zombie. She retraces those steps to the kitchen, opens the fridge, pulls out the San Pellegrino and swigs from the bottle. Flaming hangover. Yet after Harry's appalling revelation it's hardly surprising. Her eyes catch her mobile on the island. Has he been in touch? Determined to ignore any calls or texts, she left it here last night, but he's bound

252

to have sent a grovelling apology. Or at least an explanation, a plea to get in touch . . .

Quickly scooping it up, she bites her lip then looks. No messages, no missed calls, no nothing.

Resisting the urge to cry, she pads around to the sofa, absently moves the crystal decanter and spends a few minutes fixing her son's jigsaw, making the smiley elephant whole again. 'If only,' she mutters when she's finished.

I should have taken him then, made him mine. It's not fucking fair! echoes back.

Frowning, she turns to the worktop. Not one but two sparkling brandy glasses. Her dad's best Waterford, if she's not mistaken. Well, they weren't here when she stomped around fuelled with fury last night. Nor was the decanter, now she thinks of it.

54

Sibeal

Wondering what the old dragon next door might think, Sib steps from the Jaguar and walks carefully to the door. Her head feels marginally better but the nausea comes in waves. Vaguely remembering something Kat said about her father and security, she fumbles under the plant pot for keys, but Alexander doesn't appear to have noticed.

He's studying the façade, misty-eyed. 'A wonderful house. How time flies. I'm trying to work out how many years it's been.' He turns with a smile. 'Would you mind giving me a tour now we're here?'

Sib opens the door. She does mind, actually. 'Of course not,' she says. The usual smell hits, making her need to vomit imperative. 'But maybe . . .'

'After your shower, of course.' He gestures towards the kitchen. 'Could I . . .'

'Feel free. I'll be back when I've . . .'

Puked, when I've puked, she thinks wryly when the retching finally ends. She flushes the loo and kneels back, out of breath. God knows what she expelled, but it certainly wasn't food. When was the last time she ate? The image of a bagel pops into her head. Ha, she wasn't offered one this time. What did Vivienne say to Gabriel? Well, she doesn't give a toss about her absent brother. The headmaster-judge-man saved her, someone who listened and hugged and actually fucking cared.

Refreshed from the purge, her teeth-scrubbing and long shower, she pads to her bedroom to inspect her sore feet. They're pretty much shredded, but she's mentally OK. In fact, she's weirdly a little nervous and excited. She opens a brand new T-shirt, holds it out to inspect the logo, then slips it on with clean jeans. So much better already! Perhaps the alcohol is still in her system, but she feels positive and buoyant. Now she just needs a ton of stodgy food to put her completely back on track.

She trots down the stairs, scoops up the post at the door, then heads for the smell of coffee. She stops at the open dining-room door. What the hell? Alexander has settled himself at the far side of the table.

'Morning!' He nods to a mug on a silver coaster. 'Better drink yours before it gets cold.'

God, even as an adult she hates coming in here. Her earlier ease all gone, she sits down next to him.

'From what Kathryn tells me, you're progressing well with the clear-out. A ton of old newspapers, I believe!'

'Yes, we've been recycling.'

'I love converting waste into something reusable. So much better than landfill.' He absently rubs the polished arm of his chair. 'I had a bonfire when my parents passed away. Just for the likes of your dad's newspapers, things that don't really matter. But what do you do with more personal items when someone

255

dies? Correspondence, photographs, diaries? Keep them for posterity or throw them in the flames and move on?'

She thinks of answering that she doesn't know or care, that it's thankfully Gabe's department, but after a moment he changes the subject.

'Lovely to sit here again. Happy days. Us impoverished students fed like kings. I've never had a stew to match it. With home-made chunks of soda bread to dip in the gravy, of course.'

'Cooked by my grandmother?'

'No, by Imelda.' As though reliving the memory, he chuckles. 'After we'd eaten she'd play tunes on request. Anything from the Beatles to Bach.'

Finding herself flexing her fingers, Sibeal knots them into a fist.

'Your dad actually sat here, your mum near the door and Kenny was opposite.'

Still feeling tense, Sib struggles to listen, but when the conversation lapses, she tries to catch up. 'Yes, you mentioned him before.'

'Good old Kenny.' He pauses and sighs. 'Did you know your father wrote to me from the hospice?'

At his change of his tone, Sib lifts her head. 'No, I didn't.'

He rubs his chin thoughtfully. 'He wanted his contact details, Kenny's.' Then smiling wistfully, 'A last gathering of the Three Musketeers, I expect. It was a mix of emotions. So lovely to hear from your dad, but in such dreadful circumstances.' He clears his throat. 'I only had an old address for Kenny, planned to deliver it to your dad in person, but . . .' He shakes his head. 'It would've been nice to meet up like old times.'

His frown is replaced with a smile. 'I can picture him now, a big handsome lad, thick glossy hair, dark chestnut eyes like yours.'

'Who? Dad?'

'No, Kenny.' He gazes for a moment, then seems to flinch. 'Anyhow, enough of boring you about the past.' As though groping for something to say, he looks around, then gestures to the framed portrait of her parents. 'What a good-looking pair. He captured her so well in those paintings upstairs ...'

Sibeal shifts in her seat. Bloody hell, he must have been on the landing when she was in the bathroom.

'I know I've said it before, but you look so alike.' As though reading her mind, he covers her hand with his. 'Which isn't a bad thing at all, Sibeal. She was beautiful, of course, but talented too. Her singing voice and the way—'

Sharply pulling away, Sibeal stands. 'What do you know? Her "talents" didn't stretch to loving her only daughter.' She stares at the piano. She can still feel the shock of the slam, the sharp pain in her knuckles which took appalling moments to turn into pulsating agony.

He rises too. 'I'm sure you're wrong. By all accounts Imelda suffered from depression, severe depression. It can take over your life, become oppressive, but that doesn't mean she didn't love you. She'll have just struggled to show it.'

She covers her face to hide the tears. 'You're wrong.' Robin, her Robin. She didn't just think he loved her, she *knew* it. She was mistaken, she was stupid, she's so very hurt. 'You're wrong,' she repeats when she can finally speak. 'I'm just unlovable.'

Alexander snorts, but not unkindly. He peels away her fingers and looks into her eyes. 'Now you're the person who's wrong,' he says.

55

Katy

Clumsy patting on her shoulder brings Katy back from gluey sleep. She turns to the sing-song voice.

'Kat? Little Kat? Time to wake up!'

It's Sibeal Matthews, so close to her face. Is this another dream? Will her dad appear on her pillow too, smiley and relaxed? No, it can't be; the stench of alcohol on Sib's breath is too real.

'Move over, then,' she's saying, giving her a little push.

Too groggy to think straight, Katy does as she's told, hitching across to make room, just like when they were friends.

Sib wafts a fluted glass. 'Chin-chin,' she says. 'Alexander and I have been for lunch at . . . It used to be a pub. Toilets downstairs. Black and white all over.' She guffaws. 'What's black and white and read all over? A newspaper! My dad used to say that . . .' She pauses, then pokes Katy with a fingernail. 'But your dad's lovely too; so handsome and *commanding*!' She apes his deep voice. 'A booking for Alexander Henry? Fancy sitting outside, Sibeal? Such a lovely day! Yes, outside would be nice.'

Wishing she would just stop, Katy inhales to say something, but Sib drains the glass and continues to prattle.

'So guess where we ate? You're correct, little Kat. Outside!

With a "Don't tell Kathryn" bottle of bubbles.' She puts a finger to her lips. 'But it's fine; I made a little "Don't tell Alexander" digestif just now. Found Martini and gin in a cupboard when he'd gone. Now I'm shaken, not stirred, like—'

Katy finds her voice. 'So where's Dad gone?'

'To collect Joseph.'

'Joseph?'

'Not Joseph ... Milo! Silly me! All peachy and perfect like you, little Kat. Yes, time to collect *Milo* from school, Alexander said. Then what? Oh yes, "Tell Kathryn to get up." They were our master's instructions. "Tell Kathryn to get up for when Milo gets home. I have to go into town." That's what the headmaster said. Oh, and to make you a nice cup of tea. You like it strong, don't you know.' She pulls her long legs off the bed. 'Tea coming! And another digestif for me. I'll put on the kettle, little Kat. I'm superbly good with a kettle!'

Katy presses her face in the pillow when she's gone. Feeling abandoned by everyone earlier, she came back up here to read and inevitably fell asleep. But in truth it's preferable to being awake. Harry hasn't even attempted to get in touch and Sib is drunk and out of control yet again. And whatever is going on between her and her dad, she doesn't want to know. But she has to get up and make an effort for Milo. Her adorable son is the one constant in her life; however low she feels, she has to get a grip and function for him.

She heads for the shower, scrubs her body and her hair, emerging ten minutes later feeling brighter. As she throws the damp towel over the banister, chatter rises up from the hallway.

'But we've only just got home, Grandad. Where are you going?'

'I have to pop into chambers for an emergency, I'm afraid, Milo. But Mummy's upstairs. She'll be down in a minute.'

'What about my new jigsaw? It's for kids aged eight.'

'You'll smash it but I'm sure Mummy will help. Give her a kiss from me.'

The door clicks to, then another voice echoes, as slurred as before. 'Auntie Sibby is here to help little Milo! I'm superbly good at jigsaws. Is this supposed to be an orang-utan? Looks more like Boris Johnson to me.' Then, as Katy turns to get dressed, 'I was promised a boy, you know; a boy just like you! Don't tell anyone, but I sneaked into his bedroom and watched him sleep.'

For a beat Katy stands stock-still with shock. What on earth . . .? And why didn't her dad wait until she appeared rather than leave a drunk woman in charge of his grandson for even a minute? Alarm rattling through her, she dashes to her bedroom, fumbles with her bra and yanks a T-shirt over her damp flesh. When she finally hurtles down the stairs, the front door is ajar, buffeted by the breeze.

Not bothering with footwear, she steps outside and takes in the scene. Sib is in the driver's seat of the Volvo, Milo at her side. For a second she gapes, then the engine turns over.

Almost tripping in her haste, she belts over the driveway to the passenger door, yanks it open and pulls Milo out.

Sib's keening from last night pounds loud in her ears. *So perfect, so very small. I should have taken him then, made him mine. It's not fucking fair! Why should she have another when I don't have any?*

She scoops her son up and clutches him tightly. 'What the hell are you doing?' she shrieks.

Sibeal struggles from the car. 'I was just showing the boy—'

The boy. Through the anger and trepidation, Sibeal's words echo back. *I sneaked into his bedroom and watched him sleep.* The idea is incredible.

She inches away. 'A bedroom? You've been in someone's bedroom?'

'Only the boy, little Joseph.' Sibeal puts a finger to her lips theatrically. 'I crept in, but don't tell. He's all forgotten anyway. Gone, like Robin. Closure!'

What the hell, a *child's* bedroom? Barely able to breathe, Katy holds out the flat of her palm. 'Go away. Leave us alone and don't come anywhere near us again.'

But Sibeal is staggering forward and holding out her arms. 'Don't look so worried, little Kat. Milo likes Sibby, don't you?'

'If you're not gone in one minute, I'll call the police.'

A burp, a grin and another step towards them. 'You don't mean that.'

'I absolutely do.'

Her son heavy in her arms, Katy backs inside the hallway, slams the door and lifts the latch. There a moment's silence before Milo starts to wail. Then, interspersed with the loud rap of the knocker, the doorbell incessantly rings.

56

Katy

Conscious of her father's silence, Katy empties the dishwasher. She'd almost forgotten he could be like this. Even when Bridget popped by for a coffee first thing, perched at the island and swung her ankle decorously, he declined to be coaxed into conversation, leaving Katy to entertain her instead. Somewhat miffed, Bridget left after ten minutes.

'Alexander clearly got out of the wrong side of bed,' she said at the door. Then after a moment, 'Did I do something?'

Katy actually felt sorry for the poor woman. 'No, not at all.'

'Then what's upset him?'

'I have no idea. Men, eh?' she replied.

But of course she does know what's 'upset' him and it's actually pissing her off.

She returns to the snug and watches him for a moment. His legs crossed and still wearing his towelling robe, he's reading the *Sunday Times* on one of the sofas. Milo is aping him on the other, but with an atlas. She pictures her mum standing over him. Like Agnetha from ABBA, people always said, down to her blue eyeshadow, but today her blonde bob is tied in a knot on top of her head. 'Come on, Alexon darling, don't sulk,' she's saying with only a hint of an accent.

For the blink of an eye, the pretty woman is replaced with another: Harry's dark-haired mum. 'What happened to the girl you were inviting to eat my special Persian dish?' she's asking. 'She told me not to get in touch ever again, Mum, so I haven't,' comes the reply.

Katy shakes the imagined conversation from her mind. It's her own bloody fault; what did she expect? Yet she's both surprised and dismayed that Harry hasn't at least tried.

She looks at her son. 'How about that baking I promised, Milo? Jam tarts or gingerbread men?'

'People,' her dad comments without lowering his reading matter. 'Gingerbread people these days.'

Katy laughs drily. 'But "tart" is OK, is it?'

'I don't make the rules, I just implement them,' he replies, his voice reasonable and even.

'Gingerbread *people* please,' Milo says, saving his place between Cairo and Cape Town.

'Perfect. It's far more fun with the icing. And I have Smarties!' she replies.

Wanting someone on her side, she considers allowing him to bake in his dressing gown, but decides against it. Though it feels wholly unfair, she's already in her dad's bad books, so no need to make it worse.

'Chop-chop, then, Milo. Off you go and get dressed. I've no idea what happened to your apron, so you'll have to hunt for it.'

Sitting in her son's place, Katy listens to the sound of a lawnmower outside and rocks her head from the newspaper headlines on the left to an advert for financial advice on the right. Not convinced her dad is even reading the bloody thing, she folds her arms.

After a few more moments, she lifts her chin. 'Why don't you just say it?'

He lowers the paper. 'Say what?'

'That you're annoyed with me.' She shrugs. 'I don't know – that you think I overreacted or I was unreasonable. I can't say exactly because you haven't said anything . . .'

'You did the right thing,' he says, reverting to the print.

'But you don't really mean that.'

'I do. Sibeal was well over the limit; you were worried about Milo.'

Rather than leaving it there, she waits for the 'but', which is actually progress. Until this minute she'd have accepted the glaze of his words, lapping them up like a puppy rather than risking an honest or candid reply. Because truths are always uncomfortable and ugly, aren't they? But she's not a baby any more; she messed up big time with her impetuous response to Harry; she has to grow up and change to move on.

Her father takes off his reading glasses and taps his lips thoughtfully. 'You know how much fairness matters to me, Kathryn. Justice, if you like.' He sighs. 'Perhaps in the moment you made assumptions that weren't correct. Sibeal has recently lost her father and apparently a lover too, so she's a little off-course and out of sorts . . .'

Katy inhales to protest the words 'little' and 'out of sorts', but he holds up his palm. 'There's no doubt she's drinking too much and—'

'Which you indulged by taking her out for a boozy lunch.'

'One glass of Buck's Fizz to go with the food. She was down,

264

asked for a drink and I didn't want to be . . . unkind.'

'Being kind.' She can't help her sarcastic tone. 'Hmm, is that what you call it?'

'Sorry?' His brow crinkles, soon replaced by an appalled look. 'I wouldn't dream of showing anything other than fatherly concern for any of your friends, Kathryn.'

Though feeling a touch guilty that particular angst was unwarranted, she goes back to the point. 'Then you left a clearly drunk woman in charge of Milo.'

'I heard you moving upstairs and I had to rush off.' He nods. 'In hindsight I take responsibility for that. I shouldn't have put work first and I'm sorry.' He takes a measured breath. 'However . . .'

He's in full judge and jury mode, Katy thinks, as she glares. But she doesn't feel in the wrong about this; *he* wasn't there.

'To accuse her of child abduction, Kathryn. That was—'

'I didn't *accuse* her of anything, Dad. I called the police because she wouldn't leave and I was scared for my son. When they arrived I told them what had happened and it was Sibeal who was unreasonable. She became abusive towards them and they – of their own volition – decided to arrest her. I'm just a simple mum; I had, and have, no influence on what the authorities decide to do. *However* . . .' She grits her teeth. 'They were right to arrest her. Her behaviour was actually terrifying.'

'She was showing Milo the Volvo; she had no intention of—'

'So she says. Funny how she had to turn on the engine.'

'I understand you were deeply concerned. But for what it's worth, I believe her.'

Endeavouring to adopt his frustratingly passive stance, Katy takes a deep, steadying breath.

'So that's just normal, acceptable conduct in your court, is it, Dad? Even though it involved your own grandson? She's clearly unstable—'

'More unhappy than unstable, I'd say.'

'So, unhappiness makes people say crazy things? Let's take an example ... How about accusing their lover's wife of murder?'

She can't help feeling a tad triumphant at his obvious surprise. But the bloody rational mask soon returns. 'I'm no therapist, but Sibeal is deeply despondent and has been for a long time. Desperation from grief, even attention-seeking in that way isn't uncommon.' He spreads his hands. 'We see this type of behaviour getting caught up in the criminal justice system more often than we'd like.'

'And what about sneaking into a child's bedroom?'

'I very much doubt that's true, Kathryn. Wild talking, that's all.' He gives a long sigh. 'We all have our own ways of coping. Yours was to ...' He stops speaking and clears his throat. 'Well, anyway. Milo will be back any moment, so let's not ...'

'Go on, spit it out.'

'As I say, I'm no therapist.' He stands and stretches. 'It's time I got to it.'

Sudden rage pulses in Katy's temples. 'Mine was to what, Dad?'

'You chose to hide, Kathryn. And because you're so bright, you needed to justify it in here.' He taps his forehead. 'So you shut down and slept.' He smiles a wistful smile and puts his hands on her shoulders. 'I'm not saying it was a bad thing; it was perfectly understandable. Mum's death was appalling, a shock to us all. That was your way of coping.'

Through her cold anger she knows there's another 'but': *Five years has passed, Kathryn, yet you were still hiding and sleeping on Friday. So if anyone's to blame ...*

266

He looks at his watch. 'Noon already. I'd better get dressed, grab a sandwich for lunch and set out for the train around three. Don't forget I won't be back until Saturday this week.' At the door he turns. 'All I'm saying is think about it, Kathryn. When the police come for your full statement, maybe bear your ... Well, your own vulnerabilities in mind.'

Dumb from the unjustness of his comment, she doesn't move for a moment. Then she strides to the hallway. 'That isn't bloody fair, Dad. I never asked to be ill.'

He turns on the stairs, his expression defeated. 'I'm so sorry, love. You're quite right; you didn't.'

57

Sibeal

Sibeal wipes the wooden work surface one more time. She wishes it was glass or granite so her efforts would show. Gabe likes a clean house; he uses a spray then rubs it with a soft cloth until he sees his reflection. Usually she laughs or marks it with her handprint just to annoy him, but that's the old Sib, the one before Friday.

Good God, Friday. Her recall of what happened between Thursday and her arrest still hasn't fully returned, but that police station has. She could feel something strange happening within her body when she was handcuffed and in the back of the van, but her attempts to explain it when they arrived were met by the stony gaze of the desk sergeant. Once in the grimy cell, she knew for certain she was suffering a cardiac arrest. Then the walls caved in and crashed down on top of her. The next thing she saw was a pair of concerned eyes, which eventually turned into Hassan, the duty doctor.

Now winded out of nowhere again, she crouches down and lowers her head. Inhaling deeply, she waits for the anxiety to pass. In the 'moment' it's difficult to drag logic in, but she knows it's just a panic attack; she understands it will ebb, that she's not going to die. Ironic really: though debilitating and frightening, these episodes have saved her, the first one, at least.

'Try to relax by taking yourself to a happy place or moment or memory,' Hassan said once he'd helped her with 'stomach breathing' and she was able to function.

She tried, she really did, but nothing was there. The place, the moment *and* the memory would once have been Robin, but that was all smoke and mirrors. Looking back, it was obvious he'd been stringing a lie, but she'd been blinded by adoration. And need. Finally someone who'd accepted her as she was. Or so it had seemed.

'I can't,' she replied through streaming tears. 'I don't do happy; I never have.'

The doctor gazed, his hazel eyes kind. 'I don't believe that. I can see it in your face. There are people you love, your family and your friends . . .'

An image of Gabriel popped up in her mind. Her brother, her lovely loyal brother. Him frowning, her clowning, of course. Maybe not *happy* exactly, but so many loving places and moments and memories. She should have phoned him from the custody suite, but too alarmed and confused by her alien being, she had declined the sergeant's offer to call anyone.

Now studying the faded lilies on the window ledge, her pulse starts to slow. Her dusting and cleaning this morning was efficient and ruthless, but she couldn't bring herself to chuck them out. Pale and delicate, like their donor, little Kat. Her face had appeared immediately after Gabe's, but this time it *was* happiness. She'd been joyful with Kat during their short attachment; she liked her very much and cherished their friendship. But she'd casually lost it like everything else.

269

She straightens at the sound of the opening front door. Gabriel, at last. She gave him a brief résumé on the telephone when she returned to Brook House last night, but he said very little other than he'd come home today, so it was difficult to judge his mood. Apprehension prickling like a rash on her arms, she waits for him to appear but, Gabe being Gabe, he faffs in the hallway, so she rushes to him.

'Gabriel, finally! Where have you been?'

He pushes back his glasses. 'On the train, then the tram.'

'No, I mean … Never mind.' Her urgent tears surprise her. 'I'm so glad you're here.' Then, blowing her nose and grinning, 'Can you smell anything?'

'No …'

'Precisely! I've been opening windows, brushing up spiders, putting bleach in the loos.' She grabs his wrist and tugs him to the kitchen. 'Ta-da! Scrubbed or what? And even better …' She steps outside and opens the brown bin. 'Voila! Every last bottle I could find. Poured out and empty.'

Gabriel clears his throat. 'Well done, Sib. Dad would be proud, very proud.'

She puffs out another need to cry. 'You must be hungry. I've made sandwiches. You can choose.'

She hurries inside to the fridge, but Gabe speaks. 'In a minute. Let's talk first.'

He sits at the table and when she does likewise, he runs a finger over her knuckles. 'What happened, Sib? I know you told me some of it on the phone, but—'

'I was arrested and put in the back of a police van. I'm so ashamed, Gabe. They handcuffed me. Then, when I arrived at the station they took my fingerprints and DNA like a criminal.'

She smiles a wobbly smile. 'And my bloody shoes; thankfully I wasn't wearing a belt.' She pictures the weasel-faced officer who later questioned her without trying to hide his disdain. 'But apart from the pillock in charge, they were actually quite kind, especially the police doctor. He was nice; he listened. Then he gave me a lecture about the drinking, but I had already decided, so he didn't need to convince me it had to stop.'

Gabriel nods. 'But what about before then? You turned up at Crispin's on Thursday. What was that all about? I called you twenty times and you didn't pick up.' He motions in the direction of the neighbour's house. 'If it hadn't been for Winifred seeing you on Friday—'

'You actually called the old . . .' She stops herself short. Being *kinder* is another promise she's made to herself.

'I was worried. What option did I have? It's not acceptable behaviour to just ignore—'

'I know; you're right. I lost my mobile.' She takes a deep breath. Does the new Sibeal stretch to admitting about Robin, her grief, the teenage pregnancy and her obtuse stupidity? Maybe one day, but she's not ready yet. 'So, anyway, I stayed at Kat's . . .'

'OK, so you're at Katy's house on Thursday night. How did that fast forward to a police cell by the Friday, Sib?'

She covers her face. In truth, she doesn't know. The words 'loopy', 'deranged', 'delusional' and 'pathetic' stunned her, but when she saw Zoe's bump, the ground moved irrevocably. As though a huge crater had opened, she was in free-fall, not able to grasp anything solid as she tumbled.

She reverts to her brother. 'I can't remember everything. I was drunk; I'd been drinking on and off since Thursday morning. When the police arrived I resisted arrest and apparently slapped an officer. But none of that matters.' She slowly inhales, counts to four and exhales. 'What does matter is that I upset Kat. She misunderstood, but I scared her. She thought I was taking Milo, Gabe. I'd *never*, never do that. I think stupid things and they come out as words; I do stupid things when I'm pissed, but I'd never do anything like that. I would never hurt Kat's little boy; I'd never hurt her. You believe me, don't you?'

'Of course I do.'

The relief flows through her body like warm syrup. 'Thank you, Gabriel. Thank you.' She scrapes back her chair. 'Now I need to tell Kat.'

58

Katy

'Hurry up, Milo, or we'll be late,' Katy calls up the stairs.

Still trying to shake off last night's appalling dream, she catches her reflection in the hall mirror. She takes a step closer to study her face. Despite her pale skin, the bruise on her cheekbone no longer shows. Gone, like Harry. A stab of sadness hits, the same jab in her chest each time she looks at her phone. Bloody stupid hope; she wishes it'd leave.

She turns to Milo, his school bag stuffed with goodness-knows-what in one arm and the class teddy in the other. As last week's Star of the Week, he was allowed to bring the bear home, but today he must return it. How will he take handing it over to another child at morning assembly? Passing on the honours and allowing someone else to shine. She likes that, actually; it's good to let the clever kids have their turn, but not hog the limelight as she did at school. It's only fair and she's trying very hard to be fair.

Carrying Milo's lunch box, she walks briskly behind him as he charges ahead through the fragranced park. She wants to run too. Full of energy again, she wonders what to do with the yawning hours before her. They feel empty and without purpose. Sib and the house gave her that and there's definitely a void, but despite her attempts to be fair and the passage of five days, she's still angry with her. It isn't OK to get that drunk; it isn't OK to put a child in a car and turn on the engine; it isn't OK to scare someone like that. Whatever else is going on in her life, there is no excuse for such behaviour. And she still hears her shrill words about going into a bedroom and taking Robin's boy. Even if it isn't true, just saying it isn't normal.

As she reaches the school gates, she decides on a swim to give shape to the day. She'd like to try the open depths of Sale water park, to prove to herself she's not that person with vulnerabilities, but suppose Harry happened to be there? Sure, she wants 'hiding' to be a thing of the past, but her feelings about him are conflicted too. She's still dismayed that he dropped her without any fight, yet that nagging sensation has crept back. Something she saw or heard or just sensed that felt out of kilter. So even if he did get in touch, could she have faith in him?

'Katy! Hello!' A voice breaks through her mulling. It's Seher, Ollie's mum, pushing her newborn's pram. 'Are you going to the group on Friday?' She leans in conspiratorially. 'Don't tell anyone but I haven't read the book. No bloody time. But wildfire isn't going to stop me getting out for a few vinos. Have you read it?'

Katy nods. She has. It gave her focus on Monday and Tuesday, but even if she'd been busy, she'd have made time; God knows how she was invited to the slightly highbrow and exclusive village book club. She must have been in the right place at the right time.

Reprimanding herself for the self-deprecation, she comes back to her friend's wry laughter. 'You do know some people make notes and that we're supposed to score the novel out of . . .' She frowns at something beyond Katy's shoulder. 'Do you know that woman? I haven't seen her before but she's staring.'

Katy spins round. 'Where?'

Seher scans the pavement opposite. 'Oh, she's gone now. Maybe she works at the library. Sorry, despite maternity leave, I can't seem to leave the job behind; clocking anyone who looks out of place; old habits and all that.' She reverts to Katy. 'Hey, are you OK? I'm sure it was nothing. It's that gang of youths we need to worry about, not someone our age. Did you hear about them trashing the café in Abney? That's more than just antisocial behaviour now. And apparently they robbed an older guy, took his wallet and badly shook him up. They need to be caught and given a dose of their own medicine.' She looks at her watch. 'Oh sugar, look at the time. Could you see Ollie safely inside? I've got Lily's eight-week appointment at the doctors' and I don't want to be late.'

'Yes, sure thing.'

'What's a gang?' Milo asks.

He'd been chit-chatting to Ollie, so she didn't think he'd heard her conversation with Seher. 'Nothing for you to worry about.' She points to his teacher who has appeared at the door. 'I like Mrs Walshaw's new dress. It's time to go inside. Have fun!'

Taking Ollie's hand, he skips across the yard. It's a lovely sight, but Katy's mind is ticking with alarm. A woman staring. A *stranger* staring, presumably at her and Milo. She should've asked Seher what the woman looked like, what she wore, exactly where she stood. It can't be Sibeal, surely? She was told by the police to stay away as part of her bail conditions. If she's ignoring that, it's even more worrying. Then another stomach-churning notion: if she's been drinking at half past eight in the morning, who knows what else she's capable of?

59

Katy

Katy scoops up Poppy from the pavement and roots in her pocket for the keys. So used to seeing the Volvo parked outside the house, she doesn't register the movement at first. Then the driver's door swings open.

'What the hell?' she yells, the cat jumping from her arms. But it's Gabriel, only Gabriel, surrendering his hands.

'Sorry, I didn't mean to startle you.' His eyes rest on poor Poppy's spiked fur. 'Or the cat . . . Sorry.' He rakes back his hair. 'I should've called first, shouldn't I? I suppose I thought I'd just drive it away, sneak off, but once I arrived that seemed cowardly, so I decided to wait until you got back.'

Katy's heart slows. His face is pink and apologetic, but he did give her a shock, especially with thoughts of his sister prodding her mind. Oh God, she gave him a lift to Cheadle, didn't she; that makes sense of the stranger at school.

'How did you get here?' she demands. 'Where's Sibeal?'

'I came on the bus.' He frowns. 'I wouldn't dream of . . . she was in her bedroom, asleep, when I left.'

Katy sighs. She likes Gabriel; this awful situation isn't his fault. 'Sorry. I'm just a bit jumpy. Do you fancy coming in for a drink? I haven't got any plans for today, so I could do with some company. Oh, and we still have a set of your keys.'

Though clearly torn, he nods and follows her into the kitchen.

'Take a pew.'

'Thanks.'

She gestures to the coffee machine. 'Any preference?'

'You choose.'

Glancing at him from time to time, Katy busies herself at the counter. When she finally sits down, he gives a small jerk as though surprised that she's there.

'Smells good. Thank you.' He shakes himself back from his thoughts. 'Sorry about the delay in fetching the car. Sib hasn't been that good, she's been . . .' He takes a big breath. 'What she did was unforgivable, Katy. She has no excuses and I'm so sorry. But it was my fault too, I'm also responsible. I'm her older brother and we've lost both our parents, so it's down to me to be around when she needs me.'

'She's a grown woman, Gabriel, not a child.'

'I know, but still. On Thursday, without saying anything to me, she travelled all the way to Greenwich to find me—'

'Greenwich as in London?'

'Yes, that's where I stay. She was in a state, rambling and drunk. I heard her call me but a friend – Vivienne – took over and it all quietened down until she stormed out.' He takes off his glasses and rubs his cheeks. 'Sorry, I'm not explaining myself very well and I want to be honest. I *need* to be honest, just for once . . .'

Katy sips her coffee and watches the different emotions flit through his eyes – sorrow, apprehension and guilt, but finally determination.

278

'When I work in London, I stay with Crispin and Vivienne. Sib turned up demanding to see me, but Crispin tried to cover for me by saying I wasn't there. I was. I was in another bedroom with ... with a friend; it had been a very late night.' He shakes his head. 'Our friendship is in its infancy, so who can tell where it'll go ...' He clears his throat. 'The point is that Sib doesn't know about my ... I never told her. I didn't want to. Crispin and Vivienne appreciate this, so that's why they tried to steer her away ...'

'I see, but ...' So, Gabriel must be gay. It's not surprising; indeed, it seems obvious in retrospect. Yet why would Sib care? Of all people she's broad-minded. 'Why have you never told her?'

'It's complicated. Our relationship is complex. I don't think anyone else could or would understand it.' He picks up his cup, falls silent and drinks.

Assuming the conversation is over, Katy does likewise, but he abruptly speaks again, that resolve in his tone. 'I knew I was gay from being quite young. Puberty probably. Homosexuality was a sin, of course, so I buried it deeply, said my prayers like a good boy and tried to chat up girls. Unsuccessfully, thank God. Then at university I fell in love. Deeply and hopelessly in love. It was unrequited, inevitably.' His gaze fixes on hers. 'Have you ever suffered from that? It's painful, debilitating, like a lifelong illness because it never quite goes away. You think you've got a handle on it, then something happens, a look, a glance, a request ... Then the disease returns, stronger, more viral than ever before.'

He drifts for a while, but comes back to his story. 'So after two agonising years, I decided to tell Sib when I next came home. She was the only person in the world I could confide in, and at fifteen I thought she'd be old enough to understand, to help me throw off the shackles, the shame.' He laughs without humour. 'The timing was perfect; I asked him if he fancied staying at Brook House for a weekend and he said yes. Ridiculous though it was, I actually thought I was in with a chance. "I'm gay and this is the man that I love," I planned to say to Sib. But they fell for each other. Instant attraction, right before my eyes.'

The words are out of Katy's mouth before she can stop them. 'God, Robin, the boy's dad.' Then, quickly brushing over them, 'What did you do?'

'Is love between two people you adore more devastating or less?' he says, his voice far away. Then he seems to hear her question. 'Nothing, I did nothing. I stepped back into the casket. Became mummified, stuck in time. Spent my adult life looking to replicate that eighteen-year-old Adonis I fell in love with.' He smiles thinly. 'And he remained a close friend, so the infection . . . Well, it lay dormant until it didn't.'

Feeling hot, Katy nods. Thank God he didn't pick up on her mentioning Robin's name. 'It must have been tough.'

'It was; it really was . . .'

Clocking his glowing eyes, she knows there's a 'but'. Out of all this trauma, she's apparently become an expert in them. 'But? The guy you meet in London? You're smitten!'

He flushes. 'Is it that obvious? Maybe; I don't know.' He glances at her before looking away. 'With my . . . history . . . I want to be sure that it's the right thing for us both before we make it a more permanent thing. Only meeting occasionally is bloody frustrating at times, but on the other hand . . .' His expression transforming, he laughs. 'The excitement, the slow burn of anticipation is actually nice, like holding your breath.'

As though he's said too much, his grin falls and he stands.

'Sorry. I've been talking for ages, taking up your time. I'd better get back to . . . Thank you for listening. If you don't mind, please can you . . .'

'Keep it to myself. Of course. And any time you want to chat, feel free.' She catches his hand. 'I'm really happy for you, Gabe.'

'Cheers.'

She sees him to the door and watches him turn the Volvo around. Excitement and anticipation. She experienced them with Harry, all too fleetingly. With Sibeal too. She regrets her obdurate reaction to his honesty; it was impulsive, childish and embarrassing. But her? The thought of the stranger at school makes her itch with disquiet. No, Sibeal she can't trust; she doubts she ever will.

She smiles at Poppy rolling with pleasure on her back, then eventually notices that the Volvo is still stationary.

Gabriel winds down the window. 'You said "Robin, the boy's dad". What did you mean?'

60

Katy

Too agitated to go swimming, Katy locks up and heads for Bridget's house instead.

She was honest with Gabriel. How could she not be? The teenage Robin didn't have kids, so she had to come clean. She tried to backtrack by vaguely saying that Sib had got together with Robin at some point, but the damage was done.

'Apparently he made her promise not to tell you,' she finished lamely.

Confusion, anger and a strange resolve passed through Gabriel's features. But the clear hurt was the worst part; perhaps deep inside she'd meant to wound Sibeal by blurting it out, but she'd done it to him instead.

'I'm so sorry, Gabriel,' she said. 'I've upset you and that's completely out of order.'

She wasn't sure what response to expect, but his guffaw for several seconds wasn't it. When he stopped, he looked at her with the most peculiar expression. 'He never touched me,' he said. 'In all those years he never touched me.'

Now arriving at Bridget's door, she turns to her mission to be kind. She knows she's visiting to make herself feel better, but in truth she's missed their friendship and chats.

Murphy eagerly greets her, soon followed by his owner. 'Katy! This is a nice surprise. What are you doing here?'

'I thought I'd come for a cuppa. Is now a good time?'

Bridget holds out her arms. 'Of course. I can't remember when you were last here. Come in.' She pulls away after a moment and gives a strange laugh. 'Though next time give me a ring first. I might be up to no good!'

A sense of unease flutters in from her comment, but Katy brushes it away and focuses on two pairs of riveted eyes. Slightly regretting her decision to pop by, she considers what to say about the Sibeal debacle. She's already spoken out of turn to Gabriel and would hate Bridget to gossip.

Bridget duly fires in. 'I know she is, or should I say *was*, your new friend and I don't want to distress you but she was a little odd, don't you think? With Milo? The way she stared, did you notice?'

Oh God, Bridget is right; there was definitely an intensity about her when they first met. Has she been completely blind? Sucked into an inappropriate friendship through sheer loneliness? Put her son at risk?

Bridget continues to breathlessly rush. 'And Alexander always sees the best in people, doesn't he? He's still an attractive man who deserves to find happiness again one day, but a young thing like her making a beeline for him ... Well, one doesn't need a mathematician to work out what she's after.' She shudders. 'Andrew saw them outside the Albert on Friday. Said she was loud, flirtatious and all over him ...'

A jolt of alarm turns her stomach. She's been so hung up on

283

Milo's safety, she's sidelined Sibeal's astonishing behaviour before then: turning up at their house without warning, sleeping naked in her dad's bed. And all that blather about how charming and handsome he is.

She pictures his appalled expression when she hinted something inappropriate had happened between him and Sibeal. She's certain it didn't, but what's the expression? *There's no fool like an old fool* . . .

A ringing tone brings her back to Bridget's intense gaze. She pulls out her phone. It's Gabriel, oh God; she can't just ignore it.

'Hi, Gabe, is everything—'

'Look I'm sorry, so sorry. Please don't cut me off.'

Bloody hell, it's Sibeal.

'Can I see you or meet you somewhere? I know I'm not supposed to, but I really need to explain.'

Anger fires in. 'You can *explain* one thing. What the hell do you want with my father?'

'What? Nothing. I wanted to explain about Milo. I know I scared you but—'

Again, her tone steely. 'It isn't a difficult question, Sibeal. Why are you after my dad? A poor church mouse after his money?'

'I'm not after—'

'You were naked in his bloody bed!'

'Was I? I was so drunk; I can't honestly remember, Kat.'

Katy finds herself yelling. 'You turn up at your friend's home and somehow divest yourself of your clothes and you can't "honestly remember"? Oh dear, you were drunk, the universal excuse. Keep away from my son and my dad. You aren't normal, Sibeal; stay away.'

Her chest bursting with fury, she throws down the mobile

and covers her face. When her pulse finally settles, she turns to Bridget. But the intrigue and triumph she expects to see isn't there; her neat features are crumpled and sodden with tears.

61

Katy

Not bothered about wet hair today, Katy propels herself through the outdoor pool. She should be absorbing this perfect combination of sunshine and summer-fragranced breeze, she should be enjoying the suspension of all thoughts as she glides through the water. But her mind is in overdrive. Gabriel, bloody Bridget and inevitably Sibeal.

Bridget's behaviour yesterday was odd, to say the least. In the space of ten minutes she swung from gossipy to sobbing to wanting to bring back the guillotine to dispose of Sibeal, not so much for her appalling behaviour with Milo as her conduct with Dad, which 'beggared belief'. It was actually rich coming from Bridget the flirt and now a further day has passed, that aspect of the horrible situation has faded. Katy had been caught up in Bridget's indignation, and as angry as she still is, she knows Sibeal isn't a gold-digging type. The focus is back to Milo and his safety.

Flipping over for backstroke, she stares at the blue sky and tries to drag her musing to tomorrow's book club meeting. Will she come across as sufficiently erudite and pass muster? She'd normally have a giggle about it with her dad as he hates intellectual snobs, but he hasn't called or texted to check in this week, nor did he leave her the customary delicacy or two in the fridge to reheat.

His reasonable platitudes filter in, especially words such as fairness, grief, desperation. And the 'criminal justice system', a frightening notion for anyone. Is he right? Should she look more kindly on Sibeal and her troubles? Fate has dealt the Matthews siblings a poor hand in so many ways. Both their parents died and she lost the love of her life. Things seem to be looking up for lovely Gabriel, but they won't be complete without his sister.

She groans inwardly. The prickling agitation is still there, but ... Could she give Sib the benefit of the doubt? She doesn't *know* if she was near school yesterday and though the call was in breach of her police bail conditions, her voice did sound breathlessly apologetic. She'll never be friends with her again the trust has been shattered – but maybe she could put the frightening incident with Milo in the past and whitewash the rest of her drunken antics. And if she's really honest, isn't the usual intrigue – and strange pull – about the siblings still there? What on earth prompted Sibeal to travel all the way to London in search of Gabe? What did he mean by their complicated relationship that no one else could understand? And how about his bizarre comment about him and Robin never touching?

Though she's lost count of her lengths, her rumbling stomach's a sign that it's time to consume something. Pulling herself up with her arms, she hops out of the pool, perches on a lounger and pulls a banana from her bag. She's swum for at least half an hour and she isn't the least bit out of breath. She's actually as fit as a fiddle, she eats well, doesn't smoke and is sensible about alcohol. She tries her bloody hardest, which is why her dad's insinuation on Sunday made her incandescent with anger all day.

Of course he didn't mean she does it deliberately, but to suggest she's responsible for her fatigue, even at a subconscious level, is outrageous. He has no idea how debilitating it is, how many days and weeks she's missed out on enjoying her son, not to mention life in general.

The 'but' forming in her head, she swallows the too-soft fruit. But she did have a relapse on Friday. As though he might be standing at the very spot she saw him all those weeks ago, she glances around to the entrance. Was it connected to her fallout with Harry? Maybe triggered by emotional imbalance? And though it had no bearing on Sibeal's inexcusable actions, she *had* been incapacitated for hours. Nothing happened to Milo that time, thank God, but it could occur again. She can't rely on her dad and Bridget for ever. Besides, she wants to be independent at some point in her life. Sooner rather than later. A job, then a flat. Maybe one day a partner.

'Right!' she says aloud, wrapping herself in a towel.

The hardest part of a decision is making it, but made it she has. Not just one resolution, but two. Firstly she'll contact the police and say she misunderstood Sibeal's intentions on Friday. Secondly, she'll stop hiding her illness. No more occasional research on the internet or listening to Bridget's theories about it. She'll see a doctor, a psychologist, a psychiatrist, whatever it takes. Her dad's bound to know a specialist; she'll take it from there.

62

Sibeal

Sibeal pulls down the mirror flap and slips further down the seat of her SUV.

She pictures the patches of sweat seeping through the duty solicitor's shirt on Saturday.

'You're not to contact or go within a hundred metres of Kathryn Henry or her son. It's a condition of police bail, Ms Matthews. If you breach it, you'll be arrested and brought before the magistrates,' he said through the fog of body odour. 'Do you understand?' he added slowly, as though she was stupid.

'Yes. Does that mean I can get out of here?'

'It does, but if I could reiterate—'

'No need. Gotcha.'

Wondering how many metres there are from here to the primary school, she taps the steering wheel. She messed up with the bloody phone call with Kat on Wednesday. She only wanted to say sorry and explain what had happened with Milo and the car. She was caught on the hop with her questions about Alexander, so she gave the honest truth. She doesn't know how she ended up naked in his bed. Quite honestly she doesn't care; that person

289

was some woman sotted by grief and alcohol. It wasn't her, the real her.

What to do now to resolve this mess? She scratches her scalp with frustration. She doesn't even have a mobile to send Kat a message. Not that she would in the circumstances anyway. They're too long and complicated to type out; she wants to see her in person and tell the whole story. She needs to hold her, be held. She hates Kat, of all people, thinking badly of her. The imperative to sort it out pulsates in her head, has been throbbing in her thoughts since she sobered up.

Gabe was livid when she suggested visiting Kat on Sunday. 'For God's sake, Sibeal! You're an intelligent woman. What part of it don't you understand? It's a condition of bail. You *have* to stay away, whether you like it or not. Promise me now. Promise you won't go to Katy until you have permission. Promise me, Sib, or I'll leave here right now.'

So of course she had to give her word and he watched her like something between a hawk and a mother hen. But in fairness his role as jailer was outweighed by his care; he was sweet and attentive in general, but particularly good with the panic attacks, talking her through them with a low and calm voice. Then on Tuesday evening he announced he'd collect his car in the morning and drive up to Saxton for a couple of days.

'Is that OK, Sib? Will you be all right on your own?' Then, eyeballing her, 'I can trust you to stay away from Katy, can't I?'

'Do you think I'd risk going anywhere debilitated like this?' she replied breathlessly, knowing that would reassure him more than her Brownie guide promise.

Coming back to today's quandary, Sibeal watches the kids run joyously across the playground for a while. Darting, leaping and diving, some with a football, others for no apparent reason other than being five or six years old and alive. One of them might be Milo, but she'd struggle to pick him out. Boys his age all look the same from a distance – unless they're with their pregnant mum, of course. But she's not thinking about that any more. She's shelved all those cruel remarks; she's stopped trying to work out who Robin was really in love with. It's Kat she needs to see; she was reckless loitering outside the library on Wednesday morning. Kat alone is the thing, not surrounded by other parents and people.

Craning her neck, she spots the school door. Children are spilling out like skittles and . . . bingo, there's Kat stepping into view and holding out her hand to Milo. She's not stopping to chat with other mums today, but leaving the gate out of her view.

Fumbling as fast as her stiff fingers will allow, Sibeal presses the ignition, puts the car into gear and takes a left turning. Oh hell, it's a dead end. Trying not to mount the kerb near school premises like she did last Thursday, she carefully turns around. Her heart loud in her ears, she indicates and drives up to the high street.

Alert to vehicles and the spill of pupils everywhere, she steadies her speed past the shops. Though a lump clogs her throat and her chest starts to ache, she continues to navigate the traffic, her eyes scanning the pavements through her clammy agitation.

The lights are on red when she reaches the junction, so she lowers her head and tries to steady her rapid, shallow respiration. When she looks again, they're there, Milo skipping and chatting a few metres ahead. She accelerates towards them, but her heart feels so swollen, it might burst from her chest. And her hands are numb; her tongue suddenly too big for her mouth. Sheer

291

panic taking over, she swerves to the pavement and comes to a shuddering stop.

Vaguely aware of the blare of a horn, she presses her forehead against the steering wheel and tries to find her internal voice: *it's just an attack; it will pass; simply breathe, Sibeal, breathe; a long, slow breath in through your nose. Hold it, count to four . . .*

But the exhale is cut short by the click of the door. A breeze rushes in with Kat's angry face.

'What the hell are you doing? I told you to stay away.' She stares for a beat, then narrows her eyes. 'It was you on Wednesday, wasn't it? It's called stalking, Sibeal.' Her tone laced with contempt, she continues to speak. 'Look at you, you're drunk and out of control again. You disgust me.' She glances at Milo by the wall. 'What's wrong with you?' she hisses. 'What decent person drives a car in your state? Children are walking home from school, for God's sake.'

She steps away and looks to the sky. Then she sighs and comes back. 'Because I like your brother, I won't report you today, but there won't be a next time. Do you understand? I *will* go to the police and have you locked up. Now park the car properly, get a fucking taxi and go home.'

63

Katy

Katy watches Bridget chase Milo around the kitchen island, attempting to recover her shoe. This morning she'd felt, well, not exactly excited about the book group meeting, but chirpy she had a project, pleased she was actually leaving the house on a Friday night like other people her age. But she's flagged since seeing Sibeal. Not the worrying kind of exhausted, but emotionally spent.

Bloody highs and lows. She was so chuffed with her positive attitude and firm decision to do something about her illness after her long swim yesterday. When she got home she savagely pruned the bushes around the driveway to make way for a car. Because she promised herself that too: driving again would give her more freedom, allow her to extend her narrow horizons. She chatted to passing neighbours, asked Hazel if she could join her for a run one day, cuddled Pam's new granddaughter and got an invitation to Marita's 'house extension party'. She clocked Sandra pulling out her bins, so she popped over to ask how the Thursday group was going and returned ten minutes later with news of a new handsome man in her life and a slice of apple frangipane tart.

A normal, regular existence, and so heartwarming.

Then this afternoon happened: the high of watching Milo skip home; listening to him chat about his new friend – a boy with 'special' trainers who'd had his 'first legs chopped off' because he'd had 'tonsillitis' – and feeling so very grateful that Milo's hearing disability hadn't been worse. Then the low: turning to the piercing sound of a car horn, seeing the SUV skew against the pavement. Then, seconds later, realising whose car it was.

The image of Sibeal, her skin pallid and sweaty, flies in again. She had clearly been following her and Milo, but Katy's anger was stronger than her alarm. She wanted to yell; she wanted to slap her ex-friend's drunken, confused face. But her five-year-old was watching; people had stopped outside the post office to stare. So she drew on her dad's words and sought out Gabriel's hopeful smile in her head. Charity and kindness; steps forward, not back. She'd overlook it today, but there wouldn't be a next time.

Her eyes slide to Bridget. She doesn't quite know why but she hasn't mentioned the shocking incident to her. And yet . . . Sibeal was drunk at half past three in the afternoon and driving a car. Did she do the right thing by not calling the police? She turns to Milo, scoops him up and breathes in his soapy smell. God, she hopes so; she really does.

'Don't get too giddy. It'll be bedtime very soon,' she says to him. 'Are you going to read Bridget a story?'

'Like I do with Grandad?'

'Exactly.'

He scrunches his face. 'So, what will you be doing?'

'Same as you. Talking about a book! This one is what they call a "modern classic".'

She shows him the cover. During her school holidays she'd

devour at least a couple of novels each week. Back then she preferred to read than congregate with her friends in Bruntwood Park. But was that really true? Or was it just to see the delight on her dad's face when she'd finished yet another tome?

Shaking the thought away, she comes back to Bridget's inquisitive gaze.

'So where did you say this meeting was?' she asks.

Katy frowns at her customary casual yet information-gathering question. She didn't and she doesn't need to give anyone chapter and verse like a child. But in fairness, it was good of her to fill in for Alexander. 'Off Stockport Road, towards Cheadle Heath.' Bridget lifts her eyebrows pointedly and takes a breath to make a comment about the area, or perhaps the long walk there, so Katy quickly speaks again. 'Does seven thirty mean that time on the dot? Or does it really mean eight?'

She doesn't want to be the first to arrive, yet it wouldn't do to be late. And what wine should she take? Expensive or plonk? But she pushes her old meekness away. She's off out at night on her own to meet people, some of whom might be strangers, to voice an opinion, join a debate. She's going way out of her comfort zone but that's a good thing.

'Actually,' she says, 'I don't really care. This is the new me, Bridget. Are you impressed?'

64

Katy

The book club chatter still pulsating in her head, Katy slings her bag across her chest and closes the gate of the white-rendered semi. Though she went to the private primary at her end of the village, she used to have a friend from ballet who lived around here. When she was a bit older and allowed to walk alone, she found a shorter route to her house.

Remembering it took her past Milo's school, she heads in that direction and listens to the echo of her own footsteps. It's only an hour and a half until midsummer's day, but there's a nip in the air. Not that she needs to don her jacket just yet; Adele and Jo had their open fire lit. It was soothing, if a little strange, to listen to the crackle and hiss of burning wood in summer, but the front room was like a furnace. She chuckles to herself. Perhaps that's why she's slightly drunk; maybe she guzzled the frequently proffered red to quench her thirst. Ha! Hardly an excuse, but the headiness feels pleasant and it's nice to walk the muffled streets of Cheadle and admire the blue sky, albeit a deep, moody Prussian with a hint of orange now.

Certain Bridget will demand the lowdown on the attendees,

the conversation, the colour of the bathroom and the grape of the wine, Katy contemplates the evening as she walks. It was good; a bickering couple dominated the discussion, so it took a little time to get a word in, but once she did, her opinion flowed, and she was even a touch controversial about passages in the book which she considered to be benevolent sexism. As for meeting new people, answering their polite questions was almost effortless, a huge revelation of how easy life can be without crippling anxiety.

Detecting the tang of barbecued meat, she ambles past a row of pretty terraced cottages. An almost imperceptible movement catches her eye, so she stills. She's clearly not the only one to smell chicken. Bridget considers urban foxes to be a nuisance and says they should be shot, but Katy loves the occasional glimpse. 'Kathryn, quickly, a fox! They may be a bit wily, but aren't they a sight for sore eyes,' her dad used to say. A lucky sighting, like a black cat crossing the road. She does it with Milo. Passing down family traditions; she likes that.

Once she's given the animal safe passage, she inhales a different aroma, this time the sweet citrus scent of honeysuckle. A happy holiday redolence, somehow. It reminds her of the vacation her dad was researching. If he did get around to booking it, he hasn't said so, but surprises of that kind aren't unheard of. Or perhaps he's still a little miffed about her reporting Sibeal. Yet her instinct turned out to be correct; her SUV could have so easily mounted the pavement and injured someone this afternoon. Even Mr Fair and Reasonable wouldn't condone that.

A jolt of surprise strikes as she takes in her bearings. Though in the opposite direction to where she's headed, Harry's house is a stone's throw away. How perfect would it be to let herself in the front door, pad up the stairs and slip into his bed. She still has the key to his house somewhere in her bedroom, but not, it would seem, to his heart.

Disappointment surges again. She truly thought he liked her. She fully expected him to call or text and apologise profusely, but people are not what they seem, she now knows. God, she's had a steep learning curve about *that* the past week.

Her head down, she trots along the tree-lined road until the blue railings of her son's playground come into sight. As she approaches, a shiver passes through her. It's so bright and effervescent during the day, but its dark emptiness seems ghostly tonight. Sensing a loose trainer, she bends down to tie the lace, but when she straightens, she's not alone.

Their black hoods up, four boys are sauntering towards her. No, not boys, they're broader and taller than that. *Youths*, as Seher put it, oh God. Breath stuck in her chest, she quickly considers what to do. Turn back? But there's only an empty school behind her. It's better to head for the high street as confidently as she can muster. The bars and pubs will still be open, she can holler for help. And anyway, despite their steady gazes, who says they mean her any harm?

The hammer in her chest almost painful, she looks at the pavement and continues her journey. Like an automatic door, they split in the centre and allow her to pass, but just as she exhales, the sound of their footsteps stops.

'Nice watch,' she hears. 'Let's have a look, then.'

Though she knows she should sprint, her feet are glued to the ground. Then the tallest skips ahead to face her. Dead-eyed, he stares. 'Didn't you hear what he said? Show him your watch.' He pulls his mobile from his pocket and dangles it. When it catches the light, it's not a phone, but a knife.

Fear icy on her skin, Katy turns to the others. His hands in his joggers, the chubby one swaggers. 'Let's look then.'

Without thinking, she covers the Omega with her palm. 'It was my mum's,' she finds herself croaking.

'Is she as hot as you?' He grins. 'Two MILFS in one go. Nice. Come on then, let's see it.'

Yelping at the unexpected prod in her back, she stumbles towards the leering youth. He grabs her wrist and peers at the jewellery. 'Gold. Very nice. Think I'll have that for my—'

A pair of arms rocket in, bulldozing him over.

'Leave her alone and fuck off.' Then louder, 'Go on, fuck off!'

Dumbfounded, Katy stares at her saviour. Using her coat like a matador, Sibeal swipes at the two youths who had been watching. 'That's right,' she shouts as they scuttle away. 'Fuck off home, you big babies. Go and pick on someone your own size.'

As the boy on the pavement scrabbles up and backs off, a car screeches to a halt and two men tumble out. Yelling instructions, they close in on the remaining youth. His face swamped with sheer panic, he snaps around from them to Katy. Then he brandishes his knife and charges towards her.

Certain she'll never see Milo again, she scrunches her eyes. A split second later, she's thudded to the ground. Winded from shock and the impact of the fall, it takes moments to realise that Sibeal is half covering her body, that she must have pushed her from harm's way and fallen with her. Other noises filter through the rushing sound in her ears; the thud of car doors and shouting, heavy footfall and scuffling. Almost laughing at this ridiculous situation, she finally takes a breath to say something to her rescuer. But a warm sticky liquid is spreading on her arms.

The old nightmare descending, she freezes for a beat. Blood;

she knows it's blood. But clarity sets in, swiftly, suddenly. It's Sibeal's, not hers; she can feel the vibration of her chest, the rapid wheezing against her neck.

'Sib? God, Sib. Are you OK?'

Fearful of hurting her, she carefully lifts Sibeal's arm and disentangles herself from her heavy legs. Then someone speaks, so she turns. Blonde hair, middle parting and a long fringe; the woman looks remarkably like her mother.

Does this feel right? What is your gut telling you, darling?

She blinks Elke away. 'Sorry?' she asks her.

'I said it's fine; they've got him.' Then she frowns. 'Are you injured?'

Blood, the brightest red blood. 'No.' The enormity of what has happened hits her. 'It's not me, it's my friend. I think she's been stabbed. Someone needs to call an ambulance.'

A man is already kneeling by Sibeal's side. Bizarrely his chest is naked, but when Katy focuses, he's pressing his T-shirt to her side.

'The police and paramedics are on their way. Fifteen minutes, tops, they said.'

Breathing deeply, Katy nods. Thank God for that. Then the timescale strikes. Fifteen minutes? *Fifteen* long minutes? Hyperventilating and staring blankly, Sibeal's face is drained of all colour and blood seems to be everywhere.

Katy reaches for her bag and pulls out her mobile. Too shaky to do it herself, she gives it to the Elke woman. 'Call Harry, he's a doctor. He lives just near here.'

65

Katy

The noises and smells of A&E surrounding her, Katy checks her mobile again. She's texted and called Gabriel, but there's still no reply. God, she hopes it's simply him turning his phone off for the night rather than connected to their last conversation when she gave away her friend's secret. Her friend who might have saved her life this evening . . .

She shifts in the hard chair and yawns yet again. She's incredibly tired, but she couldn't nap even if she tried. Is Sibeal OK? The last she heard they were taking her in for surgery. Suppose a vital organ has been damaged? Suppose she's lost too much blood? Suppose she doesn't wake up from the anaesthetic? The thought of her death is unbearable.

The events of this evening play again in her head. It all happened so quickly. One moment she was tying her trainer lace, the next a glint of metal, then Harry was there wearing surgical gloves, cutting Sib's clothes and exposing a gash that was literally spitting out blood. He soon covered it with a large gauze pad, squeezed the top of her leg with one hand and pressed the dressing with the other. But by then the damage to

Katy's psyche was done. The mental image will be etched on her retina for ever.

Harry. It must have been only a few minutes until she heard his footfall and murmuring behind her, but it felt like an age. Remembering his 'please give me space' in the pub, she reluctantly released Sib's hand and moved back to the pavement.

'I'm Dr Harrison,' he said to Sibeal. 'You're doing really well. An ambulance is on its way with oxygen and pain relief, but I'm just going to have a look at your wound first if that's OK.'

Until then she didn't realise 'Harry' was a nickname. So perhaps she never knew him at all. Perhaps he was right to barely give her a second glance, even when the paramedics arrived. Almost drifting off with fatigue, she waited for an acknowledgement, a diagnosis or *something*, but it was only when Sibeal was settled and strapped on a stretcher that he finally turned, his eyes impersonal. 'I'm assuming you'd like to go with her?' he asked.

She nodded dumbly.

'Right, then I'm off home,' he replied.

'Katy?'

A palm on her shoulder brings Katy back from groggy sleep to the emergency waiting room. She squints at the person addressing her. His hair disarrayed, it's Harry, of all people. But the smatter of pleasure is replaced with alarm. Something dreadful has happened to Sibeal. That's why they've sent him to break the news.

'Oh God, Sibeal. She's—'

'She's fine, Katy, they've just—'

'She won't die?'

He sits next to her. 'No, she won't. She's back from surgery and

302

asleep on a ward. The artery and wound repair was successful; they stopped the bleed, so she isn't in any danger.'

The relief shuddering through her, Katy rubs her sore eyes. 'Thank God. I was so worried. I can't believe I fell asleep.' She glances at her watch, Elke's watch that caused so much trouble. 'How come you're here at this time? You said you were going home.'

'I'd had a thirteen-hour shift and needed to get back in the sack, so—'

'Sorry! There was so much blood. I was petrified the ambulance might not arrive in time. I immediately thought of you.' She covers her face, the loop of trauma tumbling back. 'God, poor Sib. I feel so bad for her. Immensely grateful too. If she hadn't lunged between us, it would've been me.'

'Christ? Really?'

She nods. 'But I'm so sorry about waking you up. I didn't think—'

'It's fine; you did the right thing. It was arterial; the blood loss could have been dangerous.'

She glances at his weary, drawn face. 'So what happened to getting back in the sack?'

He shrugs and smiles a small smile. 'Who needs sleep anyway?' Then he takes a quick breath. 'I did get into bed, actually. But you were in my thoughts, especially the last time you were in A&E. I thought it might be . . . difficult for you.'

Caught short by his comment and thoughtfulness, she interrupts quickly. 'More concerned about poor Sib; terrified, actually – so much blood and so quickly. I've been trying to contact her brother but no luck so far.'

Did the woman who helped really look like her mum? She steels herself. 'About that day I bolted from your—'

'It's fine, I understand.' He stands up. 'Right, I'll get off. Good luck with tracking down the brother.' He steps away, then turns back. 'How have you been? I mean, apart from tonight and your fall.'

She feels herself flush from the intensity of his gaze; she didn't know about the graze on her cheek until she went to the ladies'. But he doesn't mean that and it's an opening to ask.

'I'd actually like to get treatment for my ... my illness. You know, by a specialist of some sort. A psychiatrist, for example.'

'Your GP surgery is the best start, Katy. Someone young and clued up. There's a doctor called Janet who recently joined Darley Medical ...' His cheeks colour. 'Sorry, I should remember her surname, but she's sharp and a good listener. She'll probably suggest you keep a diary.' He fluffs his hair. 'I saw her about the old ankle; had to get referred for an X-ray. Madness, really.'

He pulls his car keys from his pocket and studies them for a moment. 'Do you want a lift home? Your friend will probably sleep until morning. She'll be pretty sore when she wakes, but she's in good hands.'

Katy pauses for a beat. God, he's so very handsome. How nice would it be to rekindle their friendship, to sleep in his 'sack' together. And Bridget promised to stay over with Milo 'for as long as it takes', so this is the perfect opportunity. But Sibeal took a bullet for her tonight. Sure, she must have been following her again, which needs to be addressed, but the debt is there and she has to track down Gabriel.

'I think I'd better stay.' Though she longs to kiss him, she holds out her hand. 'Thank you for everything you did for Sibeal. And for me. You've been a really great friend.'

304

66

Sibeal

Sibeal squints at the hospital clock. Only thirty minutes has passed since she last looked, but it feels as though she's been trying to rouse herself for hours. With an effort she turns to the chair next to her cot-like bed. Kat's there, still asleep. Now that it's lighter she can see the nasty graze on her face more clearly. She resembles Janus. One half looks as though it has been finely grated, the other is as pale and perfect as ever.

As though reading her mind, Kat's eyes flick open, blue and concerned. 'You're awake!' she says, straightening up. She pats her mouth. 'How lovely – dribble. I must have nodded off.'

It's a struggle to unstick her tongue. 'Your cheek, does it hurt?' Sibeal asks through the wooziness.

'You've been stabbed and sewn up and you ask me about a scratch.' The smile falls from her lips. 'Are you OK? Shall I call a nurse?'

A wave of nausea recedes. 'Maybe some water . . .'

'Sure, can you hitch up a little? Should I help?'

Sibeal slowly and painfully inches up the mattress. Apparently held in by a strip of sellotape, there's a cannula in the back of her hand and what she assumes is an identity tag. 'Sibeal Matthews', it should say, but she's not sure who that person is any more. She's turned into this meek, fragile and stupefied person, firstly in her head, and now in her body too. From top to toe she feels leaden, sore and achy, but her right hip and buttock area sizzle like sausages in a pan.

Kat proffers her a plastic cup with a spout.

'Ta,' Sibeal says. She tries to remove the lid, but her hands have no strength. 'Can you?' she asks her. 'I'm so thirsty; I need a proper drink.'

A proper drink; a proper drink. So many aspects of her life have gone away because of that. That's why she was in Cheadle last night. She needed to tell Kat it was a thing of the past; that she hadn't been boozing earlier. She could tell her now, but the effort is too huge.

The water spills on her gown as she gulps it. 'Ah, maybe that's why it's a baby's beaker,' she manages. Her voice is slurred and it's even too much to raise her eyebrows. 'Maybe they'll give me a bib too if I'm lucky.'

Kat gently dabs her chin and her chest with a tissue. 'You need to take it easy, Sib.' She wipes a tear from her eye. 'Just sleep and get better. Please. I'll be here; everything's fine.'

Gluey oblivion drags her down. 'I wasn't drunk ...' she mutters, giving in.

67

Sibeal

The clatter of a trolley brings Sibeal around again. Kat stands to one side and a uniformed woman bustles over. 'You're finally awake then,' she says. 'Is it OK to call you Sibeal?'

Sibeal considers saying no, then remembers she isn't the boss of her mind or her limbs, let alone anything else. 'Sure.'

The nurse drags a curtain around them. 'Let me have a little gander at the damage, then you can have something to eat.'

Without a great deal of TLC, she turns Sibeal on her side, peels back the gauze plaster and peers at the wound. Seeming to be satisfied, she opens a sterile packet and firmly pads the stitches with a damp wipe. The sizzle increases to a sputter and crackle.

The woman briskly re-dresses the wound, looks at her watch and jots notes on a chart. 'Looking good. Pain relief?' she asks.

'How very kind,' Sib replies, hoping the sarcasm hits home. She holds out her palm for the pills, but the nurse rolls her eyes.

'Intravenously.' She hands her something resembling a portable battery charger. 'Press this button if you need a top-up. It's just for the immediate post-operative period, so don't get too used to it.'

When she's gone, Sibeal gingerly straightens and calls for Kat.

'Well, she was a veritable Nurse Ratched,' she says when her friend's sore-looking face appears. 'Because I'm a stabbing victim, I suppose. She'll think I'm a criminal. Perhaps even a member of the baby gang myself.'

Kat proffers a mug of tea. 'Poor you. A midwife was like that after Milo was born. She shoved me on a toilet seat and wouldn't let me out until I'd done a pee in something that resembled a cardboard hat.'

Though Sibeal smiles at Kat's comment, she clocked her eyes sliding away. Sibeal Matthews the criminal, the elephant in the room. Admittedly she's 'not normal' as Kat put it, and the drinking has to permanently stop, but she didn't set out to harm her or Milo.

She sips the warm drink, yet her throat feels so dry. She swallows again. 'Your Milo likes cars; Volvos in particular, it seems. He knew all about turbos and power steering and—'

Kat puts a soft hand on hers. 'I know.'

Her nose stings at her kindness. 'I had no intention of taking him, Kat. He wanted to sit in the car. I have no idea why I turned on the engine.'

A soft squeeze again. 'I know, Sib. It's fine.'

She takes a big gulp of air to stop the stupid tears, but they flow all the same. 'And yesterday afternoon ... You thought I was drunk in the car but I wasn't. I just wanted to see you and explain about what had happened with Milo. I know I frightened you and I'm so sorry for that, but I'd never do anything to hurt you or him.' Her heart races and thumps and thuds in her chest. 'I hadn't been drinking, Kat. Really. I haven't had a drop of alcohol since Friday.'

She wills Kat to believe her, but a shadow of doubt passes through her neat features. Fuck, it's embarrassing, but she needs to come clean.

She roughly wipes her cheeks and blows her nose on green tissue. 'OK.' Her voice emerges stiff and staccato. 'In the police cell on Friday, I thought I was having a heart attack. Fainted and ended up on the floor. Long story short, it was a panic attack. Felt a complete fool when it passed. Been having them since. You know, the . . . episodes.'

Realisation dawns on Kat's face. 'That's what happened yesterday?' She slaps her palm to her mouth. 'God, I'm sorry, I didn't know.' She flushes deeply. 'How awful of me . . . so horribly selfish. I understand how terrifying they are because I have them too . . .' She pauses and corrects herself. 'Or at least I had them until recently. I'm so sorry, Sib. I really had no idea.'

The tears roll again. 'Not your fault.'

Kat plays with the edge of her blood-crusted blouse. 'It is in a way; if I hadn't called the police, you wouldn't have been there in the first place.'

'No, Kat. I deserved to be in one. I'd been drinking on and off all day. I shouldn't have been behind the wheel of a car, not even when I got up on Thursday. I'd been throwing back whisky at home in the early hours. Even talking about it makes me feel sick.' Another huge wave of fatigue crashes in. She laughs weakly. 'There's irony for you. It's like the stuff they give alkies. Di-di-disulfiram. Not that I can say it.'

'Talking of alkies . . .' Kat takes a big breath. 'You do know that amount of alcohol isn't – well – normal, and that you need to address it before I can trust you with—'

'I know, Milo. I promise.' As though there are pennies on her eyes, she can't keep them open. Kat catches her mug as it spills. 'So tired, so very . . .'

68

Katy

Guilt fizzes in Katy's chest. Panic attacks. It's as though she's passed hers on to Sib through her mean, vindictive thoughts or bad karma. She was blind to Sib's yesterday, yet the signs were all there. She should have seen them and helped rather than give her friend a mouthful of abuse. She pushes the dry hospital sandwich away. She's nibbled all the good bits and left the rest. Bad Kathryn! It was a house rule growing up: remember the starving children in the world; always finish what's on one's plate. As well as various other directives passed down from the paternal grandad she never met.

'The crusts will make the hair grow on your chest. Or something along those lines, eh, Alexon?' her mum would say, teasing her dad. 'What is it with the British and their old wives' tales?' She'd kiss him and chuckle. 'I may be a wife, but I for one never intend to get old!'

Katy smiles at the memory. The mental picture of her mother's injuries and suffering blocked this and others out for too long. Though Elke didn't get old, did she? Harry tried and failed to save her. How must that feel? She'd like to know the answer;

she'd like to ask him all sorts of questions, but she couldn't desert Sibeal. Besides, his offer might have simply been for a lift. He definitely blushed when he mentioned Dr Janet ... Oh God, is that why he hasn't been in touch? Has he found someone new?

The uncomfortable notion is replaced with another: Gabriel. Why hasn't he called back? Well, she knows the answer to that. *Is love between two people you adore more devastating or less?* And what about Sibeal – is her inability to stay awake for more than five minutes the usual consequence of surgery?

As one might do in a library, Katy lowers her voice at the nurses' station. 'Sibeal Matthews in the corner bed ... Is it normal to sleep for so long after an operation?'

'It varies. Don't worry, we're keeping an eye on her. The anaesthetic generally wears off after a couple of hours, but some people suffer lingering effects. The anaesthetist will come in later. Has she had one before?'

'Oh, I've no idea. We're fairly new friends ...'

A new friend she seems to have known for years, she muses, as she retakes her seat. Clearly that's what happens when you don't have any others. Thank God some good has come out of this terrible episode – she's reconnected with Sib and now understands what happened after school yesterday.

Time passes and eventually Sibeal opens her eyes. They take a moment to acclimatise. 'I dropped off again, didn't I?' she asks with a croaky voice. 'It's worse than a bloody hangover, which is particularly droll.'

'The nurse said it might be the effect of the anaesthetic.' She hands over the water. 'Have you had one before?'

'No.' Then, 'Actually, yes.' She flexes her fingers. 'I had an operation on this when I was little. My dominant hand, so I had to learn to do things with my right. You'd think righting the wrong of being left-handed would have pleased her, but it didn't.' She sits up abruptly, then hisses in pain. 'Where's Gabriel?'

'I've left him a few messages and texts,' Katy replies, hoping her deep blush isn't obvious. 'But I wasn't too specific; I didn't want to alarm him, so it's probably my fault that he hasn't responded yet.'

'He turns his mobile on silent when he's working.' Sibeal arches an eyebrow. 'Not that he'll have been tutoring all night.'

'Oh right,' Katy says, stumped for another reply.

'Sometimes I worry about him. He goes incommunicado, underground almost, and my fear is that he'll get into …' She appears to change her mind. 'He's gay, of course. But I don't let on that I know because he can't face it, especially not in Dad's house.' She glances at Katy. 'That's where Saint Imelda lives. She might hear. Can you imagine how she'll react? The *shame*, to be sure! Not that she'll say it to his face; she'll hold it in until bedtime, then drink Irish whiskey like a fish and hiss her hatred out.'

Her arms a little goosebumped, Katy falls silent. So, Sib knows about Gabe's sexuality. And the strange way she refers to her mum in the present tense.

'She isn't really there, of course. Though sometimes …' She sighs, looks at Katy and nods. 'The attic room. When she wasn't being a saint, she pretty much lived there. I was never allowed in, which of course made my longing even worse. I'd get home from school and sit outside the door, thinking up ruses so she'd open it. Look what I've learned, made, drawn, baked … None of those worked, so I'd feign illness, deliberately graze my knee, steal something from the sweet shop, argue with Gabe. I tried turning the knob, of course, but it was always locked. "Go downstairs,

Sibeal. I'll be there in a minute." Giving herself time to brush her hair, suck a Polo mint, spray scent and look respectable, I expect.'

Clearly far away, she pauses for a while. 'Anyway, when I was eleven, I came home and did the usual. I can't tell you how delighted I was to find it unlocked. I knew she'd done it for Gabriel's sixteenth birthday, but that didn't matter. I'd been finally let in! I was hit with a blast of perfume and alcohol and cigarette smoke, but wild horses wouldn't have stopped me stepping over the threshold.' She gestures to the window. 'Though the skylight lit her up, her face was bulging so badly, for stupid moments I didn't twig it was her. She was hanging from a wooden beam, clearly dead.' She smiles wryly. 'So I know, I really do know she's no longer there.'

69

Katy

The Tuesday morning sunshine already warm on their backs, Katy holds Milo's hand tightly and heads to his school. She's walked past 'the spot' twice now and so far she's been fine. She's not sure what she expected; not exactly flashes of red blood or post-traumatic stress, but a reaction of some kind, or at least one bigger than the blend of indignation and relief she feels. What the hell are the parents of those youths doing to make them turn into overgrown bullies wielding knives? Because that's where it starts. With the bloody mums and dads. Every time she thinks of Sibeal's tragic tale, it brings tears to her eyes. No wonder she's needy and strange at times. Katy doesn't need to be a psychologist to see that Sib's brusque exterior hides trauma and loneliness. She wasn't just brutally abandoned by her mother at eleven; she was rejected from the moment she was born. How that must feel, she has no idea. Her parents were devoted to her and each other; she was cosseted, spoilt and loved all her childhood. Perhaps that's why the shock of the stabbing incident hasn't set in; she has the support network of Bridget, her dad and even little Milo.

He now breaks free and skips through the gate. Although she hasn't spelt out in detail what happened with the stabbing, he seems to know they're both minor celebrities this week. A group from his class immediately surrounded him with eager faces and questions on Monday. Their mums were more circumspect; they're still glancing at her damaged cheek with wide eyes today, but it really doesn't bother her. If they ask, she'll tell them what happened and enjoy the attention.

'All's well that ends well,' as her dad said when she arrived home late on Saturday. It could have been so horribly different, but it wasn't and there's no point going there. Everything has worked out just fine: Gabriel finally got in touch, Sibeal's safe in hospital and Katy's made peace with her dad.

Though they didn't ever officially 'fall out', in retrospect he was wholly right about looking beyond the face of Sibeal's behaviour that day. Katy's fears for Milo were justified at the time, but the 'criminal justice system', as he put it, is most certainly not what Sibeal needs to move forward, to help with her childhood issues and grief, and not least tackle her excessive reliance on alcohol. So she duly contacted the police officer who'd given her a business card and explained she'd been drowsy and anxious, that she hadn't yet woken up properly and therefore overreacted when she saw Sibeal in the Volvo with Milo.

A waft of guilt blows in. Sensing Milo's quietness since the driveway spat, she decided to have a little chat with him about it.

'You know when me and Sibeal had that argument ...' she started.

His cheeks burning, he dropped his head. 'Was it my fault?' he muttered.

'No, of course not! Why would you think that, love?'

'Because I asked to sit in the Volvo.' He looked at Katy with watery eyes. 'Sibby is fun; I didn't mean to get her into trouble . . .'

Yet Katy's feelings of culpability are mixed with resolve. Her son clearly likes Sib – as does she – and she wants them to have a future. But a zero-tolerance guarantee about alcohol would have to be in place.

As for Bridget, her *friend* Bridget, Katy popped into see her yesterday. So tiny physically, but with a big heart. She didn't hold back the hugs or the tears.

'I said unkind things about your friend and now I feel dreadful. The poor girl. And to think it could have been you, Katy. I'm so pleased you're safe.' She blew her nose like a trumpet. 'I know Alexander pays me to look after you and Milo, but I love you so much. If I had wanted children, I would've chosen you.'

70

Katy

As Katy rounds the bend towards home, she freezes at the sight of a police vehicle outside her house, but only for a moment. They'd made an appointment to take a statement about Friday's attack; they're just a little early.

A woman winds down the window and tobacco fumes billow out. 'DS Bradford. Sorry, traffic was light. We'll knock in ten minutes.'

'No problem at all. I'll put on the kettle.'

Pleased at her equanimity, she strokes Poppy's soft fur, then opens the door, but her father on the stairs makes her jump. His face pasty and his hair disarrayed, he's obviously just woken up. He clears his throat. 'I just opened the bedroom curtains. The police are outside,' he says. 'What's going—'

'Sorry, I forgot to mention it last night. They're taking a statement about the mugging.' Still feeling bad about their difference of opinion, she hops up to give him a quick hug. 'It's nothing to do with Sibeal and Milo. That's all sorted and forgotten, like I said.'

'Goodness, I clearly overslept.' He rubs his eyes. 'Righto. I'll get dressed and come down. Happy to sit in and hold your hand, so to speak, or make myself scarce. Entirely up to you.'

True to her word, DS Bradford knocks at nine. The smell of cigarettes and a young sidekick follow in her wake. Feeling a tad nervous, Katy shows them into the kitchen.

Her dad pops his head around the door. 'Stay or leave?' he asks.

'Stay,' Katy says.

'Then I'll make myself useful by preparing the drinks.'

Once they've settled at the table, Katy describes the events of Friday night in as much detail as she can. The male officer scribbles notes, the woman gazes with grey eyes. At the end she smiles. 'I generally have a whole list of questions, but you've covered just about everything. There's only one thing. You'd been to a book group gathering alone, so how come Sibeal Matthews was there? I don't believe she lives locally.'

Katy feels herself flush. As things had turned out, Sibeal's presence was more akin to a guardian angel's than a stalker's. 'She's a friend. She wanted a chat so she came to walk with me.'

The officer nods. 'Fortunate for you she did. That's all we need, thank you. DC Dyson will read your statement back to you before signing, then we'll be out of your hair.'

Katy sees them out and returns with a grin. 'I feel like I've been given a gold star,' she says to her dad, still sitting in his place. 'They were so nice, weren't they?' He doesn't turn, so she perches opposite him. 'Are you OK? You're not still feeling under the weather, are you?'

'Not one hundred per cent, if I'm honest, but . . .' He frowns. 'Just now you mentioned calling a doctor on Friday night. Dr Harrison?'

Katy nods; she meant to ask what his actual name was,

but she was so worried, then relieved, about Sib that it slipped her mind.

Alexander steeples his palms. 'The same doctor who took you for a pub lunch? The Three-Legged Mare?'

'Yes.' She tenses. Both his mannerisms and questions feel ominous. Does she really want to know? 'Why do you ask?'

He gazes with soft eyes, but his lips are tight with concern. 'Your poor beautiful face has had a bit of a battering of late.'

To deflect the inevitable, she reaches for humour. 'Who'd have thought a road would be so gravelly? I have a few impressive bruises too.' Then after a moment, 'It's nothing compared with poor Sib's injuries.' But she knows what he's getting at. 'The black eye wasn't anything to do with Harry. I told you at the time, Dad. It was some guy called Gary, entirely by accident.' He nods, but doesn't speak, so she fills the silence. 'And Harry and I aren't an item or anything. We're barely even friends.'

'Well, I'm sure it's nothing, anyway. You know I'm a worrier, that's all.' He claps his hands. 'Right, lunch. Any special requests?'

Katy doesn't move. Her flesh is tingling. 'Worry about what, Dad?'

'Nothing; really. It'll just be my—'

'Dad . . .'

He sighs. 'I think we drove past that pub on the way to Little Bollington, but I could be mistaken. The Three-Legged Mare . . . I don't know. Mum mentioned the unusual name, that's all.'

The pinpricks increase. 'What? You mean the night . . . the night of the accident?'

Her dad sighs again, deeply this time. 'Ignore me, please. I'm making connections where there are none. That's the trouble with spending too much time on my own. Probably drinking excessively in hotel rooms and becoming morose.' He stands and pecks her hair. 'It's so good to be home on a weekday for once. I have my creative cooking head on. What do you fancy eating? Or how about a surprise?'

'A surprise,' she replies after a moment. 'But I'm meeting Gabriel at Brook House. Then we're going on to see Sib, so it'll have to be—'

'A project for dinner, then. Excellent.'

71

Sibeal

Still acclimatising from her latest flaming nap, it takes Sibeal moments to realise the two police officers are heading towards her corner bed.

'DS Bradford and DC Dyson. Do you have a few minutes?'

A sarcastic retort pops to the surface, but it isn't enough to divert the sudden hot sweat and metallic taste in her mouth.

There's a frown above the woman's grey eyes. 'Are you OK? We can come back another time.'

Sibeal doesn't reply. She's concentrating on her breathing, trying to tame the panic before it's full blown. Leaning forward, she inhales through her nose, holds it in, counts to four and slowly exhales.

'A panic attack?' DS Bradford asks. 'They're bastards, I know.' With a flick of her head, she motions her young colleague to leave.

Hoping she's caught it just in time, Sib sits back. 'You've got him well trained,' she comments.

Clearly a smoker, the officer sits. 'Graduate sidekicks have to be good for something,' she replies with an ironic smirk. She studies Sibeal for a moment or two. 'Remember to include it in your VPS. Sometimes it helps.'

'VPS?'

'Victim personal statement. It's an opportunity to describe how the crime has affected you, the impact it has made. I'm not convinced it makes any difference to sentencing, but I personally think it's a form of therapy and that's always a good thing.'

'Therapy?' She wonders what the woman would say if she knew the agitation was brought on by seeing her more than anything else. 'That's a bit right-on for the police, isn't it?'

'Not at all. I'm all for the holistic approach for both criminals and their victims.' She tilts her head and squints. 'How would you say you are doing? Physically, emotionally, mentally and spiritually?'

God knows why, but the question brings a lump to Sibeal's throat. She tries to cover it with a derisive laugh. 'Save for horrendous tiredness, I'm probably doing the best physically, which is ironic when I'm in hospital recovering from a stab wound. Nurse Ratched doesn't think it's odd that I have to sleep every two minutes but it's bloody annoying. An operation takes it out of you, apparently.'

'No temperature?'

'Not that they've told me.'

'Opioid adverse effects?'

Sibeal raises her eyebrows. 'What? So you're medically qualified as well as a counsellor and a cop?'

'I had surgery to fix a broken femur.' Clearly recalling it, the officer sucks in some air. 'My first week in the job and I got kicked in pretty damned badly. After the op I was nauseous and struggled to keep awake. Turned out it was a side-effect of the morphine, AKA opioid adverse effects.' She smiles. 'So that's physical sorted. How about emotionally, mentally and spiritually?'

Sib flexes her fingers. 'Aren't they all the same?'

The DS pulls a rueful face. 'Possibly. So let's see. Mental health: can I handle my mind? Spiritual: do I know what gives me strength? Emotional: can I use my emotions wisely?'

Hassan, the police surgeon, said something similar. Sibeal struggled to listen at the time, but he talked about internal healing: *It's not a miracle cure, but I guarantee life can improve for the better. The only catch is yourself. You have to be open to seeking help. There's all sorts out there, but no one will come to your rescue unless you instigate it. It has to start with you but you can do it.*

She comes back to the woman. She's the straight-talking sort of person Sib likes, but after her treatment at the hands of that weasel-faced officer, she's not going to trust anyone with a warrant card ever again.

'Textbook speech appreciated,' she says, folding her arms. 'How can I help?'

'Filling in the gaps about the attack on Friday.' DS Bradford motions to her waiting sidekick. 'Need to ensure belt and braces for the CPS.' She peers at Sibeal curiously. 'Saving your friend was admirable, but how come you were there?'

Sibeal pauses before answering. Booze. That's where it started. What else did Dr Hassan say? *Masking trauma with alcohol might appear to work temporarily, but you know as well as anyone that isn't true. Things happen all around us over which we have no control, but you can control that. There's plenty of help out there, Sibeal. It's down to you to take it.*

72

Katy

Raking back her sunglasses like a hairband, Katy studies the church-like stained glass in Brook House's porch. Funny how she's noticing it today. The bright sunshine is lighting the colours this morning, so perhaps that's why. Or maybe it's because Saint Imelda has been stuck in her head since Sibeal's shocking revelation on Saturday.

She lifts the latch for when Gabriel arrives and tries to shake off the shudder. Spirits don't exist; of all the things she's felt anxious about over the years, phantoms aren't one of them. And yet her skin is goose-pimpled despite the hot weather.

Poor, poor Sib. Even though she was struggling with the drug of sleep, the childhood fear was clear in her eyes. What could be worse than seeing your distended mum hanging from a rope? Her ghost, apparently; hearing it pace the floorboards above, listening to it play music below.

'It was my bloody namesake's fault,' she explained. 'At the wake someone must have whispered about where Mum was found. I guess no one had told Great-Aunt Sibeal. I was right there beside her in my best navy dress. "But that attic has no windows!" she shrieked, almost deafening me. There's the sky-light, of course, but she was right, it doesn't open.'

Not understanding the significance, Katy waited for more.

'Imelda had already committed the mortal sin of taking her own life, but no one had let out her soul.'

'And one does that by opening a window?'

'Yup. It's codswallop to you and me, but not to an eleven-year-old child.'

Katy rubs the shiver from her arms. Three sets of house keys had dwindled to just the one in Sib's coat pocket, so she's meeting Gabe here. On the bus she contemplated whether to bring up the subject of Robin or even go one step further and tell him that Sib knows he's gay.

'I think Gabe's in love with ... well, someone,' Sib had said at some point on Saturday. Her eyes flickered. 'God, I hope he's careful. Years ago he gave lessons to a boy in my year who whispered insinuations, said he'd tell his parents unless I gave him this and that. It was blackmail and completely untrue, so I ignored it.' She took a tremulous breath. 'Gabriel's highly thought of, you know. Even the hint of wrongdoing would ruin him.'

Katy inwardly nods; she's already made a huge faux pas; it's better to leave the siblings to sort themselves out. Yet the word 'wrongdoing' loiters. What was her dad fretting about this morning? What 'connections' did he mean? The Three-Legged Mare and Harry ... Nope, she pushes the discomfort away. Harry's a nice steady guy, a doctor, for God's sake. She called Darley Med yesterday and asked for Janet. Minutes later Dr Pennington phoned her back for a chat about her 'condition' and said that blood tests were the place to start. Are she and Harry an item? It's a stab in the heart, but there's nothing untoward about that.

Needing to distract herself from her pecking thoughts, Katy ambles to the kitchen to search out a brown packet Sib mentioned. Something for Milo from Gabe, she said. When she unearths it from beneath a pile of ironing – of all things – she slips out three pristine booklets of music. She opens the first, *Piano Pieces for Children*, and reads the neat handwritten dedication:

To my beautiful boy, from Mammy.

The sudden peal of her mobile makes her jump from her skin. It isn't Saint Imelda swooping down to punish her, but the doctors' surgery. The receptionist is apologetic; there'd been some confusion with names and mobile numbers – she'd almost made a date with her 'charming father' by mistake.

Finishing the call, Katy nods with satisfaction. An appointment with the blood nurse is the first step towards what she hopes will be a new start. She feels ebullient about that. In the meantime ... Smiling, she fingers the slim volume of music. It might be for kids, but it would be fun to have a go before Gabe arrives.

She lets herself into the dining room, sits at the piano and props the booklet on the stand, but on reflection it feels wrong to crease the cover, she'll let Milo do that. Summoning up pieces she once learned by heart, she decides on 'La Donna', but when she presses B, there's no sound. A little frustrated, she lifts the instrument's heavy lid and peers inside. When her eyes become accustomed to the duskiness, she spots something stuck between two hammers, so she eases it out.

Back in the light, she squints at her find. It's an envelope addressed to Sibeal.

'You weren't supposed to find that.'

326

Katy spins around to the strangled voice. It's Gabe, only Gabe. 'Gabriel! You gave me a fright. I found . . .'

Her words trail off. His skin blanched white, his face is almost unrecognisable. And his fists are clenched. 'You weren't supposed to find that,' he repeats.

'Oh, right. I'm so sorry, I . . .'

She backs away as he moves towards her. Something is very, very wrong here. His eyes are blazing with anger, with rage. Her thighs hit the stool, her buttocks the keyboard. God, she's trapped. Desperately casting around the room, she tries to devise a way to fend off the attack she absolutely knows is coming. But there's no time to move, let alone escape, so she scrunches her whole body and waits for the blow. A split second passes, then another and another. When she peels open her eyelids, Gabe is on his knees and quietly sobbing.

73

Katy

Her heartbeat still fluttery, Katy opens the door and waits for Poppy to catch her up. Then she steps into the safety of her cheese-perfumed home and lets out a huge sigh.

Her dad's sitting at the kitchen island, clearly finishing a call. 'You're back early,' he says. 'That was the court office. I might have to . . .' He studies her and frowns. 'Are you all right? Has something happened to Sibeal?'

'I didn't go in the end. Gabriel's just dropped me off.'

On autopilot, she picks up the kettle and fills it at the tap. 'Did your creation go awry?' she asks, nodding to the sauce-streaked sink.

'Sorry?' He appears thrown by her question. 'Oh yes, I promised Milo pancakes for tea but the eggs curdled and I didn't want to risk them being off.'

She absently cleans the basin and pulls out a cup. 'Oh, right. Do you want a drink?'

'I'd rather you sit down and tell me what's wrong. You look as though you've seen a ghost.'

Seen a ghost; perhaps she has. Lost in thought, she pours the steaming water on a teabag.

'Kathryn?'

She tunes into to her dad's voice.

'Yes?'

He pats the stool next to him. 'What's happened, love?'

Sitting, she groans. 'I found a letter at the house.' Picturing Gabriel's distraught face, she covers her own. 'I feel really bad about it; it had obviously been hidden. I had no business poking around and finding it.'

'Hidden by whom?'

'I don't ...'

She swallows and thinks back. *You weren't supposed to find that.* Then as he looked up from the floor with imploring eyes: *I've been a coward. I should have told her myself, shouldn't I?*

'It must have been ...' The B was fine the last time she'd played it, so Gabriel must have stashed it the day she watched him from the landing. 'Gabriel, I'm guessing. It was addressed to Sibeal. It's the one room she never goes in, let alone plays the piano ...'

Sipping her tea, she falls silent. When he'd recovered himself, Gabriel stared at the envelope as if it might explode. Yes, as though it was a bomb which could destroy his life; something to do with his sexuality, maybe. Oh God, blackmail again?

Alexander's gentle voice brings her back. 'From one of her parents, perhaps?' he asks.

'Oh, I didn't think of that.' She shakes her head. 'I don't know the answer; he didn't open it or say. He was ... well, upset, then deeply embarrassed. I think he just wanted me to leave, so when he offered me a lift home, I said yes.' Sensing her dad's roused interest, she smiles thinly. 'I know and I agree! It's frustrating not to know what's going on, but it all happened so quickly and Gabriel was so distressed, it didn't feel right to ask questions even in the car.'

Her dad pats her hand and picks up *The Times*. 'I'm sure we'll find out eventually.'

But Katy's still mulling. 'I have an idea! Do you still have the note from their dad?' she asks. 'The one he sent from the hospice? I might recognise the handwriting.' She squints. 'It was in block capitals. Maybe a bit shaky, so I guess it could be from him.'

'Elementary, my dear Watson.' Alexander's smile turns rueful. 'Despite your excellent sleuthing skills, unfortunately not. I should have kept it but I thought I'd get to see James before he ... The benefit of hindsight, eh?' He stands, pats his pockets and pulls out his mobile. 'Oh no, not again. Let's hope they've found somebody else.'

'Alexander Henry ...' he says, answering. 'Ah, I see ...'

As he ambles away, Katy zones out and reverts to thoughts of Gabriel. He was silent during the journey, but when she climbed out of the Volvo he mumbled something about Sibeal recuperating in Saxton. She can see the sense of it, but was it always the plan?

'They do want me after all.'

She looks up to her father. 'Who does?'

He kisses her hair. 'You're miles away today. That was the court office again. They called about an emergency freezing injunction earlier but I asked if someone else could step in. It seems they've had no luck. In all fairness I'm familiar with the case, so I suppose it would have been ungracious of me to pass the buck. Sums of money so huge you wouldn't believe it.' He snorts. 'Work, eh? No rest for the wicked.'

Katy laughs. His eyes are bright with purpose. 'But you love it.'

'Perhaps you're right.' He taps his watch. 'If I drive and park at Stockport station, I can catch the two o'clock. Sorry to desert you again, darling.' He gazes steadily. 'Now stay safe, both you and Milo. No bruises, no muggings, no danger. Not even walking under ladders. Promise me?'

'Sure.' Sibeal, Gabriel and now her dad. Quite honestly she feels abandoned, but she tries for a smile. 'Don't worry, I promise.'

74

Sibeal

Listening to the peal of All Saints church bells at her tiny kitchen table, Sibeal yawns and stretches as much as she's able. God knows why, but the rich sound makes her feel safe. Perhaps it's because they've chimed for hundreds of years, or maybe she's become sentimental in her old age as she's found herself thinking how heartwarming it is that two people fall in love and want to declare it to the world on a sunny June Saturday. If she wasn't in such discomfort, she'd venture out to get a glimpse of the happy couple.

She doodles on her pad. Yes, she actually admires the openness and honesty of a wedding. As opposed to the sneaking about, the illicitness and spin of an affair. 'Spin' being lies, disingenuity, or simply excuses? Well, right now she doesn't care.

She chuckles to herself. Does this mean she's cured of Robin? Hmm, that notion is undoubtedly premature, but she's definitely more steady and settled than she has been for a very long time, albeit with spontaneous emotional bouts threaded through.

She opens her laptop and frowns at the screen. What on earth is the latest WebLife password? Bloody hell, it's clean gone.

Damned frustrating when she's usually so on the ball. Even when she drank to excess she functioned pretty effectively work-wise. She pauses at that particular thought; clarity isn't clarity when it's seen through the bottom of a whisky tumbler.

Though it won't last for ever, her wine rack is empty, and she's sticking to water. Whenever she lifts her glass of best Yorkshire tap, she thinks of her lovely dad.

She toasts him now. 'Cheers, Dad! Here's to abstemious abstinence!'

Tears sting her eyes yet again. Perhaps she can blame that on the opioids too, but there's no doubt she's missing him. She felt it most acutely when Gabriel failed to turn up at the hospital for two flaming days. He always does in the end, but their dad was more reliable, less racked with angst. Yet he did smoke those cigarettes as though each one was his last. She can smell them sometimes, even here in her small sunlit house.

Her musing slides to the long arm of the law. True, her arrest led to the panic attacks which still threaten her both day and night, but it's turned out not all coppers are bad. Dr Hassan ignited some hope in her soul and the grey-eyed detective gave her several leaflets ranging from victim information to alcohol support before leaving the hospital. They were all north-west-based help groups, but surely they'll have similar here, even in torpid North Yorkshire.

Deciding on ice in her water, she swivels around to the freezer and hisses at the sharp sting. Without the pain relief, her upper buttock constantly throbs, but it's a nice ache, one that reminds her she isn't all bad. The precise events of that night are still a muddled fugue, but she saved little Kat from a stupid thug's knife and they're back to how they were before she fucked everything up. Being so far from her is the only downside of Gabriel's strangely assertive decision to return here.

It was both surprising and hilarious to witness him charge into the ward like a huffy bull and say, 'I'm taking you home!' The ward sister duly flapped her *capa de brega* but he skilfully dodged it with questions. Was his sister's operation a success? Had there been any sign of infection? Could he easily help her dress the wound? Wasn't there a shortage of hospital beds? Then what was the problem?

When she hobbled to the Volvo, a bag of shoes, her holdall and laptop were in the back seat. 'I thought we were going home . . .'

'We are. Brook House isn't our home. It hasn't been for a very long time. There isn't anything left you want, is there?'

'No.'

'Well then.'

She narrowed her eyes. 'Did you find what you were looking for?'

He looked fixedly ahead. 'There was nothing to find. Besides, you need your creature comforts, not some dank and dusty old house.'

Gabriel, her secretive brother. He was always cagey but of late . . . God, she hopes he isn't in trouble.

The password suddenly popping, she types it in and speeds through the WebLife inbox. So busy deleting bloody spam, she doesn't twig that the sound of rapping is at her door. Wondering why Gabe isn't using his keys to bring in today's shopping, she sighs and opens up.

It takes a moment to adjust. No food nor her brother, but the weasel-faced Greater Manchester police detective.

Her saliva metallic, she swallows. 'What are you doing here?' Then, more like the old Sib, 'What do you want? Kathryn Henry made a statement withdrawing her complaint.'

He moves to one side and a hefty woman steps up. 'I'm Detective Inspector Tonge. May we come in?' she asks.

'Why?'

'We'd like to talk to you please.'

Sibeal inhales to object, but her chest is tight. Sure that tell-tale beads of sweat have appeared on her forehead, she gestures to the kitchen. Why the hell have they travelled seventy miles without an appointment or at least calling her first? When they gather at the table, she tries to keep the tremor from her voice.

'Kathryn dropped the charges; there's nothing more to talk about.'

'May we sit?'

Her earlier calm eradicated by the woman's grim expression, she nods.

DI Tonge cracks her shoulders. 'It isn't the complainant's decision alone, but you are correct, Ms Henry did change her statement. However ...'

Sibeal holds on to the back of a chair. Her fingers feel numb. 'However, what?'

'Your DNA sample was processed—'

'Why?'

'Under the law we are entitled to keep it for six months ...'

'But Kat dropped the charges.'

'I know; it's ... unusual, but it happens and in this instance I'm afraid ...' She smiles a small smile of ... what? Apology? Regret? What the hell is going on? 'Your DNA sample came up with a filial match in our database, from a serious crime—'

335

'Filial?' Sibeal's palpitations lurch from a flutter to a full-blown thudding. 'Like familial? Close family?'

'There is a distinction . . .' she hears through the rushing sound in her ears. Then, 'Ms Matthews? Sibeal? Are you all right?'

Oh God, Gabriel. What has he done? DNA. Serious crime. Database. His secretiveness. Missing days and no money. That young pupil with a dog. She needs to warn him, get him away. But there's nothing she can do to help her brother right now; her legs are insubstantial, the walls caving in.

75

Sibeal

Gradually aware of low conversation coming from somewhere, Sibeal opens her eyes. She's lying on her sofa, the right side of her body on fire.

Gabriel's face comes into view, his eyes bright with tears. 'Thank God you're awake. Try not to move.' He gestures to her jogging bottoms where blood has seeped through. 'I think your stitches have burst. You fainted and fell badly.'

Realisation snapping in, she attempts to sit up. 'The police turned up, Gabe. You have to leave now, get away,' she hisses urgently. 'They have a DNA match.'

'They're still here, Sib, in the kitchen. Two officers came to me, two to you.'

Despite the shooting pain, she wraps her arms around him tightly. 'Whatever it is, you know I love you. I'll always love you and I'll do whatever it takes to—'

'I'm so sorry, Sib.' He pulls away and rubs his pallid cheeks. 'You might think differently when you hear what the police have to say. I am sorry, please believe me.'

What the hell has he done? 'What are you talking about, Gabe? For once, just—'

Her need to know more is interrupted by an officer dragging in two chairs from the kitchen. She tries to catch her brother's hand, but he steps away and hunches down on the footstool.

When the room is full, DI Tonge pulls her seat forward until she's inches from Sibeal. 'Do you feel well enough to talk?' she asks. 'We could come back another time, but we'd appreciate your cooperation now we're here.'

Cooperation? She wills Gabriel to speak, but he keeps his head down, doggedly staring at the carpet.

'What's this all about?' Several pairs of eyes stare at her. 'Do we have to have the whole bloody circus?'

'You're right, for now we don't.' The detective wipes her glossy forehead. 'Just Ms Matthews and her brother for now.' When they've finally shuffled out, she leans forward again. 'Can I call you Sibeal?'

Unlike the weasel's, her demeanour seems kind, but alarm and agitation make Sibeal snappy. 'Call me what the hell you want. Can we get on with it?'

'Yes, absolutely. Before you became ill, I explained that your DNA sample was processed and it was found to be a partial match with DNA in our database. It's what we call a filial match and it relates to an alleged sexual assault—'

Sibeal struggles upright. 'For God's sake, Gabriel, don't just sit there like a dolt. You need a lawyer. They're not allowed to do this. You're entitled to a solicitor.'

He lifts his head. 'Sib, just sit down and listen.'

DI Tonge clears her throat. 'A *filial* match from an alleged rape in Windermere thirty-four years ago.'

Processing the words, Sib gingerly takes her place. Windermere is in the Lake District and Gabriel is thirty-five, so . . .

'Filial is the term used for offspring, not siblings,' the officer continues slowly. 'It's a parent and child connection, which means the partial match must be with your mother or your—'

'My father.'

Sibeal whispers the word, but knows they're mistaken. James Matthews wouldn't hurt a fly. Almost laughing at the notion, she voices it. 'Gabriel? Dad didn't like to offend anyone, let alone . . .' Then, with anger taking over, 'Gabriel? Why the fuck aren't you saying anything to defend him?'

When he shakes his head, recall hits like a slap. Those newspapers her dad kept, those headlines she read out. She frowns in thought. The *Westmoreland Gazette* . . . A man charged with sexual assault who then had an alibi . . . Bile bubbles up. Surely to Christ not her dad? But criminals do that, don't they? They keep tokens of their evil acts and hide them in plain sight.

'Sibeal, are you with us?' The detective peers intently. 'Gabriel has volunteered a sample of his DNA to help with our enquiries, but from the information he's given us within the last hour, we believe James Matthews will be ruled out of our investigation.'

'I don't get it,' she replies, the palpitations building. 'One minute you're saying my dad was a fucking rapist; the next minute—'

'He wasn't your father,' Gabriel interrupts. His face starched white, he moves towards her. 'Not your biological one, anyway. I know this because Mum told me before . . . before she died.' Kneeling at her side, he gabbles on fast-forward. 'I never told you. I'm sorry. She was drunk when she said it. I didn't even know if it was true. You were only eleven, so it wasn't appropriate to say anything anyway. I was only sixteen myself; it was my birthday, for God's sake. Went to college as usual, then when I got back, she'd ... How could I have known? Possibly known? We got older, we had Dad. Did he know? I don't know. But we were happy, weren't we? What was the point of saying it? I was a coward, I know, but—'

'Stop, Gabriel, stop!' She takes a huge breath. 'You're saying that my dad wasn't ...'

'He was in every way, Sib, but not by blood.'

'His name is on my birth certificate. I looked at it two bloody weeks ago.'

'I know and I'm sorry you had to find out.'

She pushes hard at his shoulder, then shoves again. 'If James wasn't my dad, then who the fuck was?'

DI Tonge holds out a clear plastic bag. 'We're hoping this will tell us.'

Recoiling at her mother's handwriting on the crumpled paper inside, Sib inches away. 'What is it?'

'It's an envelope addressed to you, Sibeal. We're hoping there's a letter inside.'

76

Katy

Wondering when her dad will arrive home, Katy looks at the time. The stab of irritation prods again. Bridget, of course. She should feel grateful for her generosity and her indulgence of Milo, but right now she isn't, if she's honest. The flaming woman asked Milo if he wanted to go to Chester Zoo without asking her first. It naturally made him excited, so Katy couldn't say no when actually she had wanted to take him herself, just the two of them on a coach trip as soon as the summer holidays began. Instead they've gone off in *her* car and left her rattling around in the house until Alexander arrives back from London.

Rattling around isn't good, she's discovered. It's given her too much time for thought about Harry, or Dr Harrison, or whatever he's called. His furtive expression in the pub has been nagging. Was he confessing the connection to her mum, or was it something else? And didn't he say something about being a 'bad lad'? Not when he was little, but later. How much later? His boy-racer days? He was right about Dr Pennington's suggestion she keep a record of her episodes of illness, though. She'd sort of done that over the years anyway and she's been flicking through her diaries this morning, marvelling at how patient her dad was when he still worked in Manchester. They were frequent, sometimes two or three times a week, back then. Of course they had Bridget on hand, but nevertheless, a tiny grandson and a virtually disabled daughter must have been difficult with such a demanding job, poor man.

Sib and Gabe have been on her mind too. A text arrived from Gabriel on Tuesday evening, but it turned out to be from Sibeal.

Due a new phone delivery any minute but wanted to let you know we'll be in Saxton for a few days. Be back soon for my car. And you, little Kat! Gabe seems to think we'll never return. He's being mysterious, but don't worry, I'll get it out of him!

Katy flicks on the kettle. The envelope she found in the piano, surely? It's too coincidental not to be. Along with the collection of toy sports cars she spotted in Harry's knick-knack drawer, her mum saying 'What is your gut telling you, darling?' and that ghastly nightmare about her dad, it featured heavily in last night's dreams. By this morning she was exhausted by the different permutations. She was left with a feeling that the writing was the same as the note from 'Mammy' in the music book; but even that might not be right; one was in lower case, the other in capitals.

Intent on tidying Milo's mess whilst he's out, she carefully carries her mug of tea up the stairs and peers into his bedroom. How he and Alexander are related, she'll never know, as his toys are scattered everywhere. They're mostly tiny pieces of LEGO, the size of the blocks seeming to decrease each time he has a birthday.

Knowing there's no chance of working out which pieces go in

which box, she scoops them with her hands and drops them in a green plastic tub. Noticing two human-shaped characters are drowning in the bricks, she picks the cowboys out and chuckles. Her dad and Milo avidly watched *Cowboys & Aliens* three times back to back one rainy Sunday. Like that dreadful film, the cheeky little rascal has been mixing the old with the new yet again.

The sound of her mobile pierces the silence. Rushing to her bedroom, she snatches it up and smiles as she looks at the screen. It's from *Sibeal new phone*.

'Hi, how's the patient doing?' she asks with a grin.

A pause and then, 'Is Alexander there please, Kat? I've tried his mobile but it goes straight to voicemail.'

Though Katy knows she's being silly, a spread of pique burns her chest. 'He's on his way back from London. He should be here fairly soon.' She tries to recover herself. 'He's probably in the car now and driving from Stockport station to here, which is why it's going to . . . Is there anything I can do to help?'

'No, it's . . .' There's talking in the background, then Sib speaks again, her voice sounding peculiar. 'Alexander once mentioned a friend of his and my dad. They all went to school together. Does it ring any bells?'

'Oh . . .' Katy thinks back and pictures her dad's fond smile. 'One of the Three Musketeers, do you mean? They went away for weekends when they were students. What was he called? I can't remember his—'

'I'm fairly sure it was Kenny, but I can't remember a—'

'Philippe. He's called Kenny Philippe.'

More whispering in the background, then Sibeal comes back. 'For speed could you look him up? Maybe in an address book or similar? We're trying to track him down.'

343

'Sure. It's by the telephone downstairs.' She frowns at the peculiar request. 'What's going on, Sib?'

The quaver palpable, she replies in a whisper. 'God, Kat, it's dreadful. I can't talk now, but I think Kenny Philippe is my father, my biological father, at least.' Then louder, 'Could you have a look and call me back?'

Katy hurries down to the hallway. What on earth ...? If Kenny is Sibeal's father, then what about James? And how come she's discovered this only now? But there isn't time for speculation. Sib sounded so very shaky and serious.

She grabs the book, sits on the bottom stair and opens up. Dragging her finger down the index, she finds the letter P and carefully goes through the names and addresses. Many have been neatly crossed out and replaced, but there's no one called Philippe. She does the same with the letter K. No match.

Apprehension fizzing in her stomach, she pauses before calling Sib back. She hasn't been drinking, has she? Did she forgive her too quickly? Will it always be like this? Sensible, grounded Kat but unpredictable Sibeal?

Gabriel answers her mobile. 'Hi, Katy, did you find anything?'

'Sorry, no I didn't. But we're talking thirty years ago, so it might not be in there.'

'It was definitely Philippe, like the French? Not Philip or Phillips?'

'The name rang a bell, so I'm pretty sure but I'll ask Dad as soon as he's home. What's going on, Gabriel? Sib said—'

'The police are here.' He lowers his voice. 'They don't want us to say anything, but it's nothing for you to worry about, Katy. We'll fill you in when they're gone, but in the meantime, if your

344

dad has any contact details for this Kenny bloke, any clue where he might live, can he call us urgently?'

'OK, will do.' Katy stares at the blank screen. *Police?* What the hell? She withdrew her complaint, so it can't be that. Is it something to do with the mugging? But how is that connected to Sib's dead father and Kenny? It feels odd, surreal, uncomfortable. The sooner her dad's home, the better.

Her mind clouded with worry, she goes back to Milo's bedroom. Where was she? That's right; she was returning the wranglers to where they belong. She pads across the landing to her dad's room, opens his wardrobe and stretches on tiptoes for the High Chaparral tub. It almost hits her head, but she manages to steady herself and place it on the bed. As she replaces the errant figures, a thought occurs. The pre-Elke's-death photographs are stashed up here. They used to be in the lounge cupboard, but her dad discreetly brought them up here at some point after the accident.

She pulls out the first box, lifts the lid and peers at the familiar snap of her as a baby in Alexander's arms. Careful not to mess up the neat order, she flicks through her childhood. Like an animated film, Kathryn Henry develops into an adult. If she's to find one of Kenny, she'll need to go further back to before she was born, perhaps even pre Alexander-and-Elke-marriage.

Dragging over the navy recliner, she climbs up and peers into the back of the shelf. Only the board games stare back, so with a sharp breath of resolve she opens the door above. Still in their original packaging, her mum's hat, matching handbag and the shoes she bought for a wedding are where she left them five years ago.

After a moment she exhales. It's fine, she's fine. It's another hurdle overcome, another positive step. Pushing the items to one side, she finds chambers diaries and lever-arch folders, then finally another box. She lifts the lid. Perfect; more photographs.

Sitting down on the chair, she begins at the back. Her mum and dad's honeymoon, their wedding, then engagement. Reverse order, that makes sense. Her dad, James and Kenny were schoolfriends, so it's best to start from the front.

She begins slowly at first, but they're mostly team photographs. Football, hockey, rugby and cricket. Too many youthful faces to pick out anyone but her dad, and only because he's the tallest. She continues to glance as the other boys grow in height and eventually she finds one of James, the spit of Gabe. There's James, and James again in different laughing poses, so she skips ahead.

Beginning to get bored, she runs through her dad's university days. But she pauses and frowns. The next section comprises at least thirty images of a woman she doesn't recognise. With the backdrop of green hills, she's wearing different outfits in each and is undoubtedly pretty, but why is she never facing the camera? She puts them back, but soon hits the jackpot. James again, too strikingly like Gabriel to miss, and in any event he's at Brook House, shoulder to shoulder with her dad. Her heart quickening, she recalls the story about the Three Musketeers being fed by Imelda. Kenny will surely appear any moment. She peers at each image. James and Imelda, then Imelda and her dad, then her dad and James again. Her fingers hurry through to find one of Kenny, but the next batch is of a woman again. Wearing different outfits in each and undoubtedly pretty, she's never looking at the camera. But this person she does recognise.

Her hands no longer willing, she replaces the lid and leans back against the headrest. Her heart beating wildly, she tries to focus. Why would her dad have thirty, maybe forty snaps of Imelda Matthews without her apparently knowing? She breathes out the answer. The artwork, of course. The portraits of her lining the walls of Brook House. He must have taken the photos for James to work from.

Shaking her head with relief, she retraces her steps to slot everything back. Something rustles and snags, so she stretches to the very back until her fingers find purchase. Her eyes disbelieving, she stares at her find. What the hell? Addressed to K. A. Henry, it's the letter she mistakenly thought was for her all those weeks ago, the one her dad said he'd thrown out.

She tremulously sits and extracts the thin paper.

I'm in a hospice, I'm dying, the note starts.

Yes, she remembers that; it's as far as she read before realising it wasn't for her.

Her whole being like ice, she reads on:

So I'm not afraid of you any more, Kenny. Your manipulation, your cunning, cleverness and charm, your deviance, your lies and sleight of hand. Imelda might have put the rope around her own neck, but we both know who killed her.

77

Katy

Though Katy falls to her knees, she doesn't sob. Her mind is in overdrive, thoughts and memories clashing and colliding. However this appears, it's not what it seems, it can't be. She has to stay calm and piece the jigsaw together for Milo, her Milo, the only certainty in her life.

She paces the soft carpet. Kenny Philippe might be Sibeal's father. Her dad could be Kenny. But who says so? Firstly Sibeal Matthews who's unstable, who stalked her and Robin's boy and even sneaked into the child's bedroom. Then secondly James, *dying* James Matthews, confused and heavily medicated, no doubt. So what if Kenny wasn't in the phone book or the photographs; they were friends long ago and he might have been camera shy.

Yet the wording of the letter flies back: *cleverness and charm.* Oh God, even *manipulation* and *sleight of hand.* That's her dad, Alexander Henry, isn't it? And Sibeal . . . she's unmistakably her mother's daughter, but the images just now show a petite person with blue eyes, not a broad-shouldered, tall woman with *something* she recognised from the moment they met.

Stopping at the window, she stares out at the brilliant blue sky. They live in the leafy suburbs of Cheadle; her dad is His Honour Judge Henry KC; he's charitable and generous and kind, he's a tower of strength and respectability. She has it all wrong, there *has* to be another explanation.

She pulls out her phone and stares at the screen. Ask him. She just has to ask him. Taking a deep breath of determination, she calls his number. It diverts straight to voicemail. She tries again, then again. Where the hell is he? When he called earlier he was at Euston station; she could hear the bustle of people and a tannoy in the background. What exactly did he say after their initial pleasantries?

'Is Milo there?'

'No, he's gone out.'

'Oh, that's fine. With Bridget in the car?'

'What makes you think it was Bridget?' she replied sarcastically.

His tone was honeyed and smooth. 'You know she means well, Kathryn. She has no kids, let her enjoy him for the day. There's a new baby elephant; he'll love it.'

Her heart clatters, loud in her ears. *In the car?* Why would he assume that? With Bridget, it's normally a walk with the dog or the playground at Bruntwood. And the baby elephant ... Did Katy mention the zoo? No, no she didn't.

She calls Bridget's number. It rings out until voicemail kicks in. This time she doesn't bother trying again. Her mind is playing back the 'Euston' noises from earlier. Instead she scrambles to Alexander's side table and searches inside. No passport. His passport isn't there.

Adrenalin propelling her forward, she darts to her room,

349

opens the small cupboard and scrapes everything out. Her fingers almost refusing to work, she snatches up the sole booklet and opens the first page. Oh God, it's her own. Milo's is missing, his passport has gone.

A steely calm descending, she calls Sibeal. There's no point speaking to an operator and wasting time.

'Kat, have you found—'

'Put the police on. Whoever is the boss. Quickly.'

'Detective Inspector Tonge here. Can I help?'

'Yes, I'm Kathryn Henry. I think the man you are looking for is my father, Alexander Henry. You need to act now. I believe he's at an airport, absconding with my son.'

78

Katy

'We're leaving Saxton now, Katy,' the DI says. 'And we'll be with you in an hour and a half. In the meantime I'll send over someone from my team with a family liaison officer. OK?'

Family? *Family?* Katy doesn't understand the bloody word. She finds herself yelling. 'I don't want a liaison officer or anyone else here. I want you to get out there and find my son!'

'That's exactly what we're doing. Calls are being placed with the National Ports Office to alert all UK points of departure as we speak. We're ensuring all forces in the UK are aware that Milo is missing via the Police National Computer. All sea and airports will be alerted.'

'He's got Milo's passport. Suppose they've already gone?'

'We work with Interpol to link into police forces around the world. But I think that's jumping the gun, Kathryn. Let's take this one step at a time. I'll be staying on the line and gathering information from you whilst my DS drives us back. Does that sound OK?'

Nothing is remotely *OK*, but she has to overcome the need to shout and sob, the need to puke up her guts. 'Fine.'

'Great. Now, the UK law states that it is a criminal offence for a person connected with a child under sixteen years to take or send that child out of the UK without the appropriate consent. I have to ask whether appropriate consent has—'

'No! I knew nothing about this. Why do you think I'm tearing my hair out? And it's Katy, for God's sake.'

'Please bear with me, Katy. These are questions I have to ask, I'm afraid. So, being "connected" to the child means a biological parent, a guardian, or someone who has custody of the child. Are the potential abductors legal guardians or do they have custody of the child?'

A shiver passes through Katy. 'No, of course not.' He couldn't, could he? Her father couldn't have somehow obtained a court order behind her back? Used her illness against her? Oh God, with Bridget's backup, that's entirely possible. 'No, absolutely not.'

DI Tonge plies her with more questions: the physical description of the child and the people who have potentially carried out the abduction. Who has the parental responsibility for the child. The relationship between the child and the abductors. Any links the abductors have abroad. The vehicles the abductors have access to.

Though Katy knows it's a checklist she has to patiently answer, she wants to shriek down the line. The *child* is Milo, her five-year-old son. The *abductors* are her fucking dad and someone who is supposed to be her friend. One of the *vehicles* is hers. How can this possibly be happening? They are the people she most trusted in the world.

The doorbell rings the moment DI Tonge exhausts her probing. Deliberate timing, Katy assumes, passing over the buck now

352

the cavalry have arrived. But when she opens up, the two fresh-faced officers look no older than her.

She lets them pass and gestures to the kitchen. 'You can come in and do whatever you need to but I'm going upstairs.'

She heads for Milo's bedroom, kneels by his bed and sobs into his pillow. Where is he? Where is her son? There's a whole bigger story involving Imelda and James and 'Kenny' but she can't go there now. Her mind is so cluttered it's hard to think straight, but she has to focus on Milo. Why would her dad do this to her? Punishment, she's sure. He undoubtedly uses the 'charm' James mentioned, but everything has always been Alexander's way. He was miffed when she offered to help Sibeal with Brook House; he was quietly livid when she called the police. But why commit this astonishing act of cruelty?

She pictures his face full of love for both her and Milo. Could she have got it all horribly wrong? Did he simply use Milo's passport to book a holiday? But why not take hers too? Then what about Bridget? What did she say the other day about if she'd had a child? She was the one who took Milo under the ruse of a trip to the zoo. Has *she* instigated this nightmare? Is she doing it alone or with Alexander, as a couple?

Too frustrated by the circle of permutations, she marches to the bloody man's bedroom. Recovering Milo is the imperative, the rest can wait, but she can't stand idle so she'll search for clues. Start at the wardrobe and go through every last item he possesses. Climbing the blue chair again, she drags everything out until all the shelves are bare. Then she sits on the bed, inhales deeply and starts with the lever-arch folders.

She is so engrossed in the paperwork, it takes a moment or two to realise her mobile is ringing. Scrambling across the mattress, she scoops it up. Her heart pumps loud in her ears as she takes in the name of the caller. It's Bridget. God, it's a FaceTime from Bridget. She knows she should holler for the officers downstairs, but time is of the essence, she can't risk her ringing off.

Steeling herself to be calm and not scream in the evil woman's face, she swipes to answer.

Milo's smile fills the screen. 'Mummy!'

'Milo!' She feels physically sick. 'Where are you, love?'

'At the zoo, of course.' He pans the camera around to the elephant enclosure. 'Look, Mummy, it's the baby!'

79

Katy

Dragging herself from the sofa, Katy walks to the front door and looks through the peephole. It's DI Femi Tonge and her colleague again. Sighing deeply, she turns the key in the lock. Yesterday's adrenalin has clean gone, leaving her with a sensation of sheer emptiness. After the confusion, anxiety, terror and relief, the strength to feel anything has disappeared: no rage, no hate, not even fear. Numb shock, she supposes, similar to when her mum died. But at least then she had the resolution of her death, not this floating muffled limbo.

Femi steps in. 'I called, but you aren't answering your telephone or mobile.'

Her skin is glossy, as though she's been running. She was here until late yesterday and she's back now. Has she rested in between? Who knows. What's the point of sleep anyway? It only postpones the inevitable next day.

Without asking if her visitors would like one, Katy pours water into a teapot and places it on the table. Mugs, sugar and milk are still there from last night.

Femi studies her with a frown. 'It's been a traumatic time. Is there someone you can call? A friend or a relative?'

'Nope,' Katy replies. 'Besides, I'm fine.'

'OK. I promised to keep you informed in person, so—'

'Do you want tea? Shall I pour?' Katy asks to postpone reality a moment longer.

'Sure. Thanks.' Femi spoons in two sugars and stirs. 'So we've established further background information about your father. He was born Kenton Alexander Henry, known as Kenny at school—'

'So his name *is* Alexander.'

'Yes. He dropped the Kenton when he enrolled for the Bar training course in London ...' She dips her head. 'Are you OK, Katy?'

Not really. She doesn't want to hear any of it. But she knows it's best to let the officer spit out what she wants to say, then she'll leave her alone. 'Yes, carry on.'

'I know it's your understanding that your paternal grandparents are dead ...'

Anticipating the next part, Katy nods. Another bloody revelation. She should be stunned that he lied about them too, but nothing will ever surprise her again.

'But we had to check for obvious reasons. Your father's estranged parents are still alive and they're understandably shocked. They've lived in the Lake District since moving there when he was at university. They last saw him thirty-four years ago.' She pats her forehead with a tissue. 'As you know, the DNA on our database relates to an alleged sexual assault in—'

The pretty girl with the backdrop of green hills. Katy swallows to stop the rising bile. 'It's fine. I get it. You don't have to spell it out. So where is he now?'

'I'm sorry to say we've had confirmation that your father has left the country as we suspected. His car was found at Birmingham airport car park. At one thirty yesterday he took a short flight from there to Amsterdam. We believe he caught a connection there, but used a different passport, so we don't know where to yet. Amsterdam are going through the CCTV. As soon as I know, you will too.' She continues to gaze steadily. 'The better news is that we've interviewed Bridget Checkley with her solicitor and she has expressed her desire to fully cooperate with our enquiries. The interview was preliminary, so we'll find out much more during the course of today. The main thrust is that she had no idea of Alexander's plans and certainly not that he intended to leave the country.'

A shot of anger rattles through Katy. 'Well, she would say that, wouldn't she?' she snaps.

'And that she was an employee, just doing what she was paid to do.'

'That makes it all right, then.'

'I'm not saying it's all right, Katy, not for a moment. I'm hoping the CPS will give us the nod to charge her with conspiracy to kidnap. I'm just passing on what she told us, OK? The evidence she gives will help us build up a picture of why your father decided to—'

Her eyes flicking to the door, she stops speaking. 'So, this must be young Milo.' She smiles reassuringly. 'Hello, Milo, I'm Femi. You were fast asleep when I came here last night.'

Milo shuffles forward and stands on one leg. 'I know who you are.'

'Oh yes?'

'You're from the police.'

Her face suitably impressed, Femi nods. 'Very smart! How do you know that?'

'I looked out of Grandad's window. You came in a police car. A BMW 5 series.' He hops around in a circle. 'I was in one yesterday but that was an M2.'

'That must have been exciting.'

'I had a wee at the services and when we came out Bridget's car had broken down. But it was fine because the police were waiting to fix it. Then a lady bought me a Coke and some sweets from the shop. I knew she was a policeman because she was wearing a . . .'

He flushes deeply and Katy smiles despite herself. Carbonated drinks are banned by her dad; Milo knows he's accidentally let it slip out. But her grin is replaced by a deep, icy shudder. Her steady, honourable dad planned to steal his own grandson. And the rest, the awful, horrendous rest. Yet she can't think about any of it, for her sanity she can't. She'll hide here with Milo until it's all over. Though how that will happen, she has no idea.

She comes back to her wonderfully oblivious son.

'Bridget went on the wrong motorway, so we had to turn back. Then we spent *ages* in the monkey house,' he's saying to the constable. He rolls his dark eyes. 'It was a bit boring, but she likes monkeys the best.' He mimics her voice. '"I like them because they remind me of a little monkey standing right next to me now!"' He chuckles. 'She meant me. I like lions and tigers and leopards, but elephants are my favourite. We watched them throw straw on their backs.'

He pulls two plastic figures from his bulging pocket and puts them on the table. Then he digs around for the baby and lines her up too. 'Bridget said I could choose anything, but I only wanted these.'

'An elephant family. Was the baby very small?'

Milo doesn't answer, so Katy taps his shoulder and nods to the young man. 'He's asking if the baby elephant was very small.'

He leans against the officer's knees. 'She was bigger than me but smaller than you.'

'And whose trunk was longer?' He lifts his arm and puts it to his nose. 'Mine or hers?'

Milo throws back his head and chortles. 'My grandad does that,' he laughs.

80

Sibeal

Gabriel turns off the Volvo engine, but instead of climbing out, Sibeal gazes at Kat's house. It looks empty and lost without the sleek, handsome and dominating presence of the silver Jaguar on its drive.

'Symbolic or what,' she mutters.

'Sorry?' Gabriel says.

'Nothing. You stay here.' Hissing with pain, she swings out her legs, followed by the crutch she hates using.

'Let me help you out at least. You'll burst the stitches again if you're not careful. You're mean to be lying flat, not travelling in a car for nearly two hours.'

'God, you're such a nag,' she throws over her shoulder, yet she still waits for him to gently hoist her out of her seat. 'Love you,' she says with a grin when she's upright.

'Hmm,' he replies.

She leans on the stick. 'You're meant to say, "Love you too, dearest Sib."'

'You're freaking me out. You're far too ... Well, happy.' He

360

sighs. 'A lot happened at the weekend, Sib, dreadful things, inexplicable things—'

'That's why we're here, Gabe. But you stay in the car for now. If we're both at the door, she won't let us in.'

'It's *you* she won't let in. Not answering your fifty plus texts and calls is a clue.' He folds his arms. 'It'll be a wasted journey.'

'She's my sister; I want to try.'

Still playing with the word 'sister' on her lips, Sibeal walks to the front door. Her whole right side kills, the paracetamol making no bloody impact. She's not one to beg but she'll use that excuse if she has to. She reaches for the knocker, but the door flies open.

'I saw you from Grandad's window!' Milo skips from foot to foot, apparently delighted to see her. 'Mummy's in the shower and I'm really bored. Bridget usually comes with Murphy, but she's gone on holiday.' He crinkles his nose. 'Who's that in the car?'

'That's my brother. He's called Gabriel,' Sibeal answers, hopping into the hallway before Milo can break free and run to the Volvo. She doesn't want to risk *that* happening again.

'Wow, you have a brother! Isn't he coming in too?' His eyes widen. 'Does he like jigsaws?'

Sib laughs. 'Probably, knowing Gabe. He might come in in a—'

'Milo?' Kat's voice echoes from above. 'If you look in the fridge, you might find a treat.' When he's gone she speaks again, her tone devoid of emotion. 'Go away, Sibeal. I don't want you here. I don't want anyone here.'

Her face pale and pasty, she's perched on the top stair. 'Go away,' she repeats, but this time there's a hint of emotion. 'Please. I don't want to see you.'

'Tough,' Sib replies. 'I'm not going anywhere. Besides I'm in agony, I need to sit down.' She gestures towards the lounge. 'See you in there.'

Wondering if Kat will appear, Sibeal sits on the sofa and pulls up her legs to ease the pressure on her buttock. She would have come before now, but she spent most of Monday in the local A&E. After being passed from pillar to post, a young doctor finally made the decision to add more sutures. 'It might make the scar more pronounced,' he said apologetically.

'Go for it,' she replied, holding down the bubble of nausea. She didn't have any plans to get naked with anyone again for a long, long time. The last time she had didn't bear contemplation, especially as full recall tumbled back late one evening, so she decided not to go there in her head. Ever.

Finding a reasonably comfy position, she finally stops shuffling.

'Please, Sib ...'

She starts at the sound of Kat's thin voice. Her arms wrapped around her chest, she's just out of reach.

'Please, Sib, go home. I don't want to think about any of this. It's too painful, all of it.' Her blue gaze falters. 'I realise you must be shocked too, but there's too much to deal with. Apart from ...' She swallows. 'Apart from *him*, Bridget was supposed to be my friend.'

'She was, Kat. She had second thoughts and turned back with Milo. She even carried out her promise to take him to the zoo. And some good has come out of this shitstorm. We're sisters. Me and Gabriel are your family now. We're here for you and we're not going away.' She pulls a daft face. '"Family" means you have to put up with us whether you like it or not.'

Tears splashing her cheeks, Kat holds out her palm. 'Please, Sib, stop. I can't.'

Sib struggles to get upright. 'For God's sake, Kat, I'm in flipping agony here! Can you please just sit down.'

Kat lowers herself onto the carpet.

'I meant here, next to me, so I could give you a hug.' She studies her sister's wretched face. 'Look, there's nothing we can do to change the past. I was shocked, stunned, mortified. I had another major panic attack in front of a roomful of bloody cops. Fucking hell, I don't want to be the offspring of a . . .' Willing her to understand, she takes a big breath. 'But there was relief, Kat, huge relief. I grew up thinking I had done something wrong. Constantly. I never knew what it was; I felt flawed and ugly, I was deeply frustrated and unhappy, didn't like myself, couldn't make friends . . .'

Tears burn the back of her eyes. 'So I was pleased that I wasn't just unlovable.' She peers at Kat intently. 'We have to walk on with our chins held high. We've both lost so much but we've found each other. Chalk and cheese maybe, but there was always that attachment, wasn't there? I'm your big sister; I'm here to help you; I'm not going to let you hide.' She pauses. 'What have you told Milo?'

'That his grandad is on holiday.' Kat frowns. 'Why?'

Sib brushes the nap of a velvet cushion. Unlike the old renegade Sibeal would have done, she's stroking it the right way. 'I'm no expert on kids, but secrets are corrosive. Bloody hell, look at Gabe.'

Wiping her face, Kat looks at her enquiringly.

'I'll be kind and tell you in thirty seconds what it took me hours to squeeze out of him.' Her wry smile falls as she orders the scrambled tale he imparted once the police officers had left.

'So . . . On his sixteenth birthday, Imelda told Gabe he was now a man, old enough to learn that his dad and mine weren't one and the same. Then she gave him the letter, the one you found addressed to me.' The heat of anger rising, she frowns. 'Bloody awful woman. She put all that responsibility on his shoulders, a *child's* shoulders, then she killed herself. He's been tortured by those secrets for the last nineteen years.'

'Secrets?'

'My paternity and his horrendous guilt. She handed him an envelope, Kat. People don't do that out of the blue for no reason. At the time he was irritated that she was giving me something when it was his birthday. Once she was discovered dead, it became a desperate cry for help he ignored. Can you imagine how it grew, how he played with it in his head? If he'd paid more attention instead of bolting away, if he hadn't gone out with his friends after school, if he'd mentioned it to Dad, if he'd given Dad the missive . . . I would have destroyed the damned thing long ago and tried to forget it, but he kept it as a self-inflicted punishment. That's my theory, at least.'

Falling silent, she thinks back to the hospice and Gabe's delirious laugh. What did he say? *Thank God it's all over.* Of course! He'd been protecting James too, damned if he spilled the beans about her paternity, damned if he didn't. Poor bloody sod.

She comes back to Kat's gaze. 'Personally, I think Imelda was selfish and only ever thought of her own misery and needs, but Gabe doesn't see it that way. They were incredibly close and he's one of those people who . . .'

'Who what?'

364

'When they love, they love deeply, probably too deeply.' She flushes at the notion. 'Though who am I to talk.'

Inching forward, Kat takes her hand. 'You both had really tough childhoods, so maybe that's why. What did the letter say?'

Sib snorts. 'After all that bloody grief, the envelope was empty. My guess . . .' She thinks the options through. Alexander when she found him in the dining room at Brook House? Or Gabriel? Because there's still something he isn't telling her; she can feel it in her gut. She goes for the option she hopes for. 'Yeah, my guess is that James got rid of it to protect me.'

'So Kenny . . .'

A big handsome lad, thick glossy hair, dark chestnut eyes like yours. 'It was just a guess based on what Alexander had told me.'

She watches the recoil in Kat's face. 'Don't go there, Kat. Don't you dare feel an iota of guilt for reporting him. Alexander is evil. His DNA is on the database in connection with a sexual assault. We don't know what went on between him and Imelda, but innocent people don't have a false bloody passport. They don't try to take a child. Yes?'

'I know . . .'

She thinks of his sly but prying questions at Brook House about her parents' personal effects. What would Imelda's diary have revealed? A fling with Alexander and all the Catholic guilt that went with it. Or rape? 'In all likelihood I started the ball rolling by getting arrested. He'll have known his days were numbered when the police took my DNA. Maybe that's when he arranged the passport, money, flights and whatever else—'

'No, it was earlier than that. James wrote him a letter from the hospice.'

'That's right; Alexander mentioned it. Something about Dad

wanting to see Kenny before he . . .' She grimaces. 'More bloody fiction. What did it really say?'

Her head down, Kat picks at the carpet. 'I can't remember exactly. I guess the police have it now . . .' She takes a shuddery breath. 'But it mentioned your mum. Said something along the lines that he was responsible for her suicide.'

Sibeal blows out a long puff of air. 'So James definitely did know. All those teenage years when I was a nightmare, rude and wilful, testing the boundaries. He never let on. I didn't realise until recently, but he remortgaged Brook House so I could buy my little place.' Her nose burns. 'He was always there for me, patient and kind. Despite not being his biological child, he still loved me.'

Kat's tears pool on her knees. 'I thought my dad did too. It's still so unbelievable. I keep thinking that maybe we've got it wrong. What do we know about the original allegation? It could've been a genuine misunderstanding . . .'

'He absconded, Kat.'

'Perhaps there is a real Kenny somewhere out—'

'No, Kat.' Sibeal waits for eye contact. 'Everything he did, each clever little fabrication he created, each charming lie he told, was calculated and horribly self-serving.' She thinks about her research last night, not only about *him* but the pseudonym he chose. 'Did you know Philippe was the name of the protagonist in *The Man in the Iron Mask*, you know, by Dumas? He must have thought that was funny. He's a narcissist, a sociopath, a bloody psychopath, probably. That man is a monster.'

Kat plays with the clasp on her gold watch for some time. She eventually looks up. 'But he's also the father I've loved all my life.'

81

Sibeal

'Did you hear that?' Sibeal says to Milo. She cups her ear. 'It's the sound of keys in the door so it must be Uncle Gabe. It's time to hide!' She lifts the tartan throw on the Chesterfield. 'Quickly, he'll never see us under the magic blanket.'

Savouring his breathless excitement, she holds Milo tightly. Though his hands are squashed over his mouth, she can feel the tremor of laughter bubbling up through his skinny chest.

The parlour door creaks. 'Hmm, there's no one in here,' Gabriel says. 'Where can Sibby and Milo possibly be?'

'We're here!' Milo replies, bursting out. 'We were in here all the time. We were under the magic blanket!'

Sib's lips twitch at Gabe's attempt to look surprised; actor, he isn't.

'Ah, magic! That's why.' He looks pointedly at her. 'I see you're resting.'

'Absolutely. Just like the doctor ordered.'

'So I spotted through the bay. I assume jigging around is part of the therapy.'

She gestures to the coloured circles on the floor. 'Twister

Dance, actually.' She pulls Milo onto her knee. 'We were pretty hot at it, weren't we? Anyway, it has been three weeks, so I'm—'

'Less than two since the infection.' His eyes sweep the room. 'I see you're still helping the economy by replacing all the toys we chucked out.'

'From when you were little?' Milo asks. He doesn't wait for an answer. 'Did you have the High Chaparral? Grandad let me play with his cowboys and Indians even though they were old and very special.' He frowns. 'Do you think he took them with him when he ran away?'

'Maybe,' Sib replies. 'That's why we went shopping with Mummy for—'

'You've been driving, Sibeal? You're not supposed—'

'Kat drove. Don't worry, Sergeant Major, we arranged insurance. She's out in it now, having some time out from the ...' Holding back the word 'shitstorm' just in time, she goes back to Milo's downcast expression. 'I think grumpy Uncle Gabe needs a hug.' She whispers in his good ear, 'And you can show him your surprise.'

Breathing away the surge of emotion, she watches her gorgeous nephew hold up his arms. She understands Gabriel feels shy, but she senses Milo's need for another man in his life. Wrapping his legs around his new uncle's waist, he clings on for some time.

When he pulls away, he grins. 'We've been baking but it's a surprise.'

'I thought I could smell something delicious. What are we waiting for? You lead the way.'

They settle at the kitchen table. 'Guess which bun is yours,' Milo says.

'Tricky . . .'

'The one with the . . .' He wrinkles his nose in thought. 'The treble clef on it.'

'That is one pretty good musical notation.' Gabriel takes a bite. 'Delicious buttercream too. What a good baker you are.'

When he's finished his, Milo licks the gloopy icing from his fingers. 'Sibby helped.'

'Are you sure?' Gabriel laughs. 'Do you mean the same Sibby as the one sitting here?'

'He's cheeky, my big brother, isn't he? Have you had enough cake? Upstairs to the bathroom with those sticky hands. A really good wash, please. Squeaky clean.'

'You're good at this,' Gabriel says when he's gone. 'Despite your protestations, maybe you're mum material after all.'

Ignoring the comment, Sib picks the crumbs from her plate. 'We were going to make gingerbread people, but we got into the story itself and it became alarmingly topical. You know, his grandad running away like the gingerbread man had. He wanted to know whether Alexander had done something naughty.' She laughs drily. 'And of course the whole fable is about trust. The cookie believed the fox when he promised he wouldn't eat him. So I guess it was the gingerbread man's own fault; his misguided trust led to his downfall. Oh, and Alexander liked "wily foxes", apparently.'

'Yeah, of course he did.' Gabriel rubs the table. 'The minefield of trust and downfalls.' He briefly glances up. 'I think we've all had our share.'

'True.' She studies him rubbing his glasses with a tea towel. What is Gabe keeping from her? Yet, as ever, who is she to complain? How can she expect him to spill if she doesn't do it herself?

She's only been to one AA meeting so far, so it's early days, but she knows honesty is key to recovery.

'My protestations, as you put it . . .' She takes a sharp breath. 'I was pregnant once. Twice, actually. The first was nothing, scraping away a bunch of inconvenient cells at eighteen. But the second time, I desperately wanted to keep it. I welcomed the sore boobs and puking. I even gave up the booze; never felt so bloody happy. But at eleven weeks I had a miscarriage. I was at a business meeting and felt the blood inside my knickers.'

Gabriel sits back. 'God, I'm sorry, Sib. I had no idea.'

'It was Robin's. Both were.'

Her heart starting to race, Sibeal inhales deeply. But she already feels lighter for spitting the words 'miscarriage' and 'Robin' out.

Gabriel's brow furrows. 'Why didn't you tell me?'

'Robin was married to Zoe for starters. I didn't want to tempt fate until twelve weeks had passed, so he didn't know about it either. Then he broke the news about her baby. I lost mine; she didn't. As for our . . . relationship . . . he asked me not to tell you.'

'Right.'

Though Gabriel plays with his cup, she catches the shot of emotion which passes through his eyes. Sorrow? Anger? Pain? But not surprise.

'You knew about me and Robin?'

'Nope. Not then.' He flushes. 'Katy told me recently. She didn't intend to. It just slipped out.'

'Gabe?' Alarm flutters in Sibeal's belly. 'There's more. What aren't you telling me?'

'Nothing.' He briefly looks up. 'Really.'

'For God's sake, Gabriel . . .' she begins, then she quietens

370

as the sound of piano music filters in. Not her dead mother today, but Milo's attempts to perfect 'Amazing Grace'. It feels weirdly symbolic.

She lowers her voice. 'I know it's in the past and complicated, but . . . You kept a huge secret from me, Gabe—'

'You said you'd forgiven me and that we'd—'

'Look forward from now on. I know and I have. But we also spoke about honesty. There's still stuff you haven't told me.'

His inward struggle plays out on his face. They had the 'I'm not an idiot, Gabriel, I know you're gay' conversation in the car when he insisted on dragging her back to Saxton. But the strange glance between him and Zoe at Robin's wake still nags. And what did the woman derisively say when she confronted her in the car? *If Robin was in love with anyone, it was . . .*

Incredulous realisation burns, deep in her chest. 'You and Robin? You were an item?'

'No.' Gabriel frowns. 'Not an *item*.'

'Then what? Was he in love with you?'

'That's actually funny.' He guffaws. 'God, no. Robin was only ever in love with one person and that was himself.' When his laughter dies down, he rakes his hair and sighs. 'I was simply his dolt, his fool, his puppy dog, his . . . lifeguard.'

'Lifeguard?'

'He was into autoerotic asphyxiation even at uni. He loved the high, the euphoria, dizziness and so on before losing consciousness. He had some kind of rescue mechanism to stop the deprivation of oxygen once he'd climaxed, but at some point it failed and he had a close call. He freaked out and stopped doing it for a while but . . .'

Christ, breath play. Picturing Robin's yellow tie, Sibeal

371

touches her own neck. Had it not been for Imelda's mode of death, she would have agreed to try it. She would have done anything for Robin. So, it would appear from her brother's deep blush, would he.

'But he missed the exhilaration, I guess.' Gabriel smiles thinly. 'So he decided on a "close friend" to keep him safe. Who else but pliable, pathetic, besotted Gabriel?' He swallows. 'I agreed to watch him masturbate whilst he strangled himself with a tie or a scarf. Looking but not touching. It was sheer agony.'

'You were in love with him?' she asks quietly.

'Yeah. Pitiful, unrequited love from the moment we said hello in the uni flat.'

'And this arrangement, did it continue . . .?'

He nods. 'From time to time. I was grasping at straws, but it was something.'

Sibeal puffs out long and hard. It's so left field, she doesn't know how she feels. 'I didn't have the first clue. God, how oblivious was I?'

'He played us both.' Gabriel scoffs grimly. 'Saxton isn't exactly close to Wilmslow, is it? I didn't realise until that last . . .' He takes a shuddery breath. 'Once or twice I glimpsed his car parked outside your house but I thought nothing of it – popping in for a coffee before his "fix" at mine, I assumed. But it turned out he was getting value for the cost of his petrol. First you, then me, Sib.'

It takes a moment for that revelation to settle. Yet this time she does know how she feels: sheer disgust. 'The fucking animal. How did you know he'd been with me?'

'I could smell you on him. I asked and he admitted it.'

Narrowing her eyes, she pictures him scrambling from her

bed, then hurrying to dress without taking a shower. She knows precisely when that was but she asks anyway. 'When was this?'

Her brother nods gravely. 'The night he died.'

82

Katy

Katy taps her fingers on the steering wheel and waits for the temporary traffic lights to turn red. God, she wishes the 'temporary' stretched to how often they change. It seems they let two vehicles through her end, twenty the other and during that time her eyes keep slipping to the passenger dashboard and the letters printed there. SRS AIRBAG. No wonder they call it branding because that's how it feels: seared in her head, on her brain.

Of course she could play with the radio or glance at her mobile, she's stationary, after all, but she's new again to driving and this isn't her car. Bridget still has hers. She offered it back via her lawyers 'now that her contract of employment is at an end'. It came with a personal letter from the woman saying she felt dreadful about what had happened, that she had no idea about Alexander's intentions nor his past, that he asked her to drive Milo to services near Birmingham as some sort of surprise. That she changed her mind when repeated messages came through from a number she didn't recognise. That she misses her and Milo terribly. She just did as she was told and regrets it every moment of each day.

'Yeah, like the Nazis were just doing what they were told,' Katy said to Femi.

'By all accounts your father is a very charming and persuasive character,' she replied.

Katy knew the DI was backtracking from her previous assurances that Bridget would be charged. 'Clearly Bridget is "charming and persuasive" too,' she commented wryly.

She understands the officer is just the messenger; it isn't her fault the CPS don't know what to do about the bloody nurse-cum-abductor. Katy fumed for days. Getting away scot-free after what she'd put her through, not just the act itself and the lies that went with it, but the breach of their friendship and trust; that dreadful and debilitating sensation of the ground moving beneath her feet. Yet now time has passed, she's glad. The historic allegation of sexual assault and the search for her dad hit the headlines. Thank God she was able to persuade the police press officer via Femi that it wasn't in either Milo's or the public's interest to know about the attempted abduction. She didn't want her son in the news. She did not want him to be the subject of pointing or derision or pity. With Sib's help, she's personally gone about her business with her chin held high, but Milo is only a child. She doesn't want his life to be shaped by this appalling event, so although she's being as truthful as she can with him, the doses are very small.

As the lights turn to green, she smoothly accelerates towards the motorway. She likes driving this smart SUV. She might buy one for herself; as things have turned out, she has money and quite a lot of it.

She'd already seen much of the paperwork during her frantic search in Alexander's wardrobe when Milo was still missing. She only registered one or two alarming snippets at the time and didn't want to delve further, but with Sib's gentle coaxing that only the truth would 'set her free', she went back to the disarray and discovered her home was free of any mortgage and in her name, and that she had various savings accounts. The only question was why.

The red folder she'd hidden from the police was a whole different ball game. Containing cuttings from every newspaper that reported it, ambulance, vehicle examination and post-mortem reports, photographs of the damaged car and the scene, it should have been labelled 'Elke's Death'.

Once she started going through it, she couldn't stop. She examined each image, every document and report, read all the correspondence from Alexander's solicitors. Because the crash had been caused by an unidentified driver, Elke's estate had an unanswerable claim for compensation against the Motor Insurers' Bureau, the body that covered such cases, they said. Surely he'd want to pursue it? Then there was the malfunctioning airbag. The car was less than a year old; a successful civil action against the manufacturer was almost guaranteed. Agreeing to the write-off and destruction of the vehicle was premature; Alexander might change his mind.

Each reply from her father was polite but to the point: 'No thank you, money isn't everything. We're putting it behind us; it's what's best for my daughter and her unborn child.'

Katy now sighs. It's plausible, very plausible. She was undoubtedly traumatised and paralysed with grief, she can't deny that. And clearly they already had plenty of money in the pot. Indeed, her financial security means she can sell up and move as Sib has suggested, buy somewhere new, start afresh. So maybe some good has come out of the darkness.

'Really?' she asks herself in the mirror. 'Really?'

Does this feel right, darling? What is your gut telling you?

She blows out a long puff of air. The scaring-off of boyfriends, the control and manipulation, the lies, the back-handed compliments and anxiety-inducing criticism about her weight, her looks, her academic abilities behind that honest, reliable and loving façade . . . Who the fuck is she kidding?

The shock and numbness will wear off and the enormity of everything will strike at some point, but it's vital she keeps it together. All she can do is take one step at a time. Later today she'll instruct an estate agent to put the house on the market. But first she's going for a swim.

83

Sibeal

Sibeal knows from Gabe's frozen demeanour that she finally has her answer to how Robin died.

'So he did have a cardiac arrest. From strangulation, I'm assuming?'

He nods. 'I had a caller at the door so I told him to hold off until I'd got rid of them. When I returned to the bedroom, he was unconscious. I immediately called an ambulance, but he died on the way to the hospital. It was horrendous.'

'You went with him?'

'Yeah, watched the paramedics do their stuff. They really tried.'

She frowns. 'But what about Zoe?'

'She was at home with Joseph. I called her, obviously.'

'So, how did that go down?' God knows why, but the thought of the poor woman's discovery takes Sibeal's breath. 'Her husband had died eighty miles away from home. Bloody dreadful enough. But from autoerotic asphyxiation in another man's house . . .'

'I know, but . . .' Gabriel lifts his hands. 'She didn't say it outright, but I think she knew about his proclivities and preferred to take a blind-eye approach. I don't know her that well but when she arrived at the hospital in York, I felt really sorry for her.'

'Her husband had just died, Gabe, so I'd have thought "feeling sorry" would be the bare minimum.'

'I didn't mean that. She felt deeply humiliated.'

'And didn't want the truth getting out?'

'Yes. And in fairness to her, she has Joseph and another child on the way. She didn't want them to ever know how he died or have the stigma. So between the two of us, we hatched a more palatable version of his death, you know, for public consumption.'

Another tune from little Milo wafting by, Sibeal drifts and mulls on the ability – or more aptly the curse – of loving someone as deeply as she and her brother had loved one man. Obsession like that is truly terrifying. Good God, she's a case in point: drinking excessively, stalking and spying, having irrational thoughts. But Gabriel? She glances at him. That snap of anger he can have, coming out of nowhere . . . She isn't convinced there was a random caller at his door so late at night, but that's fine by her. Robin was a shit; a complete and utter shit. All those insults Zoe hurled at her would have come from him; he fed many lies about her too. Then hopping from one sibling to another for a double helping of sexual gratification . . . She just hopes his death hurt horribly.

'So Zoe isn't a complete bitch, then?' she asks.

'I think she loves her kids and wants only their happiness. And can you imagine all that denial behind the smile? All that pouting and posing for the camera when she's probably broken inside? Yeah, I feel really sorry for her.'

'The trouble with you is that you're too nice.'

379

'I wish.' He takes Sibeal's hand and traces the fine scars on her fingers. 'I wish I could turn back the clock and undo this.'

'It was a moment of madness; we all have them. You were a child, you were angry; you didn't mean to hurt me.'

The memory is always the same, that shocking crunch of the piano lid on her knuckles. Yet the sheer devastation Gabriel could do that to her, so much worse than the pain.

Batting the past away, she props her legs on a chair. 'Just remembered; I'm supposed to be recuperating and I'm ready for lunch.' She playfully pushes him. 'Come on, dearest brother, get to it.'

84

Katy

The July sunshine warming her shoulders, Katy makes her way towards the glinting lake.

'Have you been open-water swimming before?' the guy at the counter asked.

'No, but I thought I might just take a look and see how I feel about it. Would that be OK?'

'Yeah, sure. We recommend swimming in twos to begin with, so if you do decide to take the plunge, come and have a word and we'll see if someone is available to go in or spot you from the banks.'

'OK, sounds good.'

Inhaling a honeyed warm smell, she watches a bee go about its innocent business, transferring pollen from one flower to another. And there's a red admiral, dancing from white to purple to butter-yellow. Were there actually more butterflies in her childhood? Or does that thought come more from that insubstantial cloud that swings from sweet nostalgia to murkiness?

She mentally pinches herself. Keep it together, stay strong; the future is what matters, not the past.

Sitting on the jetty's edge, she slowly slips her feet into the dark depths. She anticipated it would be extremely cold and it is. But as she closes her eyes and feels the water ripple around her goosebumped flesh, there's already a sensation of cleansing, of purging the voices in her head.

Does this feel right, darling? What is your gut telling you?

And those deeper tones:

So beautiful, so compliant, your skin like alabaster.

Why on earth wouldn't you want a beautiful addition to our family?

You do know how deranged that sounds, don't you, Elke?

You're overwrought with anxiety, that's all. Perhaps take a Prozac to calm you down?

She splashes them away and turns to the old nightmare she longs to expunge, but someone from behind interrupts her contemplation.

'Hi, are you the woman looking for a swimming pair?'

She turns and looks up. A towel in one hand, cap and goggles in the other, Harry's kitted out for a swim.

'Hello,' she says, 'I didn't know if you'd come.' She didn't; she really didn't.

'A text asking if I wanted to be your partner was hard to turn down.'

'*Swimming* partner,' she replies, blushing despite herself. 'It's safer to have one, apparently.'

'It is indeed.' Smiling thinly, he sits down beside her. 'If it's the right person.'

'That's very true.'

Gazing at the greenery all around, she falls silent. Why did she message him? Loose ends, she supposes.

'Can I ask you a question?' she says.

'Sure.'

'What's your real name? Your real first name?'

'It's Bijan. How come you're asking?'

Of all her bloody worries, it's strange this one popped out. 'I wondered why you call yourself Harry.'

He smooths the scar on his chin. 'Short for Harrison, of course. Bijan wasn't a great name growing up. You know, kids shortening it to Bi ...' He sighs. 'That's what I told Mum and Dad anyway. The truth is I was teased about it at primary school. I hated the foreign name; I was embarrassed about my mum's accent; I just wanted to be normal. So at high school I changed it and introduced myself as Harry.'

The next loose end rushes out. 'Is that why you were a bad lad?'

He looks into the distance. 'To prove my whiteness, I got in with a bad crowd for a while.' He grimaces. 'You met one of them in Phil's pub. It's a time I'm not proud of. Ashamed, in fact.' He comes back to her. 'You remember me saying that?'

So beautiful, so compliant, your skin like alabaster.

'I remember more than I think I do.'

He peers at her thoughtfully. 'I heard about your father,' he says softly. 'I'm so sorry, Katy. It must be incredibly hard for you and Milo.'

She takes a sharp breath. 'Why didn't you get in touch after I stalked out of your house? I know I was angry and that I reacted impulsively, but I thought you'd message to see how I was. I was completely out of order, but I thought you'd understand.'

'I did text; I called and texted several—'

'There was nothing on my phone.'

'You replied and told me to stop . . .' He lifts his head skyward. 'Why did you post my keys back?'

'I didn't! They're still in my . . .'

Her protest trails off. What did James's letter say? *Manipulation, sleight of hand.* That clearly included responding to and deleting Harry's messages, as well as visiting his home. And of course feeding in those alleged 'connections'. The Three-Legged Mare, red cars, country roads and fast drivers. Deceptive, distorting. Clever and cunning.

Clearly reading her thoughts, Harry nods grimly. 'Phil said he'd been in the pub, casually asking questions about me.'

'You knew, didn't you?' Katy turns to look him in the eye. 'You called my dad Kenton when we were looking at his car.'

'Kenton Henry. That's the name I was given when he was admitted to A&E. From his driving licence, I guess, but . . .' He frowns. 'I didn't *know* anything, I still don't. It's just . . .' He appears to search for the words. 'Nothing quite added up.'

Katy swallows; she has to keep it together; she has to find out what he knows. 'What didn't add up?'

He massages his forehead, his expression pensive. 'I was told your dad was brought in unconscious, that he was still unresponsive when you arrived; you confirmed that when we talked about it. But I'd seen him before then in a side room, sitting up and on his mobile. My beeper vibrated, so I hadn't gone in. I didn't think about it at the time, but I recognised you when we met at the fair.' He smiles a small smile. 'You aren't easy to forget.' He spreads his hands. 'I'm sure it means nothing, Katy. It was just odd, that's all.'

She eases out her trapped breath. When she went through the 'Elke Death' folder, her father's impatience to dispose of the 'faulty' vehicle stood out a mile. Of course she'll never know for sure, but a sixth sense tells her that he tampered with the passenger airbag. Praying the high dose of Prozac they found in her mother's body lessened her fear and pain, she shredded every last document in the file. Though the police's investigation is focused on the sexual assaults, she can't take the risk they'll turn their attention to Elke; she can't expose herself, and especially Milo, to more trauma.

'And how have you been?' Harry's low voice brings her back. 'Have you been well?'

Euphemisms like her dad, but that's fine, she needs to address it. 'Reeling from recent events, obviously, but no tiredness, no lethargy, no episodes for quite some time. I don't want to tempt fate, but for now all is good.'

When she properly studied her diaries, the pattern of her 'fatigue' was unmistakable; she was only ever ill when her father was home. Drugging her with strong opiates is her guess, sleeping draughts in those delicious sauces he was so delighted to prepare just for her. As well as his curries, porridge, night-time cocoa and God knows what else. It must have been a bonus she was opioid adverse like her sister and took longer to recover from the stupor.

The clotted voice swipes in again: *So beautiful, so compliant, your skin like alabaster.*

She shudders deeply inside. To control her and keep her biddable like a pet, that's all. That is all, surely? The disgusting dreams are just dreams; her mother's surprising insistence she have an abortion simply sensible; the arguments she overheard and the proximity of her pregnancy to her mum's death coincidental. And Milo? His deafness, his cryptorchidism and tendency to catch colds could apply to any kid. Bridget was at his birth to support *her*, wasn't she? Not there to count his fingers and toes.

She'll never let on she glimpsed the destination that man was researching for the 'holiday', and she destroyed James's letter and the word 'deviance'. The abduction is under wraps, so there's no one left to query why he would snatch his grandchild. And grandsons look like their grandads all the time. Don't they?

The old nightmare prods: *So tired, too tired in the car next to Dad. The flash of his features and the comforting smell of his after-shave in the dark.*

'*Stop. Dad stop! You have to stop!*'

And inevitably the weight, constricting her chest and her body, pinning and pushing her down.

She inwardly sets her jaw. She will obliterate it, she will. She'll plunge into the cold water as many times as it takes and swim the evil out.

She returns to Harry's soft gaze. 'Seeing as I'm finally maturing at twenty-eight, I think it's about time I . . .' She gestures to the sparkling lake surrounding them. 'Dive in at the deep end.'

'Not even dipping your toe in first?'

'Nope.' She likes this guy, she really does. 'I'm ready if you are.'

'I absolutely am. Let's do this.' He stands and offers his hand. 'Katy Henry, may I have the pleasure of being your partner?'

ACKNOWLEDGEMENTS

Huge thanks to:

Anna Boatman, Christopher Sturtivant, Hannah Wann, Beth Wright, Lucie Sharpe, Rebecca Sheppard and the rest of the fantastic Piatkus team.

Liz Hatherell, my delightful copy-editor.

Authors Angela Marsons, Helen Fields, Lisa Hall, Heleen Kist, C. J. Cooper, Karen King, Elisabeth Carpenter, Alice Hunter, Amanda Robson, Diane Jeffrey, Louise Beech, Marion Todd, Heather Burnside, J. M. Hewitt, Stephanie Sowden, Amanda Brittany, Caroline Corcoran, Stephen Edger. Thank you so much for your fabulous quotes.

Brilliant friends, including the Didsbury runners headed by the intrepid Sue; the bookclub-without-a-book and cake-date ladies; the Prosecco duo, Chris and Alison; my afternoon tea pals, Bo and Fran; my forever friends, Sara and Liz; the GNO stronghold, Belinda, Jan and Yvonne; Mr Roddy Macleod; writer buddies Cath, Rosie, Tricia and David, and of course the perfect dinner companions, Andy and Lorna, Mike and Cara, George and Laura.

Libby, Sam and Carolyn, my author rollercoaster-ride comrades.

Early readers Kate Johnson and Sue France.

Ian, John and David from my local bookshop: E J Morten Booksellers of Didsbury.

All the generous people who helped me promote my 2022 books:

Joanne Goodwin, editor of *Cheshire Life*

Sue France (AKA Cheshire's Queen of Connections)

Daniel Blewitt of Avid Readers Club

Kerry Ann Parsons of Chat About Books

Sandra Foy at Urmston Bookshop

Daksha, Dale, Eileen, Gail and Sofia at Didsbury Library

Jenny Martin and the team at Leigh Library

Danny at Manchester Central Library

Darcey and Sarah at Huddersfield Waterstones

Emma at Wakefield Waterstones

Sam, Caroline and the team at UK Crime Book Club

Wendy, Emma and the team at the Fiction Cafe Book Club

Julie Harrison at UK Gossip Girls Cheshire and Sth Manchester

Chris Johnson AKA CJ Harter, editor and author

South Manchester Writers Workshop

Sarah Williams of Crime Fiction Fix

Rob, Chris and Sean of Blood Brothers Podcast

Carol Taafe-Finn from the Matlock Luncheon Club

John Cavey and the team at the Repton Literary Festival

The Slug & Lettuce, Didsbury

The wonderful book bloggers, in particular those who so generously stepped up to travel on *The Sinner* and *The Shadows of Rutherford House* blog tours.

Every single fellow author, blogger, reviewer, reader or online book-group member who has championed my books.

Last, but not least, the reading public! Thank you so much for buying my novels, investing hours of your time reading them and posting such heartwarming reviews.

January 2023